The Guardians of Peace

By Jeffrey Caminsky
  The Guardians of Peace series
    The Sirens of Space
    The Star Dancers
    Clouds of Darkness
    The Guardians of Peace

The
Guardians of Peace

A Novel

Jeffrey Caminsky

NEW ALEXANDRIA PRESS
LIVONIA

Published by New Alexandria Press
PO Box 530516
Livonia, Michigan 48153
www.newalexandriapress.com

Hardcover Edition:
ISBN-10: 1-60915-007-4
ISBN-13: 978-1-60915-007-5

Softcover Edition:
ISBN-10: 1-60915-0082
ISBN-13: 978-1-60915-008-2

Quantity discounts are available on bulk purchases of this book Special books or book excerpts can also be made available to fit specific needs. For information, please contact sales@newalexandriapress.com or send written inquiries to New Alexandria Press, PO Box 530516, Livonia, Michigan 48153.

Printed in the United States of America
First Printing May 2012

10 9 8 7 6 5 4 3 2 1
First Edition

2012908250

To our children's children's children.....

Author's Note

DESPITE THE AUTHOR'S best intentions, unforeseen developments seem set on preventing the reader from gaining a further historical perspective of the events chronicled in this and previous volumes. In fact, the Publisher has suspended, at least temporarily, any further efforts to educate readers about the state of humanity's future— and has threatened to halt distribution of future volumes on most planets to the east of Isis itself. While unfortunate, the Author hopes to remedy this deficiency in future editions, and is confident that, for the sake of the public interest, the Publisher will relent and permit more ready access to its own warehouse of knowledge in the future.

Benjamin Franklin once observed that it is often possible to do well by doing good. Let us hope that commercial self-interest will never lead us to forget that education is among the greatest of common goods, as it lays the foundation for enlightened thoughts and deeds.

IT IS 2557.

With war raging across the known Galaxy, a lonely world finds itself preparing for a battle it hoped would never come. As in countless centuries throughout human history, the descendants of Planet Earth find themselves fighting among themselves...one side seeking to reclaim what they believe is rightfully theirs, the other fighting for their homes, their families, and their future.

A Word from the Publisher

WHILE IT IS rarely in anyone's interests to point fingers or go casting blame, occasionally a failure to respond—even to the least credible of allegations—may, given the imperfections of human nature, be taken as an admission by credulous souls. This being so, to forestall any misunderstandings arising from the uncharacteristically uncharitable representations being made by certain persons associated with this Work, the Editorial Board has deemed it advisable to take the unusual step of offering a few words of its own upon the release of this fourth and final volume of *The Guardians of Peace* series.

In point of fact, many of the texts cited in the introductory notes to earlier parts of this work appear to have vanished completely. Curiously, they have disappeared not only from the Grand Library but from the Company's secured database as well, along with sizable portions of our catalogue from the years 2100 through 3200. These missing documents include entire sections dealing with early interstellar exploration and travel, as well as non-terrestrial life forms and the early political conflicts between the sentient races found in a particular quadrant of our Galaxy. Despite our own best efforts to locate the missing materials, some of these sections now contain only an indecipherable trail of atomic particles, and algorithms written in mathematical syllables that are not yet translated or understood. Oddly enough, all of the missing volumes from the Library have been traced to a single Old Earth library card number which, records show, expired nearly a hundred years before the beginning of the Cosmic Era.

As a result, we are presently reexamining our generous policy of providing ready access to all of our works for scholars, researchers, and interested members of the public. This policy has served the interests of all concerned for quite a long time, and we are confident that it will do so again in the future. We will, we are certain, resume our past practice once we have put a few appropriate safeguards in place.

The Guardians of Peace

A nation that draws too great a distinction between its scholars and its warriors will have its thinking done by cowards, and its fighting done by fools.

Thucydides
Old Earth Historian

Prologue

Prologue

A ND STILL THE QUESTION REMAINS," snapped the young man. "Is *Khu'ukh* dead, or is it a trap?"

Taking a deep breath, Ga'Glish calmed himself enough to continue. "You see our predicament, Zatar. The longer we delay, the more suffering our people must endure and the further the Terran fleets will push into the surrounding skies. Yet if the reports are meant to deceive us—"

"Yes," interrupted the slender young Crutchtan. "But whatever once passed between them, and however wise the Veshnan Solan may be, his speculation about the matter can be no more productive than our own."

As Ga'Glish snorted impatiently, Zatar of Ib'leiman could only smile in grim amusement. He had heard much about this young Crutchtan, whose gifts had brought hope to the Alliance just when all had seemed lost. Yet the lad seemed to care little for the niceties of form that had always made visits with Crutchtan dignitaries seem so endless. It was a refreshing change, though it did little to improve the humor of their small gathering. The fact that the young man was right made the mood even more somber.

"After our guest has traveled all this way to lend us his insights," hissed Ga'Glish, "you cannot even have the courtesy to hear what he has to say?"

Before the lad could respond, the Veshnan intervened to rescue the youth from the lad's inexperience and breach of etiquette. "I draw no insult, my old friend," Zatar smiled pleasantly. "Please take no offense on my behalf. And young fa'Shenali is quite right—for while I came to know the Terran quite well, the culture of his people was, and remains, a mystery to me. I know only that deception forms a large part of their dealings among themselves. And in battle, it seems that my Terran friend proved to be quite a master of the art himself—so much so that, I must confess, his actions were those of a stranger to me."

"So you agree," said fa'Shenali, his voice little more than a whisper. "This could well be the sort of deception that *Khu'ukh* might engineer, drawing us into the open so that he can strike a final, lethal blow. One from which, given the fact that our reserves are depleted and we have no margin for error, we would never recover."

Zatar drew a deep breath and closed his eyes. He could scarcely imagine the horrors that would follow in the wake of such a disaster. It was apparent that the young Crutchtan spoke directly from his heart. Despite the success of recent weeks, Zatar had no doubt that they remained in mortal danger, and one misdirected step could bring destruction to all they had ever known.

"That sort of deception seems alien to me," Zatar replied at last. "So alien that I cannot discount the possibility, even as it seems to make little sense."

"There is another facet to our problem," Ga'Glish added.

"And what is that, my old friend?"

"We have actually intercepted two separate reports from Terran transmissions, Zatar—which offer conflicting and contradictory explanations for his absence from the fighting. Both report the same result, but I find myself wondering what each may say about the future."

"The first report," fa'Shenali interjected, "says that the One Called *Khu'ukh* is missing and presumed killed while traveling from a consultation with senior commanders to the battle of *Denlubi*, lost in the eddies of the nearby vortex. It is the explanation that the Terran military leaders have passed among themselves. And we have intercepted similar reports in many different sectors— "

"As have others of the Alliance," added Ga'Glish.

"The other report," fa'Shenali whispered, "we have intercepted only once— "

"Though on a high-security channel, one that we have been able to penetrate only intermittently."

"All these reports have come only on military channels, not on their civilian broadcasts," the younger Crutchtan snapped. "And all could easily have been left unencrypted just to ensure that we would be able to decipher their message."

"Far be it for me to interrupt," Zatar tried to intercede.

"The fact that these reports appear only on military channels means nothing," countered Ga'Glish.

"It means everything!" retorted fa'Shenali."It means that the information is entirely under the control of their commanders, and is not being told to their people. Given what is at stake, it means that I will give neither report any credence. Not unless we find some way to confirm it."

"The second report...?" Zatar tried once again, astonished at his hosts' display of temper. Crutchtans were ordinarily so outwardly stoic. Even filtered through the translators, this was an unprecedented display of emotion for any Crutchtan to show.

Nodding in silence, the younger Crutchtan lowered his head. Ga'Glish took a long, deep breath and continued.

"The second report contains the seeds of mystery as well as promise," said the elder. "We have one source, consisting of an intercepted conversation between two high-ranking military officials, discussing the manner of his death. But this account suggests that the Terran leadership killed him themselves, while he was traveling a great distance to the west...and seeking to aid his home planet in a rebellion against the central Terran government."

"What!"

"Our linguists have checked their translations, and are positive that this interpretation is correct...."

"They are certain that they understand the gist of the conversation," added fa'Shenali, his voice now milder and under control. "The truth of account, however, is open to question."

"For obvious reasons, we are releasing none of this," said Ga'Glish. "Rumors of this sort could have wildly unpredictable results. And if fa'Shenali's worries prove correct, they would have a devastating impact on our morale at a time and place of the Terrans' own choosing. And we have no doubt that the time they chose would be precisely when another change in fortunes would prove most disastrous for the Alliance."

"What are the implications—," Zatar began.

"We have other references in their civilian broadcasts to some sort of uprising or insurrection— " Ga'Glish interrupted.

"—of unknown size and origin," added fa'Shenali.

"—suggesting that there may be some Terran elements sympathetic to our own cause."

"We don't know where, or how we might contact them— "

"But we think we have enough evidence to believe that they exist, either now or in the recent past."

"And if he was trying to join them....," Zatar whispered.

"From a strictly military standpoint," said fa'Shenali, "it makes no immediate difference how he died—so long as he is, in truth, dead. Whether by accident, or at their own hands, if he is no longer able to assume command of any Terran fleet, then we are free to press our attack without fear that he will appear at our most vulnerable moment and destroy us. As soon as we can confirm that he is no longer a threat...well, then all things are possible."

"But in a larger sense," said Ga'Glish, "it makes a great deal of difference to know whether *Khu'ukh* died returning to the battle, or was murdered by his own kind. For if he was willing to join some kind of rebellion, then the discontent among the Terrans may well be more widespread than we allow ourselves to believe at present. It means that some elements of Terran society may be willing to help us. And it may give us additional options for the future."

"More than this," Zatar nodded thoughtfully. "The knowledge that at the end he had joined with us would give us an inestimable boost to our own flagging spirits." Privately, he had the passing thought that it also meant that he could mourn an old friend, rather than rejoicing at the death of a merciless enemy.

"But at present, this is all fond hopes and idle speculation," said fa'Shenali. "It solves too many of our problems, and toys with too many of our emotions, to make me think that it is anything but a Terran ploy."

"And so...?"

"And so, if you have any opinions to offer...."

"I am afraid, my friends, that all I can offer are good hopes for the future, and wishful speculation."

As his elders continued their discussion, Fa'Shenali took a deep breath and looked at the floor in contemplation. They had accomplished much, but there remained much to be done. And so long as this particular phantom remained in the shadows, he was determined to keep their progress cautious and slow, no matter how much Ga'Glish and the rest of the High Command called upon him for action. Even across the gulf of space and war and culture, the One Called *Khu'ukh* had proved an inspired teacher, even if his lessons were always written in blood. And though fa'Shenali had learned those lessons well, he still felt like a young one in his first year of school. He would risk much when pitted against the slower, duller students in class; but he alone knew how terrified he was at the thought of confronting the headmaster.

Though hailed as a hero by his own people, and called a savior by the Imperator himself, the young man felt lost and alone in a universe that seemed to know only sadness and tragedy. Like Zatar, fa'Shenali was surprised to discover that among his fondest hopes was that this alien teacher of his had died not as an enemy, but as a friend. Yet in his heart, the young man's greatest fear was that the master would soon return to show his most pretentious student just how much there was to the art of war that remained for the young man to learn.

Let's all gather in the valley
  Where no earthly sins have trod,
Where sweet hope abides forever
  And sleeps in the unbroken sod.

Come and camp beside the river,
  The shimmering, crystal-clean river.
Gather with your friends along the river
  That flows from the heart of God.
                                    Isitian Hymn

I wish I could have come home to happier times, but the future is always uncertain and hazy, and life comes with no guarantees. I can offer no promises about what lies ahead, except that like everybody else, I'll try my very best.
  I just hope I don't let everybody down.
                                    Roscoe Cook
                                    Remarks on returning home
                                    January 3, 2557

Chapter 1

THE MESSAGE FROM the computer sounded its sterile monotone: "Main body of Isitian Fleet showing on screens: Range, one-hundred fifty astrokilometers."

"Divert two wings to either flank; five squadrons are to remain in reserve. Prepare to attack the center of the enemy line."

The readings on the monitor came as no surprise. Greg Garrity, his plump, jowly face hanging over the collar of his dark blue ensign's uniform, looked over his shoulder to see the bored expressions on the faces of his companions, clearly visible in the dimly lit room. Above them, the chronometer displayed the time: ten minutes to go, he thought; just another ten minutes. Adjusting his headset, he spoke clearly and firmly into the microphone.

"Execute," he said. Immediately, the screens showed the massive columns of the Terran armada moving into position, preparing to deliver the fatal blow to the defenders. The swirling storm clouds, guarding the passageway to the rebel planet, loomed in the distance as a reddish haze, superimposed over the green markings of the tactical monitor. On the monitor face, reflections from the doorway showed a company of junior officers, passing down the corridor.

"This is ridiculous," called a whiny-voiced engineering student from New Alexandria Tech. Garrity cringed whenever the pretentious twit opened his mouth. Between those judgmental blue eyes, and that obnoxious, swaggering walk, the man reminded Garrity too much of his older sister. Garrity looked forward to the next rotation, when he and Reed could rig the computer to stick him with some other poor slob, whose life wasn't miserable enough.

"Of course it's ridiculous," said Garrity, his eyes gauging the course of his attack. Unsatisfied with what he saw, he entered a minor correction into the configuration, then reissued the "Attack" command. "This whole exercise is ridiculous."

Pressing the accelerator key on his control board, he speeded the course of battle. Just before the contending forces engaged each other, he cancelled the acceleration mode, and the two fleets slowed their movements accordingly. Soon the melange of battle engulfed the screen, and the grand conflict melted into the thousand small, life-and-death struggles that have always been the true battlegrounds between races. Through it all, the five young officers of Battle Group 71-B watched with a detachment born of endless repetition. Before long, the bottom of the monitor became an endless string of alert prompts, each demanding the young man's attention.

<<ALERT: Engagement, Sector Six, Unit A15>>.
<<ALERT: Engagement, Sector Five, Units U12-Z09>>.
<<ALERT: Engagement, Sector Six, Unit X17>>.
<<ALERT: Engagement, Sector Four-->>.....

"Voice on," Garrity said into his microphone, trying to react to the overload of information displayed on the screen, and becoming angrier and angrier in the process.

"Just how in blazes does he expect us to keep all this information sorted?" demanded Tom Reed, the tall, reedy ensign looking over his hometown friend's shoulder. "I don't understand any of this. Just how— "

"Shut up, Tommy!" Garrity barked, turning away from his screen to glower. "I can't hear myself think with you jibbering away like that!" His gaze returned to the screen just in time to see the defenders shatter his left flank, and the Isitian ships begin streaming through the gaping hole in the Terran battle line. As the battle raged, the monitor showed the attack line unravel, until the ragged Terran lines were no more than a jumble of isolated squadrons, trying desperately to fend off the swarming Isitians.

"Perhaps discretion is the better part of valor," droned the computer's monotone. "The Isitian commander would be more than happy to accept your surrender."

"You shut up, too!" Garrity snapped, pressing the "Surrender" key. Soon, the display on the monitor registered his score. It was an embarrassment, the young ensign thought, as his companions began the usual catcalls and ribald speculations about the missing parts of his reproductive system. But, he sullenly reminded his friends, his was still the highest score in the group: McFarland and Lund each had yet to reach double digits; the others could barely find the On switch.

<<TACTICS: 28>>
<<STRATEGIC DESIGN: 27>>
<<ISITIAN CASUALTIES INFLICTED: Craft destroyed: 126; craft damaged or disabled: 207>>
<<TERRAN CASUALTIES SUFFERED: Craft destroyed: 909; craft damaged or disabled: 1955>>
<<OUTCOME: 11>>
<<   Terran surrender places fleet under Isitian control; Central Command is preparing a general court martial. You might be wise to seek asylum>>
   <<Do you wish to try again?>>

"No, you miserable electronic cretin!" Garrity shouted at the monitor screen. None of this made any sense to him. Quite beyond the Navy's damnable insistence on chopping a normal, Isitian day into decimalized tenths that didn't even add up to twenty-four, they all spent four hours a day in groups, drilling at bridge stations; two hours in a simulator, pretending to sail around the skies; six hours in some sort of mind-numbing classroom; and two hours in these infernal groups of five, running computerized simulations of a Terran attack. The constant activity was driving him crazy. Absolutely crazy. There was no time to read—no time to rest—and precious little time to blow off any steam. To top it off, the regulations on battle simulations were very strict and quite specific: their two-hour simulations were all run from the Terran perspective. The real attack could come at any time, and they were too busy playing games to practice the things they'd need to know when the war finally came to Isis. But the computer simply wouldn't allow it; trying to log on as the Isitian commander would result in an annoyingly loud and lengthy bleep, as the screen displayed a suggestion that the errant ensign reread page twenty-six of the Training Manual. It made no sense at all.

   "All right, whose turn is it? What prat-head gets his skull bashed in next?"

The bell sounded, signaling the end of their mandatory drilling session. From every cubicle up and down the training station, a loud cheer rose from the throat of every cadet and ensign on the base.

"Free time!" hollered Garrity and the others, logging off the computer as quickly as they could. Securing the station, as they had been trained to do, they raced down the corridor and into the interior of the base to join hundreds of their companions, all experiencing a similar case of neural overload and recreational deprivation.

A few stayed behind at the simulator, left alone in the Strategic Cubicles by their peers, who considered them harmless, if somewhat antisocial eccentrics. But it was, after all, part of the Isitian tradition of tolerance. Everyone was free to pursue his own interests, in his own fashion, so long as nobody else was bothered. And as far as the typical young Naval officer was concerned, anybody so wrapped up in the insanity looming in the skies off Zarathustra that he couldn't break away from his studies was one to be pitied, not condemned. None of them knew how much longer any of them would be around. Most preferred to spend as much of their last few months as possible in the company of friends, rather than trapped in a dark, lonely room, with only a viewing screen and computer for company.

* * *

THE STERN face of the middle-aged man looked up from his watch. Lifting his whistle between his teeth, he blew long and loud.

"Time," he barked.

As the assembled volunteers collapsed on the gym floor, Yeoman Sergeant Colin Boyd checked off a dozen more names on his clipboard. Those twelve, now stumbling toward the finish line or gasping for air along the side, were now classed as "Washouts," too physically unfit for the new standards the Navy was enforcing on its new recruits.

Not that he really objected, Boyd thought to himself. Before volunteering for the Home Guard he'd been a fitness instructor at the largest high school in Bristol, capital of the Isitian northlands. In fact, he was all in favor of fitness, as a general rule and approach to life. Isitians tended to be a soft lot, and a little exercise never did anyone any harm. But with the Terries doing God-knows-what off

Planet Zarathustra, it seemed an odd time to be getting fussy. Isis needed all the help she could muster. And their motley crew of volunteers wasn't even aiming to be real spacers, much less piloting one of the Navy's better ships: they'd all signed up to do grunt work. It seemed a waste of enthusiasm to tell them they weren't needed, just because they couldn't do enough pushups or run a mile fast enough to suit the Brass.

He hoped to God the Admiral knew what he was doing. All the old yeoman knew was that he'd started out with a hundred-fifty volunteers. Pruning those with no mechanical aptitude cut the group by a third. Those failing the physical tests put them well past the half-way mark. And they still hadn't come to the real killer: the gravity scrambler. Less than half the people who entered the large, circular hall emerged with their stomachs intact. The changing gravity was supposed to simulate travel on a ship in space, so they told him. Boyd wondered if it wasn't an excuse by some sadistic button pushers to inflict suffering on their countrymen. He himself had barely passed: his stomach was starting to give way just as the power drained from the machinery, ending the exercise. Each time he took another group to Testing Area G, his own insides started protesting. He felt as if he were leading a herd of cattle to the stockyards.

But the scrambler wasn't until tomorrow. Today, the survivors could keep their pride as well as their lunch. He'd just keep running them through the rest of the drills.

Anything to keep them busy, the Admiral had told them.

Anything to keep their minds from wandering.

* * *

//cc144.7012.6/TO/HQ/FR/reynolds,ltcmdr/
QLQ OP ALPHA, POST INFORUN. CLOSE APRCH ZarCom cl PSc.
CG MANVRS TRACKNG LIST B. CONFRM STRSHP PRSENCE
ZarCom, ##s INDETERMINABLE THIS RNGE. NXT INFORUN, PER
LIST C. NXT RPT, PER TABLE B.

PAUSING TO reread his message, Lieutenant Commander Doug Reynolds hoped that a Terran monitor station would find it as confusing as he did. The Admiral himself had compiled all the various Lists and Tables to minimize the amount of actual data broadcast over subspace radio, and shorten the time spent transmitting. So the Terran Fleet would never be "practicing flanking maneuvers," or "perfecting their Transport approach." Instead, they'd be "tracking List C," or "lagging List D," or some other damn thing. Of course, the Terries themselves would know perfectly well just what it was they were doing, so the whole thing seemed pointless. But at least they'd never know what was on the List. So long as the Terries didn't capture an Isitian ship intact, the system was close to foolproof.

Foolproof, perhaps, Reynolds scoffed. That wasn't the same as idiot proof. If he made a single mistake in entering the information into his own computer, he'd get a false rendering of the listings—and false information sent back to Isis. It might not matter much if his next report came earlier or later than Headquarters expected, but his commanding officer had made clear just how vital it was to keep track of the progress of enemy maneuvers. Hoping he hadn't made an Isitian hash of things yet again, he entered the twin keyboard stars needed to direct the communications computer at Headquarters to read the next three letters as the code sequence. Then he keyed the final command sequence to send his message on its way:

```
/**AZB/djreynolds/enter/Xmit//
```

The computer clicked and whirred, and the young commander looked out his forward window. He stared into the clear, black skies of western Terra, trying to recall happier times. He'd visited Zarathustra many times as a boy. His mother's family still lived there, and always did what they could to make their own house feel like home to him.

Now a fleet of Terran warships was on maneuvers in Zarathustran skies, maneuvers that could have only one purpose: the invasion of his home. Each day, with every reconnaissance pass he made, he saw hundreds of Terran frigates simulating battle formations, or troop transports practicing approaches for landing an army.

In his heart, he knew his sensors would never lie to him. But it was hard to imagine that war could intrude on memories of his boyhood, or come between him and those he loved as family.

* * *

THE SIMULATION hall was deathly quiet, except for the clattering of a lone keyboard.

<<Wasser, Arnold J, cadet>>, read the entry on the computer screen. <<Load AJW.005>>.

As the simulator located and recalled his program, the young cadet leaned back in his chair and sighed deeply. Tall and wiry, his black hair still cut short from his induction physical, he felt out of place in the light gray uniform of a cadet. Most cadets were too busy with their mandatory drills to get much extra practice on the simulators. But Nielsen, the arrogant twit from the Central Highlands who lived two doors down in the dormitory, had actually beaten the machine. To celebrate, the fool had spent the last two days lording it over everybody on the floor. If an idiot like that could beat the program, thought the young cadet, then anybody could. Wasser spent hours on the system, even before Nielsen's singular triumph over electronics. And if the Admiral wanted them to practice the enemy's tactics, then he'd do his best to master them. Even if it made no sense to anyone in the Cadet Program.

<<Program loaded>>, reported the computer.

<<Run program\speed 10>>.

As the progression of maneuvers from his best effort to date began running at superhuman speeds, Wasser watched the battle unfold before him. He saw his left flank make its charge toward the Isitian right, only to be cut to ribbons by a pivoting enemy center, which battered his advancing forces before turning to confront the bulk of his fleet. Soon, the battle ended and the screen flashed his score: a final outcome of twenty-two points for the Terrans, and a recommendation that he try something less demanding as a profession. The computer kindly suggested that "hotel valet, junior grade" might not be beyond his capabilities.

<<Repeat program\speed 5>>

The computer replayed the battle once again, this time at a slower speed. Wasser found himself drawn to the quick, thrusting pivot of the Isitian formation—which he knew, from painful experience, would both cut off and pin his attacking flank, and permit the enemy flank to batter it unmercifully.

"Pause," he said, into the microphone; at once, the computer froze the action in place. The young cadet stared into the monitor, wondering how anyone could make sense out of it all. Suddenly, he sat upright in his seat: the Isitian pivot was, after all, little different than the same maneuver they all practiced at the bridge simulations; only the perspective had changed. And if the computer could do it for the Isitians, Wasser thought, nothing prevented the Terran fleet from doing the same thing.

Pressing the "reenter" command, Wasser slowed the computer down to a manageable speed, and ordered his advancing flank to execute a pivot of its own, opening a gap to let the charging Isitians through. Once they passed, he pivoted again to turn the enemy flanks, swinging his ships hard to close the trap and push them away from the action. With the battle raging fiercely along the left flank, he sent the bulk of his remaining forces charging through the gap in the Isitian lines, shattering their communications and causing a wholesale retreat. Trapped in the middle, isolated from friendly forces, the Isitian advance wing was quickly destroyed, and the computer stopped the simulation.

<<Darkness descends on the Universe>> read the printing on the monitor, as the scene faded to a black background. Wasser leaned back in his chair with a weary smile. It might not be much, he told himself, but at least now Nielsen's incessant boasting wouldn't drive him crazy. He was about to sign off the computer when a familiar face suddenly appeared on the screen.

"Congratulations," said the equally familiar voice.

"Jesus!" the young cadet muttered under his breath, marveling at just how closely the Admiral was keeping tabs on things.

"You have passed your first major hurdle," continued the voice, paying no attention to Wasser. The young man relaxed. It wasn't really the Admiral, he realized; it was just a computer image.

"Understanding your enemy is often as important as understanding yourself," continued the Admiral. "And understanding the enemy's tactical problems will make you a better officer, and a more effective warrior.

"Even so, you're probably not ready to confront the challenges we'll be facing in a few more weeks. Therefore, I want you to keep studying the tactical problems the Terran fleet will confront, when they try to attack us. Once you've beaten the computer a second time—this time, at its second level—it will let you look at the problem from our perspective.

"One final hint," smiled the image. "Don't try the same tactics that worked this time. The computer is programmed to take account of your success, and will defend against the battle plan you've just used. You have now beaten the computer's first level, but you'll have to be even sharper to beat Level Two.

"Good luck. And keep up the good work."

"Ahh, crap," muttered Wasser, as the Admiral's image faded and the screen returned to its login display. That was the last thing he needed, right now. Another fool's challenge, before he could actually start practicing for what lay ahead.

* * *

PROGRESS REPORT: *Small Craft Retrofitting*

DATE: cc: 144.7277.9
TO: Adm. R.C.Cook
FROM: Comm.A.J.Landis
SUBJECT: Weekly Summary

As you ordered, I have passed along to Repairs and Maintenance the new specifications for the small craft we commandeered for the war effort, and have directed the Personnel Office to continue processing volunteers to man the additional 2,500 ships you requested. Estimates range from six to ten additional weeks to retrofit the additional ships, and retool those we had already finished, and a similar period of time to train the additional personnel. This, in turn, means that the earliest departure date for the Fleet is now late April or early May, rather than the middle of March, as originally planned.

I must, at this time, record my dissent from your recent directives. While each additional ship will, in a literal sense, augment our Fleet, given their limited utility I can see no need for additional civilian craft beyond the 2,000 small craft we commandeered originally. We seem to have all that we can handle trying to track and control this number of ships, particularly since they will, of necessity, be manned by largely untrained commanders and crews. In my opinion, we would be better served by trying to perfect the resources already at our disposal, rather than seeking to expand them in unproductive ways.

In this regard, I willingly concede the need to augment our capabilities in any practical manner possible. Nevertheless, reading your most recent communication, I do not understand it to call for enhancing the weaponry or shield strength of the small craft which have already undergone retrofitting—a course I would gladly undertake, if it were physically possible. Rather, your newest directive seems aimed at inflating the radar or sensor imaging of each ship, and confirms your order to install a debris-dispersing mechanism into the standard air locks. As I do not understand how such devices increase the fighting capability of the sloops, yachts, and other small craft that are presently within the Chancellor's Executive Order of Conscription, I cannot permit such a diversion of our already limited resources to pass without comment.

Presently, we have completed retooling 523 ships, leaving 1,477 ships to redo, under the new specifications—and as many of the additional 2,500 ships as our repair crews can manage to complete, before the Terrans sail. I am doubtful that we can accomplish all this, as well as train the additional personnel needed to man them all. But, as that is your directive, I shall do my best to see that we accomplish as much of it as time and circumstance permit.

Chapter 2

COMMODORE COOK?"

Janet Mendelson Cook turned toward the sound of the noise to see a tall, dark-haired young man hurrying toward her, snaking his way through the human maze filling the small concourse. The old base had been cramped and crowded when CosGuard knew it as I-Com—or Isis Command. Now that it was Isitian Naval Headquarters, they seemed to be living on top of each other. Running herself ragged seemed to be standard procedure these days, and she stopped to wait for him. She wasn't looking forward to the meeting that was waiting for her at the other end of the hallway, and was grateful for the interruption.

"What is it this time, Commander?" she smiled.

"Sorry to interrupt again, Ma'am," said the young officer. "But before you go in to meet the wolves I thought you should see this." He handed Janet a copy of the latest dispatch from the scouts. The message included a facsimile of a Zarathustran news report, outlining what the Terran government had released to its citizens as the latest in a series of Isitian demands. The Terrans claimed that Isis wanted nothing less than full annexation of the Planet Zarathustra, as well as the surrender of all warships presently moored at ZarCom, Cos-Guard's command base for the planet. It was all nonsense, of course; but these days, nonsense seemed to spread faster than truth.

"Has he seen this, yet?" Janet asked, motioning with her head toward the hallway leading to the Technological Laboratories in the Eastern Wing of the space station.

"No, Ma'am. He left strict orders not to be disturbed. You're the only one who can ignore that order without having to grow a new hide."

Janet laughed brightly. Rank might have its privileges, but some privileges had little to do with rank.

"Thank you, Lieutenant," she replied. "This may come in handy. And I'll make sure he gets the word, sooner or later. Now return to your duties, Mr.—?"

"Barnes, Ma'am."

"Mr. Barnes—that's right. Thank you."

"Yes, Ma'am."

As he watched the Commodore turn and walk down the Main Concourse, Commander Christopher Barnes wondered how they could pull it all together. He knew little about the trouble brewing down on the planet, and cared less, but time was running out on them. If the witless wonders on the ground couldn't see it, then they were as blind as the Terries. They could at least give the Navy the credit for an ounce of brains, and then let them do their best to pull this miracle off. Politicians and their nitwit assistants had enough trouble keeping things functioning groundside. Even before this whole hash started, it taxed their collective abilities. Trying to second-guess the Admiral might prop up their egos, but given the track record of most politicians it would only add a few more decimal places to their odds.

As the Commodore disappeared down the hallway leading to the Command Center, Barnes turned and headed toward the Simulators. His current assignment—Naval Intelligence—might be where the real action was at the moment, but he went off duty in twenty minutes anyway, and his Second could page him if something important came up on their screens. He was already looking toward the future. As he told all his subordinates, if you want to contribute to the effort, you have to pay the price. He had another hour left on the Simulator for today, and still had to make up for missing half his session two days earlier, when the scouts were making their last close pass at ZarCom. The Terries wouldn't wait forever; and when they finally came, he'd be ready to do his part.

"DAMMIT!"

"What's wrong, Charlie?"

"Ow—dammit!"

Charlie Kozlowski shook his hand violently, trying to shake away the pain coursing through his lower arm. His glove, now blackened from its encounter with the fusing torch, lay smoldering on the floor.

"Hey, nobody said this would be easy."

"Nobody said it would hurt, either!"

"Charlie?"

"Oh, Jesus!"

"What's wrong, people?" asked Yeoman Sergeant Ken Cutler, the shift foreman. Walking toward the sound of the disturbance, Cutler was expecting the worst. Ever since the Admiral had returned to Isis, the morale of his construction crew had never been better. Perversely, it also led to no fewer than ten accidents in the last month, all from trying to finish this new ship before the Terrans came to call. A month earlier, he'd thought the task hopeless; he still felt the same way, but now everyone was determined not to be the shirker whose lack of effort cost the Admiral a second starship.

"Not you again, Kozlowski?"

"Sorry, Sarge."

"What is it with you Northlanders?" he barked gruffly. "You can't keep your heads down, or your minds on your work. I swear it comes from those cold, lonely nights in the winter, when you've nothing better to do than dream your life away waiting for the ground to thaw."

As his men laughed, Cutler cast a knowing eye up and down the line. Cable wires still hung from the sidepanels; and there were still empty holes where the hallway display terminals were supposed to be. It looked no different than it had the previous day, and it would probably look about the same tomorrow. As hard as they worked, they never seemed to make any headway. In the days ahead, it might be hard to keep his crew motivated if they had no sense of progress.

"Anyone remember," he said, stepping over the tools Kozlowski had scattered on the deck, "how many of these things we've done this past week?"

"Doesn't do much good," snorted one of his crew, a tall, gangly teenager from the South Shore area. "The halls go on forever, and we just keep stringing wire after wire. After a time, you sort of lose count, Mr. Cutler."

"Well, I just went back to check over our work," replied the sergeant. "We've done the wiring on sixteen corridors on four different decks, spanning a combined total of nearly five-thousand linear feet—and laying the innards for sixty-four display monitors."

Cutler looked to see eyebrows raising on his crew. "That, gentlemen, is damn impressive. And that's the pace we have to keep, if we're going to get this ship ready in time for the Admiral to use it."

Hearing the fire in their shouts, Cutler smiled to himself. A month ago he had to be everywhere, browbeating his men like a nagging mother-in-law. It had been exhausting—for his crew, as well as himself. Now, with Admiral Cook in charge of the Navy, it was all he could do to keep them from working themselves to death each day, and stapling their fingers to the sidepanels in the process.

"Now listen to me good: we can't keep getting careless. Kozlowski could have lost a hand trying to hurry. We don't want to hash up this ship like a Bristol Stew. Keep a constant pace. And stay at it. That's what'll get her done in time—and that's what'll keep you all in one piece.

"You got that, Kozlowski?"

The young Northlander grinned sheepishly and nodded his head.

"Good. Now, back to work."

As the crew turned back to their tasks, Cutler's ears drew him toward a loud crash from the other end of the corridor, where the systems technicians were trying to place the hallway monitor screens.

"Crap!" he muttered to himself. He ran down the hallway, toward the sound of the disturbance. Nothing was going right: everywhere he turned, all he saw were mistakes and sloppy workmanship. A month ago he'd worried that his crew was the biggest collection of oafs and lard-brains that could ever come from Planet Isis. Now, he was beginning to worry that maybe they weren't.

* * *

"Unacceptable!"

"Excuse me, Minister, but— "

"Do you hear me? That is completely unacceptable!"

Janet's face flushed a deep red. She wasn't used to putting up with such bull-headed arrogance. Not that she didn't have plenty of experience handling it, but she didn't usually have to put up with it. Dealing with her usual source didn't require nearly as much tact.

"Excuse me, sir, but I'm just the messenger. If you wish, you may express your concerns to him directly. I can put you on the list, and he'll get back to you as soon as he has a free moment."

Reginald Ross, Minister of State, snorted in disgust. His eyes bulged and he began pacing about the room, sputtering to himself. Janet exchanged a glance with George McKenzie, the gentlemanly Minister of Defense, who shook his head sympathetically, but said nothing. As the tantrum abated, the defense minister rose from his seat. It wasn't easy, McKenzie thought, standing between two mammoth egos. And it didn't seem likely to get any better, any time soon.

"You know, Reggie," he smiled. "We did, after all, come unannounced. Perhaps— "

"Unannounced?" Ross spat angrily. "I damn well told him I was coming two days ago."

"You didn't speak to him yourself, though?"

"I spoke directly to the Commodore," Ross said, pointing an accusing finger at Janet. She was about to say something she knew she'd regret instantly when McKenzie intervened.

"And we both know that Mrs. Cook would have certainly conveyed the message to her husband. But we never got a confirmation, did we?"

"What the hell difference— "

"And with all the responsibilities he has to tend to—well," he said, turning to Janet with a smile. "Far be it from us to intrude. Perhaps we can reschedule the meeting?"

"We have a meeting of the full Cabinet next week," Ross said archly, his dark eyes glaring at Janet. "I want him there. Without fail."

"As soon as I can corner him," Janet replied, desperately grabbing the opening, "I'll try to arrange it myself."

"Splendid," McKenzie said, as grandly as he could. "Now, Reggie, we had best be on our way." He ushered his younger colleague toward the door, only to stop just before leaving, promising to join up with Ross at the pneumatic tubes that would carry them to the shuttle bay. He walked briskly back toward Janet.

"I'm sorry, George."

"He can't keep this up, you know. I barely got wind of Lord Fauntleroy's little excursion. I hate to think what might have happened if I hadn't been here to calm him down."

"I'll try."

"You'll have to do more than that. Despite what your husband thinks of him, Ross is no imbecile. He is a highly respected member of the Chancellor's Party, and controls a good third of our side of the House. He may well be Chancellor himself, some day. Like it or not, his concerns reflect a good deal of worry, groundside. And until he's satisfied, he'll make more and more trouble for all of us."

Janet nodded glumly. She should be used to it by now, but somehow it never seemed to get any easier. As the soft-spoken McKenzie's smile returned, and he took his leave, she was left to wonder whether she'd go crazy before it was finally over.

Hurrying to catch up to his colleague, McKenzie's mind raced with problems of his own. Fairly or not, he knew that he'd be blamed for all of the Admiral's failings as a bureaucrat, and groaned at the thought of answering yet another round of unanswerable complaints at the next Cabinet meeting. As Defense Minister, the Navy was his responsibility. And as the first instinct of any politician was to pin the blame for any potential disaster on somebody else, nobody else in the Cabinet would be willing to take the heat if dealing with their temperamental commander proved to be impossible. But if it came to a choice between his neck and the Chancellor's, he had no doubt where his duty would lie.

After all, this was—or would be—war. If he could help save Isis by sacrificing his career, it would be a small price to pay. Even for a politician.

* * *

"SQUADRON SIX, hard pivot, one hundred degrees."

As the order faded into silence, the bridge crew of the *Delta Miss* huddled over their instruments, trying their best to bring the old girl into position as they maintained formation. The squadron struggled to keep their line straight, knowing that everything they did, every communication entered, and every maneuver mastered or flubbed would be instantly logged and forever remembered by the tracking computers.

Holding position as the rest of the battle group moved to execute their own orders, the ten ships of Squadron Six stood fast while the maneuver proceeded, as it had for the past two hours. Squadron Seven would ease past them, heading toward the rally point twenty klicks to the rear; Eight and Two would stay behind as a rear guard, then fall back. As the last ship from Squadron Two passed the pivot line, Seven's line moved forward with charged guns and a slow, steady advance, until the ships from Squadron One showed on the forward screens.

Soon, the clearing bell sounded, and the overhead lights returned, announcing the end of the round. Through the windows, a few spectators from the next session were clearly visible, watching how Team Blue handled the problem they were all facing, day after day—or napping in their seats, trying to fit as much sleep into the day as their tight schedules permitted.

"Awaiting final analysis," the Admiral's voice announced over the speaker. "Maintain your stations."

"What'll he find this time?" wondered the ensign at the weapons station, a short, stocky young man with quick, clever eyes and a quiet, intense voice. For the last week, the maneuver hadn't changed one whit; only the roles of the squadrons had varied. Yet every time, something new was added to the critique. It was driving him to distraction. No matter how long or hard he practiced at any of the bridge stations, there was always something else for him to learn, something new for him to consider.

"Oh, stop worrying so much, Nielsen," scoffed the lad seated for the moment in the command chair. "You know, it isn't really Cook at all, doing these evaluations. He can't be everywhere, for God's sake, so they use his voice to make us all nervous. It's just some damn computer, using our own input to dish out the critique according to some preset formula. A rotting waste of time, if you ask me."

"Whitcomb, you're a fool!" snapped Eric Nielsen, his dark eyes flaming indignantly. "A fool and a disgrace to your uniform!"

"Really? You'd really rather be doing this, when we could be out doing real maneuvers with real ships? Keeping us locked up in the simulators is one thing. But cooping us on base for maneuvers is a real piece of work. If we ever do face the Terries across the masterboard of some piece of electronics, I suppose it may prove worthwhile. But I doubt they'll shy away from facing off against us in space. It would be nice to practice sailing around for real before we square off against the Terry fleet, don't you think?"

Nielsen sighed harshly. He didn't care whether the Admiral really sat through maneuvers with them, though he found the thought vaguely comforting. But he hated the cynicism that Whitcomb and others like him brought into the simulations. He didn't like spending all his drill time on base, either. But they had lots to do, and little time left to do it. If the Admiral thought they could do more at a simulator station, it wasn't their place to question the order. And if malcontents like Whitcomb thought differently, they could make better use of their time by complaining less, and practicing a good lot more.

"Evaluation completed," announced the voice over the speaker. Each ship's critique would be tailored to its squadron assignment, strategic role, and tactical performance. Nielsen knew full well that the Admiral couldn't do it all himself. But he also knew whose insights controlled the computer. If morons like Whitcomb couldn't take advantage of their commander's experience, it put more weight on his own shoulders to take up the slack.

"Squadron Six—your line formation was substandard at the outset. Your spacing was scattered and non-uniform, and you made no attempt to adjust. Once the pivot order came, your maneuvers were splotchy and uneven. While excusable under fire, a dry run offers no excuse for the failure to maintain synchronized movements. Though this is primarily the helmsman's responsibility, the officer in the command chair is ultimately in charge, and should notice when the ship is not maintaining proper formation.

"*Delta Miss*," the voice continued, the computer smoothly moving its analysis from squadron to individual ship without interruption. "Performance at the Weapons and Systems stations showed improvement. Tracking sensors showed a smooth progression from the charging sequencing to target acquisition mode, and the information display network showed a smooth transition of sensor data to all stations. Helm and navigation showed modest gains, particularly in plot-time and execution; however, maintaining formation in battle exercises usually takes priority over optimizing your individual station performance, and this was the weakest component of the exercise. The command chair failed to notice the bridge crew's tendency to rush the formation, and neglected to direct modifications accordingly; in addition, clearance orders on prompt by other stations were often tardy, suggesting a need for greater attention to detail.

"Crews on all ships will change stations, and run the exercise again."

Slowly, sullenly, the drilling team rose and started toward their next station. For most officers in the Isitian Navy, bridge simulations were among the least favorite parts of the day. The Quarter Watch team for the *Delta Miss* was no exception.

"A waste of time."

"Attention— !"

"Whitcomb—shut up."

"—the simulation will begin in one minute."

"Right. And I suppose Mr. Goody-Two-Shoes thinks this is a marvelous way to spend his time."

"Eyes front and quiet on the bridge."

"Oh, give us a break, Nielsen."

* * *

PROGRESS REPORT: *Starship Construction*

DATE: cc: 144.7282.2
TO: Adm. R.C.Cook
FROM: Comm.A.J.Landis
SUBJECT: Daily Update, Weekly Summary

We have overcome most of our electrical problems and are making steady progress rewiring the ship according to the new specifications. As you predicted, the delay caused by reconfiguring the main computer appears unlikely to affect the installation date, now that the changes in the wiring have converted the computers into self-contained units. In addition, reprogramming the units as individual cells should allow easier deck-site access, more than compensating for the small decrease in available memory for the entire system. I anticipate finishing preliminary wiring within the next two days. Following a day or two of diagnostic testing, we should be able to begin downloading all necessary data whenever you are ready. While final testing will require several additional weeks, you should be able to begin using the electronic systems immediately thereafter.

Attached are the unit reports, for your review. As you can see, work is proceeding slightly ahead of schedule. If we are correct in assuming that the Terran fleet needs at least three additional months to prepare for offensive actions, we will have plenty of time; if an attack comes before the end of March, our chances of readying the ship in time for action are less than 50%.

In any case, as you directed, the *New Alexandria* will remain operational for the duration and will forego her scheduled repairs until after the crisis is past. I do, however, continue to believe that we can undertake both repair operations simultaneously and highly recommend that you reconsider your recent order to the contrary. While replacing her computers has eased much of the strain, her electrical system remains in need of overhaul, and her hull tiles and sensor banks still need replacement. In the absence of adverse intelligence reports, I adhere to my opinion that, if done immediately, the ship would be back on-line within the month, and that her enhanced battle-readiness would justify both the additional cost, and the dislocation of present training schedules.

Chapter 3

S EATED AT THE conference table, George McKenzie felt his heart sink. The squabbling had gone on for the better part of the month and showed no signs of stopping. But he was tired—tired of fighting this battle all alone. And tired of grappling with his own doubts, his own fears. He had nothing to go on but faith in their cause, and in their commander. And faith, it seemed, was in short supply these days. He was one of a dwindling number of friends the Admiral still had among the Inner Sanctum. He was even starting to wonder whether the Chancellor might be harboring second thoughts about the matter, as well.

The sun, low in the crisp, morning sky, cast a warm glow into the inner office. Looking smaller and frailer than McKenzie had ever noticed before, Irene McGinnis, the Chancellor, peered out through the large bay window onto the gardens, damp from the winter rains. She seemed preoccupied, as if paying no attention to the bitter argument raging among her most trusted advisors.

"I'm telling you, it is a catastrophe in the making!" thundered Reginald Ross, the energetic young Minister of State. "Mark my words. History will not be kind to us, Irene. To have come so close—so very close, indeed—only to waste our chance like this. If it weren't so tragic it would be downright laughable."

"And to top it all off," agreed David Henderson, the Chancellor's Chief of Staff, "we can't even breathe a word of this. Every way we look, we're simply cut off. Confront the problem publicly and we start a panic."

"Ignore it," continued Ross, "and we may be little more than accomplices to our own destruction."

"And let's not forget who's standing in the wings," added Henderson, "just waiting for us to stumble. He may have changed his tune in the last month—he can't undercut us now, without going after his own flesh and blood, thank God for small favors. But his stock across the aisle has risen fast in the last few weeks."

"Well, David, you don't have to explain the facts of life to the Chancellor."

"No, Reggie, there's where you're wrong." The Chancellor turned and walked back toward her bickering senior advisors, her eyes set like granite. For the first time in ages, McKenzie thought, it was the Irene McInnis of old returned to them. "I'm afraid you're going to have to spell it out completely for me. Because, you see, I'm just a foolish old woman. And I'm not about to let this one slip by me because I'm not as quick on the uptake as I used to be. So please explain yourself, if you would."

Now it was Ross' turn to feel the gnawing of uncertainty. But his misgivings weren't about whether he was actually right or wrong. It was so clear to him. So simple, so inevitable, and so devastatingly logical. His only real doubt was whether he would win this battle for the Chancellor's ear. For the first time, he sensed the depth of her own feelings in the matter.

"A number of things disturb me, Madam Chancellor," Ross said, his eyes hard and uncompromising. "His refusal to meet with us, I suppose we could ascribe to temperament— although, as you recall, I predicted that he would stand us up again, today. His refusal to answer any of our questions— "

"Any of *your* questions," the Chancellor corrected, with a wry smile.

"It does not appear that he is forthcoming about his plans, his schedules, or his intentions," Ross continued. "And that makes me extremely concerned about the direction he is taking us."

McInnis walked to a large chair beside the fireplace, and bade her senior advisors to do likewise. "You know what I think, Reggie? I do believe that you are jealous. You and David both. And I think this whole episode is nothing more than resentment over the fact that he cancelled your project to refurbish the *New Alexandria* without troubling to let you and your friends from Highland Technologies talk him out of it."

"*Madame Chancellor—!*"

"Oh, put your eyeballs back in their sockets, Mr. Minister," laughed McInnis. "I have seen more jealousy these past few weeks than I have in my whole career. And that includes," she continued, her eyes full of mischief, watching for the Minister of State's reaction to what she had to say, "more than a decade in Covington, watching the Terran Senate in their annual backstabbing rituals, grubbing for Federal money and preening for the cameras. I have no illusions, Reginald Ross—not about you, not about me, not about anyone involved in any aspect of any government, anywhere in Creation."

"Have you forgotten exactly who his uncle is?"

"Cornelius Cook is a great many things," the Chancellor replied coldly. "He is, in my estimation, the shrewdest member of the Opposition. He is also a rogue, an opportunist, and a political chameleon. He will say or do anything for partisan advantage. And he is now, poor soul, finding his chickens coming home to roost in a flock, ever since his nephew assumed command of the Interstellar Navy. He cannot attack our preparations for defense without looking like an ingrate and an idiot. But he cannot make people forget about his loud and windy opposition to funding the Navy in the first place without attacking our preparations as somehow inadequate. It is, Mr. Minister, a politician's nightmare—and frankly, I don't think Senator Cook is worth one jot of bother at the moment, whatever the opinion polls might show."

"If he gets wind of the cancellation— "

"Well, Reggie, I'm certainly not going to tell him."

"It will come up in the annual budget...."

"Mr. Minister," the Chancellor scoffed, "by next year's budget report, I fully expect that we will all be heroes—and the last thing the Opposition will want to talk about is whether we managed to spend quite all of the money we twisted arms hither and yon getting the Senate to authorize. Either that, or we will not be troubling ourselves very much about partisan politics, because we'll all be dead at the hands of a Terran invasion force, or rotting away in some Terry prison awaiting trial for treason."

"And what about his nephew? Can you be sure of his real reasons for the cancellation? And don't you think he's likely to leak this whole business, if only to pass a crumb to his own flesh and blood?"

Smiling sweetly, the Chancellor leaned forward, her dainty hands folded demurely across her lap, her steel-blue eyes skewering the soul of her Minister of State.

"Minister Ross," she began quietly. "Among your responsibilities are state security, and in that capacity I have full confidence that you will bring to my attention anything that might pose a threat to our young and fragile Republic. But before you continue, I wish to share something with you.

"I have met and worked with thousands of men over the years. I have been impressed by few, and have admired fewer still. For your future reference, you should know that Admiral Cook happens to be the bravest, most honest man I have met in my lifetime. And I will hear nothing said against him in my presence.

"I don't know why he scotched the renovation project. He hasn't seen fit to share it with me—and I, for one, am reluctant to take up his time just now, dealing with what is, in the final analysis, largely a matter of politics. It would have been splendid, if he could have joined us today. I am sure that we all would have found whatever he told us to be positively exhilarating, if a little on the daunting side. But I am also quite unwilling to trouble him about the matter. For you see, Mr. Minister, I *understand* what it means for him to have the weight of a world crushing down upon his shoulders. And I will do nothing—*nothing!*—to increase that weight by so much as an ounce."

Ross flushed a deep crimson and took a deep, bitter breath.

"Now, have I made myself sufficiently clear?"

"Yes, Madam Chancellor," he replied.

"And was there anything else you wished to say on the subject?"

"No, Madam Chancellor."

As proudly as they could, Henderson and Ross took their leave, and left the Chancellor's office to walk down the Grand Hall, toward the Ministry of State. The Chancellor waited until the door had closed behind them before sinking back into her chair and closing her tired, misting eyes.

"I'm too old for this, George," she sighed, her voice hiding the hint of a quiver. "I should be off somewhere, tending my garden and spoiling my grandchildren."

"It should be over in a few months, Irene," McKenzie said softly. "You can hang on until then. If you can still make the likes of Reggie Ross feel like a naughty schoolboy caught peeking up a little girl's dress—well then, I'd say Old Ironpanties hasn't lost all that much, over the years."

McInnis opened her reddening eyes and smiled. "It's been years since I've heard that name."

"I'm sure they still fit, you know. Granted, you're a bit older than that sunny, ravishing lass of years past. And I fancy you may have drooped a bit here and there. But you really haven't gained all that much, near as I can tell. And you still have the prettiest legs of any girl in town."

"Oh—stop it, George!" the Chancellor sniffed, hoping very much that he would do nothing of the kind.

"I don't know how we've come this far," he whispered. "But nobody else could have kept it all together. And I don't know anybody else on this planet who can keep us all pulling in the same direction.

"Just hang in there, Irene. A few more months, that's all we need. Then, you can finally be glad you waited all these years to finish your memoirs."

The Chancellor closed her eyes and nodded, wishing to heaven that she could just crawl into her nice, warm bed and sleep for a hundred years.

* * *

"TIME."

As the gravity scrambler whirled to a halt, Boyd shared a grim smile with his lieutenant. Nodding across the way to the other drill sergeant, the two of them opened the hatch door and quickly stood aside. About half of the four dozen recruits, all desperate to escape what they all perceived to be a modern-day torture chamber, poured out of the hatch, and quickly dropped to the floor, looking to all the world as if they were trying to keep the old starbase from spinning. Moans filled the antechamber, joining the sounds of retching that wafted pitiably from the floor of the chamber of horrors.

"Recruits, stand at attention!" barked Boyd. Both drill sergeants stood with clipboards in hand, observing each survivor for fatal signs of weakness. Twenty or so bleary-eyed recruits struggled bravely to their feet, standing as stiffly as they could manage. Marking them off at once, the two sergeants quickly ushered them to one side, then motioned for the rest of the detail to help tend to the washouts.

"Oh, my God," moaned one of the survivors. One of the women,

Boyd noted. She'd probably be on track to become an officer, if she made it through the rest of her training. A pretty one, at that—at least, she would be, when she was through looking green. Too few of them around these days, he smiled to himself. But life was tough all over.

"All right," grunted Boyd, rocking each survivor by the shoulders, testing to see just how steady he might be. "All of you are at ease. And you don't have to stand at ease, either. Stay close to the ground, bend over, and breathe deeply. It might help to keep your eyes closed. Remember, you can still get bounced, if you loose it." He tried to phrase it as gently as he could; the Admiral had, after all, warned against mentioning food at this point in the procedure—and, as always, the Admiral was right again.

"We'll be back in a few minutes, after we tend to your unluckier friends over there."

As the two sergeants ambled off to supervise the rescue of the remaining recruits, the successful applicants soon found their wits and senses returning to them. Before long, most had taken to sitting upright, leaning against the wall and watching another of their erstwhile comrades helped from the gravity machine. Some had recovered enough to be steadied by a single enlistee; others had to be carried, often still wailing piteously from the ordeal. The stench was everywhere; but to their collective surprise, most of the survivors felt no nauseous aftereffects.

"Congratulations," said the smiling lieutenant, as he stepped toward them. "Although I'm sure none of you feels quite like celebrating just yet."

The subdued laughter was enough to break the mood. The young officer motioned for them to stand.

"I am Lt. Dyer," he said, after a short pause. "I will be supervising the next stage of your physical training." He motioned to his left, and yet a third young sergeant appeared, leading a hovercart filled with boxes.

"You've just finished the screening portion of your basic training," he continued, intoning words he'd said dozens of times to hundreds of servicemen. "Since you've survived with most of your innards intact, you're ready to embark on the biggest challenge of our lifetime. Each of you can be proud, for our screening is tighter now than it's ever been. But don't get to feeling important. It could just as easily have been you losing your breakfast in the Scrambler. It doesn't make you any better, or them any worse. You just happen to have a tolerance that's useful in combat, one that we can't teach and don't have time to compensate for, or train away.

"Effective tomorrow, each of you will have a new training regimen. You'll find it posted at 500 Hours today, in the personnel office and on any bulletin board on any of the base computers. Until then, each of you is free to stand down—and I suggest you take advantage of the time to get some sleep. Until this business is over, you won't have much free time, and right now sleep is the most valuable commodity in the Navy.

"When you report for duty tomorrow, you will wear your new uniform, which I'll distribute right now. Notice that they're of two types—a gray cadet's jersey, and a full enlistee's issue. Whether you realized it or not, this group of survivors contains both officers and enlisteds. That's because the Admiral wants you to know that you're all the same in the eyes of the Navy. Your responsibilities will be different, and from now on your training will be different, but the Navy needs everyone. You went through the Scrambler as a group, and you came out as a group. Officer candidates may have some special skills we need: a grasp of spatial relationships, perhaps; or advanced training in some scientific specialty. But grunts have always done the real work in any military force, anywhere, at any time in history. It won't change in the Isitian Navy. Space plays no favorites, and neither do we. From now on, you are part of a team. You think, work, and train as a team. And when we finally manage to stop the Terries, we're going to do it as a team."

As the washouts were getting the attention they needed, the sergeants returned to the small group of survivors and the lieutenant concluded his remarks. Nodding to his senior noncom, Dyer stepped to the hovercart and removed a large box, and two smaller ones from the top of a pile.

"Ronald Atkins, Crewman," he barked; a tall, young man stepped forward, and the large box was handed to him. As he took it, and peeked inside to see the pressed, dark blue crewman's uniform folded inside, the sergeant whispered, "Go salute the lieutenant." Atkins did so, smartly, and the lieutenant snapped a salute in return.

"Crewman Atkins," the lieutenant smiled, extending his hand, "welcome to the Isitian Navy."

"David Bartholomew, Cadet; Al Cameron, Crewman; Geoffrey Jason, Cadet...."

* * *

REYNOLDS ADJUSTED the receiver on his radio, trying to home in on the signal. Winking at his navigator, he smiled when the voice from Zarathustra finally came in strong and clear. It was exactly noon in New Aruba, the planet's capital and largest city, and time to hear what was happening in the rest of the Universe. He'd just finished sending his latest report along the relay chain back to New Alexandria, and thought Headquarters would like some insight into what Covington was telling the rest of Terra. Besides, he and his navigator, Eddie Williams, both thought the news reader on the midday news sounded cute. They had an ongoing debate over whether she sounded blonde or brunette. He set the controls to record, and sat back to enjoy the music of the woman's sweet, soothing voice.

> "On Isis yesterday, the Senate voted to continue the grain embargo. Chancellor McGinnis vowed that so long as Terra continued the war in the East, no further food shipments would be forthcoming from her planet. Before the War, Isis supplied nearly half of all Terran grain exports."

"Where do they get this stuff?" Williams wondered aloud. "It's like something you'd find on an off-channel back on Earth. You know, right between the documentaries on 'Beauty Queen Marries German Shepherd,' and 'Boy Raised by Man-Eating Sharks.' "

"Hush," ordered Reynolds. "You're insulting the girl I love."

> "While elements friendly to the Terran League voted to rescind the ban, the ruling coalition defeated the effort by a wide margin. Meanwhile, demonstrators outside the Isitian capital continued their protests, amid growing signs that a crackdown against pro-Terran elements is imminent."

"Coalition?" scoffed Eddie. "When is the last time the Government coalesced around anything? Other than a pay raise for themselves, I mean?"

"Hush!"

"And now the War News Update, courtesy of the Central Terran News Agency: Terran forces pushed ahead again yesterday, capitalizing on a narrow breach in the line of Glincian forces. Eager to maintain an unbroken front, several attack wings slowed the pace of their activities in recent days, but the general retreat among the enemy has sources in Covington's Central Command convinced that it is only a matter of days before the Terran fleet resumes its advance.

"Meanwhile, there was renewed fighting along a broad front in the Crutchtan theater of battle. Covington reports heavy enemy losses, and a continuing consolidation of Terran gains. Yesterday, heavy fighting forced the main body of the enemy fleet to stop more than twenty parsecs away from the strategic outpost at Girshoona, and a source in the Terran High Command confirms that the enemy offensive has stalled well short of its objective. With additional reinforcements arriving daily from the starbase at Looking Glass, Central Command points to the widening gaps in enemy supply lines, and expects that the expanding Terran counterattack will isolate and destroy the foremost enemy divisions within a short period of time."

"What do you make of it?" asked Eddie, tapping the control buttons to transmit the recording to the next communications station.

"Who knows?" answered Reynolds, taking a deep breath. He checked the chronometer: it read 500 hours; another hour, and they could pass off to Lt. Landon's ship. The Navy had arranged the scouts in teams so they'd have help in case of trouble. It occurred to him that it was nice simply to have the company. Landon and company might not have the charms of the newsgirl of his dreams, but at least they gave Eddie and himself a sounding board for their complaints.

"Who the hell knows anything, anymore?"

"Right you are, Eddie. Right you are, indeed."

JOGGING DOWN the rampway, his legs unstiffening with each step he took, Jack Markham didn't know whether to be disappointed or relieved. Washing out of the Navy was not the achievement of a lifetime. He knew that sitting around, unable to do anything to protect his wife and children, would drive him crazy. On the other hand, he had lots of company. At least he wouldn't have to face a lifetime of doubts and self-torment, just because he didn't give it a try. Juggling his bag to keep it from falling as he ran, Jack smiled lamely at the young woman manning the turnstile, who was urging him on with a wide, beckoning wave.

"Hurry!" she shouted. "You've got just enough time to make it!"

Unfortunately, his duffle bag had other ideas. As he stepped up his pace, the seam in his bag gave way, spilling the contents along his path and tangling his feet among a cascading pair of sweatpants. Plunging headlong onto the rampway, he landed face-first at the feet of the pretty girl who was doing her best to keep from laughing at the young man who had just fallen in defense of his homeland.

"Let—let me—let me help," she stammered, trying to let the washout keep as much of his dignity as possible. Reaching down to help collect his belongings, she couldn't stand the strain any longer, and collapsed in laughter onto the ramp. The clearing bell sounded to announce the departure of the shuttle to Isis.

Rolling dejectedly onto his back, Jack reflected that this was one day he'd rather forget. His only accomplishments had been washing out of the Navy, and missing the ship home. It was a fine thing, escaping the chance to die at the hands of the Terries only to give his wife an excuse to kill him, for keeping her waiting at the spaceport.

"When does the next— " he began.

"Not until tomorrow, I'm afraid," said the young ensign, helping Jack collect his things.

"Is there any place— ?"

"Just go back to your barracks. They'll be glad to put you up for one more day."

"This isn't— "

"The first time this has happened?" She smiled and shook her head. "People miss their connections all the time. Of course, not many manage to do so with quite as much style."

Jack felt his face turning red as he chuckled along with his companion. But everyone always said that laughing at yourself was better than letting others laugh at you alone. He was starting to have his doubts about that.

"This has to be the most embarrassing day in my entire life," he said at last, hoping that his pretty young companion would take some pity on him. "Christ—I doubt very much more could happen to me today."

"Actually," began the turnstile keeper, only to stop in midsentence. Jack knew at once that he should let things lie. Despite what his wife and family said about him, he had a keen sense of people and his surroundings and sensed that the turnstile attendant was doing her best to spare him further grief. It was just that damned curiosity. That's what always led him further into trouble. Not a general obtuseness, as his wife always told him.

"What?" he demanded. "What is it? You may as well tell me. Things can't possibly get any worse for me, you know."

"Well—you didn't just miss the shuttle."

"Of course I just missed the shuttle. Got tied up by some damn fool pencil-pusher with a wad of paperwork to fill out. Then I got shunted to the back of the mess line—only to have them run out of corn, leaving us standing for an extra twenty minutes while they boiled up some more. One minute earlier, and I wouldn't have had to rush quite so much. And if I hadn't been rushing...."

"No, I mean, the shuttle wasn't all you missed," the young lady winced visibly as she smiled. Jack could tell he'd regret asking, but couldn't stop himself.

"So what else went wrong for me?"

"You missed him. He was here. He sometimes comes to thank the washouts for their efforts, you know. Today was one of those days. He stopped by to help send off the shuttle."

"Who?"

"Well, the Admiral, of course."

Jack groaned to himself. Now his day was complete. One chance to make the Navy—one chance to make it back home—and one chance, probably his only chance, to see the man trying to reconstitute the whole hash. Three chances up, three chances gone. Just like a game of rounders, except that rounders didn't make him sick to his stomach.

"How often...."

The young lady smiled sadly. "Not very. Once a week, sometimes twice. Sorry."

"Well," Jack snorted, swinging his duffle over his back, "I hope the Navy has better luck with the Terries than I've had with the Navy."

"Couldn't be much worse, you know."

"Thanks, Missey," Jack laughed, starting back up the ramp toward the main concourse. "You're a real boost for morale."

"We each serve in our own way, you know."

"Yeah. And I bet they don't do it this way in the Cosmic Guard, either."

"At least you got the lingo down pretty well."

"It was the only thing about this ordeal that didn't involve sending something spinning. Whether it was my brain, or various body parts."

"Good luck to you."

"These days, we all need some, Missey. The whole planet needs some."

* * *

"Goodnight!"

"We'll see you tomorrow, then."

"I don't see how you do it. You must be exhausted."

"So are both of you. Now, off with you! We have a lot to do tomorrow."

The door closed behind her, and Janet stepped into the darkness. She could have turned on the lights, of course, but she didn't feel like struggling with the brightness. Stepping gingerly around the furniture, she came to the oversized couch that they'd received as a wedding gift from her new brother-in-law. Lying down quietly, she stared into the blackness until her eyes welled with tears and her throat tightened until it hurt.

This was not how she imagined her life, she thought. Not how she imagined marriage. Certainly not what she expected out of a life together with the man she loved. She felt hurt and betrayed. Mostly, she felt alone.

That was what hurt the most. More than any of his thoughtless remarks, more than the belittling little jokes at her expense, or his way of making her feel so foolish she wanted to shrink into nothingness. She was so alone that it felt like a prison—a horrid, steel prison of her own making. Worst of all, coming after the closeness of their escape together, their endless days of sharing each moment and every danger, the past few weeks made her feel that life had passed her by in one hurried rush. She felt too neglected to feel like much of a wife; and Heaven knew that her chosen man, her dear sweet Skipper, had not been much of a husband.

Taking a deep breath, Janet did what she could to drive such thinking out of her head. She knew what they were up against, as well as anyone. Maybe as well as the Skipper himself. It wasn't callousness that drove him to exhaustion every day. But each day that passed was one less that they had to spend together. If the future was really as bleak as she feared, then these days were all that they had. The hopelessness of their efforts wouldn't change the fact that the days were rushing by, and they were letting them slip by as foolishly as two teenagers, convinced of their own immortality.

But it wasn't his fault, she told herself. She'd chosen to follow him; come what may, she'd do it again.

It wasn't his fault, she reminded herself over and over again. No matter how she felt about it, it wasn't really his fault.

Nervous as a schoolgirl, Janet sat with the others in the commander's outer office. She'd been looking forward to meeting him for quite some time, she smiled; and she'd been stunned to realize that she'd drawn the CONSTANTINE as her first assignment, and the mysterious Commander Cook as her first skipper. She'd followed his career with interest, ever since her first days at the Academy, and found herself flustered beyond all reason at the prospect of meeting him.

"The Skipper will see you now," said Jennifer, the yeoman who served as the commanding officer's secretary and orderly. Janet was the first to her feet, and made sure she was in position to be first into the office. Making a good impression with the new commander was always a priority; that's what they told her at the Academy, and that's exactly what she intended to do. She'd spent half the morning getting just the right touch of makeup, and the optimal bounce to her hair. It irked her to realize that, owing to the stronger elbows of her fellow tyros, she found herself at the back of the line, behind the two other young officers also joining the CONSTANTINE at Demeter—two bumbling oafs who struck Janet as better suited to wind surfing than helping to run a CosGuard cruiser.

Bounding into the office, she was struck at once by the mound of papers on the Commander's desk, and by the oddly familiar look to his face. She'd seen it before, she was sure—only to chide herself for being such a fool: she'd seen his picture dozens of times—at the Academy, and in some of the briefing papers on the Hawkins Massacre. As he shuffled absently through the papers on the desk, his mind seemed light years away from the mundane, administrative task of greeting the newest additions to the crew. Janet smiled at the realization that such a brilliant mind could find itself lost in a fog of its owner's making.

"Ensign Rico Cardinale, reporting for duty, sir," said the first young officer in line, a dark, handsome man, who spoke with the barest trace of an Earther's accent.

"Ensign Robert Drinan, reporting for duty, sir," said the second young officer, a tall, reedy Babylonian. Janet had known Drinan at the Academy and had taken an instant dislike to him. He was pushy, arrogant—and always convinced that he was right.

"Ensign Janet Mendelson, reporting for duty, sir."

At the sound of her voice, Cook's head snapped up; a look of astonishment on his face, he looked directly into her eyes. In that heartbeat, Janet forgot about everyone else in the room, and could feel herself beginning to blush. Though her heart began pounding furiously, she didn't know whether she wanted to laugh, or to cry. It was him—without the beard, and without the sand. But it was him. He'd even said his name was "Skipper." As it all fell into place, she began to wonder whether she hadn't really know it all along.

"Hello, Miss Mendelson," the Skipper said, smiling wryly. "I guess it really is a finite Universe, after all.

"Welcome to the CONSTANTINE, everyone."

Chapter 4

AS IT HAD every day since he'd returned home, awareness eventually began to clear the fog in his brain. Grudgingly, Roscoe Cook stirred, struggling to find the energy to lift his head and commit himself to another day. At once, he felt a sharp, searing pain in his neck, the result of sleeping while seated on his lab stool, with his head on the table. Cursing silently, he forced himself to stand, rubbing his neck and stretching his stiff back.

Slowly, snippets of the past day crept back into his consciousness. After all this time in the lab, after weeks of driving himself to find an answer, he'd finally found out what had killed Captain Fitzgerald and the *Magellan* an eternity ago, on a doomed mission in what now seemed a different reality.

Rubbing the sleep from his eyes, Cook sat back down and turned his attention back to the computer screen. Everything was just as he'd left it: the lab table was the same tangle of equations and sketches; the monitor showed the same outline of a starship. He would run the program again, just to make sure he hadn't overlooked something, but his heart knew the truth. What he'd found wasn't likely to help them. Not this time. Not one damn bit.

Entering the parameters of his experiment, Cook ran his projections once again. He watched as a tiny oval appeared on the screen, representing a small gunship, and moved toward the larger disc symbolizing the *Magellan*. The two ships glowed red, as each charged its guns; firing simultaneously, and directly amidships, he watched the smaller ship explode—and the starship register a complete systems failure. The charge from the smaller ship's guns had tracked a power vacuum caused by the big ship's blasters, leading straight into the gun batteries and directly to the power source. There, overloading the starship's engines, it caused a massive power surge that crippled the powerful ship.

Cook shook his head. It was easy enough to fix: a small surge buffer in the guns would take care of the problem. That it had escaped the attention of engineers throughout Terra was a testament to the power of orthodoxy, for a flaw like this would never come to light unless someone was looking for it. And it was obvious that the Crutchtans hadn't discovered it either, for the glitch would have neutralized every starship in the Terran fleet. At least temporarily—until CosGuard made the necessary adjustments.

Cook smiled—briefly allowing himself a touch of pride. After all, his signature technique of shifting power from gun battery to gun battery to confuse the enemy about his intentions also eliminated the problem. Quite by accident, he'd managed to diffuse his ship's power, preventing the surge and making it impossible for the effect to work.

But none of that mattered very much. The effect required a massive power source, far more massive than the typical frigate or cruiser that formed the bulk of the Terran Fleet. In other words, the source had to be a starship—and as the energy stream had to go directly down the mouth of an open gun battery that had just fired, it could only come from a ship in the process of taking a direct hit. Perhaps in a few years he could isolate the energy patterns needed to replicate the effect; if controlled, it might provide them with a powerful new weapon if Terra threatened them again. For now it did them precious little good, and he'd wasted enough time and energy tracking this particular wild goose.

Yawning, Cook entered his calculations and impressions into his log, and into the *Manual of Battle and Tactics* he was compiling for his Navy to use in training. He summoned his next task to his screen. It was his first chore every day for the past month, and would be among the first things he'd do every day until the crisis was over. His eyes still bleary, he called up the tutorial program he'd devised to train his recruits, and checked to see if anyone had come up with a Terran attack plan he hadn't anticipated. Seeing nothing to worry about, he set the program for a speed and complexity setting reached only by his personal password. For the next two hours, he ran simulation after simulation on the computer, wargaming his ragged, overmatched fleet against as many new enemy formations as he could imagine.

* * *

ARNOLD WASSER felt his heart racing. He wanted to shout, but didn't want to make a fool of himself. It was nearly shift change, and there were already several other young officers in the simulation room. The last thing he needed was to attract a crowd to watch him squander another chance to beat the computer.

Freezing the action on the screen, he stopped to consider the problem: the furious battle raging in the middle of his screen. The computer, playing Blue—Isis was always blue; it was the Admiral's favorite color— was pressing the attack, throwing all its reserves into the center of the Red line. It was the same problem that was giving everyone trouble: the Computer was a master at concentrating its attack and finding the weakest point in the Red defenses. If he moved a regiment of Red frigates from his flank toward the center of battle, he might tip the balance. But if his line buckled, as it always did, one flank would be badly undermanned and no match for a concentrated enemy assault, as every ensign in the fleet had discovered. On the other hand, the center of the Red line was already showing signs of stress; if Blue kept attacking, the enemy forces would eventually puncture his defenses. And yet his own force outnumbered the remaining Blue fleet by a substantial margin. There should be a way for him to beat the machine this time, he thought. There simply had to be a way.

"Save screen," he told the computer; instantly, the battle etched itself into the vast electronic brain of the Central Computer, letting him experiment with another approach. Shaking his head in frustration, he decided to press ahead.

"Resume—no, freeze!"

Suddenly, Wasser had an idea. No, he told himself—not so much an idea as a hunch. He remembered the informal talk the Admiral had given his training class, and his lesson on the advantage of doing the unexpected. If redeploying from the flanks would lead to disaster, and holding the line would lead to disaster, then the answer had to be something else. Something so obvious that everyone would miss it. Fighting every instinct in his head, he decided to cede the center of the line to Blue and withdraw his ships to either flank. Taking a deep breath, the young cadet entered the order codes, and resumed the battle. As he watched the Blue ships pour through the opening, he suddenly saw how to beat them: with their enemy gone from the center, the point of the Blue formation had nothing to stop it. At once, he gave the command for his ships to attack—and watched as the Red fleet proceeded to destroy the distended enemy line.

As the computer took control, sending the Red ships after the remnants of the Blue fleet, the images of battle faded, replaced by a familiar face.

"Well done," said the image of Admiral Cook. "This is your second victory over the Blue fleet—or, to put it more precisely, the second time you managed to avoid defeat. And that, more often than not, is what separates the hero from the imbecile, the successful commander from one who dies along with his command."

"You've passed the first major hurdle on your way to becoming a real combat officer. You've learned to analyze the enemy's problem, and see things from his perspective. Now you're ready to experiment with our side of the problem.

"Your access code will now let you command either fleet—Red or Blue—at your discretion. I know that every young officer wants to do his part to beat back the Terran threat. Now you have your chance. I ask only that you not share your code with any of your comrades. Like you, they have a lot to learn, and little time left to do it. But advancement in my Navy must be earned. If they can't master the problem from the Terran perspective, they won't be much help in developing solutions to our own tactical dilemmas.

"One last thing—and I say this only to keep you from getting too cocky. These battle simulations can help prepare you to face the Terrans when they finally come. I've devised many of the problems myself, and some of them come from actual battles. You can also set your own battle scenarios from now on, to experiment with tactics, practice problems that are giving you trouble, or see how some of the maneuvers you're practicing will look when seen in the grander scheme of things. But always remember this: the computer can play at twenty different levels for these simulated battles—and there are five more levels beyond that, requiring my own personal password to enter. Each level is more demanding than the last. You just passed Level Two, and the computer will never let you practice that level again. From now on, the machine will get better and faster with each step. And we don't know which level will approximate the Terran commander.

"Of course, I have my own opinions about the matter," the Admiral's eyes twinkled. "But that's none of your concern."

Suddenly the image on the screen, the stern but patient face of Admiral Cook, seemed to look directly into the young man's eyes.

"Congratulations, once more," the Admiral said, a hint of amusement in his voice. " Now, Ensign—enough of this chit-chat. It's time for you to get back to work."

As the image faded, Ensign Wasser felt himself soaring through the heavens like a mighty starship. For the next three hours, he kept plotting battle after battle on the screen, never noticing how quickly the time was passing.

* * *

> *The Galaxy's bound for disaster*
> *And colder than Death is the Sky,*
> *But I volunteered to be up here*
> *So what kind of prat-head am I?*
> *Isis—Isis*
> > *We'll raise up a bottle to thee, to thee.*
> *Isis—Isis*
> > *We'll raise up a bottle to thee.*

ENSIGN GEOFFREY JASON plopped down on his bunk and closed his eyes, the sounds of laughter and singing from the hallway still ringing in his ears. Without doubt, this had been the worst day of his twenty-two year old life. Dragged out of bed while his brain was screaming for sleep, he'd spent the next eighteen hours running in lockstep with a whole company of officer candidates—from drill station to drill station. Without a second to call his own, his brain was pummeled on all sides by formations, protocols, and battle tactics—all attacking relentlessly, giving him no time to absorb what was going on around him. He'd foolishly spent his two hours of free time running a simulator drill, trying to lead the Terran attack fleet against the Isitian Navy, and doing rather a poor job of it. He wondered if he'd been better off hanging out in the galley, instead—though it seemed to him that the mess hall food was designed largely to keep the recruits at the simulators. Now that he finally had some free time, he was too tired to do anything but drift off to sleep.

> *The Heavens hold dangers and sadness*
> *And storm clouds and rocks and debris,*
> *And we all signed up for this madness*
> *So what kind of prat-heads are we?*
> *Isis—Isis*
> > *We'll raise up a bottle to thee, to thee.*
>
> *Isis—Isis*
> > *We'll raise up a bottle to thee.*

Jason took a deep breath to relax, and felt himself drifting— drifting off to sleep....

"Ow—ww!" he cried sharply, awaking to find some idiot's foot rising off his stomach. Pulling down sharply on the offending leg, he soon found himself engaged in a tug of war with its owner.

"What the devil do you think you're doing?" came a voice from the upper bunk.

"Who the hell told you to use my belly for a trampoline?"

"Let go."

"Come back down here and learn to get up properly."

"Let go."

"Come down here, before we're both washed out of the service."

As his roommate eased himself off the bunk, and the sleepiness left his head, Jason found himself feeling quite foolish. Obviously, the oaf didn't mean to wake him. By the looks of it, the poor fellow was just as tired as he was, and probably would have preferred not climbing into an upper bunk.

Taking a step back, the young man smiled sheepishly and extended his hand. "Lund," he said, his voice carrying a trace of a Highlander accent. "Jay Lund. Sorry if I disturbed you. I didn't mean to wake you."

Jason grinned and shook the fellow's hand. "Jason," he said, shaking his head. "Given the workout they gave us today, I doubt if I'd do much better."

"Southlander?"

Jason nodded. "New Alexandria, born and bred."

"I'm from the Hill Country."

"You seem to have a problem scaling heights, Lund."

The young man laughed, then took a step back, and leaped up to the top berth with a single bound, giving the bunk quite a jolt as he came to rest. Peeking down from the upper bunk, he laughed roughly.

"I was really trying not to disturb you, you know."

"What group— ?"

"Company 17, Battlegroup J."

"I'm Battlegroup A. As in asleep, sound asleep. I hope our schedules aren't going to clash. I'd hate to go through this every day."

"I'm too tired to worry about it just now."

"You're not the one who's going to have his stomach trampled."

"You're the one who chose the lower bunk."

> *With future uncertain and hazy*
> *The Terries are heading our way.*
> *Invading a planet that's crazy—*
> *Now what kind of prat-heads are they?*
> *Isis—Isis*
> *We'll raise up a bottle to thee, to thee.*
> *Isis—Isis*
> *We'll raise up a bottle to thee.*

THE WARNING BUZZER sounded, letting Garrity know that his shields were buckling. Trying to ignore the sounds from the nearby bar, he focused his attention on the lone enemy escort, approaching from astern. He'd already given up trying to muscle his way through the exercise once again. Now, he just wanted to keep his streak intact. No other ensign had managed to avoid destruction for more than ten consecutive missions; he'd already passed number eighteen, and had his sights set on twenty. But first, he had to escape the trap the computer had set for him.

The game terminals were a popular gathering spot for off-duty officers and enlisteds. The bar at the other end of the room served the coldest beer and least objectionable food on the base. Once done with their drills and training for the day, those of all ranks never tired of joining one another for food and company. But no matter the hour, there were always one or two young naval officers who couldn't pass up the chance to show off. Especially when some of the prettier female officers showed up, dressed in civies and ready for a night out.

> *Greener than green are her forests*
> *And bluer than blue is her sea,*
> *In all of Creation the fairest*
> *And home to such bounders as we—*
> *Isis—Isis*
>   *We'll raise up a bottle to thee, to thee*
> *Isis—Isis*
>   *We'll raise up a bottle to thee.*

Pulling his own ship into a wicked turn, Garrity passed out of the killing zone as his last shield collapsed, narrowly missing a full broadside from the enemy leader. Staying just beyond range of the enemy's wing, he focused his approach on the single escort blocking his escape route. If he could blow past it, he knew, he'd live to fight again, and keep his string going; if not, he had to start over, with a new record to shoot at—this time, his own.

"Look at him," came a female voice, from over his shoulder. "He's doing it again."

"Naw," scoffed one of his own buddies. "He's about to self-destruct. Watch."

Ignoring the distraction, the stocky young ensign concentrated on the escort laying just to port. As it banked over, trying to intercept him, Garrity gunned his engines and veered sharply—first to starboard, trying to get the computer to commit to an attack, then to port, cutting behind the escort and into the open skies beyond. Suddenly, the escort lay directly before him, its open broadside beckoning to his own still-charged guns. Pulling the trigger, he saw the image of the enemy escort explode on the screen. Finally, he steered his own ship through the electronic dust and smoke, and out of danger.

Some things can never be righted
And some things can never be wrong,
So let's go where all are invited
For laughter, companions, and song.
Isis—Isis
 We'll raise up a bottle to thee, to thee.
Isis—Isis
 We'll raise up a bottle to thee.

"Lucky bastard!" one of his friends shouted, slapping him on the back. "Steps right into it, and still comes out smelling like a rose. I think he's forgotten how it feels to get his ass kicked."

Garrity leaned back in his chair, and locked his hands behind his head. "Can't help it," he grinned, winking at the young female officer candidate hovering at the edge of the crowd. "Of course, some things you never forget."

"I have ten credits that say you can't make it all the way to twenty-five," said his friend.

"If your money's as dumb as you are, Randy O'Dell, it'll be like stealing from a kid."

"Your luck running out?"

"You're on."

"And somebody fetch this bounder a beer—we may need to handicap him to keep down the odds!"

* * *

"WHAT DO you mean, 'he's making rounds?'"

"I mean, he's making rounds."

Seated alone at the communications console, Ross did his best to control his temper. The young ensign appearing on the monitor in front of him was hardly to blame, he kept telling himself. For her part, the radio officer squirmed uncomfortably in her chair on Base One, looking as if she would have been quite content to have lived her life without the honor of speaking to high government officials, and hoped the distinction would pass as quickly as possible.

"Excuse me, Ensign," Ross said at last. "I'm not blaming you. But I want to understand this. What, precisely, does Admiral Cook do when he's 'making rounds?'"

"It varies, from day to day," came the reply, a bit more impatiently than Ross had expected. "Mostly, it's just walking around, seeing what's going on—helping out, if needed. You know—just making the rounds."

"He, of course, realizes that he is due at a meeting right now."

"I wouldn't know about that, sir."

"A meeting with myself, the Chancellor, and a number of other high officials in the Defense Ministry."

"I don't know what the Admiral's schedule is, Minister Ross."

"Well, Ensign...can you convey a message for me?"

"Certainly, sir. What is your message?"

Ross stared angrily at the pleasant, if insufficiently intimidated young woman on the screen. No, he concluded, he could not say what he wanted. Not to this cute, innocent-looking young lady. The thought that Cook probably knew this—and assigned the girl to screen his calls for precisely that reason—infuriated him all the more.

"Never mind, Ensign," he snapped. "Just page him, and tell him to call me the minute he is free. It is very important."

"Yes, sir. I'll let him know at once."

For all the good it will do, Ross thought, as he signed off the screen. How anyone so irresponsible could command a fleet was a mystery. Whatever the Chancellor saw in the arrogant, mule-headed Northlander, she wasn't sharing with her Minister of State. Obviously, Cook thought it more important to strut about his base, playing peacock to his little fleet of teenagers, than to brief the leaders of his own Government about his plans to defend the Planet.

Such insolence could not be tolerated, Ross told himself. But if he couldn't make the Chancellor see reason, his only recourse was to make the matter public.

Ross slammed his fist against the console, and rose to his feet, walking nervously about the room. Of course that would never do. It would only scare everyone. And it would play right into the hands of the Opposition. The very thought made him even angrier.

The Chancellor was blind, he thought. Either blind, or too old to see the truth. The name Cook had always been anathema to the Party, for more than a generation. Cornelius Cook was just the latest to cause trouble in the Capital of New Alexandria. How she could think this younger Cook could be any different was beyond belief—especially since he'd so neatly boxed them into a corner. The Admiral had all of his family's instincts for the jugular. He knew the Government would stand or fall on his slightest whim. He was simply toying with them, trying to goad them into doing something rash, so that his uncle's Party would be seen to come to the rescue—garnering the credit and riding it to victory for the next generation or two, if by some miracle they managed to avoid destruction at the hands of the Terries.

Ross sat down. He rubbed his weary eyes with his hands, then placed his head on the console. He could feel his heart pounding wildly, and he took a few deep breaths to calm himself. He was scared, he finally admitted. Like everybody else, he was scared to death. Everywhere he looked, he saw nothing but blackness and destruction in their future—blackened buildings, blackened fields. And blood—the blood from millions of shattered lives, staining the streets and running until the rivers flowed crimson.

They were all crazy, he thought. Crazy to think they could beat the Cosmic Guard. The same Cosmic Guard that kept beating the heavens bloody on the other side of the galaxy. No matter which way he turned, the answer was always the same. Nothing could stop the Terrans. Not the aliens, not broadsides from the press, not common decency. Not even the great Roscoe Cook. This would be the last spring any of them saw—the last blooming lilacs, the last nesting songbirds, the last season of renewal, and hope, and love. No matter what he did, it would never be enough.

Taking a deep breath to compose himself, he rose and strode from the room. They still had their meeting, and he was still the Minister of State. No matter what Fortune had in store for them, he would do his duty. That duty meant planning for every contingency, every twist or turn of fate.

And it would only be a cruel Fate that defeated them. If they were going to be destroyed by the Terries, it wouldn't be for lack of trying, no matter what the cost. Not so long as Reginald Ross had a breath left in his body.

* * *

"COMPANY—HALT!" barked the drill sergeant. "Lessinger—on the floor, and give me twenty."

Lisa Lessinger, bringing up the rear of the team of rookie ensigns, had endured all she could from the uncouth sergeant leading her company in fitness training. Every day, for a whole hour, they had to run—then stretch—then run again—then do calisthenics. And then run some more. It had precious little to do with piloting a space ship. And that, after all, was the whole point behind the Interstellar Navy.

Lisa stood stiffly in place, and the sergeant stormed toward her, looking as if he intended to rip her to shreds.

"I said," snarled the sergeant, pressing his face toward hers, until she could smell the onions he'd had on his meat patty for lunch, "down onto the floor, and give me twenty pushups. Now, Missey!"

"I outrank you, Sergeant," Lisa said haughtily. "I also don't like pushups—I don't feel like doing any pushups—and the sooner you stop behaving like you own us, the better off we'll all be."

"Ensign—!"

"We are in the Navy to defend Isis, Sergeant, not to cower before the likes of you. And to be quite frank, I have had more of this than I care to stand."

His eyes bulging with anger, the drill sergeant was about to unleash his full fury on the young ensign when he spotted a familiar figure, standing beside the door leading to the Men's locker room.

"Company—attention!" he barked, and all the officers scrambled into formation.

Striding into the gym, the Admiral walked slowly around the company, his eyes quick and alert, searching for the slightest flaw in any member of the assembly. Completing his circuit, he turned and walked to the head of the group. As he neared, the sergeant saluted smartly.

"What seems to be the problem, Sergeant?" Cook asked gruffly.

"Sir!" answered the sergeant; he stood stiffly at attention, eyes front, and spoke without a trace of the numbing fear coursing through his entire body.

"There is no problem, sir!"

His brow furrowed, his gaze cold and merciless, Cook circled the drill instructor, then walked over to young Ensign Lessinger.

Standing directly in front of her as she stood at attention, he took his time examining every aspect of her appearance before speaking.

"Is there a problem, Ensign?" he demanded.

Lisa hesitated a moment, before she replied.

"Permission to speak freely, Admiral?"

"Certainly," Cook answered, without a trace of good humor.

Taking a deep breath, Lisa decided to press ahead, whatever the consequences.

"Sir—in my opinion, we are spending far too much time in physical training, with the result that we are neglecting other things that would be far more helpful."

"Such as?"

"Actual maneuvers in space. Increased time on the simulators. More flight time in actual spacecraft."

"Interesting point, Ensign," Cook said, smiling coldly. "I happen to disagree—though I will note what you have to say on the subject. Now, I believe you owe the sergeant some pushups."

"Sir—with due respect, I fail to see the purpose behind permitting the physical abuse of officers by enlisted personnel."

"I stand corrected," Cook said, his eyes going down the neat lines of the assembled officers. "The rest of the company has twenty pushups to do."

"Admiral—that's hardly fair."

"Fifty pushups," said Cook.

"*Admiral*— !"

"One hundred pushups."

Her face now a bright red, Lisa found it impossible to think clearly. She knew only that what was happening was wrong, and that somehow she had to put a stop to it.

"Admiral—you can't do that!"

"Two hundred pushups," Cook said sternly. "And you, Missey, will return to your quarters, pack your things, and catch the next shuttle home. You have just washed out."

The rest of the company kept an astonished silence. Alone and without a word, Lisa walked off the gym and down the rampway leading to the lockers, tears coursing down her face. For all her quirks, she usually had one of the highest scores on any tests the company was given. Among the female officers, she'd always been the leader. One of the few in the bunch with the nerve to speak out, when given the chance.

As the disconsolate young officer disappeared from view, Cook turned to face the company. "I believe all of you owe the sergeant some pushups," he said, smiling tightly. "I suggest you get started." At once, the assembly was on the floor, straining and counting in whispers as they complied with the order.

"Sorry, Admiral...," " began the drill sergeant; as much trouble as Lessinger had been to him, he suddenly felt quite sorry for her.

"Don't worry about it," Cook snapped, loudly enough to be heard by the first two rows. "Your job isn't to babysit them, Sergeant. You're here to teach them humility, give them the stamina to withstand 48-hour shifts in combat, and get their butts moving—preferably in the same direction. I don't punish people for their ideas—or for disagreeing with me. She's dismissed for the harm she caused her comrades, not for failing to appreciate a little exercise. Space is unforgiving, and so am I. With that attitude and lack of judgment, she'd have gotten good people killed. We don't need officers who think they're more important than their mission."

"Begging the Admiral's pardon," panted a young ensign, busily engaged on the floor.

"What is it, Ensign?" Cook replied, his eyes stern and merciless.

"Well," the young man continued, struggling not to break his rhythm. "I couldn't help but overhearing—and if the problem was Ensign Lessinger's—lack of judgment—well, if that problem is resolved—and if there's no further need for us to— "

"Nice try—what was the name?"

"Ziegler, sir."

"Nice try, *Lieutenant* Ziegler. Your loyalty to your fellow officers is commendable. But the order stands."

An audible murmur coursed through the sweat and strain of the tiring young officers, as each officer wondered if he'd heard correctly. But no one else dared to speak.

"Carry on," Cook said sharply. "Sergeant, if you'll accompany me, please."

As they stepped out of range, Cook's demeanor abruptly changed, from harsh to concerned. "I'll need Ziegler's full name and serial number for his promotion. Send it to my office as soon as you're done. And it looks like you have about a half-dozen women in the company?"

"We have four left, Admiral."

"Will they make it through two-hundred pushups?"

The sergeant shook his head. There was no way any of them could do it. Even Schultz, the strongest of the lot, would collapse before she was half done.

Cook nodded gravely, considering the problem. "Don't suggest this to them, but if any of the men volunteer to take up the slack for them—to do however much of their penance the women can't finish—you can let them."

"One question, Admiral?"

Cook smiled, looking rather skeptical. "Just one?" he laughed. "Sure—go ahead."

"I'm sure there's a method to your madness—I mean, not that you don't know what you're doing."

"Oh, there's a method, all right. Though to tell the truth, I often suspect I haven't the foggiest notion what I'm doing."

"Ziegler's the brightest one of the bunch—and the most sensible. Of this bunch, he's the ensign I'd most want to take orders from, if it were up to me. But he's usually one of the quietest. And why in the world—why promote him, now?"

Cook chuckled to himself. "Ziegler's getting promoted a few weeks early, that's all. He'd already earned his promotion— "

"But how— "

"How is none of your concern," Cook smiled, but his voice was quite firm. "Let's just say I have my own scouting system, one that I don't care to reveal, at least not yet. As for why—well, let's say that the good Lieutenant owes your temperamental young lady a debt of gratitude. And the two of them gave me the chance to teach several lessons all at once."

"I'm afraid I don't understand, sir."

"Good!" Cook laughed. "Then you can't spoon feed it to them, either. Carry on, Sergeant."

"Aye, sir."

The drill sergeant watched the Admiral walk down the rampway to the locker, the spring and swagger to his stride makinge him seem taller than he actually was. He'd talked to the Admiral twice before.

Each time in private, like just now. Both times, the Admiral surprised him. Not by any grasp of tactics or commanding presence; the sergeant himself dealt in strength and fitness, and knew nothing about anything having to do with space. But he respected the Admiral for his unpretentiousness, and the quiet irreverence of his personality. There were plenty of officers the sergeant never much cared for, egos a parsec wide and filled with notions of how empty the Universe would be without them. The Admiral was too level-headed for such nonsense. Despite his reputation as a dreamer, the Skipper seemed to have his feet planted on something solid. And, the sergeant suspected, the Admiral had little patience with fools who never acknowledged the laws of gravity, or took life too seriously to laugh at themselves once in a while.

Mostly, he was impressed by the fact that someone everyone worshipped like a god would care a jot about the deadening arms of his junior officers—or take the time to crack a few heads himself, just to help some lowly aide maintain discipline.

Suddenly, a voice called out from behind him.

"Sarge!"

The sergeant turned, his face resuming its hard, callous visage. "What is it this time, Papineau?"

"Have a heart, Sergeant. We aren't cut out for this kind of punishment."

"Admiral's orders," the drill instructor scoffed in return. "He thinks the lot of you are too soft. And, dammit, he's right. I haven't pushed you nearly hard enough. Now, quit complaining or I'll double the punishment myself, just for the hell of it."

* * *

"EXCUSE ME, Madam Chancellor."

As she took the note from her junior aide, the Chancellor noticed that the young man seemed rather tense. Smiling, she patted him on the hand and smiled. She'd seen it before, in many of her new assistants. Now that the crisis was getting worse the effect was even more pronounced. No matter how well-schooled they were, some of the younger staff members were awed at confronting the assembled leaders of the planet. The grandness of the Cabinet Room, with its cathedral ceiling and wood paneling, the fine tapestries and portraits of past leaders, was enough to humble all but the most egotistical of them.

"Oh, we're not all that horrible, are we Patrick?" she chided him gently.

"It's not that, Ma'am," Patrick replied, smiling nervously. "I just don't like to be the bearer of ill tidings. I've heard that some of the Ministers have gotten rather testy over messages like this one." Still smiling, he bowed politely and departed. McInnis lifted her glasses to read the note; at once, she realized why the young man was so anxious to leave the gathering. Leaning forward, she apologized to the Minister of State for interrupting his presentation.

"I'm afraid that the Admiral will not be with us, today," she announced, smiling blandly at the chorus of groans that greeted the news.

For once, Reggie Ross managed a chuckle of inner satisfaction. He had his own agenda for the day, and it did not include having to contend with Roscoe Cook. It was nice to see the Admiral so obliging, though his absence was so habitual as to be part of their routine. There was no excuse for Cook's disrespect for the Cabinet, or his continuing absence from meetings that were shaping the fate of the Planet. But the young minister's anger at the Admiral's indifference had slowly crystallized into contempt, for if Cook were this predictable in battle their cause was already lost.

"As I was saying," Ross continued, after the murmurings had abated, "in my opinion we are squandering a valuable defensive resource, simply through a failure of organization. We have more than fifty-million able-bodied men on this planet, and we are fully capable of mounting a resistance to any Terran invasion force. My proposal simply would charter a series of regional militias, under the Ministry of State, to serve as a military defense force in the event it becomes necessary."

"Hunting guns and target pistols are hardly a match for Terran artillery," pointed out the defense minister.

"And what about the cost?" asked the Minster of Finance. "The Opposition is already calling for a general review of our military budget. How can we justify diverting funds from the Navy, just to let some of our overgrown adolescents strut around playing soldier? And it goes against so much of our own tradition, don't you know."

"I understand," said Ross, meeting their gaze with a grimness his colleagues had never seen before. "But right now we are placing all of our eggs in a single basket, and it makes me uncomfortable. Suppose Cook really isn't a magician, after all. Suppose the Terries rout the Navy and we awake one day to see them landing soldiers on our soil. Would you really want us to be defenseless? And remember—however large an army they send against us, this is our home. We'll always outnumber them, and they can't be everywhere."

As she listened to her ministers argue the matter back and forth, the Chancellor found her mind drifting back to quieter, happier times. She smiled at the memory of her son's wedding, her daughter's first day of school. Twenty years earlier, she would have dominated the meeting unless she consciously refrained from doing so; today it was all she could do to focus her attention on the matter at hand. She was painfully aware that she hadn't the slightest idea what to do about any of it. She was tired; she was confused; and on top of it all, she was as scared as anybody. Between the costs of training and the costs of procurement, it seemed like an awful lot of money. Especially since the Navy had pretty well drained the coffers already. But it all seemed terribly important to Reggie Ross.

Then again, she smiled to herself, these days everything seemed important to Reggie Ross. Perhaps it was best to let him carry the day, every once in a while.

* * *

JANET FELT her heart quicken as she entered their quarters. A quick look at the mess in the living room confirmed her first instinct, and filled her with warmth and anticipation.

He was here tonight: the thought made her feel like a schoolgirl. It had been ages since they'd had any time together. Any time at all. But he was here tonight, and that was all that mattered. The rest of the universe could wait; for the next few hours, they would be alone—just the two of them, Mr. & Mrs. Roscoe Cook. And they could act like newlyweds were supposed to act. It would do wonders for her own self-esteem, she giggled.

A few steps from the doorway, the foyer opened into a large living room. Janet stepped to the mirror they kept next to the door, and checked her hair. She grimaced at the way she looked: of course, if the inconsiderate slob had only called to tell her he'd actually be home on time, she could have made sure she was presentable before leaving the office. Not that he would have noticed, of course, but it would have made her feel prettier. And she wanted to feel as pretty as an Isitian meadow tonight.

"Skipper?"

Hearing no answer, she stepped quietly through the living room to the back hallway. The hall was darkened; if her husband ever noticed a burned-out light, she thought, he'd probably never admit it. But she smiled to see the light coming through the closed bedroom door. She took a deep breath and, quietly as she could, opened the door.

There, face down and motionless on the bed, half-dressed and dead to the Universe around him, lay the great Admiral Cook, tattered underwear and all, sleeping like a baby.

Shaking her head, Janet smiled, even as she felt the tears welling up in her eyes. Stepping lightly to the bed, she covered him gently with the extra blanket he'd always teased her about, the quilt her grandmother had given her for the nights she felt chilly, during certain times of the month. Then she leaned down and kissed him on the head.

It was probably the first good sleep he'd had in weeks, she thought. He was lucky not to be sick—sick from exhaustion, or from overwork, or from worry. And he needed rest more than anything.

She changed her clothes as quietly as she could. Turning off the light, she snuggled next to him in the dark and closed her eyes, listening to him sleep, and stroking his hair every now and again.

Chapter 5

"READY WITH THE next one?"

"Mainframe Circuit, panel 126, number Z15-B, ready to test."

"Commence test sequence."

"Commencing."

A surge of power transferred from the portable generator to the computer panel they'd isolated for testing. Nearby, the young crewman—an engineer second class, half-way through his sophomore year at New Alexandria Tech—watched his monitor closely, expecting to see all sorts of trouble. The testing program was truly first rate: they'd secretly copied it from the Terries before the Cosmic Guard closed down I-Com, and had refined and improved it ever since. Even the Admiral was impressed.

The computer clicked and whirred as it raced through its tests, checking the relays and hunting for internal loops and glitches. The only trouble, the engineer thought to himself, was that the program was proving to be too good. Because it sought out each and every flaw, no matter how minor, it spit out problems that made no difference to the electronic brain itself. This, in turn, sent them scrambling to correct bugs in the machine that wouldn't affect its performance. They'd already wasted two days trying to track down a stubborn problem with the peripheral power dispersers, only to find that the culprit was a single repeated command on some secondary circuit. It would never be operational, unless something went wrong with the main power train. And even then, it would add less than a nanosecond to the response time.

"What a colossal waste of time," he scoffed at his team leader.

"You might want to trim your tongue a bit," smiled the older, sergeant. At last, the green light flashed, and he marked off the circuit on his checklist. "You never know who might be sneaking up behind you."

"Achh—if the Admiral wants us to work with a will, he'd better expect to hear an earful every now and then," the college boy shot back. "Now are we going to stand here all day, or do we still have some time to waste checking a few more billion circuits before lunch?"

"Testy this morning, aren't we?"

"Testy every morning, Sarge. At least, until this nonsense is over."

"Ready? Of course, you know once we're done here we still have the Terries to look forward to."

"Mainframe Circuit, panel 126, number Z15-C, ready to test."

"Commence test sequence."

"Commencing—and you know, if I've a choice between boring myself to death like this, and facing the Terries...."

"Yeah?"

"Well, the Terries are looking better and better, every day."

"You're crazy—you know that? Stark lunatic crazy."

"Well, you've heard all about Heaven protecting its lunatics, haven't you, Sarge?"

"Doesn't apply to idiots, Crewman."

* * *

THE WHOOP of triumph made heads turn all across the Main Concourse.

"Chris—what is it?"

Beaming from ear to ear, Christopher Barnes folded the piece of paper and tucked it in his pocket. He looked at the collection of soft curves and long, brown hair standing in front of him, and slowly shook his head.

"Sorry, Mary Beth," he grinned, knowing it would drive her crazy. "I'm not at liberty to say."

"You're horrible."

"Flattery only gets you so far, you know."

"You're simply horrible."

Turning on her heels, she stormed off. He watched intently as she wriggled her way down the concourse, heading toward the main briefing room, her bearing as alluring as her anger. As part of the Command Staff, they both had a mandatory meeting in twenty minutes. She would probably be calmed down by then, Barnes thought devilishly. If not, she'd be even more fun that evening, when they both had free time scheduled. Orders or no orders, he'd want to make the most out of it.

As she disappeared into the crowd, Barnes marveled at his luck, but was cynical enough to wonder if he'd come to regret his good fortune when war finally came to Isis.

COMMAND DIRECTIVE

DATE: cc:144.7776.0
FROM: Admiral Cook
TO: Lt. Christopher Barnes
SUBJECT: Change in Duty Assignment

Report to Briefing Room A today at 750 hours; until further notice, you will discuss this Directive with no one.

Barnes took a deep breath, almost afraid to look at the paper any more. As one of the Admiral's top aides, he found himself inspired beyond all rationality by Cook's untiring example of work, work, and more work. He'd turned into such a recluse that he rarely saw any of his friends, anymore. Except for Mary Beth, of course; but then, these days he'd come to regard her as a delicious distraction, more than anything else.

But he knew exactly what the Directive meant. He knew how few of these were circulating. Most importantly, he now knew that all his long hours of practice and sweat, accumulating skills as a pilot and tactician, had not passed unnoticed.

He hadn't the foggiest idea how he'd been selected. The Admiral shared few of his secrets, and this was one of the most closely guarded secrets of all. But right now, he knew that these thoughts should be the furthest thing from his mind. Far more pressing was the matter of the new intelligence from out East.

And the matter of keeping himself under control, until 750 hours.

* * *

JACK MARKHAM felt his heart skip a beat the moment he saw the headline: "GOVERNMENT FORMS GROUND FORCES — Volunteers Needed to Man Garrisons."

Grabbing the newspaper from the stand on his kiosk, Jack read the article avidly. It was a second chance, he thought. A second chance to do something— anything—to keep his family safe, and his home secure.

Even as far south as New Alexandria the early Spring rain still carried a hint of Winter, and his fingers quickly grew cold. Looking up from his paper, he saw a crowd of people, coming up the escalator from the Underground into the cold gray dawn. Quickly, Markham put down his reading and turned his attention to his customers. The Home Garrison could wait until after rush hour, he told himself. Keeping his family fed was almost as important as keeping them safe; and with the winter fruit harvest now flooding the market, he stood to make a small killing with his stand, as long as he didn't daydream the day away.

"Fresh fruit for lunch," he said with a smile as the crush of commuters approached his small stand. "Finest in all the City. Home Garrison forming—read all about it."

* * *

//cc:144-7784.2/TO/HQ/FR/reynolds,ltcmdr/
QLQ OP BETA. CG MANVRS OFF ZarCom, DAY TEN AND
COUNTNG. STILL NO CONFRM STRSHP ##s, BUT Adm ESTIMATE
TOTAL CG WRSHPS APPEARS ON MARK. CONFRM MULTIPLE
TRNSPRTS, NOW ENGAGD LANDNG MANVRS. BATTLE MANVRS
NEARNG END LIST C, CG SUPPORT SHPS MVNG TO STAGING
ZONE A. ESTIMATE ADDL 3-4 WKS BEFORE DEPARTURE; WILL
POST ANY CHNG.
/**AZB/djreynolds/enter/Xmit//

Alone in the quarters she shared with her absent husband, Janet closed her eyes and took a deep breath. The message had come twenty minutes ago, yet each time she reread it, renewed horror coursed through her bones. She could feel the room closing around her, and time pressing on her shoulders. For weeks, she'd tried to play the skeptic. But if the Cosmic Guard was practicing landing maneuvers at ZarCom, then Skipper was right all along: they actually meant to invade and occupy Isis. If they were practicing the block battle formations of Skipper's "List C," they meant to crush anything standing in their way. And if the scout's other estimates were correct, the Terran fleet would be ready to sail in three weeks—and a week or two later, the ragtag Isitian navy would be fighting for its life. Walking to the nearby washroom, she splashed water on her face and tried to calm herself.

They'd never be ready. Not in a million years.

No matter what they did, no matter how hard they worked, they'd never be ready. There was too much to do, too little to work with. The Cosmic Guard was the most devastating fighting force in History, and would never simply unravel. The Terrans could sleep for a hundred years, and tiny Isis still wouldn't be ready.

She looked up, staring at herself in the mirror. How had it all come to this, she wondered. She would die with the man she loved and thousands of others, their ashes cast to wander eternity through the emptiness of space.

It was so senseless.

Everything seemed so hopeless.

When she looked again, she saw the tears running down her cheeks, and heard the sounds of her muffled sobs echo off the walls. The image on the mirror seemed like another person, a distant reflection of her life, and everything that might have been.

"Lt. Mendelson?"

"Mendelson, here."

"The Skipper would like to see you, Lieutenant."

"On my way."

Janet took a deep breath, then stepped to the mirror to neaten her hair. Skipper had been distant for too long, she thought, and it was about time she demanded some answers. They'd be arriving at Ishtar soon, and she didn't like the thought of being left alone with the other women aboard to tend the ship. Especially if he'd be leaving her alone to stew with her own sense of inadequacy. Shaking her head in disgust at the creature she saw staring back at her from the mirror, she decided that it was a lost cause, and hurried out the door and down the hallway.

She arrived at the elevator and entered the code for the Conning Deck. Not that they hadn't had some rough times before. It was, after all, something Regulations frowned upon—

although somehow the forbidden aspect to their romance did add the spice of excitement and adventure. The need to keep things hushed did complicate things an awful lot. But the last week or two had been nearly unbearable. He'd said very little; in fact, he hadn't said much of anything at all, unless she brought something to his attention. She didn't know whether to ascribe it to his Isitian temperament, or to something more troubling. Something she simply refused to think about.

Arriving on the Conning Deck, Janet headed down the central spike toward Skipper's quarters. Stepping into his outer office, she was surprised to see that Jenny was gone from the secretary's desk, but that the door to the main anteroom was ajar. Opening the door, Janet saw Skipper's chair facing away from her, toward the wall. Stepping inside, she started when his chair swiveled. Without warning, she saw the misery-laden eyes of the only man she'd ever loved, staring at her like someone about to lose his best friend.

In that instant, she knew; she didn't know how, but she knew. Tears rose in her heart, and her throat began to tighten. It was etched into his face, and she felt so wretched and alone and abandoned that she wanted to crawl into a hole and die.

"ALL RIGHT, time to call it a day," barked the yeoman. "Spencer, coil that wiring; we'll need it again tomorrow. Benish and Liss, start picking up all the loose crap we've managed to dump. The rest of you, collect the tools and calibrators, and put them in the tool caddy. The next shift won't appreciate having to look hither and yon trying to find everything they need."

As his work crew began gathering the assorted tools and trash they'd managed to scatter about the bridge, Yeoman Second Class Dennis Drake cast a watchful eye over his charges. They were all good men, he thought, though some of them, being office workers in civilian life, were a tad on the impractical side. But they came to the Navy with at least a minimum amount of technical skill, and not one of them had ever shirked a job or failed to work with a will. A crisis would do that to people, though on the whole, he'd be willing to swap a little enthusiasm if they could make the Terries go away.

So much for being practical, he chuckled to himself, only to stop in mid-thought. A puzzled look on his face, he saw one of his charges still busy at work, feet dangling out from under the navigation console, oblivious to anything going on around him, his ratty old coveralls stained with oil and half-covered with bits of electrical tape. Without stopping to check which of his men was deaf enough to ignore the order to stand down, Drake went over to the navigation desk, picked up a shaft of conduit piping, and rapped the miscreant flush on the soles of his sneakers.

"Wha—*ow*! What the hell's going on up there?" called the absent-minded crewman, his voice muffled by the large console.

"Up and about, Mister," Drake grunted. "I won't have one of my crew holding up the works. Next shift's due any time, and we still have to get the bridge tidy—Admiral's orders. I won't have the rest of us waiting because you can't be bothered to clean up after yourself. Whatever it is can wait until tomorrow."

"All right—all right. Just trim your damn engines."

As the workman began scuttling out from under the navigation console, Drake ran his eyes over the rest of his crew, to see which one was causing all the trouble. But when he counted them, he realized that all seven were already accounted for. He was starting to sort out the puzzle when the troublemaker emerged from under the console, and Drake turned white as a ghost. Without realizing it he began to recite a prayer he learned in Sunday school long ago. He stopped only to notice something warm and wet trickling down his leg.

It was the Admiral himself, rising to his feet and dusting himself off, a scowl on his face and his eyes narrowed fiercely. Drake saw his hopes and ambitions passing before him like a lost dream. It took all his courage just to keep from fainting.

"I— I—I— "

"All right, Yeoman, what's the problem?'

"I— I—I— "

Cook cast a sharp glance at the assembled work crew, and immediately felt his temper subside. The young man hadn't meant to disturb him, he quickly realized. In fact, the poor slob was probably trying to get his work crew to tidy up the place, not even realizing that there was an extra worker on the bridge. Now the trick would be to let the yeoman come away from this with at least some shred of dignity intact. The hint of a twinkle crept into his eyes; he caught the gaze of the most intelligent-looking crewman of the lot, and winked.

"I see your point, Yeoman," Cook began, gravely. "Rules are for everyone, after all. And I shouldn't be exempt, merely on account of rank. Wouldn't be very Isitian, now would it? And you're quite right. It's a bad example to set for the rest of the Fleet. So, my apologies and all—didn't mean to interfere with your command. Although the last crew chief didn't mind at all. Simply let me work right through into the next watch. And that means— "

Cook's eyes suddenly went wide with dismay, as he suddenly realized he'd quite lost track of the time.

"Yeoman—what's the hour?"

"I— I—I— "

"Anybody—what time is it?"

The crewman with the intelligent eyes was the first to respond.

"Watch change, Admiral."

"Yes, yes, yes," Cook said impatiently. "But which watch? What is the hour?"

"Nearly midnight."

"Cosmic time—what's the cosmic time?"

The crewman looked at the chronometer by the systems console. "High-watch, most nearly, sir," came the reply. "By the Cosmic Clock—it's five after the Hour."

"For the love of..." sputtered the Admiral. He was late, he suddenly realized. He was already late, and this was one meeting he didn't want to hold up. He'd never make it on time—Hell, Cook thought, he'd be lucky to be twenty minutes late—and he hoped that everyone would have sense enough to wait for him.

"Yeoman—do me a big favor and stash my tools and other gear. Anywhere on the Bridge will be fine. I've got to run."

"I— I—I— I— "

"Thanks—that's a sport. Now I'm running late, or I'd be glad to help. Nice to see you all. Keep up the good work."

With that, the great Admiral Cook dashed off the bridge, down the exit ramp and into the interior of the new ship. Yeoman Drake, still in shock, stared after him dumbly. The rest of his crew stood in place, waiting for their orders and enjoying every moment.

* * *

"MINISTER ROSS!" snapped the Chancellor. "Please calm yourself."

"What do you mean, he's not here?"

"I mean..., " began the tall, slender naval officer the Chancellor had just introduced to the full Cabinet.

"Just who the Hell does he think he is?"

"Well, Minister, you see— "

Dismissing the hapless courier with a wave of his hand, Reggie Ross fumed as he paced around the Great Hall. Ever the diplomat, the Chancellor patted the young man on his shoulder as she escorted him to the door.

"We're all under a strain, you know," she explained with a matronly smile. "The Minister of State in particular. He takes the Terrans quite seriously."

"Everyone I know takes the Terries seriously, Ma'am," grinned the young man, flattered by all the attention and awed by the number of famous people surrounding him. As he left, he took one last look at the gathering—Ministers, sub-ministers, Senators and business leaders, all come together in a single room, for a purpose never explained to him but which he could well imagine. Coming stiffly to attention, he snapped a smart salute and was gone.

"Well, Madam Chancellor—I hope you're satisfied!" snarled the Minister of State. "This gathering was— "

"Not now, Reggie," McInnis smiled blandly, her steely blue eyes conveying the message quite clearly that Ross had better curb his temper at once. As he sputtered impotently, she turned to address the rest of the assembly.

"Unfortunately, the press of business has kept the Admiral away from our little gathering," she said pleasantly. "So I'm afraid we'll just have to proceed without him."

His eyes bulging, Ross could scarcely contain himself. In the past week they'd committed the Government to spending more than a hundred million credits, to organize, train, and equip their militia. Now the obstructionists among the Opposition, as well as their own cost accountants, were trying to scuttle the whole program. Cook might—just might, mind you—help them carry the day, if they could lean on him just the right way. But once again, he was too damn busy playing with his ships to drop by. Worse yet, not even the

Chancellor seemed to have the slightest clue about the Northlander's thoughts on the subject, or why he chose to absent himself from yet another cabinet meeting. And she seemed completely uninterested in calling him to account.

To top it off, the door hadn't even finished closing when the Crier appeared along with the last man Ross wished to see at this meeting.

"Madam Chancellor," called the Crier, his polite tones polished to haughty perfection, "the Assistant Minority Leader is here."

"Good morning, Senator," McInnis smiled, nodding politely to the latest arrival. "It's so nice of you join us on such short notice."

"Always a pleasure, Madam Chancellor."

"Your nephew won't be joining us today, I'm afraid. He certainly is busy these days, as well we can imagine."

Cornelius Cook chuckled politely, and took his chair on the Opposition's side of the conference table, next to the Minority Leader. His stride was a dead match for his nephew's, the Chancellor noted: bold, confident, as if afraid of nothing under heaven. But while the two shared the same family features, the face of Senator Cook was creased by many more frowns. And it was in the eyes that she saw the real difference between them. The Senator and the Admiral both had the same fierce intelligence burning in their eyes, but Cornelius Cook showed none of the warmth and humor of his famous nephew, and she felt none of the gentle, self-mocking wisdom she sensed whenever she saw the Admiral in person. Though pompous and self-important, Senator Cook had helped carry his party through the crisis with the ruthless charm and cunning that made him a legend in the Northlands. She sensed none of that in his nephew; but every day, she wondered if she wasn't seeing a mirage born of her own desperation.

"Well," began the Minority Leader, "I believe we're all here now. Perhaps we can commence."

The participants took their places, and Reggie Ross leaned forward from his seat at the Chancellor's right.

"Senator Cook," Ross began, wasting no time on pleasantries, "perhaps you can explain your loyal opposition to our only real means of defending our cities on the ground. We have no standing army, you know. And if the Terries do manage to land, it will be rather difficult for us to raise an objection to their presence, don't you think? They will hardly be in the mood for talking out our differences."

"We continue to have objections," smiled Senator Cook, speaking for the Opposition in a mild, but unyielding tone of voice. "We object on a number of grounds. The organizational muddle, logistics, and whole damn expense of the thing strikes us as just a tad half-baked, to be quite honest about it. But our main problem seems to be our insistence on looking reality squarely and calmly in the face. You cannot recruit, equip, and train an army in a matter of weeks. It's impossible. No matter how much we might wish it were otherwise, we would simply be arming a mob of untrained civilians to no useful purpose."

"I beg your pardon— " Ross began, to be silenced only by the Chancellor's heel digging sharply into his foot.

"If the Terrans land," the Senator continued, leaning forward, his hands folded on the table, "this 'home guard' army of yours will be massacred. From a military standpoint, all they can possibly do of any consequence is inflame the Terries just enough that they won't stop at massacring our army, but will find it such jolly fun that they'll continue their efforts when they get to our cities. While I wish my nephew all measure of success in his efforts," he went on, his voice wavering slightly as he spoke, "I cannot see how, if they beat him in the sky, we can possibly hope to fend off the Terrans on the ground. We would be sending thousands of Isitian men and boys needlessly to their deaths, and trusting the Terry soldiers not to take their revenge on our helpless civilian population.

"That, we believe, is neither prudent nor wise. Although we will not say so publicly, that is the real reason why we oppose it so adamantly. And that is why we will continue to do all we can to block final approval of this ill-conceived scheme in any way we can."

"I might remind you," said the Chancellor, "that it was your Party that blocked our efforts to raise an army and augment our Navy two years ago, when we first raised the possibility. 'Alarmists,' you called us, as I recall. It was all we could do to keep you from scuttling the starship project."

"Hindsight is always perfect," replied the Senator, behind a bland smile. "We prefer to live in the present. And right now, we have more productive ways to deploy our resources."

"But no way that is more pressing."

"That is in the eye of the beholder."

"Your eyes appear to see well only after the fact, Senator."

The smile disappeared from Senator Cook's face, replaced by cold, studied fury. The Chancellor had seen the look before. Cornelius Cook did not like to be called a fool, and did not forgive insults easily.

"You forget yourself, Madam Chancellor," he said acidly. "We are not menials to be cast off like yesterday's rubbish. We are all Isitians—every bit as patriotic as anyone in this room, and just as concerned about the fate of every man, woman, and child on the face of this Planet. If you are trying to obtain our cooperation, or settle our differences behind a common front against a common foe, you have rather a self-destructive way of going about it."

With no further discussion, the entire Opposition delegation rose to leave. By reflex, the Chancellor opened her mouth to say something, but decided to save her breath. The maneuver was too smoothly executed not to be preplanned. If the entire meeting was just for show—something to give them cover, if the decision turned out badly and word were leaked to the press—then nothing she could say would make the slightest difference. She wouldn't give them the satisfaction of seeing her squirm.

As the large, wooden door closed behind the last departing member of the Opposition, McInnis leaned back in her chair and emitted a low, dull moan. She was as scared as anyone. And for all his bluster, she realized, so was Cornelius Cook. Through any of his faults, he was still a patriot at heart. But a blind patriot was still blind. If the Opposition wouldn't help them pull Ross' home guard together, they'd have to do it themselves. And to hell with the damn accountants.

"How long do we have? Reggie—how long—?"

"Thirty or forty days, according to the reports I've seen. If we're lucky."

"Can you really pull it together?"

"I don't know," Ross shook his head. For the first time since this crisis started, the Chancellor noticed a catch in his voice. "But I won't give up. And if we won't even try, how can we ever hope—how can we dare to pretend that things are going to turn out for us?"

Taking a deep breath, the Chancellor rose to her feet, helped by her Ministers of State and Defense. She never felt so old and helpless, she thought. Or so very, very frightened.

"Gentlemen, do what you think is best," she said, as the attendant came to escort her back down the hall to the Chancellor's Office. "I know each of you is doing that, every hour of every single day. But it is worth remembering, from time to time, that our survival is at stake here. Not our careers or our petty ambitions, but our very existence. Let us conduct ourselves with pride and with dignity. And treat the Opposition with all the courtesy you can muster, no matter the aggravation. It really costs us so very little. And if we do manage to pull this thing off, we'll have the rest of our lives to lord it over them. Spare no expense, if you think it will help. Despite what the croakers say, if we're destined for ruin it will hardly matter in the end."

The attendant steadying her arm, the Chancellor shuffled off, looking every day of her seventy-seven years, leaving all her Ministers to their public duties, and their own private fears.

As THE door to the conference room swung open, the three young officers started, then leaped to attention.

"Sorry I'm late. Got tied up with the blasted navigation computers. By the way, avoid new ships like the plague. Damn sight more trouble than they're worth, if you ask me."

Cook looked up, to see the three young men standing stiffly as he fussed with his charts and disks and papers. Smiling inwardly, he allowed himself the look of one quite lost in his thoughts.

"Oh—sorry. At ease, you three. Been so long since I've had a formal briefing, I quite forgot the protocol."

Looking a bit uneasy, the three officers glanced at each other warily. After so much strict regimentation in recent weeks, they weren't sure what to expect.

"Go on—sit down. All of you. Sit."

Nervously the three men, all newly promoted lieutenant commanders, took their seats. Cook, rummaging through his stack of things, found what he was looking for and put it onto the computer projector at the far end of the table. Mumbling to himself, he began entering some commands and data of his own into the machine, apparently forgetting about his captive audience. Finally, one of them could take it no longer, and loudly cleared his throat.

As Cook looked up, Christopher Barnes, shifting uncomfortably in his chair, felt himself blush under his commander's stern gaze, and immediately regretted his momentary impatience.

"Barnes, isn't it?" asked the Admiral.

Barnes swallowed, hoping to moisten his dry throat. "Yes, sir."

"Get the lights, if you would, Mr. Barnes. We have a bit to discuss today, and we're already well behind schedule."

"Yes, sir."

As he reached across the table to the controls, Barnes was surprised and flattered that the Admiral had remembered his name, until he remembered that this was, after all, a very small group. Chastised by his own conceit, he sank back into his chair in the darkness, forgetting for the moment just how select the group really was. As the image of Isis appeared on the screen, all his fears and inadequacies melted away.

"As we all know, we are in the midst of a crisis. An historic crisis, perhaps, if we're able to have a say in how the history books write it all up. But a crisis, nonetheless."

Humming away brightly, the computer changed the projection to the display of the military problem the Navy's entire class of officers was forced to confront for two hours every day.

"From the enemy's perspective," the Admiral continued, taking a laser cursor to draw their attention to the areas he wished to highlight, "taking Isis is deceivingly simple. Protected on the east by a stormy bank of clouds, a single passage controls the approach to the planet—Gutterman's Gap. Two sets of shoals prevent a clear frontal assault through the opening. The Donnelly Shoals..."

Cook circled the larger body of rocks and debris, which guarded the eastern edge of the passageway.

" — though larger in size, consist of smaller rocks and ice. The Paddington Shoals—the smaller of the two—contains larger, planetoid-sized rocks, and small, trace amounts of interstellar gases. Together, they require anyone traversing the passage between the Greater and Lesser Nakahashi Storms to weave first to center, then anticenter in the pass itself. And as the passage narrows toward its western terminus, the surrounding storms intensify, making radio contact difficult, and sensor probes through the opening impossible. Therefore, the challenge to the Terrans is clearing the passageway in order to deploy a sufficient force into the clear skies beyond the Gap to secure the channel—and permit an attack from either side against any force sent to defend the planet. Once you accomplish this, the battle becomes a simple one of attrition. And that sort of battle, Isis simply cannot win. If you recall, it was only after you began to draw the home fleet out into the open that you were able to master the problem in the form I first gave you. That is the key to understanding the enemy's likely tactics, when the war finally comes to us. And that will be your key to understanding the orders I'll be giving, during the course of battle."

Quickly, Cook changed the focus of the problem, from the offensive perspective to defense. Each of the men in the room listened to their Admiral intently, though none of them could keep up with what he was saying.

"This is the aspect of the problem you started studying after you showed some aptitude for the Terran's strategic dilemma—the problem of defending Isis against a superior force. You began with a more realistic allotment of forces, though still overly generous to our side, and a computer that I programmed to be unforgiving. I note that none of you have yet solved our own little tactical dilemma...."

Looking away from the screen, Barnes saw a trace of a smile dart across the Admiral's lips.

"But your attempts to devise a solution have been more creative and less predictable than any of your compatriots. That is one of the reasons you three are here today."

Cook shifted the perspective from Gutterman's Gap to a display of Isis and her surrounding heavens, and moved his cursor from the pass to the Planet Zarathustra—some sixty parsecs away through the cosmos, reduced to the far right edge of the computer's display.

"Using Zarathustra as a staging area for their fleet, the Terrans will proceed west for forty parsecs, before meeting the eastern edge of the Nakahashi storms. Convention—the strategic orthodoxy of this day, and days past—cautions against dividing their own forces so close to their objective. Choosing to go around the storms permits a more open approach to the planet, but adds another forty parsecs or so to their route. It also poses the risk of an endless series of attacks by an unseen enemy in unfamiliar skies, around any of a number of bends in the clouds."

Cook directed the cursor at Gutterman's Gap, his voice warming to the problem. Barnes, fascinated by the display and struggling to follow the Admiral's train of thought, stared at the images in wonder.

"Therefore, the conventional approach to the Terrans' problem suggests that they will do what each of you, and every single one of your comrades, have done. They will try to storm the Gap, concentrating their entire fleet to force the passage, and expecting us to oppose them with our forces massed to defend the easternmost opening. That is what the textbooks will tell them, and that is what the textbooks have all told you."

"You said our simulation is overly generous," said one of the young officers, a Northlander named McAllister.

"I'm sure it doesn't feel that way," the Admiral said. The three young officers could sense the Admiral's smile, and heard the gentle humor in his voice. "But at your current level of difficulty, I have programmed our forces for two divisions—roughly equal to the Terran invasion force. To give the Terrans a slight edge, I've given them two extra starships, and an extra brigade of frigates."

"What do you expect?"

"That's a state secret, you know," Cook laughed. "I haven't even told the Defense Minister yet, and I'm reluctant to tell my wife because I don't want her to worry, though she probably remembers her tactics classes as well as I do. But even given their probable estimate of our strength, they will probably devote two full divisions to the invasion. The way the numbers work—five companies to the division, five squadrons to the company, five warships to the squadron—I am expecting approximately two-hundred fifty Terran warships. Each company is usually headed by a cruiser, each division by a starship. I wouldn't be surprised to see them toss in an extra starship or two—and that would greatly complicate our lives. But the invasion force on your simulation is a good approximation of what we're likely to face.

Cook walked to the other end of the table, activated the lights, and stepped to the front of the table.

"On the other hand, our forces are exaggerated considerably in the simulation you're using," he smiled wryly. "That makes your job to date a bit easier than mine."

"Do we know yet," Barnes began, "how many ships— "

"How many ships we can muster?" Cook concluded the question, slowly shaking his head. "If you want to know, I'll tell you. But trust me—you really don't want to know."

"You'd actually tell us?"

Cook nodded grimly. "You three have just passed a major hurdle. You've made it past training, and are now part of my command structure. I won't tell you everything, but I will tell you whatever might help you fulfill your assigned role in the Navy. And in any case, as part of my staff, I think this is something you're entitled to know. If you really want it."

Barnes and the others exchanged a quick glance. Barnes noticed the pride in the eyes of his comrades, a pride he felt himself. Better than most, he knew that the Admiral took very few into his confidence. Making it this far, against greater odds than he realized at the time, was the biggest accomplishment of his young life. Each of them felt it; and each felt he was ready to tackle anything under heaven.

"I think we'd like to know."

"Don't say I didn't warn you," the Admiral said. Barnes noticed that the warm humor of the philosopher was gone from his eyes; in its place was the cold steel of the warrior.

"Presently, we have one starship, and a second one should be ready in time for battle. We have nearly one company of starworthy frigates—twenty-three, to be exact, with another eight or nine possible. The precise number depends on the success of repair crews working around the clock at the dry docks. And we have as many small craft, yachts, and schooners as we can handle, capable of being retrofitted to carry at least one disrupter cannon. Today's report listed our present compliment at just over two thousand, and the shipyards are converting at the rate of approximately one-hundred per day. If we sail in twenty days, we should have about four thousand small ships to add to our fleet."

Barnes felt sick to his stomach. To his surprise, he saw what appeared to be a flash of sympathy in the Admiral's eyes; a heartbeat later, it was gone.

"You mean," said McAllister, "that we have one company of frigates to face two CosGuard divisions?"

"It's actually worse than that, Mr. McAllister," replied the Admiral, his tone at once ironic and stunningly self-assured. "One of you three will be the company commander. The others—together with two more officers I'll be naming in the next few days—will be my frigate squadron leaders."

"But one company?" repeated Barnes.

"It's more than a single company, Mr. Barnes. You will have about four-thousand other ships standing beside you. True, their biggest, and perhaps only real use will be to confuse the enemy. But don't disregard the force of sheer numbers on the enemy psyche. Don't disregard the element of surprise. Don't disregard the edge that fighting for your homeland will give you. And don't ignore your Admiral's facility with a starship. I have studied the likely effect of a second starship on the battle, and have immodestly assigned a total strength of one division to our fleet. And with one division, I have no problem beating the computer against a conventional enemy fleet. Even at the levels I play the simulation, one division is more than enough for us to defend successfully.

"But that's down the road," the Admiral said, a wry smirk on his lips. "For the time being, I have another problem for you three to work on. A problem I've been grappling with for weeks."

Cook killed the lights, and returned to the computer.

"Watch the screen," he said grimly. "This simulation, I have dubbed 'The Admiral's Nightmare.'"

Transfixed, Barnes watched the battle unfold, stunned by the complexity of motion on both sides and exaggerated by the compressed speed of the engagement. As it sailed from Zarathustra, the Terran fleet aligned itself into three columns, each comprising about a third of the entire formation. Halting well before the first wisps of the storms, one column moved to circle centerside of the storm clouds; another, proceeded anticenter. As the two flanking columns neared the far bend, the Terran center started down Gutterman's Gap, moving to engage the overmatched Isitian fleet.

"Freeze simulator," Cook barked, and the computer obediently halted the movements. Barnes looked at the display carefully. The Isitian forces, now divided between the Pass and the Planet, seemed so small as to be nonexistent.

"None of you—actually, nobody who's logged onto the computer to run the offensive simulation—has deployed the Terran forces like this. And the reason is quite simple: it violates nearly every rule anyone has written on the art of war in the last three thousand years, and every lesson you're likely to learn in any textbook on tactics. You don't divide your forces—you don't divide your forces near an engagement—and you certainly don't divide a superior force on the eve of battle in hostile territory. You lose the advantage of numbers, and risk giving an overmatched foe the chance to beat your forces in turn. Conventional military wisdom holds this to be foolhardy, and no CosGuard commander I know would even think to do this. But the first time I played the offensive simulation, this is precisely the deployment I chose for the Terrans. And it is the one line of attack I have never beaten. What's worse, the regular simulator program doesn't even begin to reflect our real dilemma. When I compensate for that, the tactical situation becomes hopeless."

Cook moved to activate the lights. "And believe me, I've played this situation through day and night, several times every day. And it still haunts my dreams."

"Why is it such a problem?" asked McAllister. "If the enemy divides their fleet, then all we do is— "

"The theoretical problem is simple," interrupted Cook, smiling patiently. "At less than division strength, our forces lack the critical mass needed to blunt a thrust, and mount a counterattack. That's why the Cosmic Guard is organized into divisions in the first place. To put it simply, if I divert enough ships to block the Pass, I don't have enough to protect the Planet; if I mass sufficient strength to defend the Planet, the Terrans can force their way through the Gap and attack me from the rear. On the other hand, if I seize the initiative and try to beat all three columns in succession, the first enemy column just has to keep retreating, drawing us further away from the Planet until the other two columns can rendezvous and attack. Of course, we can always assume that the enemy commander is an idiot, and would simply proceed to fight us on our own terms. But underestimating the enemy is the best way I know to invite disaster, so I chose to assume that we'll be fighting them at their best. Any way I approach the problem, the Planet falls as long as they divide their fleet in the open skies east of Nakahashi. But even this understates our real tactical challenge."

Cook moved to the head of the table, and in turn, looked each of his new squadron commanders in the eye. "If we adjust the simulator to reflect the real world," he said sternly, "we find that our actual forces are all but indivisible. Most of our strength in battle comes from a single source—my own starship. But I can't fight the battle alone, without support. The pillar of this support is our second starship—and Heaven help us if it isn't ready in time. I can detach as many ships as I want from the main body of our fleet, but they'll be wasted unless the detachment includes a starship—fried where they stand, with few enemy casualties and no effect on the course of battle. But if it does include the second starship, I lose the one prop that makes my own ship worth a whole division. If I can use the second ship to pin down some of the enemy, my ship can wipe the skies with the rest. But if I have nothing to keep some part of the Terran fleet at bay, they can simply surround and destroy me—and then massacre the rest of us.

"And that, gentlemen, is the problem I want you to study."

"But how can you expect us— "

"To solve it for me?" Cook laughed. "You can't. Plain and simple. What I want from you are ideas, not solutions. I'm fresh out of ideas on this one, I'm afraid, other than hoping that the enemy commander will prove to be a fool—and I don't have any more time to spend on the problem. You come up with the right idea, I'll turn it into the right battle plan."

"But I—we—haven't even beaten the defensive simulation yet."

"Acch—don't worry about it. You're not doing these things to earn points. I've had you doing it to give you some glimmer of understanding the battle you'll be fighting. You three have had enough of that. Actually, you probably have more understanding of our situation than you'll find good for your own mental health, but that's beside the point. And to be honest, your efforts on this little obsession of mine are probably wasted, because no Terran commander I know has the balls to do anything of the sort. Once again, I'm probably sparring with my own shadow. Nevertheless, this is what I want you to do."

Cook rose to his feet, and yawned; Barnes thought he saw a brief hint of fatigue cloud the Admiral's eyes. But it passed as quickly as it came, and he dismissed it as the product of his own imagination.

"Now, follow me," Cook motioned grandly, and started off toward the conference room door. "We have one more thing I want to do today. Then, I'll leave you to your work."

Warily, the three men rose from their seats and followed their commander out the door. Each man felt flattered to be part of the Admiral's grand plans. But each was beginning to wonder if the reward for all their hard work might not prove to be more than they'd bargained for.

* * *

"GOOD—GOOD. Very good."

Slowly, Janet walked past the carrels in the training deck, looking for any signs that a pilot trainee might need help. Of all the tasks that her husband assigned her, she reflected, this was the one she hated most of all.

"No, no—don't overcompensate," she said, moving toward the controls of one particularly ham-handed ensign. "Remember, there's no drag in deep space. No friction. Once you set your ship in motion, there's no stopping it. Not without using more power to correct your mistake. When you're near a planet, you can sometimes let gravity iron out your goofs—but not here. Watch—"

Bending over the controls, Janet gently guided the simulator toward the base formation appearing on the screen—first angling back past the center of the squadron, then easing off as the direction indicator approached the intended heading.

"See—a light touch—correcting before you shoot past your target...always thinking ahead."

"Yes, Ma'am. Thank you, Ma'am."

Janet smiled, with as much warmth as she could muster. "Just relax, Ensign. You'll get the hang of it yet."

As she continued her stroll down the aisles, Janet knew full well why she hated this part of her work. It wasn't that she didn't enjoy getting to show off for the class. Sharing her knowledge with the students was the one part of her job she actually enjoyed. But when she thought about what the future held for these young kids—children, they seemed, for they looked so much younger than she remembered anyone being when she was that age—it was enough to break her heart.

Cannon fodder, she shivered. That's all they were. That's all any of them were. Not talented enough to compete for a chance to command one of the Isitian Navy's aging and near-derelict frigates, or to be considered for a position on one of the two starships, all they could do is train as pilots, to steer one of the many small craft they'd be taking into battle against the Terran fleet.

They were all so eager, she thought, so anxious to learn. So willing to devote these precious hours of their young lives to mastering a skill that would probably kill them. Despite what Skipper might tell them—or tell her, in the few and fleeting moments they could spend together—she had few illusions about what their fate would be. Despite all their practice and hard work, all their sacrifice and dedication, she was sure they would all die. Every last one of them. In the first few moments of battle.

Just before the Terrans turned the attack on the rest of the fleet.

Against the Isitian starships. And against Cook.

And in that moment, she realized, their passing would be no more than a prelude to her own.

* * *

HIS EYES bleary and aching, Ensign Jason shuffled his way down the corridor leading to Company 17's quarters. After all his extra hours on the simulator, he'd beaten the machine only once. And even that, he was coming to conclude, was a bit of a fluke. He knew too little about tactics to avoid most major mistakes, but once, for some reason, one of his mistakes happened to send the Blue Fleet reeling. He still didn't understand what he'd done. With most of his simulator time coming when he was dead tired, he was beginning to have his doubts whether he'd ever understand anything, ever again.

Pausing to focus his eyes on the number above the door, he opened the door and stepped inside, moving quietly so he wouldn't disturb the sleeping, snoring cadets he roomed with. Careful to avoid the foot lockers and assorted junk that would litter the floor until tomorrow's inspection, he found his bunk and eased onto the mattress.

"Jason?"

"What is it, Lund? I'm dead tired."

"Did you know Rose? From Company 71—you know across the hall?"

"Not really. What's he look like?"

"Tall, thin. A little on the goofy side."

"Doesn't ring a bell."

"His mother died today. Some sort of accident, I think."

"Oh, no. That's too bad. Is he— "

"I don't know. But a bunch of us were going to take a collection. He comes from a pretty poor family. The funeral's tomorrow."

"Is he leaving?"

"You mean, washing out?"

"Yes."

"I don't know. Would you?"

Jason leaned back onto his bunk and tried to think. The exhaustion was blurring his thoughts together, and he found it impossible to concentrate. But this was one question he couldn't reason his way through. The answer was emotional, not rational. He was certain what he would do.

"No."

"I don't think I would, either."

"Good night, Lund."

"That's too bad, though."

"Good night, Lund."

"Makes you really stop and think...."

"Good night, Lund."

* * *

"THIS IS Blue Leader. That was awful, you know. Keep it smart this time. Keep the formation snappy, but don't rush things. Just take your time and let the ship do the work. Let's try it again. Pivot left, two hundred degrees by 10 north."

The distant clouds of Nakahashi stretched like the blood of forgotten ancestors against the blackness. Everywhere, silence and emptiness stretched into Eternity.

"Roger, Admiral. Blue-1, acknowledged."

Four small, lonely ships slipped through the skies, their pilots drifting with their thoughts and their fears.

"Blue-2, acknowledged."

As the command squadron practiced formation after formation, building arc after looping arc, time seemed to slow from a torrent to a slow, still lake. The rigors and torments of the future faded into oblivion as the stars and clouds drifted through Eternity, as they had through the ages. Their leader led them to dance and soar in the Cosmos, and soon they were one with the heavens.

"Blue-3, acknowledged."

Chapter 6

L OOKS LIKE RAIN. I'm packing your raincoat, just in case."
"I'm sure they'll give us rain gear."
"It's just plain foolish to be going off in weather like this.
They waited this long, they can pick a nicer day."

Jack smiled and continued eating his breakfast. Pancakes and
bacon was a welcome change from the juice and slice of toast he
usually gobbled down before heading off to tend the little shop that
he called a business. If the drill sergeant at the training camp where
he was headed didn't run it out of him, it might just last him until the
government bought him lunch.

Or, what passed for lunch at these militia camps. Stale bread,
scalded coffee, and something vaguely resembling meat by-products
were the usual fare. All you could eat, too—which, for most, was not
very much. Even after eating his fill at the camp, he never failed to
return home, tired and hungry.

It had gone on like this for nearly a week. Ever since the papers
had reported the camp locations, the makeshift military bases were
swollen with volunteers. Though the food had been passably
mediocre for the first two days, the Government wasn't prepared for
the onslaught. In the space of a week, New Alexandria had become
almost a ghost town. Until the crisis passed it would probably remain
one, unless the Government did something to keep the crowds
down to a manageable level. Twice-weekly drills were under
discussion, he'd heard. Or limiting each day's call alphabetically. Or
by birthday. Something—anything—to get the numbers down.

"Well, dear...," he began, getting ready to leave for the day.

"Hush. The news is coming on," his wife replied. Keeping his
smiles to himself, he kissed his wife on the cheek and returned his
attention to breakfast. Soon, the monitor screen filled with snippets
of stories past and present, fading into the image of the friendly,
handsome, news anchorman.

"Good morning," smiled the face on the screen. "While claiming success across most of the battle front, it appears that the Terrans have lost a major battle just east of Girshoona, threatening their grip on that key stronghold. Here at home, a lack of funds threatens to hamper efforts to ready the world to fend off a ground attack. But first, an update on today's weather."

As the newsman droned on, Jack let his mind drift to the upcoming day's drilling: target practice and marching; marching and target practice; field maneuvers and target practice. All in the mud and the rain.

Julie was right about one thing, he grinned, watching his wife gaze intently into the monitor screen. It was a foolish way to spend the day. It broke his heart to leave them, even though he'd left them to go to work every day before the War threatened, and would do so after the threat was over. But it reminded him that nobody knew the future; and one day, if things turned out badly, he might never come home.

Before long, his breakfast finished, he gathered his gear by the door. Kissing his wife, and hugging his daughter until she squealed, he left through the big front door like he did every morning.

And just like every morning for the last week, tears filled his eyes as soon as he crossed the street and headed toward the Underground stop that would take him to the training camp.

* * *

COMMAND DIRECTIVE

DATE: cc:144.7791.1
FROM: Admiral Cook
TO: All Fleet Personnel
SUBJECT: Change in Duty Assignments

With the completion of basic screening, we are moving from basic training to active preparation for battle.

New assignments are posted on all bulletin boards, and are being transmitted to everyone affected. They are effective immediately, and will continue until further notice. All officers and crew assigned to battle duty should make arrangements to ship their excess belongings back to the Planet. Maneuvers commence in earnest tomorrow, and there will be no turning back until the battle is won.

Please keep up the good work: Isis needs you. We need every hand manning every station to make our stand against the Terrans. No one will go into battle alone, and each of us has a vital role to play in whatever fate has in store for tomorrow.

* * *

GREG GARRITY folded the letter from his kid brother, and leaned back onto his bunk. Scott was seven years old, and jealous that his older brother was going off to space. Poor kid was just old enough to see what was happening, but too young to understand the danger. Like any little boy, he saw only the excitement; he was too young to realize all the work that came with it.

Taking a pen and paper, Garrity decided to send his brother a letter of his own. He'd sent lots of letters home to his family, but never one addressed to The Squirt. He promised himself to write more often, before things got serious.

Dear Squirt:
I enjoyed your last letter. It's nice to know people care, and that you're proud of your big brother. I hope all of us can make a lot of people proud, once the Terrans come to call.

I think you wouldn't like it here. We're living together in a big dormitory—fifty guys to a room, twenty rooms to a floor. We have to stand in line to wash, take a shower, and eat. And we have so little time to do anything but drill, that it's easy to put off keeping in touch with friends and family. I'm sorry I haven't written sooner. I promise to try harder in the future.

Orders just came out today, giving us our assignments against the Terries. I've been assigned to command a small schooner, as part of the Militia brigade. I've done pretty well in the fighter drills, so I'm happy someone finally noticed. I just hope that I get enough time to practice in space, so I don't embarrass myself when the shooting starts.

Garrity paused for a moment. He didn't want Scott to start worrying needlessly; their parents were probably worrying enough for the whole family. And he didn't want the kid to remember him only as his principle tormentor in the Garrity clan, but words were difficult. He didn't like writing, and had a date for later in the day. A very promising date, he smiled to himself, so he finished as quickly as he could.

> Say 'hi' to everyone for me, and give Mom and Dad a hug. I'm sorry if I always seemed to tease you, but when I was younger it seemed like that was what big brothers were for. Maybe when I get home, I can be a better big brother as you grow older.
> Your pal,
> Greg.

* * *

"HELM, COME to 220 north 15; Weapons, charge the shields, prepare to charge the forward guns."

"Yes, Ma'am."

Janet turned the command chair on the simulated bridge to face the portside screens. The simulation was turning into a disaster: none of the kids manning the bridge posts had the slightest notion of what to do. Anticipation meant nothing to them. They could barely anticipate their own bowel movements, let alone orders from the command chair. Nobody did anything without being told; they just sat there like lumps, waiting. And not a single one had the foresight to bring their lunch with them.

Like Nielsen, the rookie weapons officer sitting at his post with a confused look on his face. Obviously, the order to charge the shields had come as a shock to him. Otherwise, he wouldn't have spent half a minute looking for the right switch when he had five whole minutes of helm maneuvers to ready his post for the simple act of activating the ship's deflectors. Or Wasser, the systems officer—a nice enough kid: bright, intense, eager to please. But so reluctant to say anything without an invitation. Eisenberg, the navigator, seemed too addled to navigate his way out of a water closet. None of the more experienced people from the *New Alexandria*, their sister starship, seemed to know their way around a bridge, either. Fortunately, Tony Landis—the nitwit to whom her own husband had given command of the other starship—was drilling his people in Simulator Room Five, across the hall and mercifully out of earshot.

She didn't know how the Skipper hoped to do anything with such a group, and she didn't know what she was supposed to do with them, either. The thought of leading them into battle made her sick to the stomach. It didn't help matters when Skipper disappeared for days at a time, leaving her to face every disaster all by herself. And he was a great one for leaving messages. Always leaving notes and little bits of paper stashed here and there. Do this—try that—try some other silly thing, they'd all say. But just try to find him when there was work to be done. Or when something went wrong.

"Overtaking target," reported the young systems officer. "Range one klick and closing."

"Shields up, Commodore."

"Charge all forward gun batteries."

"Aye, Ma'am."

"Range one-half klick and closing."

"Fire in the hole, Ma'am," called the weapons officer. Janet looked at the weapons display on the armrest, to see that the forward gun batteries were now fully operational.

"'Guns amain' is the proper prompt, Lieutenant," said Janet, wondering if they'd actually hit something this time. She never got the chance to find out. "Prepare to fire on my command."

"All hands, attention!" barked the security officer. As every other officer in the room scrambled to his feet, she heard a reassuringly familiar voice—though it reassured her only for a passing moment.

"Acch—as you were," said the Admiral, smiling mysteriously as he moved toward the command seat. He squeezed Janet's hand, and motioned for her to stay where she was. Momentarily flushed with delight at getting to see him, Janet was soon mad as a hornet at the interruption. She glared at him so angrily that Cook mistook the look for passionate devotion and smiled, moved at his wife's display of affection.

Cook nodded, his sharp eyes moving from face to face as he studied and memorized the features and manner of each member he'd chosen for his bridge crew. Until now, he'd known them only from their work—the silent record of the progress of each officer, kept by the computer he'd programmed just for that purpose. He'd picked three for each station, and was still unsure whether this kind of blind selection would actually yield results. Personal profiles and simulated performances were handy tools, but they could never tell him how much steel was in anyone's backbone, or how deep the blood flowed in someone's heart. But he had no real choice. Time was short, and he had no other way to cull through the thousands of volunteers who'd flocked to join his Navy. And anyway, letting them sort themselves seemed like a good idea at the time. He tried his best to keep his doubts to himself, and smiled confidently as he addressed them. He'd always found the best way to face his own fears was to laugh at them, and was determined to help his bridge crew do the same.

"Good day to you all, and welcome to Panic Central," he said, grinning as the room filled with nervous laughter. "First of all, let me apologize to each and every one of you, for dragging you into this. Usually I try to reward hard work, ability, and dedication, not punish it. And I won't make any pretense about what we have facing us. It will be lots of stress, mind-numbing drills, and endless repetition. And at the end of it all, we get to let the Terrans try to kill us. Actually, now that I think of it, that's not the sort of graduation party I'd ordinarily plan to attend."

Cook looked around the room, letting the rising spirits of his crew begin to take on a life of its own. He could see that laughter was having an effect on his people, and smiled inwardly in satisfaction at the thought that he could still sense which strings to pull. "I suppose that wouldn't be so bad, by itself," he continued. "But it doesn't give us a lot to look forward to. And of course, after we do somehow manage to live through it all, we'll get to listen to all the preening politicians congratulate themselves on having the courage and vision to face down the Cosmic Guard. Maybe even allowing from time to time, that—well, yes, perhaps the Navy did have a tiny role to play in the whole affair. By the time it's over I suspect it'll be more than any of us will be able to stomach.

"Well, then," he turned to wink at Janet, who was, for some reason he couldn't understand, now glowering at him. As the crew's laughter subsided, he shrugged and kept plodding along. "I suppose it's time to get down to basics. As of tomorrow, we begin maneuvers in real ships, and out in real space. I'll expect and demand more from this group than any other.

"I selected each of you for a particular reason—either a specialized skill I need, or a particular skill you've shown. Like any other assignment in my Navy, until the crisis has passed your job here will be the focus of your existence. Because you'll be working at tasks that are among the most important in the whole Navy, I expect you to put your heart and soul into your efforts. You will arrive early for each day's drilling; and you will stay late practicing, to remove any deficiencies that come to light during the day. You will—each of you—excel at your assignments, because I will tolerate nothing less, and because if you are not brilliant at your assigned task, Isis will crumble like dust in the heavens. And no matter how much despair you feel during the days to come, you will also look back on these next weeks as the most exciting, exhilarating, and inspiring days of your lives. You are part of a noble cause—one of the noblest in human history, like Old Earth's crusade against the Nazis, or the American war against slavery. Every moment you spend honing your abilities and perfecting your skills is one more slap in the face of tyranny. And when the fighting starts, and Terran guns start blasting away, every second you've invested in yourself will come to pay dividends. In the heat of battle, everything you've learned will come pouring back into your hands and minds with amazing clarity.

"In three weeks, you'll be able to stand against the best the Terrans have to throw at us. The Commodore and I will see to it—and mark my words, we will not let you shortchange yourselves, your homes, or your families. You may well come to hate us in the coming days. But when we lead you into battle, you'll fight as warriors have always fought—with hearts aflame and heads held proud. And we mean to see that when the day of battle finally comes, each of you will have the tools and skills to battle on to victory."

Cheers ringing in his ears, Cook turned to look at Janet, who was now smiling proudly despite her best efforts to stay annoyed.

"Now, I need two volunteers to man the systems and weapons stations. You two— ," Cook pointed at the hapless pair still seated at the designated stations, holdovers from the drill Janet was conducting when Cook finally made his appearance. "You two stay where you are—and do try to pay attention. I get rather testy when my bridge crew fails to keep up the pace. The rest of you sit back; the Commodore and I will show you what a starship can really do."

Cook stepped toward the navigator's station, and motioned for Janet to join him at the helmsman's console. As they took their seats, an audible murmur filled the entire bridge.

"I hope you know what you're doing," whispered Janet, as she settled into her station. She knew exactly how unprepared the bridge crew was, and winced at the thought of having two rookies manning the weapons and systems stations.

"We haven't done this in some time, you realize," she went on. "Those poor fools can barely strap themselves into their seats, and I doubt we'll impress anybody merely by snapping off a few of your fancy turns on the simulator. You covered that maneuver in the briefing book, and half of them have it mastered already. At least they have on the computer. I have my doubts that space will be quite so forgiving."

"You underestimate their hunger to be impressed," replied the Admiral, grinning wryly as he entered the code for a new battle problem. "And don't forget who wrote all these simulations. It's just too bad I can't program the Cosmic Guard to be as slow moving, witless, and easy to hit as the three starships we'll be going up against in the next few minutes."

Despite herself, Janet found herself chuckling as the new simulation appeared on the screen. In all their years together, and whatever his other faults, the Skipper had never failed to keep her life interesting and exciting. At times too exciting. He might be stubborn, opinionated, and too absent-minded to remember to come home for dinner. But even if he was leading them to death and destruction, at least she wouldn't die of boredom.

* * *

PEEKING THROUGH the clouds, the golden sun warmed the afternoon air, and the hillside was alive with wildflowers. The day was muggy, and the grass was still damp from an early spring shower. The subtle fragrance of renewed life was drowned by the acrid smell of burning air.

"No—-no—no!" screamed the drill sergeant, straining to be heard over the din of weapons fire filling the air from the target range, just over the hill.

"Company halt!"

The assembly pressed and grunted its way to a clumsy mass of more or less stationary men and boys, all shuffling under the strain of standing still. The sergeant, a physical education teacher in civilian life, closed his eyes and counted to ten. Then to twenty. When his temper subsided enough to speak in coherent sentences, he strode to the front of the group and threw his daypack onto the driest available patch of ground.

"This is the most miserable, God-awful group of nitwits, fools, and bunglers I've seen in my entire life!" he shouted, glaring into the face of each volunteer as he walked down the line. "A bunch of third-graders would have a better sense of organization. Kindergartners have a better attention span. And a slumber-party of teenaged girls would be less inclined to jibber-jabber! What in God's name are you morons doing that you can't pay attention?"

As the sergeant's shouts rose with the gentle spring breeze, Private Jack Markham of Delta Company, Isitian South-Central Militia, unshouldered his weapon and took a deep breath. It was uncommonly warm for this time of year, and all things considered, he'd rather be at home playing with his three-year old daughter. Soon, his mind drifted to his wife's baked bread, and their summer cottage on the lake. He missed the sergeant's order to resume marching, and was surprised to find himself suddenly at the bottom of a large pile of bodies, all cursing like spacers at the latest muddle to greet the proud lads of Delta Company, Isitian South-Central Militia.

"Jesus H. Christ— !!" hollered the sergeant, pulling the militiamen away from the mess. "I told you—the next screw-up would cost everybody! And—dammit—I'm sick and tired of yelling myself hoarse!"

As the company fell to the mud and began their penance of pushups and sweat, Jack found himself growing angrier and angrier with each ache of his muscles. The sergeant, playing on their inadequacies as well as their pain, kept drumming away at their clumsiness, insulting their manhood and intelligence, until every one of them was ready to storm Central Command itself. The Terries were the cause of it all, the sergeant kept telling them. If it weren't for the Terries, they'd all be with their families—lounging around their living rooms and drinking beer, while their wives fed them grilled steak and buttercakes. Soon his groans blended together with those of his comrades, and he found himself wanting nothing more than to have the Terrans land—in downtown New Alexandria, if they had the balls—so that he could even the score.

* * *

MOVING HIS eyes slowly, trying carefully to keep them in focus, Lt. Steve Eisenberg glanced at the chronometer. "750 Hours," it read. Eisenberg let out a slow, silent stream of air.

It read 200 Hours when they began, he remembered. They had been drilling ever since, if you could call what the Admiral put them through "drilling." Fifteen hours without a moment's peace, and Admiral Cook had seemed as fresh as when they began, even bouncing down the walkway from the bridge when they finally broke for the day.

Looking across the bridge, Eisenberg saw nothing but exhaustion. Exhaustion and despair.

Not that it wasn't exciting to watch the Admiral at work. Eisenberg had practically grown up on a ship. He'd had been sailing the skies of home for as long as he could remember, and after volunteering for the Navy he'd been the star of their crash course in navigation. But the Admiral's ability to pull navigation plots and course headings out of thin air was humbling, and enough to make him feel foolish. And seeing what a starship could do in the hands of a master was awe-inspiring. Almost frightening.

In fact, he mused, it was almost as frightening as seeing just how many mistakes the rest of them could make. They seemed to have an inexhaustible supply of those. And he suddenly wondered how many "masters" the Terries might be sending after them. It was enough to make him want to crawl into bed and sleep for a thousand years.

"All right, people," called Nielsen, apparently the brightest among the weapons officers. Sturdy and strong, Nielsen was one of the smaller members of the crew, barely five and a half feet tall, with the loudest voice and biggest mouth of the entire bridge team. Eisenberg had heard that Nielsen, like the Admiral, was quite a musician: in college, Nielsen had toured the whole planet with the Central Tech glee club. But the little jerk was hitting all the wrong notes as far as the rest of them were concerned.

"Time to get moving," the cocky Central Highlander continued. "Tomorrow will come soon enough, and we all have lots of work to do before we're ready to take the new ship out of port."

Seeing nothing to throw at him, and being too tired to try in any event, Eisenberg slumped in his seat, staring dumbly into his own mental fog. Others might want to rush off to the simulators, he scoffed as a handful of his bridgemates rose and reluctantly started the long journey toward the simulation room. For himself, all he wanted was a warm bed and a long sleep.

And he'd get it, he promised himself. Just as soon as he found the energy to get out of his chair.

"QUITE A SESSION, wasn't it?"

Cook lay back into the chair, reliving each moment of his first bridge session with his new crew. Unlike the first session on the *d'Artagnan*, this time he'd wanted to lift the spirit of his people, not teach them humility. And the effect on him was invigorating. The adrenalin was surging, his combative juices were flowing. For the first time in weeks, he found himself too pumped up to collapse from exhaustion, too awake to go to sleep—and, at last, home early enough to spend time with his wife.

"Quite a session, wasn't it?" he repeated.

"Yes."

"Aren't you just amazed? Those kids are green as an unripe banana, but they sure put their hearts into it. And did you notice how much they improved in one session? I'd be willing to bet that in five days—one week, tops—they'll be so sharp we'll be mistaking the lot of them for crusty old spacers."

"I suppose."

Rising from his chair to stretch his legs, Cook found his mind racing past the immediate task at hand to contemplate the future in all its unknown permutations. Gone was the numbing weariness that kept pulling at him, day after day. It was enough of a struggle to keep despair at bay. In his darker moments, even he would have his doubts—although everybody looked to him for answers, and if he even hinted that all he had were questions, everything would collapse like a house of cards.

But not tonight, he smiled. Tonight, he could conquer anything.

"Any ideas for tomorrow?"

"No."

"I was thinking about dividing them into teams."

"Go right ahead."

He sat down on the couch beside Janet, and stroked her hair. Her response caught him unprepared.

"You know what I find infuriating?" she snapped angrily, glaring at him with enough venom to make his spine prickle with alarm. "Besides the fact that you don't care about anything or anyone, I mean. And probably never have."

He was about to ask why she was so dead set against dividing the bridge crew into teams, but Janet fired another volley before he could open his mouth.

"Nothing is ever good enough for you, is it?" she demanded. "You find fault with everything, and never give anyone the slightest pat on the back. Those kids—and in fact, your entire Navy—do everything they can to make you proud of them. And what thanks do they get? What thanks do any of us get? We get more work piled on us. Then you leave for days at a time. Never letting anyone know whether they're doing a good job. Never letting anyone know what fool thing you'll have them doing next. And then you waltz back into the room, like you did on the bridge today, and expect everyone to cheer. Like you're some kind of god. Heaven's gift to Isis. Is that it?"

"What, exactly— ," he began.

"Like tonight," she continued. "Everyone on the bridge was dead tired, including me. We'd all been drilling for two hours—two mind-numbing hours, you know. Going over every single element of protocol, every aspect of each and every station, in excruciating detail. And then you march in and keep them at it forever! How in God's name can you expect anyone to have any energy left, much less any enthusiasm? How can you watch while the rest of us kill ourselves, just to have you ignore our every effort? And how can you just sit there, with your mouth open, and not say anything at all?"

His head spinning, Cook realized that he had to say something. Unfortunately, trying to sort out what Janet was saying he was paying more attention to her words than to the tears forming in her eyes.

"I think you were all wonderful, on the bridge today."

"Oh, so that really is all you care about," she retorted. "It really hasn't changed very much. That's all you ever care about."

"Janet— "

"You know, it might help to have a real husband every once in a while," she said acidly. "One who is really flesh and blood, instead of just a memory." Rising to her feet, she left the room, slamming the bedroom door behind her.

Left alone on the couch to ponder his many failings, Cook sensed that she was right, whatever she was trying to say. He hadn't been much of a husband, he thought. The fact that there wasn't anything he could do about it wouldn't make her feel any better.

Slowly, he rose to his feet and walked to the bedroom. He knocked gently on the door and, hearing no response, quietly stepped inside. Tonight she needed a husband. Even if, tonight, being a husband simply meant being around to be yelled at.

* * *

"WHAT IS the head count? The precise head count?"

The Chancellor leaned forward and looked down the table. Immediately, she knew that the news was not good. Jerry O'Hara, the Assistant Majority Leader, squirmed uncomfortably in his chair. He was a good man, and a superb headcounter. Unfortunately, he was not as skilled at the less refined talents that politics sometimes required: arm-twisting and emotional blackmail were arts that somehow eluded him, even as he'd ascended the ladder of power in the capital city of New Alexandria. Persuasiveness and honest charm might have been all he needed to bend the Senate to his will in the past; but as their day of reckoning neared, and fear began to work its way onto the Senate floor, reason was becoming as rare as an honest man in Covington. Rumors of the impending Terran attack were already rampant in the capital. They needed an iron hand to keep the croakers from causing a general panic, and she was much too tired to keep them all in line by herself.

"We're still waiting, Senator," she smiled sweetly.

"This is just a preliminary count, you understand," O'Hara hedged, hoping to soften the news.

"We are all realists, Senator," replied the Chancellor sternly. "We have no time to play games."

"If the vote is taken tomorrow," O'Hara said, knowing that there was no way to postpone the vote any longer, "we can count on only forty votes. Forty very reluctant votes, I might add. If nothing changes in the remaining week, the measure will fail, by a vote of fifty-six to forty. Nobody, it seems, wishes to risk infuriating the Terries. The Northlanders—even our own people among them—are all putting in with the Opposition. Party discipline, I'm afraid, is not what it once was."

"That will require new elections," Ross observed, sinking into his chair. "And we cannot have an election in the middle of a war. Can you imagine trying to confront all the wild rumors and accusations as fighting is raging around us? It would be chaos."

"We can't postpone the vote?" asked the Chancellor.

"The vote was scheduled three weeks ago," replied David Ruskin, the Majority Leader. "The date was agreed by unanimous consent, and I dare say, we will not see unanimous consent to change it. Not unless we begin arresting certain members of the Opposition—and then, we will have our own loyalists up in arms with cries of a dictatorship. No, I'm afraid the vote cannot be changed."

"Can't we amend the motion, to continue funding of the militia for only a few months more?"

"By then, the main event will be settled, one way or the other," replied her reluctant chief of staff, hating to be the bearer of bad tidings. The Chancellor might be practical enough to see reason, he knew; he was not so certain about Minister Ross. "Our choice is to back down completely, or put the matter to a vote. And we are likely to lose the vote."

As her ministers discussed the matter, the Chancellor noticed the approaching panic in their eyes, and heard the edge of fear in their voices. She found herself wondering how they had come to such a turn—a planet, dedicated to reason and honor, come to the brink of ruin at the hands of madmen bent on mindless destruction, and unable to do anything about it but squabble mindlessly. Not for the first time, she wondered whether the human race had learned anything through the eons, if Man was ever bred for anything but death and darkness.

* * *

THE DISTANT clouds loomed to the east, billowing in the blackness.

High above the troubled planet, several small ships slipped their moorings and drifted off into the nearby skies. First five—then ten—then fifty ships left the docks, dodging and soaring, weaving together and apart amid the emptiness. As the small world turned slowly on its axis, the tiny ships danced in the night sky like fanciful stars, until they faded with the dawn.

Chapter 7

//cc:144.7797.4/TO/HQ/FR/reynolds,ltcmdr/
QLQ OP BETA. CIVILIAN RADIO BROADCAST MONITORED, THIS
DAY: ZARATHUSTRA RADIO REPORTS CONTENDING FLEETS
ENGAGED IN SKIES OFF CRUTCHTAN PLANET GIRSHOONA.
TERRAN GOVERNMENT IS CALLING BATTLE A VICTORY, BUT
CASUALTY FIGURES ARE ABSENT FROM BROADCAST RE-
PORTS. ON SECONDARY FRONT, TERRAN OFFENSIVE STILL
STALLED. COSGUARD CONSOLIDATING GAINS INTO GLINCI AND
ATKVALO SKIES. FULL RECORDING WILL FOLLOW PER NORMAL
CHANNELS. TERRAN MILITARY BROADCASTS REMAIN INDECI-
PHERABLE. SUGGESTIONS RE NEW CODE HELPFUL, BUT HQ
ANALYSIS AND DECRYPTION WELCOME. FACILITIES HERE TOO
PRIMITIVE FOR TASK.

   OPINION XO: SETBACKS ON OTHER FRONTS MAY DIVERT
COSGUARD BRASS ATTENTION FROM ISIS. OPINION CMDR:
SETBACKS WILL ACCELERATE TERRAN TIMETABLE TO DIVERT
PUBLIC ATTENTION AWAY FROM EASTERN FRONT.
   /**ZTT/djreynolds/enter/Xmit//

* * *

"So, THIS is it?" said Minister Ross to no one in particular, more in resignation than anger. "This is how we go down fighting—at one another's throats?"

Smiling sadly, Ross glanced at the rest of the Cabinet, assembled to go to the Senate floor and record their votes for posterity, each determined not to take the blame for it. But the fiasco was his own idea, Ross admitted to himself. He could hardly fault them for scurrying for cover as the Government collapsed around them.

Rising to his feet, Ross stepped toward the large, second floor bay window overlooking the Capital Gardens. The sky was overcast and gloomy, and a driving rain pelted the glass. The Senate itself was buzzing with rumors, and the fear was growing with each passing moment. The poor fools in the streets outside might still be hoping for the best, but in the Senate chambers their leaders were on the verge of panic. Ambling along, he tried to pass the time left before the vote by looking at the portraits of past Isitian leaders that filled the walls. He'd once dreamed of having his portrait hanging among them; now, he'd settle for having the Grand Hall survive the next month without rising in flames. He tried to ignore the whispers of his colleagues, avoiding the stares and glances that followed as he passed. It was several moments before he realized that everyone else was standing silent and still as a statue, staring off toward the massive doors that guarded the entranceway.

Lifting his eyes to look for himself, Ross felt his heart skip a beat.

Walking very slowly through the entrance was the Chancellor, dressed in her silken robe of office, ready to face the Opposition in the Senate Chamber.

Beside her, taking her aging, frail arm like a favorite son escorting his mother to church, was the Admiral himself, clad in the midnight blue uniform he'd designed and eyeing the gathering with a mixture of amusement and scorn.

"Greetings, to all of you," said the Chancellor, as the junior aides rushed to find her a seat. "I thought we might want to have a little chat before we convened the full Senate, in order to avoid any misunderstandings."

Waiting until the murmurs died down before dropping her bombshell, the Chancellor smiled sweetly. "And then, I thought we might arrange a small press conference, to let our citizens know exactly what it is we're going to be voting on. Heaven knows, I certainly have trouble keeping these things straight myself."

For a moment, for a brief moment, Ross dared to hope things might somehow turn out all right. The Chancellor was trying her best to turn things around. As old and tired as she was, she wasn't going to let her Government go down without a fight. And however she managed it, bringing Cook along might be enough to do it. At least, it might if the temperamental Northlander was willing to help.

"If the leadership would be so kind as to join me in the Conference Room?" the Chancellor said, straining to be heard over the murmurs.

As the Cabinet and party leaders began to filter into the adjoining room, leaving Admiral Cook behind to mingle with the junior senators, Ross felt his heart racing madly. He knew that this event would probably make or break his career, but the thought of how much else was at stake left him ashamed of his own conceit. He took the chair at the Chancellor's left, and began to wonder exactly how much he really mattered in all of this. How much any of them mattered.

It was probably a fatal flaw in a politician, he thought. And the realization probably came too late to redeem himself as a human being. But as he turned to watch Irene McInnis slowly make her way to the table, he realized exactly how little most politicians really understood, and how rare someone like the Chancellor was in public life.

"ALRIGHT, UP and at 'em! One more time—to the attack!"

Fighting the urge to curl up and go to sleep, Jack Markham rose to his feet. Together with the rest of his unit, he howled at the top of his voice, charging through the mud and rain toward the top of a hill that seemed to recede further with each step he took.

"Company—hit the dirt!"

Jack threw his weary body to the soggy ground, taking care to keep his weapon out of the mud, and adjusting his helmet so he could see in front of him. He was tired and hungry. The rain, now drumming incessantly against his helmet, had already left him as wet as he could get. The wind blustered and whipped against his face, and he squinted to get a good look at what might lie ahead.

Today, the top of the hill held only militia officers and damp tents filled with coffee and something warm to eat. Someday there might be Terrans on top of the hill. And as he thought of the little girl, warm and dry at home, who might someday forget her father because of them, a burning rage made him ignore the rain and the mud, and filled him with hate.

"Company—attack!!" screamed his sergeant.

Screaming as loudly as he could, Jack didn't feel the weariness of his legs, or the sting of the wind-driven rain. Along the entire line, Delta Company rose and charged the last fifty yards toward the command post, faster and stronger than when they started at the bottom of the hill.

* * *

"I SUPPOSE there is no point denying our present predicament," the Chancellor began. Patting Ross on the hand, she smiled maternally across the table at two of the junior majority whips—the two rumored to be spreading dissention among the rest of the Northland delegation, and throughout the Party. Her eyes were hard as tempered steel, and the tone of her voice told the two young rabblerousers that they were in serious trouble.

"The Minister of State has encountered substantial resistance to continuing the funding for our ground forces."

"Actually, it is not the ground forces that caused the problem," one of the Party's whips responded, a young Senator named Wilcox, whose calculating eyes were softened by an habitually jovial manner. "Inept as they are, they do seem to be trying their best."

Surveying the room with the arrogance of youth, Wilcox was unintimidated by the array of Party elders around him. Despite the circumstances, he found himself buoyed by the scent of opportunity.

"Rather," he continued, "it is the untimeliness of the proposal, the incompetence of the Militia's existing command structure, and the lack of time for adequate preparation that is the source of the trouble. Unfortunately, the Minister could have prevented the entire problem, merely by making his proposal a year ago."

Before Ross could remind Wilcox that he had done exactly that—though he'd called it an 'army' then—the Chancellor tugged at his arm and shook her head, to tell him to let the point drop.

"Nevertheless," the Chancellor continued, "our Government cannot back down. Not this close to an engagement with the Terrans. It would demoralize the fleet, as well as our population, and all at the worst possible time. That is why the Admiral is here. He can explain whatever military questions you may have. And he is prepared to speak publicly against any attempt to bring the Government down now, on the eve of battle."

"He's willing to go along with whatever we propose?" scoffed Wilcox. "Even if it costs his flesh and blood the chance to rise to power?"

"He is willing to speak his mind," the Chancellor replied archly. "On most days, that is more than I dare say about most of us in this room. And let us not flatter ourselves needlessly, Senator. I rather doubt that he can assure the public that we are not such fools as we appear—only that they are better off sticking with the fools they have at present, than by importing a entirely new lot of fools to run things, just now."

"So where do we go from here?" asked Wilcox.

"I propose that we invite the Admiral to join us. And I've scheduled a press conference in half an hour. If nothing else, it should enliven the vote."

The Chancellor signaled her aide to fetch the Admiral. Ross, his palms sweating profusely, turned to face the entrance. Soon, the conference room door swung open to the sounds of laughter. The Admiral, standing in the center of a fawning circle of politicians, was smiling wryly amid a chorus of bellowing mirth. Looking toward the inner conference room, he seemed to exchange a nod with the Chancellor. Excusing himself, he began to walk toward the smaller assembly of party leaders. In the space of a heartbeat, Ross saw to his horror, every trace of amusement and warmth had left the Admiral's face, and Cook's eyes bore the look of a stern and remorseless killer.

Ross turned away and slumped in his chair. He knew now that his career was over. No matter what the Chancellor might think, in the end Cook was no different than his uncle. He needed the attention and the cheers, just as much as the rest of them did. Obviously, he was not above making a backroom deal. Otherwise, he'd never agree to the elaborate charade of strutting him before the Party, as well as the public. And Cook was not the type to pass up the chance to crush an adversary. After their bitter rivalry over control of war preparations, Ross had no doubt that Cook considered him an enemy.

So his career was going to be the price of victory, he mused grimly. If so, it might well prove to be a bargain. But the Chancellor was refusing to go down without a fight. He'd be damned if he'd give up without fighting to the last, either.

* * *

"Mr. Jarvis—tell Company B to pivot left and advance ten astrometers."

"Aye, Ma'am."

From the command seat on the Navy's mint-fresh flagship, Janet watched the monitors in horror. The motley collection of converted pleasure craft and freight haulers that the Skipper had rushed through retrofitting seemed to be moving in all directions at once. Everywhere she looked, the skirmish lines were so sloppy as to be non-existent. Wincing as she watched her order carried out, half the small ships of Company B advanced before pivoting—half of them pivoted before advancing—and four dozen sloops and starjammers barely avoided ramming one another in the process.

"No! Halt!" she screamed at the flagship's young radio officer. "Have them halt immediately."

"Yes, Ma'am."

As the maneuver ground to yet another halt, Janet found patience eluding her. Directing the operations of their naval militia, she knew she was not working with their best recruits: the best officers and crew were assigned either to their company of rusty old frigates, or to one of the two starships. The rest could barely find their way to the head and back, much less carry out full-scale battle maneuvers without risking a collision. And, as always, Skipper was nowhere to be found. It seemed to be his custom wherever there was any real work to be done.

"Mr. Fredrickson, come to heading 140, sublight, one-quarter ahead. "Let's see if we can get at least one group of these lunkheads to get it right."

"Yes, Ma'am. Bearing 140—mark!"

As the flagship sputtered under power from its still-unripened engines, Janet sank into the captain's seat. She had to make due with what they had, she told herself; it was the same thing Skipper kept telling her, over and again. There was nowhere else to go; they had to work with what they had.

* * *

"So you are, in fact, willing to stand with us against the Opposition."

"No, Senator Wilcox," Cook replied coldly. "I care nothing about politics. With few exceptions, I regard politics as a calling uniquely suited for incompetents, charlatans, and outright liars. I am, however, willing to stand with Isis. And I will do whatever is necessary to give us a chance—a fighting chance—against the Cosmic Guard."

"You really think we stand much of a chance?"

"Our chances would be better if I could tend to my Navy, instead of cleaning up your muddles here on the ground. And I won't know how good a chance until the battle begins. But yes, we stand a chance."

"One chance in two? In three? In twenty?"

"I'm not a bookie. And I'm not a politician, so I don't feel comfortable just making things up. But it's the Terrans who are attacking, Senator, so we don't have much choice in the matter. I'm not going to waste my time worrying about something as silly as calculating the odds."

Ross leaned forward to speak. But now that he actually had the Admiral here to answer his questions, Ross found himself uncharacteristically reluctant to talk. After all, the Militia would be useful only if the Terrans managed to land troop ships on Isitian soil. He sensed—he knew—that the Admiral would never admit that the Navy might not be up to the task. As he tried to work up the courage to ask the question, his rival pressed his own line of attack.

"How, then, do you plan to do it?" asked Wilcox.

"Do what, Senator?"

"Beat the Terrans, Admiral! Surely, you haven't forgotten about that already?"

Ross noticed that Cook's lips were spread in a tight smile, as his calm, steady voice seemed to mask the sharp edge in his message. But there was no humor in the Admiral's eyes, and his merciless gaze was making the arrogant young party leader addressing him squirm.

"I don't make plans for the sake of looking busy, Senator. I won't know how to beat the Terrans until I see what they're throwing at us. And so I think it's more productive to drill my Navy on the basics of interstellar combat, rather than devising intricate plans that won't last beyond the first thirty seconds of battle."

"You mean to say," said Wilcox, concern etched across his face, "that you haven't given your battle plan a moment's thought? That you plan to go into this thing without the slightest notion of how you're going to accomplish your mission—that you're simply going to wing the whole operation?"

The Admiral leaned forward, arms folded across the table. "What I mean to say," he said quietly, "is that I don't really mind leading a bunch of amateurs into battle against the Cosmic Guard, because I have no alternative. But I'll be damned if I let a bunch of amateurs look over my shoulder while I'm doing it."

"Admiral, you misunderstand—"

Cook stared directly into the frightened eyes of the young Northlander from the district next to his uncle's.

"No—I understand perfectly, Senator. But so that you don't misunderstand me, let me make it as simple as I can for you. I don't have time to waste. If you don't like how I choose to prepare the Navy for battle, then call the press and demand that the Chancellor relieve me. If you don't have the balls to do that, then get the hell out of my way."

"And that means," the Chancellor interjected, sensing the opening just given her, "that we cannot permit ourselves the luxury of losing the vote this morning. I believe I speak for the Admiral when I say that a change of government at this juncture would be, shall we say— "

"It would be a criminally stupid thing to do," Cook interrupted. "Whether good or bad, morale is highly contagious. Optimism is a potent weapon, and enhances the power and effectiveness of any fighting force. Bad morale, or any emasculating sense of hopelessness, is the enemy of victory. Voting down the Government—now, of all times, on the eve of battle—would be among the most irresponsible things anyone could do, even for a bunch of witless politicians. I will do anything I can to stop it."

"But you do, of course, know the source of the controversy, do you not?" asked Mallory, the other young whip rumored to be among the renegades. "Minister Ross has backed us into quite a corner, with his little militia. How can we, in good conscience, support a plan that places our entire civilian population at risk? Unless, of course, you are willing to assure the public that his Militia will be effective in combating the Terrans."

"What is your opinion on the matter, Admiral?" asked Mallory.

"My personal opinion—," Cook began, only to have Mallory interrupt.

"Personal opinions are cheap in this town," he said haughtily, trying his best to control the direction of the Admiral's remarks. "We are asking for your professional judgment, Admiral. That is what we value, and that is what we require—for it is upon that, that our fate depends."

Ross steeled himself against hearing his own project lambasted by the very man he'd hounded unmercifully himself. Cook, smiling coldly, looked not at him, but at the two majority whips who seemed to be causing all the trouble.

"Very well," the Admiral said, leaning back in his chair. "The battle for Isis will be won or lost in the sky, not on the ground. In my professional judgment, given the current state of preparations and the time remaining, the Militia will have no impact on the final outcome."

"You are certain of this?" asked Wilcox.

Cook nodded grimly. "If the Terrans do manage to land a troop transport through my Navy," said the Admiral, "the Militia will be, at most, a minor annoyance—much like a swarm of mosquitoes confronting a bulldozer. In the foreseeable future, it will be militarily ineffective in any engagement, and will pose an insignificant threat to any substantial invasion force."

"You have a press conference scheduled in ten minutes. If asked publicly...."

"I'm not a politician, Senator," Cook said acidly. "My opinions—personal or professional—are not for sale."

Ross took a deep breath and prepared for the worst. He was surprised when the Chancellor, seated next to him, squeezed his hand and smiled at him. Then, he started when the large double doors swung open, and the crier entered the room.

"The quorum call is sounding, Madam Chancellor," announced the courtly old gentleman who had been the Senate's crier for longer than anyone—except perhaps the Chancellor and Minister McKenzie—could remember. "The vote will begin in thirty minutes."

"If we want our news conference before the vote, we'd best get along," observed the Chancellor.

"Reggie," she continued, "do help me to the Briefing Room."

As Ross helped the Chancellor to her feet, he watched Wilcox and Mallory scurry out the door. Probably dying to beat Cook to the press room, he thought. The scent of blood was too strong not to set the sharks to feeding. With the press of events crushing down upon all of them, he could hardly blame them. Fear and jealousy were powerful emotions; when blended with ambition, the mixture could be intoxicating, even dangerous. The future of Isis, an island of sanity in a Universe gone mad, was being blown and tossed by the winds of fate. And against such winds, it was hard to believe that anyone could resist whatever course self-preservation might urge upon him.

The walk to the Briefing Room was the longest he would ever remember. He'd later recall how he understood, for the first time, how a condemned man felt on his way to the gallows.

"COMMUNICATION COMING from the Flagship."

"On the screen," ordered Sammy Rose, the nominal commander of the *London Dancer.* The Orders of the Day had placed him in charge of the refitted sloop, but he didn't feel in command of anything. Between avoiding collisions with the other ships in the Company, and making sure the navigator wasn't daydreaming again, he seemed to be doing nothing right.

On the other hand, few of the other ships in the company were managing to avoid making an Isitian hash of things, either. Certainly, the Commodore felt that way: on the screen was the face of the Admiral's wife, scowling darkly at the collection of mistakes, missed directions, and misadventures they'd just finished.

Her litany, Rose soon realized, was all too familiar: he'd heard most of it before, when Company A was on the mark. The change in personnel hadn't changed the Commodore's mood.

"Exactly what do you clowns think you're doing?" the Commodore demanded. On the screen, her eyes seemed ready to pop out of their sockets, and her long, brown hair made her face appear as pale as bleached flour.

"A college fraternity party would be more organized than this company of clowns," she went on. "How do you people expect to do anything but die like squashed spiders, putting that little effort into snapping off your pivot? Any spacer worth his whiskers could drive a freighter through a line like that! Now regroup and try it again. This time, pay attention to what you're doing."

As Rose steered the ship back toward the staging zone, he sighed deeply. It seemed like they'd been doing this forever—first on the simulators, for hour after hour; now in the blackness of space, for day after endless day. He was tired and depressed; he wanted nothing more than to crawl into a hole and hide. He didn't know how long he could keep it up. He knew only that he had to try.

For the sake of everyone back home, and for the family of his own he hoped to have, one day, he had to try.

THE BRIEFING ROOM was rarely filled to capacity, but today there was barely space to breathe. At the Chancellor's side on the podium, Reggie Ross looked out over the mob and shook his head bitterly. All these months of trying to get Cook to come to a meeting, and all it took was a room filled with reporters. He could have saved himself a lot of trouble and worry over the past few months, it seemed, simply by scheduling a press conference.

As Cook stepped to the microphone, Ross took a deep breath. Whatever else he did, he told himself, he wouldn't give them the satisfaction of seeing him buckle. He'd take his fate like a man; and if his hide was the price of keeping the Government intact until the crisis had passed, no one—no one but his wife, perhaps—would ever hear him complain.

"I'm not a politician, so I don't have much time to waste," said the Admiral, nodding modestly at the polite laughter. "Perhaps we should just begin."

An older man, in his fifties, balding with the beginnings of a pot belly, was the first to speak.

"We haven't heard very much about preparations for the Navy," he said, his baritone voice gravelly and gruff. "What can you tell us about how the Navy is coming along, and whether you think we'll be ready for the Terries, if and when they come?"

"The Navy's doing just fine," the Admiral smiled. "Though I'm sure I'm driving my bridge crew to distraction, morale is generally good. In fact, from what I've seen since coming down here, morale is probably better up there than it is in the Senate."

"I do believe he's enjoying this," the Chancellor whispered across to George McKenzie, the Defense Minister who was standing next to Ross.

"I told you, Irene," McKenzie replied, ignoring Ross for the moment. "Don't underestimate him. Not when he's finally put his mind to something."

"As for whether we'll be ready for the Terrans," Cook continued, "I suppose readiness is a relative state. I doubt any commander in History ever thought his forces were actually ready for anything. The real question is whether we're readier for the Terrans than they are for us. On that score, I may have an answer for you in a few weeks."

"What do you think the answer will be, Admiral?" asked a younger reporter, an awestruck lad with a marked Northlander accent.

Cook's eyes twinkled, and his cocky grin lit the room like sunshine melting the fog. "I expect if I'm around long enough to give you one, we'll have gotten it just about right," he said with a wink. As he looked around the room, the anchorlady from New Alexandria's most popular public affairs program elbowed aside a younger colleague and caught his attention.

"How confident are you that we'll be able to beat back the Terrans?" she asked.

"Confident enough not to be on a ship heading west," Cook shot back. As the surprised laughter rose in the old hall, he held up a hand to bring the roars of approval back down.

"More to the point," he added, his eyes twinkling, "I'm confident enough not to have my family on a ship headed west."

"How do you think the Terrans will attack?" called a pretty young reporter from the far side of the room, struggling for her moment in the spotlight. "I mean, what plan of attack are you most afraid of?"

"Young lady," Cook mocked, with the gruffness of one of his drill sergeants, "that is a question that only a fool would answer."

Seeing the poor girl blush terribly, Cook took quickly took pity on her. "We'll let you redeem yourself later, if you want to try again," he smiled, looking across the roomful of raised hands and eager faces. "And don't be afraid of coming up with something interesting. I'm no politician, you know—so I don't dance my way around questions. Like most people, I use language to communicate, not to hide."

He pointed to the Cabinet officers and party leaders behind him on the podium. "Politicians use language like I use my ships: bob, weave, confuse the enemy. Win the battle, and live to fight another day. So this may be your one chance to get some straight answers.

Just stay away from State secrets, Missey." He pointed at another reporter and nodded.

"Admiral, it's been nearly four months since you returned to Isis," said Don Danielson, a noted commentator from the capital, and the bane of every local politician for the last twenty years.

"Seems like only yesterday, Mr. Danielson."

"—and since your arrival, you have not allowed anyone from the Navy to return home."

"Only the washouts."

"Don't you think it would be a good idea to let them come back home, Admiral? I mean, just once, if only to say goodbye?"

"No," Cook smiled, and be began looking for another reporter.

"Well, sir—why not? I mean, isn't it only right to let them say their goodbyes? After all, with all due respect, sir, we may never see them again. And some of them, surely, will die. Aren't you being needlessly cruel with your own people, Admiral?"

Ross watched as Cook took the measure of Danielson. Ross knew the reporter for a pompous ass, but a pompous ass who was sharper than any other reporter in town, with a hairpiece nearly as big as his ego. From the podium, the galaxy's most legendary warrior glared angrily at the hapless journalist with a mixture of contempt and cold, focused fury. In a heartbeat, the overmatched reporter turned visibly pale.

"I haven't seen my own family since shortly after I arrived," Cook began sternly, and a hush took hold of the assembly. "I said my goodbyes right after the holidays. This is my first trip back here since I assumed command—and I won't see them this time, either, because I won't break ranks with my troops. If they can't see the people they love, then neither can I.

"If you think that's being cruel, so be it. But then, you really haven't seen very much of the Universe, have you, Mr. Danielson? And I rather doubt you'd have much stomach for combat. You haven't lived with death as your bunkmate, or watched your best friend blown apart before your eyes. We, on the other hand, can't indulge ourselves quite as daintily as some. We have no use for your brand of false compassion, that lets you feel good about yourself for the moment and morally superior to everyone in range of your sanctimonious preaching—and yet accomplishes nothing.

"Everyone who volunteers for the Navy is told to say their goodbyes before they molly up to join us," Cook continued relentlessly. "And when they leave the Planet, they know that if they pass muster into the service there are three things they'll have to do before they can ever see home again: they must *fight* the Terrans; they must *beat* the Terrans; and they've got to *survive*. It may have somehow escaped your attention, Mr. Danielson, but we've a lot to do up there, and not much time to do it. So *that* is, in part, how I motivate my troops. *That* is how I make them strong and tough and angry, and ready to storm the heavens against longer odds than I'd wish on my worst enemy. And *that*, Mr. Danielson, is how I will bring as many of them back home with me as I possibly can—despite the sentimental nonsense from some quarters here on the ground that seems to be masquerading as compassion, these days."

As the assembled journalists rose to their feet to cheer, Ross looked at Cook in admiration. The Admiral, glowering mercilessly at the ashen face of the most obnoxious journalist on the face of the planet, had done what no politician had ever been able to do—get a pack of reporters to cheer over the carcass of one of their own. It was enough to make Ross forget his own troubles, until Cook lifted his eyes and called on the next reporter, a dark, handsome anchor-man who looked and sounded considerably more timid in person than he ever did on the screen.

"Admiral—if I may—the recent dispute in the Senate. You are aware that there is a vote scheduled for today, on whether to change the Government, and call for new elections, over the question of funding for the militia."

"So I've heard."

"Do you have any comment, sir? I mean, what is that likely to mean for your preparations for battle. If it passes, I mean?"

"I never believed that the Senate would be that irresponsible," Cook replied, his voice carrying a measure of relief, "especially since there was no need for it. They could, after all, vote to postpone the vote, the Opposition could abstain, they could choose to make their vote temporary, and review it again after the dust of battle settles. I'm sure, if I had the time to read the Senate Rules, I could come up with a dozen other things they could do. But obviously, any change now would have an immediate impact on morale—and that is something we obviously cannot afford. I'm just glad they've found a way to postpone their little games for a few weeks. And that the vote, when it comes, will be one of support for the Navy."

"But the vote—it's in fifteen minutes. And the Opposition. I mean, your own uncle announced just yesterday— "

"My uncle is a patriot," Cook said firmly, his face registering mild surprise, but his tone of voice suggesting that the matter was closed to further discussions. "Obviously, he would do nothing to jeopardize the war effort."

The newsman looked astonished; and he was not the only one. On the podium, the Chancellor and half the Cabinet were trying to keep their mouths from hanging open.

"You mean, you've discussed the matter with him?"

"My uncle and I have discussed a great many things," Cook said coldly, his impatience now poorly concealed. "And I am not one to put words in his mouth, or steal his thunder on anything he wishes to announce himself."

"Does that mean...?"

"That means I will say nothing further on the subject."

As an astonished murmur swept through the assembly, Cook made a point of looking at his watch.

"How about the issue that started the whole controversy?" came a voice from the back. The Admiral looked up and was glad to see the young girl he'd embarrassed earlier, a look of terror on her face as she forced herself to speak up.

"Which issue was that, Missey?" he grinned.

"The Militia, Admiral. What do you think of the Militia? Majority Whips Mallory and Wilcox came out against it in this very room, not ten minutes ago—and issued a call for the Minister of State's resignation as a way to resolve the issue."

At last, Ross thought to himself. He steeled himself for the fatal blow to his career, his dreams—his chances of rising through the ranks, any time in the future.

"You know," Cook chuckled, shaking his head. "I've been waiting for someone to ask me that very question. If you want my *personal* opinion...."

The young woman nodded, vastly relieved, and very pleased that the great man wasn't going to make her feel like goose droppings again.

"My *personal* opinion," Cook said, carefully stressing his words, "is that it is a positively *splendid* idea. It can't help but increase morale up in the sky to know how strongly everyone down here feels about standing up to the Terrans. Quite frankly, I wish I'd thought of the idea first—and, in my own defense, I'll only say that I've had a lot on my mind these last few months, and the subject of organizing our defenses on the ground just never occurred to me. But I'll do what I can to help, once my schedule clears."

Vaguely conscious of the low murmurs that filled the hall, Ross remembered nothing of the rest of the press conference, except for the wild crush of reporters at the end of it all, as they dashed madly from the room. Numbed by the blur of events around him, he would recall only how hard it was for him to keep from crying.

MINUTES LATER, back in the conference room, the mood was poisonous.

"You forget yourself, Senator."

"Like hell I forget myself, you goddamn son of a bitch. You stabbed us in back." Mallory moved forward until he stood nose to nose with Cook, who glared back with a coldness in his eyes that drained the anger from the politician's face and drove the senator back, weak-kneed and sweating profusely.

"You stabbed yourself in the back," Cook said sharply, not flinching an inch from where he stood. "I only handed you the knife. When you had the chance, you yourself cut me off because you didn't really want to hear my opinions—you just wanted to use them. So you heard exactly what you wanted to hear, before running off to make a self-dealing, cowardly attack on one of your own people, hoping to claim the credit for keeping the government together. Whether from cowardice or ambition, that qualifies as desertion in my book."

Cook narrowed his eyes coldly. "In my Navy, I'd have you shot for you what you did, Senator," he continued sternly. "These days, Isis doesn't need cowards. She needs heroes."

Mallory sputtered impotently, then retreated, red-faced and humiliated, looking for a reporter—any reporter—to have a chance to give yet another spin to the story. As the Chancellor and her party approached, he relaxed. Looking closely, Ross was struck by the abrupt change in the Admiral's manner. The cold, ruthless anger had left Cook's face, and he turned to face them with a shy, almost embarrassed smile.

"I hope I helped," Cook said. "I do tend to be a something of a ham. Always overdoing everything."

"We've already received word that the Opposition wants to put off the vote for another half hour," grinned McKenzie. "I think we can handle things from here."

"Thank you, Admiral," said the Chancellor, patting Cook's shoulder. "You don't know how much help you've been, though you could have saved us all a lot of grief simply by telling us about your uncle's change of heart ahead of time."

"Oh, that," Cook said, shifting uncomfortably on his feet. "Well, I didn't really have a chance, you see. Besides...."

He looked at the Chancellor and chuckled mischievously. "To be perfectly honest, I thought I should really let him know about it first. And I do hope he was watching—though the scramble to reschedule the vote makes me think he probably was. I'm sure it's what he would have done if I'd had the time to ask directly. Eventually, at any rate."

"I beg your pardon?"

Cook scratched his head and laughed broadly. "Well, I suppose I should be running along, now. I've probably caused enough trouble for one day. And I'd hate to be caught down here when Uncle Neil finally comes down from the ceiling."

The Chancellor and defense minister soon joined in the laughter; Cook simply shrugged his shoulders and turned to leave.

"Admiral?" It was Ross. Still shaken by the whole affair, his face was pale.

"Yes, Minister Ross?"

"I'm really quite grateful— "

"*Acch—,* " scoffed Cook.

"What I don't understand is, why the change of heart?"

"I beg your pardon?"

"You have a reputation for blunt honesty," Ross continued, trying not to seem ungrateful. "How could you change your mind about the Militia, all in the space of twenty minutes."

"He didn't, Reggie," said the Chancellor.

"I don't understand."

Cook laughed ironically. "You know, Minister Ross—I'm not sure I like you very much," he said. "You strike me as opinionated, narrow-minded, and self-important. And like most politicians, you're too busy yammering away to make sense of the Universe around you. But for some reason I can't understand, the Chancellor is quite fond of you—so perhaps, I can afford to spare another few minutes of my time."

His eyes twinkling mischievously, Cook winked at the two elder politicians. "The Chancellor is a better listener than the fools you have as party whips," he continued. "When she asks me what I think, she actually wants to hear what I have to say. And she wants to hear everything I think about the matter, not just the part that agrees with her.

"You see, Minister—you and my uncle are quite a bit alike, actually. Far more than you realize. You both think tactically, not strategically. And on the issue of the Militia, you two illustrate the stopped clock principle at work: you were right for the wrong reason; he was wrong for the right reason."

"Stopped clock...??"

"The battle for Isis," Cook went on, "will be won or lost in the sky, by the Navy, and we have exactly one chance to do it. If we lose, and the Terrans land their army, the war is over, and you should order your troops to lay down their arms to prevent needless bloodshed. Your little Militia can't possibly affect the outcome, for there isn't enough time to train them as a fighting machine. But after we win, I'm not so naive to believe that we're out of danger, now and forever. If we win today, the Terrans can still return, tomorrow.

"Someday—a year from now, perhaps; maybe five years, maybe ten—the Navy will be strong enough to absorb a defeat, regroup, and mount a counterattack. From that moment on, having a force on the ground may spell the difference between victory and defeat. Because, you see, I can defend the planet from the sky, and I can destroy the planet from the sky—but I cannot *liberate* the planet from the sky. Only a ground force can do that."

"But then why—?"

"We are at a defining moment in our history," Cook continued, his voice crisp, his eyes narrowed. "We'll either be utterly destroyed, or we'll become a nation—strong, proud, and united. If the Militia is seen, rightly or wrongly, as part of our salvation, we can use it as the basis of a planetary defense force in the future. And if Isitian colonies take root and Isis grows beyond a single planet, we can use a planetary militia on each and every planet, under local control, to protect against invasion, and to provide a check on what will become, if I have anything to say about it, a rather formidable interstellar space force."

"You really think," Ross said warily, "that we have to worry about the Navy taking over the government?"

Cook looked him straight in the eye. "Not as long as I have a say in the matter," he replied coldly. "My dreams don't include playing Caesar, or Napoleon. I'm a scientist and a philosopher—and I'm a soldier only because I have to be. But I see our Navy much as the early Terrans dreamed about a Cosmic Guard—a force to protect human life of all races, keeping the peace throughout the galaxy.

"I will not permit my Navy to pose a threat to anyone except those who mean to destroy us. But in a hundred years, I won't be around. And if you put all that military power into a single pair of hands—well, I've read a lot of history, Minister Ross. And I think the more prudent course is to decentralize that sort of power as much as possible.

"No, the Ministry of Defense is where you place the Navy, to defend Isis against invasion. The Ministry of State is where you place the Militia, the department in charge of planetary security. In a crisis, the Chancellor can coordinate all the forces available to the nation, to meet whatever danger might arise. But defusing power like that should keep anyone from getting dangerous ideas—and would, as a practical matter, make it impossible for any one military commander to be in a position to topple the government, single-handedly."

Cook chuckled ironically, and shook his head. "In the end, I guess my uncle is too worried we'll lose to risk putting more lives in danger. And you're so worried we'll lose that you want a contingency plan in case the Terries destroy my Navy. Well, I'm not particularly worried about any of that. Even if I were, there's no way to avoid it being rather a bloody affair if the Terrans do beat us in the sky. But whatever the future holds, I'm a dreamer at heart. And I'm enough of a romantic to prefer spending my remaining days in this Universe planning for the future, rather than wringing my hands over the present."

"You're not worried? You're really not worried?"

Cook grinned a cocky grin, and laughed roguishly. "Ask McKenzie about our chess game," he replied with a smirk. "In the meantime, I've a war to win—and we're still far from ready. You know, they say Heaven protects lunatics and children. I'm willing to bet there's something in there about Isis, as well."

The three leaders watched in silence as Cook gave them a jaunty salute, then turned smartly, walked down the marble tiled floor, and left the conference room. When Ross turned to look at the Chancellor, there were tears in her eyes. And yet, instead of the tired old lady he'd seen that same morning, he saw once again the grand political warrior that he grew up admiring.

"I tell you, George," whispered the Chancellor, "he's almost convinced me that we can pull this thing off."

"Well, Heaven help us if he ever turns to politics," McKenzie laughed. "He has a voice like thunder, the aura of a Greek god, and the killer instincts of a paid assassin. In all my days, I've never seen the press whipped into submission like that. In two years, we could be thinking of Cornelius Cook as a rank amateur. If the Opposition runs him—"

"They won't," the Chancellor smiled mysteriously, as if privy to a secret. "He doesn't have the stomach for politics, George. He's a man of principle. Stubborn as a mule. And too damn honest."

"Honest? You didn't see the way he hung Wilcox and Mallory out to dry—not to mention turning the tables on his own uncle? All in a single stroke!"

The Chancellor smiled broadly, and waggled an index finger at her old friend. "That's one of the things that's making me a tad more optimistic about the war, George," she replied. "As we were walking down the hallway to the meeting—he was late, you know; I'm told he often is.... "

Ross rolled his eyes, but held his tongue. He was too grateful to the man for saving his career to say anything about the Admiral's habit of never showing up for briefings. For the first time since he was a teenager, he felt too foolish to risk saying anything.

"Well, he asked me what I needed from him. Three things, I said: I needed to keep the Government intact, at all costs. Well, at least until the next election. I wanted to keep the Militia together. And if there was some way to spare poor Reggie from this sordid mess, I wanted to do that, as well. Then I mentioned, as a casual afterthought and not being entirely serious, that if he could ever make Mallory and Wilcox just go away, I would be forever in his debt."

The Chancellor laughed—and it was a laugh from the old days, McKenzie would recall, the gleeful, positively wicked laugh of a master politician savoring the poetic justice that Fate had just bestowed on a rival. "And I'll be damned, but in the space of twenty minutes he carried off one mission after the other. As brilliantly as if he'd been bred for politics, and as smoothly as if it were one of his bloody training exercises.

"But what's all this," the Chancellor chuckled, "about a chess game?"

"First time we met," McKenzie grinned, putting his arms around the Chancellor and Ross as they walked, "I asked whether he thought it was hopeless. Man-to-man, and all that, you know. We were going to be badly outnumbered, I remember telling him, and our naval militia was proving rather difficult to organize. If we were facing certain destruction, I said, we needed to make plans for the inevitable.

"Looking around, he spotted a chess board," he continued. "The chess board in my office. You know, the one I always keep ready for whenever Henderson or Denton comes by the place. 'How good a chess player are you?' he asked. I consider myself reasonably good, you know—though by no means championship caliber—and he challenged me to play a game. Well, I took white, he took black, and he told me to take both his rooks, both his knights, and any four pawns I wanted off the board. I made my first move—and he responded by making, over my howls of protest, the next four, and promptly declared checkmate. 'That's not by the rules,' I said to him, for it certainly was not very Isitian. 'In battle, I make my own rules,' he replied, then pointed to the chess board. 'Here, the rules I need to win tell me to make as many moves as I wish.' Well, I said right then and there that if this were a real match, I'd simply refuse to play by his rules."

McKenzie laughed, his mirth a combination of irony and admiration. "Well, he looked me cold square in the eye, smiled that devilish smirk of his, and told me that if this were a real war, and I refused to play by his rules, he'd simply kill me."

The Chancellor chuckled and shook her head. "You think he can really pull it off?"

"He told me that if there was a way, he'd find it."

"Well, I believe it. I'm actually starting to believe it."

* * *

THE MOON Diogenes shone brightly through the window. Outside, the breeze rattled the branches, and Jack could hear the distant howl of a native scroungelle through the open window. The rains had melted away with the late evening's warm front, and the night air smelled of Spring.

Holding his wife as she slept, Jack stared through the darkness at the bedroom ceiling, kissing her forehead as it rested on his bare chest, stroking her arm as it rose and fell with each breath he took.

He'd come to savor this time. He'd come to treasure each moment he could hold those he loved in his arms. He didn't know how many more of them he had left. And if he couldn't bring himself to explain to Alana, his little girl, exactly why Daddy kept getting teary-eyed whenever he gave her a hug these days, he hoped he'd get a chance to tell her, when it was all over.

If not, he knew the wonderful woman he was holding in her arms would do so. Every chance she had, she'd make sure their daughter wouldn't forget him.

JANET FELT terribly foolish, but she couldn't help herself. No matter how hard she tried to stop, the tears flowed out of her eyes like a rushing river. It had been so long, she told herself; there was so much bottled up inside that she couldn't stop. She knew there was more to it than that, but it felt so good that she didn't want to let her mind intrude. It would be just like him to want her to explain herself just now, when any fool could see that the best thing to do was to keep his mouth shut.

"Janet?" came the inevitable voice in the darkness.

Resolutely, Janet just clung to him more tightly than ever, refusing to let him go. Her arms wrapped tightly around his neck, she struggled against his efforts to ease back, and kept him wrapped as warmly and tightly as she could manage.

"Is everything all right?"

Soon, he gave up struggling and just let her go, sobbing and sniffling until the wave of emotion finished and she finally let herself relax. Rolling free, he stroked her damp cheeks and kissed her puffed eyes.

"I'm sorry," he whispered. She sniffled in amusement: it was so like him to apologize, even if he didn't know why, as if it would change anything. But he meant well, so she said nothing. Before long, she no longer felt quite so foolish, and raised her hand to stroke his face.

"What's the matter?" he asked, concerned.

She shook her head and smiled. Her throat too tight to reply, she kissed him softly and buried herself in his arms again.

"Just thinking too much, I guess," she replied in a thick voice. "Don't worry, nothing's really the matter."

Janet rolled Cook onto his back, and came to lay atop him, her head resting on her hands. She smiled and pinched his nose playfully. Relieved, Cook started to dry her cheeks with his fingers.

"Things actually went well, groundside?" she asked. "You're not just saying that to keep me from worrying?"

"I think so. At least nobody was yelling at me when I left. I guess that's a step in the right direction. But with politicians, there's always some other muddle to fix before very long."

"How long before— "

"As I told them downstairs," Cook grinned playfully, "not nearly long enough. But believe me, it's nothing to worry about. It's out of my hands now, and I'm not going to waste my time worrying about how it will all end. We'll find out soon enough, and we'll adjust accordingly."

"Brave talk, for someone who spends so much time working that he forgets to go to sleep."

"That won't last," Cook smiled, combing her hair with his fingers. "Another few weeks and it'll be over. Maybe we can even go on a more conventional honeymoon. You know, not every man takes his bride to war. I'm still not sure I should have dragged you into this."

"You didn't," Janet said, resting her head on his chest. "Anyway, I let you drag me. I didn't have to tag along, you know. But I do have a few choice words to say to the Fates, if I ever get the chance to meet one of them."

Cook chuckled lowly. "Well, you know, I think it was me the Fates were really after. You just got caught in the dragnet. I still think it was selfish of me to bring you along."

"Mr. Modesty, I presume," Janet laughed. "My God—you are so full of yourself, these days. Maybe you just don't get enough roughage."

As she grinned a playful grin, Janet saw him get that distant, maddening "I'm-off-in-my-own-little-Universe-and-you-can't-find-me" look in his eyes. Her feminine instincts instantly roused, and sensing that he was getting drowsier by the minute, she pressed in for the kill.

"All right," she said, coyly, running her hand across his chest. "What is it this time?"

"What's what?"

"What are you off dreaming about, now?"

"Nothing."

"Skipper?"

"No—nothing, really."

"*Skipper!*"

"Well...," Cook leaned back, and stared at the ceiling. Janet saw his lips turn up in one of his mysterious smiles, then saw him shake his head as he realized he had no place to hide.

"You'll laugh."

"No, I won't." Janet knew she wasn't really lying: at least she wouldn't laugh just then. Depending upon what he said, she might not laugh at all. But he was hiding something, and she had to know what it was.

"Well, all this talk about Fate and everything. It just reminded me about something."

"Reminded you of what?"

"Nahh—never mind. It's silly."

"Skipper..."

"Well—it just occurred to me as we were orbiting the planet that first day back, getting ready to disembark. The whole trip home, I was surprised at how little I was really worried about anything, and kept wondering when it would all hit me. Then I just—realized—and I knew it wouldn't. At least, not until it was all over."

No longer so playful, now curious and intrigued, Janet refused to let him off the hook.

"What did you realize?"

"Well...," Cook sat up, and leaned against the bedpost. He looked at her, his eyes filled with amazement, his smiling face radiating peace for the first time since they'd met.

"All my life, I've wondered—why me? Why did I always have such an easy time of it? Why did I understand Math before anyone taught me about numbers, or Music before anyone explained anything about notes? And why did I choose space over music or philosophy or any other science? Why did I understand navigation, or tactics, or deployment, before I knew any of the rules? Why did everything come so quickly, so naturally? How can I pick navigation plots out of thin air, and see them in the sky just by imagining? Why do I always know when to turn—when to attack, when to retreat—when to flag, when to billow? How do I always smell danger in space, and know exactly when, where, and how to escape it? And how did I, of all the people in this Universe, come to every turn in my life, every choice I've ever made, facing obstacle after obstacle, without a clue as to how to do it, but knowing—actually knowing—that everything I did, no matter how hard or dangerous, would always turn out right. That somehow I'd always find a way.

"Then, once we started this thing...once we came home to a half-finished ship and a planet filled with hopeless souls who needed to be whipped into something resembling a fighting force—suddenly, I knew. I just *knew*."

"Knew what?"

"You said it, Janet: *Fate*. *This* is why I am here. *This* is the reason for my existence—why I was born with the gifts I have, why I left Isis when I did, why I knew exactly when it was time to come back home. Whether I knew it or not, I've spent my whole life preparing for this very battle. And as soon as I saw that, I just knew."

"Knew what, Skipper?" Janet was trying her best not to get impatient. She knew that this was all very important to him, even as he was making himself impossible to understand. And for some reason she didn't understand, she was beginning to feel frightened.

"Don't you see?" Cook smiled gently. "Whatever gave me the gifts I have has brought me to this exact time and place. Live or die, this is the reason I was born. Once I understood that, I knew that there was no way to escape it—no way to avoid it—no reason to hide from it. So all that's left is to get us as ready as I can, and trust to Fate. And hope that whatever brought me here didn't mean for me to lead you to your death, at the same time."

Janet wrapped her arms around him, and tears welling in her eyes again, rolled him over on top of her. She was worried and upset by his detour into metaphysics, yet quite willing to surrender herself to the hope that he might be right, just one more time. And as he'd often told her that he didn't care to live in a Universe without Isis, she couldn't imagine living in a Universe without him.

Chapter 8

"LOOK SHARP, BOYS. The Admiral's on his way."

On McAllister's warning the five squadron commanders scrambled about, stowing their lunch bags and hiding their disposable cups from sight. The last time the Admiral had barged in on them they had to endure a ten-minute lecture on the need to keep things in trim, and two hours the next day helping a company of grunts shipshape the old *New Alexandria*. They didn't want to risk a repeat, but Cook burst through the door before they could finish.

"All right, people," the Admiral said, tossing a folder on the table nearest the door. He pulled five file jackets from inside the folder, and began passing them around. "We haven't got much time today. You've all got new assignments—and I'm due at the new ship. They have some new glitches to iron out, and I'm afraid they're going to turn my navigation desk into an Isitian hash."

Barnes looked at the file that was thrust into his hand, and immediately lost his appetite. "Company Commander," it read; alone among the group, his assignment carried the Commander's title. He remembered how proud he'd been when first selected for the command group. Ever since, he'd felt as if he were dangling from a pier over water filled with carrion sharks. Now the Admiral had weighed him down with lead and cast him over the side.

"Each of you now has a squadron to command," Cook said, his voice crisp and clear. "From now on, and until further notice, your only task will be to drill your squadron—and drill, and drill, and drill—until your people can snap into any maneuver you order, and move smartly into the next and the next and the next. You are to report to the docks immediately, take command of your frigate from the dockworkers who are still duct-taping it together, and sail into the South Polar clearing as soon as you can muster your squadrons. I want you to devote at least two hours every day to joint maneuvers, and the rest of your duty hours to working your squadron until every turn of every ship becomes automatic—and each crewman knows every inch of his vessel as if it were his wife's body. We don't have much time left, and I'll need my frigates as sharp and tough as you five can make them."

Abruptly, Cook turned to leave and headed toward the door. Barnes, now reeling from the thought that he would be in charge once the Admiral left, found his head drowning with questions.

"Admiral?"

Cook spun on his heels and looked Barnes straight in the eye.

"Make it quick, Commander."

"The simulation," Barnes said, trying his best not to babble in front of his troops. "The three-pronged attack on Isis. What should—I mean, do we continue...?"

"Acch—forget the simulation, Mr. Barnes. You now have more important things to do with your time."

"You've solved the problem then?"

"Of course not," Cook snapped. "The damn problem's unsolvable. If the Terrans come at us like that, we're probably fucked. Plain and simple. So don't worry about it anymore."

"But what do we— "

"Stick to your drills," Cook said, then turned and motioned his entourage toward the door. "I'll be watching—and in five days or so, I may join you. If my own damn ship manages to hold a charge without overheating, that is. And if my keel guns don't melt the new engine cables.

"Carry on."

"Aye sir."

Cook strode out the door, leaving the squadron leaders confused and dazed. Ushering his new subordinates out of the laboratory and toward their new assignments, Barnes felt sick to his stomach. Brusqueness might well be one of Cook's hallmarks as a commander. But Barnes was willing to bet that the speed of this particular change had more to do with the latest intelligence reports than any real improvement in the Navy's rate of progress.

* * *

"JUST WHAT do you think you're doing?"

As much as she detested the grinding routine, Janet was not pleased at being dragged away from her bridge drills just now. The rookies were finally starting to come together as a team, and showing signs of progress. When she burst into the conference room she was fully prepared to give her husband a piece of her mind. But upon entering, she knew at once that this was not one of his mindless interruptions. Her face turned a deep crimson; this was no time for her to complain.

Standing around a table, surrounding a star chart of the eastern skies, were Cook and most of the senior command staff: Commodore Landis, the commander of the *New Alexandria*; Captain Decker of Logistics and Supply; Captain Crane, of Naval Intelligence, along with two of his senior aides; Commander Malik, of Engineering; Commander Hodari, of Personnel; and several others she knew from their technical work on the new ship. Silently, Janet sidled her way next to her husband, hoping to get a look at the chart and see what was going on.

"The latest report said what?" asked Landis. He was a tall man, with thin, graying hair and a lean, haggard face. The crisis had taken a particular toll on him, Janet knew: his wife died just before she and Cook arrived, and he was still grieving.

"Reports have the Terran fleet massed about here," said Cook, pointing to a stretch of open sky just west of the base at ZarCom. "They completed their last maneuvers three days ago, and our last report was that they were forming into columns. That tells me they're about to sail—and we're about to go into business for real."

Cook pointed to a trinary star system two parsecs anticenter-west of ZarCom, just beyond a nebulous cloud of condensing gasses.

"I've ordered our scouts to deactivate our communications relays, and lay to," he said, holding up a hand to quell the protests from Crane and his subordinates. "I want them available to report on enemy movements from the rear, if needed, and I want them positioned to kill the enemy's relays, once the Terrans enter the Nakahashi storms. Now that the enemy fleet is moving into position to intercept our messages, I don't want to compromise the location of our scouting teams or communications buoys. To be frank about it, I see no need to do so."

Crane stiffened visibly, but said nothing. Janet guessed that the Skipper had just stepped on one of his pet projects.

"I expect them to take another day in the staging area, then move out," Cook continued. "From ZarCom to Nakahashi is just over thirty-seven parsecs. Assuming a pace of two parsecs per day, it should take them another eighteen days or so to reach the outer clouds."

"Enemy scouts?" asked Crane. He was a short, dark man with fiercely intelligent eyes. He wore a small moustache, which made his face look sterner than his voice suggested.

"That's a possibility," nodded Cook. "But we don't need to worry about any scouting parties until they reach Nakahashi, and most Terran commanders won't send their scouts out of communications range. Especially here, where they have detailed charts of the skies, and probably have discounted our ability to offer resistance. My guess is that they'll approach the cloud, dawdle another day or two, then edge their way through the pass—perhaps letting their scouts lead the way as they head into the bend.

"But that's in the future. For now, we've got to get our own ships mobilized, and begin maneuvers in earnest out in space. I've already ordered the frigates to commence joint maneuvers in the southern skies. I want our Irregulars to start maneuvers in the north, tomorrow."

"But the readouts!" protested Hodari, the personnel director. "The computers still haven't sorted— "

"I know we haven't finished culling through the data, yet," Cook cut him off. "If we had another month or two, we could devote the same care and attention into our smallcraft pilots we gave to the starship and frigate assignments. A lot of good ones came in with the latest recruits, and we can't do them all justice. Some could do well commanding a frigate—others might even bump some of our bridge officers. But we don't have the time. And, to be blunt, it isn't worth the effort any longer. They'll have to do the best they can, but they won't be the ones to carry the day. All they can do is confuse and harass the enemy. Beating the enemy will fall to the actual warships. And, heaven help us, we've still got a long way to go before the new ship is ready. Perhaps now," he continued, nodding at Landis, "you'll understand why I didn't want both starships down for repairs at the same time."

"We could have finished the *New Alexandria* well before this," Landis sniffed.

"Taking the repair teams away from the new ship—and ensuring disaster if the Terrans sailed before we were ready? Not on your life."

"Well, I'm getting sick and tired of talking about this 'new ship,'" Landis shot back. "'New ship' this, and 'new ship' that. Why not name the damn thing, for crying out loud? At least then we'll be able to put a name to all our complaining. And you won't have to take five minutes distinguishing between the two starships."

"Actually," said Cook, rising to his full height, "I've been giving that matter a lot of thought." He walked from the table toward the doorway. Janet knew the look in his eyes; it made her want to crawl into a hole and hide.

"I've checked through the registry records, and poured over all the possibilities," he said gravely. "And I believe I've come up with the perfect name." Walking to the head of the table, he calmly collected his papers, and placed them in his leather case. Janet closed her eyes, and promised herself that she wouldn't wince.

"*Rosinante,*" he announced grandly; Janet swore silently.

"I beg your pardon?" said Landis.

"The ship will be called the *Rosinante,*" Cook said firmly. "Mr. Hodari, I'll leave the registry details to you. Commodore Landis, you will muster your crew within the hour, and commence space maneuvers. Mr. Decker, you will prepare a report for me by the end of the day tomorrow, detailing all the provisions each ship should stock—assuming that we sail in five days, and will be gone for two full months. Mr. Crane, I want a full intelligence report on my desk by the end of the day, and then you can pack your things to sail.

"That will be all, people. I'll be meeting with each of you individually, tomorrow." Turning abruptly, he left the meeting alone, leaving his subordinates to sort out the minutiae themselves. As the door closed behind him, each one had the same overriding concern.

"*Rosinante?*" sputtered Landis. Everyone in the room turned to look at Janet for an explanation. She just smiled.

"It's Don Quixote's— "

"Yes," snorted Commodore Landis, "I know—it's Don Quixote's horse. What the hell kind of name is that for a starship?"

"He likes old literary references."

"I've noticed that."

"Well, why can't we just come up with something better?" Janet went on, hoping to rally the troops. "I mean—really now. It shouldn't be all that difficult."

Though buoyed by the fact that everyone seemed to agree, Janet knew she still needed an idea. Since time was short, she seized on the first thing that popped into her head. "All right—what was that silly old adventure show all the boys used to watch when we were younger?" she asked.

"You mean *The Cosmic Avengers?*" replied Crane.

"Why not pick a name from there?" offered Janet. "In fact, what's wrong with *Avenger?*"

The command staff mulled it over for a while in silence, before Landis stated the obvious problem.

"You know, it's not what he told us to do."

"Look—do you like it better, or not?" asked Janet. Everybody nodded in agreement.

"Then enter *Avenger* on the registry," she told Hodari, "and write out the work order to put the name on the hull. We'll have it all done before he notices the change. By then, it'll be too late to do anything about it. And he'll probably be very grateful, you know. He can always tell a good idea from a bad one. Well, eventually, he can."

"Just as long as I don't get into any trouble," the personnel officer said skeptically, scribbling himself a reminder.

"They'll be hell to pay," Landis snorted, shaking his head warily.

"Just leave the Skipper to me," Janet said, dismissing his concerns with a wave of her hand. "He'll come around—believe me."

At least, Janet thought, he'll come around sooner or later.

That is, if he knows what's good for him.

* * *

"CHOW TIME!" called the Mess Sergeant, drawing back the cord blocking the entrance to the mess tent. Soon, the shoving began in earnest, as the militiamen elbowed their way into position for an early place in line. Near the front of the line, Jack was content merely to try to keep everyone else's elbows out of his ribs. The food was hardly worth the aggravation, he smiled to himself. Whether he started passing gas now, or five minutes from now, it wouldn't really matter.

"Any news from skyside?" asked the young man behind him.

"Not as far as I can tell," replied Jack.

There was a news monitor in the mess tent, but it was impossible to hear anything over the noise. It never stopped the rumor mill from grinding out its own version of the news. And Jack had found, much to his amusement, that the rumor mill was every bit as accurate as the highly paid journalists appearing on the monitors. The broadcasters could have saved themselves a lot of money and been just as wrong about everything, simply by letting the militia take over the news.

"Man, I thought they'd be all over the planet with it by now. I guess the world really is full of incompetents. And that goes for the press, as well as the rest of us."

"All over the planet with what?"

"The Terries, that's what. I heard the Terries have sailed. There's a big scramble skyside, trying to get ready."

Jack suddenly lost his appetite. "Where did you hear that?" he demanded. Everyone around them turned, intently following the conversation. "How do you come off, starting these rumors?"

"It's not a rumor," the young man answered, looking very self-satisfied. "I happen to know a girl who works in the capital. It's all over the Senate office building, you know. The Terries are putting out to space, and Cook's trying to pull the fleet together to go meet them."

As bodies scrambled around the mess tent, trying to locate an open phone line from the base to the outside, Jack found his own thoughts lost in the ensuing din. So soon? he kept repeating to himself, over and over again. It seemed like a bad dream, yet he tried his best to keep his head clear. Panic wouldn't help them. Isis needed strength and bravery, not mindless terror. If the end was really coming, he didn't want his last days alive spent wandering around in a trance, or wringing his hands over something that they couldn't avoid.

* * *

THE CHANCELLOR looked tired, thought Ross. Tired and preoccupied. He remembered how well-preserved and sturdy she looked when this whole thing began. Today, she looked particularly haggard and frail. It seemed she'd aged another decade in the space of five minutes.

"What other steps should we take?" she asked, after a long pause. Ross saw McKenzie nod at him, encouraging him to speak as freely as he wished.

"I've already activated the home guard," he said, "and have drafted an order declaring a state of emergency and nationalizing the police force, for your signature if the need arises. We can have troops on the streets by dusk, if things get out of hand. But frankly, I doubt that there'll be any trouble. I've seen no signs of any disturbances, at least nothing the local police can't handle. Mostly, we have a planet full of scared people, desperate for reassurance. And since Admiral Cook has his hands full, that source has to be you."

"Meaning?"

"Meaning," Ross continued, "you need to address the nation—today, tonight, as soon as possible. Rumors are rampant in town, and I'm sure the news broadcasters will jump on the story as soon as they get some hard information. I've traced the rumors to a leak somewhere in the Government. Probably some panicked senator, or a junior staffer without the wit or common sense to hold his tongue. But people want to believe we have things under control, and that everything will turn out fine."

"I'd like to believe that myself, Reggie," the Chancellor said wickedly.

Ross blushed, and the Chancellor immediately felt sorry for her thoughtlessness. But she also felt the old instincts stirring inside her. Fear was a potent motivator, as potent as greed and every bit as deadly, if allowed to rage unchecked. She had no doubt that Isis would remain calm, whatever the circumstances, so long as people had some reason to hope. If her people needed a leader, that was the job she was elected to do. And modest as she tried to appear on the surface, she knew that nobody on the planet could do it better.

"Reggie," she smiled, as sweetly as she could, "perhaps you could jot down some ideas for me. But don't be too maudlin. I hate it when a speaker sounds mawkish, and I don't think sentiment is really called for, just now.

"Certainly."

"Reserve time for me some time tonight," she continued, patting her Minister on the arm. "And please don't take it personally, when I change everything around, after you've done your very best to make me sound like Churchill or Cicero."

"I never do, Madam Chancellor."

"I just really do prefer to do my own writing, you know."

"Yes, Madam Chancellor."

* * *

"ENGINES STALLED again," said the chief engineer, over the intercom. "The readout says there's still an energy leak, somewhere in the engine coils."

"I know that, Mr. Malik," said Cook, glaring angrily at his intercom display. "That's what it says on the dials, and that's what I can feel with my own senses. I don't need you to tell me we still have a problem. I need you to fix it."

"But, Admiral— "

"Fix it, Commander!" Cook snapped. "I don't have the time to nursemaid you through it. I'll be down at 700 Hours to see how far you've come toward a solution."

Turning off the intercom, Cook glanced around the bridge to see the worried looks of his bridge crew. Today's drills were not going as planned, but they were about what he'd expected. He was trying to think of something clever to say, to take their minds off their troubles and assure them that unglitching a ship was always a chore, when a message came over the speaker that put him into an even fouler mood.

"Commodore Landis of the *New Alexandria* calling the *Avenger*." Cook recognized the voice: it was Ron Ehrlich, radio officer on the other starship and one of the few veterans to be found among the Navy regulars. The Admiral didn't need the interruption, and he certainly didn't relish another chance to resurrect the controversy of the day. He delayed his response until Jarvis, his own radio officer, started getting uneasy.

"The *New Alexandria* is waiting for a response, Admiral," said Jarvis, a round-faced young man whose physique suggested that he'd barely passed the physical screening. He was an whiz with communications equipment, so Cook had picked him for the bridge station. Today, the lad's high-pitched, whining voice was beginning to grate on the Admiral's nerves.

"Lieutenant Jarvis," Cook said, looking at the young man sternly; he would later regret his impatience, but for the time being he resented the reminder about his recent failures—and Janet, under the ruse of assisting Landis with the militia drills, had taken the infuriating precaution of removing herself from the ship, making her unavailable as a scapegoat. "I do not like having my drills interrupted by a message from another ship. Commodore Landis is a skilled commander, and an accomplished skipper, but I still expect you to screen all messages for us. Do I make myself clear? "

"Yes, sir."

"All right," Cook said, having rescued enough of his pride to continue. "Put Landis on the screen."

The image of Landis settled on the overhead monitor; Cook stewed silently as he saw Janet clearly standing in the background to establish her alibi.

"What is it, Commodore?"

"We've completed all the maneuvers you scheduled for us," said Landis, scowling from the screen.

"My chronometer doesn't show 600 Hours, yet, Commodore. In fact, it doesn't even show 500 Hours."

"We've done all the maneuvers; in fact, we've done them a dozen times. Attack—retreat. Attack—retreat. Pivot—retreat. Pivot—attack. Attack—retreat...."

"Is it 600 Hours yet, Commodore?"

"Of course not, Admiral. But what does— "

"Janet—, " Cook called to the image of his wife, who was doing her best to stay out of sight, and out of the squabble, "would you say that the Naval Militia has mastered this phase of their maneuvers?"

"No, Admiral. In fact, they haven't gotten it right yet."

"And does *your* chronometer register 600 Hours?"

"No, sir," said Janet, trying not to show her own anger at being dressed down in front of both starships, and wondering why men took such delight in demonstrating to one another which one of them was in charge.

"Well then, I'm afraid I just don't understand the reason for the call, Commodore Landis. I am, of course, always glad to hear from you. But I am quite busy. And, from the looks of it, you are, too."

"Admiral...."

"Tend to your drills, Commodore," Cook said coldly. "We can discuss the matter at another time. *Avenger* out."

Cook turned to face his bridge crew. This was the first time, he realized, that he'd referred to his new ship by her name—or, more precisely, by the name he'd had foisted upon him by those who lacked his sense of history and appreciation for literature. He wasn't done sulking about it, but to his surprise the name seemed to fit quite nicely.

"All right, people," he said, gruffly. "Enough chitchatting. Just because we can only maneuver on thrusters right now is no reason to let the frigates off a-loafing. Jarvis—send a message to all squadron leaders: it is their responsibility to set and revise the patterns for attacking, and retreating—to set and revise all rally and pivot points— and to keep and revise all other standing orders which may be affected by a change in orders or battle plans. This next series of drills will be a test of their ability to coordinate, as well as an exercise to see whether their people have learned to execute a maneuver without running into each other."

"Yes, sir."

"Give the order to regroup at the skirmish line, and wait for my command."

"Yes, sir."

Cook watched as the squadrons formed their battle lines. They were still tentative and sloppy. But they'd come a long way in the past two hours. In a few more days they might actually be able to follow a sequence of orders like a company of professionals.

"All squadrons at Formation One, Admiral," reported Lt. Wasser, the present occupant of the system's station.

"All squadrons acknowledge Formation One," confirmed Jarvis.

"Clear the zone!" barked Cook. As Jarvis relayed the command, he watched the old, creaky frigates move away from the skirmish line, trying their best to hold their formation steady.

"Attack!" Cook said sharply, a minute later.

Abruptly changing course, the frigates came about and began charging toward their original positions. Shaking his head, Cook ordered the leaders to keep their people in something resembling a line, whenever executing a maneuver.

"It is your responsibility to keep your lines intact," snapped Cook, staring into the communications screen. "I don't really care how you do it—although I suggest you have your systems officer formulate a program to compensate for maneuvers. Either that, or I may have to start looking for a new set of squadron commanders.

"But— ," began one of the squadron leaders. Cook silenced him by signaling his radio officer to close the channel. Then he rose to stretch his legs. It had been a long session, and he sensed it would seem a lot longer before the day was over.

"All squadrons, pivot west two hundred degrees, reform battle lines, Formation Two," Cook said as he stretched and waited for his radio officer to relay the command.

"Clear the zone!" Cook demanded, as soon as the last, tardy frigate inched into formation.

* * *

THE CHANCELLOR looked confident and strong, Jack thought. Hands folded demurely on the desk in front of her, there was fire in her quick, intelligent eyes, and her image spoke from the screen as if she were speaking directly to him. He realized, of course, that everyone on Isis probably felt the same way. But it didn't make him feel any less heroic, any less courageous, any less a part of the crusade to keep the planet free.

"Among the many rumors that have gripped our world tonight," the Chancellor said, her face smiling pleasantly, her eyes filled with stern resolve, "is word that the Terran fleet has sailed from Planet Zarathustra, and is now heading toward Isis. This rumor, I must tell you, is a slight exaggeration—but it is, nevertheless, quite true. The day we have dreaded for longer than we care to remember is at last upon us, and we must meet it as bravely as our ancestors met any other crisis in our History.

"Six centuries ago on Old Earth, another brave people faced the danger of another darkness in the depths of the Bloody Century—the bloodiest century ever known to Man, until our present era. Then, as now, a small island of reason stood, alone and surrounded, amid a rising tide of rabid barbarism that seemed to hold all Creation in its thrall. From their lonely watchtower, those brave people mustered forth as the sentinels of all civilization, and staunched that monstrous tide before it could sweep truth and decency forever from the face of the Earth. Today, this same tide is rising in our eastern skies. Whether it will crest before it drowns us shall, in the end, depend upon our courage, our daring, and our resourcefulness.

"We are, by nature, a peaceful, honorable, and industrious nation—a people who wish no harm to others, who wish our fellow creatures happiness and prosperity, desiring in return only the chance to live, love, and dream in peace. We have not chosen this battle; it has been thrust upon us. And yet, for all the fears and doubts we each may harbor in our souls, our hearts should be untroubled by the perils and anguish that lie ahead of us. Our conscience is clear—and so is our purpose.

"The chance to protect a loved one from danger or misfortune is perhaps the noblest calling we may ever need to answer. Yet we as a People are now called upon to rescue more than our homes and our children: We are consigned as the guardians of Civilization itself. That is a dire, difficult burden for any generation to carry. But it is the burden that has fallen to us, and like the festival torch that we pass from generation to generation, *we will not let that burden fall.*

"Our Navy has trained for many long, hard months, and is blessed with the greatest commander in human history. They are the champions of all we hold dear, now and forever. They, and you, are fighting for the very soul of Mankind, and for all that we know and love. In these frightening, terrible times, let us not shrink into a selfish timidity, nor sink into some hand-wringing paroxysm of desperation and despair. Let us face our future with bold defiance, confident in our Cause, and in our Champions. Let us—at this, the start of our most perilous hour— proudly proclaim for all time our devotion to peace, and honor, and decency. And let us wish our Navy godspeed, secure in the knowledge that, whatever else may lie ahead, Heaven and History will always smile upon our efforts; and that with faith and hope in our hearts, bravery and courage will now carry our cause forward, and will soon carry the day in the black and fiery skies of battle."

* * *

THREE DAYS LATER, the Navy sailed.

Coming together just beyond the sixth planet of the Isitian star system, the four thousand ships of the Naval Militia formed into four large columns. One after another, the columns trailed the single company of two-dozen rusty frigates sailing in a small battle wedge.

At the head of the company, the *New Alexandria* sailed alone, its dull finish contrasting noticeably with the shining point of light at the head of the procession. Leading the entire fleet, her new and untested heat tiles gleaming in the sunlight, was Admiral Cook's starship, the *Avenger.*

Sailing smartly in tight formation, the fleet headed toward the Isitian sun, using the star to pull them faster and faster as they moved through space. Nearing their home planet, the fleet sailed across the night sky, emerging across the terminator just at sunset over the west coast of the most populous continent on Isis, heading toward the distant battle beyond the sun, awaiting them in the east. The Admiral had insisted upon giving his troops a last parade over the planet. And though nobody ventured the thought out loud, everyone on and over the tiny planet felt the need to say a last goodbye.

"LOOK, DADDY!"

The small butterfly in his daughter's hand went unnoticed. His wife, her head resting on his shoulder, moved to stroke the girl's hair, and told her to run and play before the last light faded. Like their neighbors, the Markhams had come outside to watch the Navy; like everyone on the planet, Jack kept his doubts to himself.

Watching the small dots of light fill the clear, darkening sky, for the first time Jack knew in his heart that it was hopeless. No matter how much he wanted to believe in miracles, the truth was screaming at him from above. He saw it just by looking at the difference between the big warships, and the little sloops and brigs that made up the bulk of the Navy. No matter how many tiny ships they sent into battle, the Terran ships were bigger, stronger, faster. No matter how many Terran ships they destroyed, the Terrans could always find more. And no matter how brave or gallant the Navy might be, the Cosmic Guard had already proven itself in battle.

"But Daddy—!"

Smiling through his tears, Jack picked up his daughter and held her in his arms. Only three years old, little Alana was much too young to know what was going on. He wished that everyone could be so young, forever.

"Look at all the ships, Kitten," he whispered. "Isn't it pretty?"

"I already saw the ships, Daddy," the little girl said in a soothing voice, aware that all the grownups around her were sad, and trying her best to be grown up about it all, herself. "But maybe you should really look at my butterfly."

"Just a little longer. Just a little while longer."

"Maybe it will make you feel better."

"Maybe it will, Sweetheart. But just a little while longer."

Chapter 9

S-623— REPORT?"

"Storms abating in this sector. No signs of the enemy. S-623, out."

"Roger; *Avenger*, over and out."

* * *

"WHAT DO you mean, the guns are out again?"

"I mean, Commodore," Malik tried to explain, though not really sure he understood it all himself, "we still seem to have a slight problem with energy transference. Transferred energy storage, to be precise. The engine coils are just fine, you see. It's just—well, it's just that we still have problems getting the main guns to hold a charge. Five seconds—ten seconds, tops—and the charge dissipates."

Janet was livid. Without the guns, the ship was helpless. Given the odds they were facing, it might not make any difference at that. But the fact that nothing seemed to be going right made her want to lash out at anyone within range. If Skipper was nowhere to be found, then this poor engineer would have to suffice.

From the central catwalk in the Engineering Control Room, the two of them looked down on the rest of the Engineer's crew. Two-dozen young men, and one young woman, were working feverishly, trying to sort out the problem—checking the wiring, checking the relays, checking the fuser bolts that tied the equipment together.

"Commander Malik," she said, her eyes flaming angrily. "I presume you know exactly how crucial guns are to a warship."

"Yes, Ma'am. That is why we are— "

"And you know it would eliminate whatever advantage we might otherwise enjoy by having the Admiral along on this particular excursion, if we end up going into battle without any weapons!"

"Commodore— "

"I don't care how you do it!" she snapped, her words slapping the young man's ego as her hand slapped his arm. "Get those guns working, and get them working by tomorrow!"

"Yes, Ma'am."

As Janet stormed away from his Engine Room, Malik was once again able to relax. Admiral Cook had warned him about dealing with the Commodore when she was on a rampage. But the Admiral also told him quite clearly to worry about clearing the remaining glitches from the shields first, before turning to the guns. A five-second charge, he could live with, the Admiral had said—so long as it was five seconds on the guns; he'd just adjust his tactics accordingly. Five seconds on the shields were another matter.

"One thing at a time," the Admiral had smiled; trying to calm the welling panic in his own belly, the young engineer could still hear Cook's voice: "We have plenty of time to fix the ship. We just need to do it in the right sequence. So do what's most important first—and take it one step at a time."

Malik took a deep breath. He hated when two superior officers told him to do two different things. But he knew instinctively that the Admiral's course was better. As long as he could keep out of Commodore's way for the next few days, he was sure he'd see the problem through to its finish.

"DAMN!" BELLOWED Hennessey. Rising quickly to his feet, the young crewman dropped his glove to the floor and shook his hand vigorously, his language turning as blue as his thumb.

Pushing him off to the side, Cutler, the shift foreman, stooped over to look at the problem. The fuser bolt, which blended the relay circuitry with the hallway sensors, was stripped. That was the problem, plain and simple. Hennessey, the hot-shot college boy, couldn't be bothered to work the faulty bolt loose; he had to try to muscle it out of its socket. So the young fool not only ruined the few connections that the bolt had managed to complete: he'd made the damn thing almost impossible to remove.

"Hennessey, you twit," Cutler snapped. "Go fetch the magnidrill from Central Maintenance. If they don't have it, sit on them until they find it."

"But, Sarge...."

"Move it, Mister. And don't come back until you either find the tools or the brains you need to fix these damn things."

As the young crewman disappeared down the hallway, Cutler sat back on the floor and looked dejectedly at the rest of his repair team. They'd been at this for three years, some of them. That's how long it had taken to bring the *Avenger* from the drawing board into space. Others had joined along the way—or like Hennessey, had joined the Navy since the first of the year.

None of them had ever seen battle, nor done anything on so grand a scale on so short a timetable. None of them knew how long it might take them to iron out this latest little flaw. And none of them had any real sense of how close they might be to pulling the ship together. They knew only that they'd been at it forever, and there was still an incredible amount of work to do.

They were also running out of time.

GARRITY STRAINED to hear the Admiral's voice over the subspace interference. Outside, the reddish glow of the Nakahashi clouds was broken, here and there, by white flashes from the dying ionic disturbance. The clouds were still a few days away, yet the effect of the storm was upon them. It would be several days before the skies cleared, and the radio channels were back to normal.

Garrity was sick with frustration. He knew that what the Admiral was saying was vitally important—to them, to their homes, to their chances against the Terrans. It was maddening not to hear him clearly. But Cook was there, on one of the small sloops in the advance column, helping with the day's maneuvers and doing what he could to prepare the weakest part of the fleet for battle.

"**peat, you people are not frigates," he heard the Admiral say. "You are not regular warships, and your tact*** cannot be *** **** as those of regular warsh***. Your mission is distraction and confusion. Think of yoursel*** as fish in *** ***—*r migrating birds, evad*** * predator. If we're ***ky, your compa*ies will be the domi***t readings on the ene**** sens** **reens. Your maneuvers should be as disconcerting to the observer as ****ible. ***ember, you are try*** to confuse the enemy. Use your guns sparingly— they will just draw **tention to you and your ship, and **** you a likely ****et. Fire only whe* *** must -- and then, only a* sh*** **thin range. And **** thi* in mind: because of your differing missions, the frig*t**' **** strength is in concentrated **wer; yours is *n dispersal.

"Second—********— "

"***************__****************!!"

Frustrated at losing the signal entirely, Garrity fussed with the radio controls until Tommy Reed, his navigator, eased him away and reset the radio to its original channel. If the static was too much, there was nothing they could do. They'd have to piece it together on their own, with the ship's computer—or rely on somebody closer, who'd gotten a more complete transmission.

Damn! Garrity thought, sinking bitterly into his seat. It would have been nice to have the Admiral's insights and advice for the coming fight. Now, all he could do is wait for the signal to resume the day's drilling—if the commands could make it through the storm.

* * *

"IT IS AN abomination, I tell you. It is likely to cost us dearly in battle, if our luck is bad. I cannot understand how your husband tolerates it."

Nodding politely, Janet sipped a cup of tea while listening to Commodore Landis complain about his ship. Tall and thin, Landis was hardly an imposing figure, especially on the monitor screen. In person, his sad eyes had always evoked some measure of sympathy in her heart. But on the screen those eyes faded into the sharp contours of his face, and his voice took on undertones of whining. That was one thing Janet could not tolerate today. She had to deal with too much of that on the *Avenger*. She didn't need any more of it in her life.

Janet held few illusions about the man sitting across the screen from her. He was, she thought, a fool—without sense enough to realize just how foolish he was. Anyone who'd complain about the shortcomings of his own ship to someone trying to iron out the wrinkles in a brand new one obviously lacked the wit needed to command. She looked at Jennings, the young ensign assigned as her personal aide; Jennings shook her head and shrugged.

"Perhaps your problems seem more insurmountable than they really are," said Janet, wondering if Landis would take the hint to keep his problems to himself. "I'm sure you can solve a great many of them simply by applying yourself."

"Don't misunderstand me, Mrs. Cook," Landis smiled sorrowfully. "I appreciate all that you and your husband have done for this planet. All of us do, and all of us understand the pressure he's under. But it seems to me that we missed a grand opportunity to refurbish the *New Alexandria* when we had the chance. And since many of my present problems stem from bad wiring and old, malfunctioning equipment, I would appreciate anything he could do to loan me some of his people, to help get my ship ready for battle. A second starship will come in quite handy, you know."

Janet stiffened in her chair. A second starship commanded by someone who knew how to fight would certainly be an asset, she thought. One commanded by a fool was simply be a waste. She could not understand what the Skipper saw in this sniveling incompetent. Especially when there was, in her own modest estimation, another quite gifted commander sitting right under his nose.

"I'm sure the Admiral will give the matter careful consideration," Janet said, smiling tartly. "I will relay the message to him as soon as I can."

Looking uncomfortable, Landis managed a polite smile and nodded, as he signed off the air.

"As soon as he has nothing else to worry about," Janet added, to the blank screen. She turned to face Jennings, shaking her head in disbelief.

"I can't believe the nerve of that man!"

"Really, now."

"As if we don't have enough of our own work to do. And he wants us to drop everything and run off to put his ship in order. Incredible!"

The bustle of repair crews continued outside the door to the *Avenger's* administrative office. Team after team of crewmen combed every last inch of the ship, trying to eliminate the last flaw in the great ship's machinery, or wiring, or circuitry. And in the end, Janet and Jennings found thirteen different reasons why Commodore Landis shouldn't expect any help, trimming his ship for battle.

* * *

THE CRAMPED QUARTERS of the small sloop didn't bother him nearly as much as the interstellar static.

"Damn storms. It's a wonder Gutterman ventured through the damn gap in the first place."

"I beg your pardon, Admiral?"

Cook turned to look at the frightened young lieutenant commander who was serving as his host. The kid looked like he was just out of high school. He should be chasing girls, not chasing about the sky trying to get himself killed.

"Never mind, Mr. Jason," Cook smiled. "I'm just raging against reality again." Soon, the static died down again, and he could try running another drill with the militia.

"Company Bravo," he said into the communications microphone.

"Bravo Leader, acknowledged."

"Swing your company full about, Bravo Leader. Come to Heading 250, by 15 degrees south. Prepare to swirl and flurry."

"S-n-F, acknowledged," came the reply.

Cook watched his monitor screen closely. The screen was blurred by static, and he knew he couldn't follow the maneuvers precisely. Still, the militia company would try to do what he wanted; he hoped to see enough on the monitor to tell if it was worth bringing the lot of them along.

Landis, he knew, thought he was crazy. For that matter, he laughed, so did Janet—although her view of the matter seemed to be more a matter of principle than anything specific he might say or do. But he couldn't pretend that the Navy was stronger than it was. That approach might work in politics, where partisan gain was the driving force, but not in the world of life and death. He'd have to fight with whatever ships Isis had on hand. And if Fate had given him a multitude of tiny ships to work with, then by God he'd find a way to use them.

"Execute maneuver," he said, as the images on his screen eased into focus. He watched as Bravo's two hundred or so tiny ships fanned out, spreading until their formation reached nearly a full astrometer across—one second's worth of distance, at the speed of light. But something didn't quite look right, He couldn't quite put his finger on it, but it felt like the ships were too widely dispersed. Even if their mounted guns and laser cannons could cover the distance between them, there were too many gaps in the formation. Too much space between ships for the Terran warships to penetrate. It might be enough to confuse the Terrans when they were a thousand klicks away, but by the time the enemy came within firing range, the Terrans would have time to compensate. Without knowing why, he knew that he needed something else. Something the Terrans would never expect.

"Halt!" he said into the microphone. "Try it again, Bravo Leader. This time, compress the formation by a factor of four. No—make it a factor of 40. Let's try pairing up—two ships per team, right next to each other. And run the maneuver at quarter-speed. I don't want you people ramming into each other. At least, not until the shooting starts."

Cook settled back in his seat, smirking at the befuddled look on the face of his young companion. "Don't worry, Mr. Jason—your turn won't come unless Sotzen and the rest of Bravo Company can manage it. By then, I'll know if we have something worth using."

"If you say so, Admiral."

Cook laughed roguishly, then turned to look at his monitor screen. Jason wasn't his best commander; he'd arrived on the scene too late to master the battle manual or the simulator drills, and still had much to learn about the art of warfare. But he was one of the brightest. If this young man couldn't figure it out, maybe the Terrans wouldn't, either.

Of course, he mused, it would help if he could figure it out himself first, but the Universe was far from perfect. And if this didn't seem to work, he still had a few more days to try something else.

"STEP LIVELY! Here she comes."

As the half-dozen crewmen of his repair team dashed into the shadows of the surrounding alcoves, Cutler took a position just beyond the bend in the corridor and turned off the work lamp. Peering through the mesh that shielded the head from view, the yeoman sergeant watched as the target came into range before continuing down another corridor. Signaling his team to wait until he gave the all-clear, Cutler stepped away from his post, walked down the hallway, and looked around the corner. The rest of the team, upon seeing him relax, immediately came out from their hiding places and resumed work on the hallway lighting fixtures. One of them, the young Northlander, tip-toed quietly down the hall, stopping right next to his supervisor, who was still keeping a watch on the next corridor.

"That was a close one, wasn't it Sarge?" whispered Kozlowski.

"Too close for comfort, Charlie. And I don't like the looks of it. If she keeps prowling the decks until the Admiral gets back, we may never get this finished."

Kozlowski nodded gravely. The Admiral seemed to be everywhere, often appearing out of nowhere, just as things were turning to Isitian hash. But he always had something helpful to say—a joke to make them feel better, or a suggestion to help with the work. Whenever he left the ship, his wife took over his rounds. And the last thing any repair crew wanted was for her to be standing over their shoulders.

Not that they weren't fond of Mrs. Cook. She could be very pleasant. At least, that's what they all told themselves, since they couldn't imagine the Admiral standing for a mate with an attitude problem. But she did have a tendency to make them feel clumsy and foolish whenever things went wrong. And since repair crews were never needed when things were going right, she seemed to do nothing but complain at them.

"All right, I think she's gone," Cutler said, moving away from the corner. "Barringer—quick now. Keep watch on the next hallway. No telling when she'll be making the next sweep. Rashid, Wachler—finish up on this light and Kozlowski and Hennessey, you take the next one. We'll want to get back to the computer hook-ups as soon as possible, and we can't report back to Mr. Malik until we finish up here."

As his crew scurried about their business, Cutler kept a watchful eye on the corridor. These were perilous times, he realized. But it would be oddly comforting when all they had to worry about was the enemy.

* * *

"S-779—REPORT?"

"The storms are well past in this sector, *Avenger*. Skies are clear as a bell. Been that way for the last five hours. As a matter of fact— "

"We need your report, S-779. Not the latest gossip."

"Right—well then, still no sign of the enemy, *Avenger*. And—well—nothing else to report. S-779, out."

"Roger; *Avenger*, over and out."

* * *

The bay door closed, and the hangar filled with air. The small sloop glided gently onto its assigned place along the dock, where it was surrounded by a horde of mechanics and staff officers. After a few minutes, the loudspeaker ordered everyone back to let the ship's crew disembark. Soon the door slid open and the whole crowd gave a loud cheer as Admiral Cook stepped onto the launch pad. He wore the flight suit the Navy gave to all small craft commanders, grinning boyishly at the loud greeting by the assembly—which only made their verbal salute all the louder.

"Clear the dock area," called the hangar deck officer over the speaker, vainly trying to be heard over the noise. "All personnel clear the dock area."

"You won't believe the progress we've made," Commander Malik shouted in the Admiral's ear, as he finally broke through the cordon of security guards trying to push back the crowd. "I think we've finally gotten the shield problem nailed. We may have the guns powered up for testing today, if we're lucky. Even the damn tracking computers are starting to fall into place."

"Acch—I told you not to worry so much," Cook shouted in reply, clearly enjoying the mob's enthusiasm. "Most problems take care of themselves, if you let them. And I'll let you in on a secret, Commander. No ship comes from the factory without problems down to the septic tanks. But your construction workers did a magnificent job on this ship. Nothing here comes close to the headaches we had to sort out on the *d'Artagnan*."

"Thank heaven for small favors, sir."

Laughing, Cook clapped the young officer on the back, and moved along toward the airlock leading to the interior of the ship. If he'd taken the time to look, he would have seen that everyone on the deck was feeding on his mood, responding to whatever they sensed in his eyes, or his face, or his walk, hungry for his approval. But today he was too excited to worry about it. He'd seen exactly what he'd hoped to see. Through the static and the fog, he knew what his Navy could do. Getting them to do it might be a problem, for he had no idea how they'd respond when the enemy guns started blazing. But he'd seen enough to discard the remaining doubts he had.

He stepped smartly through the opening in the crowd his crewmen made for him. Soon, barely noticing the repair crews and technical teams he greeted good-naturedly as he passed, he neared the main bank of elevators, heading for the bridge. Now, if only the Terrans would cooperate, he smiled as the elevator door closed behind him. Mercifully, that aspect of the problem was out of his hands. He wouldn't know the answer for a while yet. And, he reminded himself for the hundredth time today, he'd be a damn fool to fret about it in the meantime.

"NO—YOU IMBECILES! Keep the lines straight as you attack," Barnes shouted over the shoulder of his radio officer, into the microphone at the console. "Wobbling lets the Terries have that many more openings to attack. We attack as a unit, not like a bunch of preening prima donnas. Now, re-form the company and do it again. *Bristol Bay*, out."

As the frigates came about to regroup, weaving their way through the regiment of small craft that had been assigned to him for the day's drilling, Barnes patted his radio officer on the shoulder. "Sorry, Gates," he smiled. "I guess I'm just getting edgy."

"Everybody's getting edgy, sir," the young ensign replied. "Don't worry about it."

Barnes shook his head and returned to the command chair. Picking up the latest communication from the *Avenger*, he read it again, trying to understand what it meant. Ever since they'd left Isis, each frigate squadron had drilled as a unit, coming together only for an hour or so each day, under the Admiral's stern gaze, to practice attack formations. Today, the new orders were to practice joint maneuvers for the duration, and to rotate among the militia regiments each day, until the battle. He had no idea what the Admiral had in mind, for the small craft were now crowded together in tight formations like canned nuts. It was hard enough for them to weave through the tiny openings without running into each other, let alone try to do it in something resembling a formation.

"Company regrouped, and standing by," reported Addison, systems officer for the *Bristol Bay*. "I sure hope we're doing this right, Commander. Without the Admiral.... "

"The Admiral can't do our fighting for us, Mr. Addison," Barnes replied coldly, trying to hide his own sense of inadequacy. "It's about time we started taking charge of our own duties and responsibilities.

"Gates?"

"Yes, Sir."

"Signal the attack."

"Aye aye, Sir."

"Helm—come about to Heading 230; Weapons—raise the shields, prepare to charge all guns."

"STABILIZERS ON."

"Check."

"Diversion switch on."

"Check."

"Magnetic insulators on."

"Check."

"Intake regulator on."

"Check."

"Interrupter circuits clear."

"Check."

"Surge suppressor on, this time?"

"Check."

Yeoman Sgt. Ted Silarski took a deep breath. The air reeked of fused circuitry and human sweat. His crew was tired and out of patience. The last time they'd tried to test the weapon circuitry, they'd nearly fried a whole section of the engine coils. Now, nearly a week away from home, they were almost out of replacement parts and running out of time. If this last series of repairs didn't do the trick, he didn't know what else to do. He hated the thought of telling the Admiral that he'd just have to face the Terries with a glitch in the ship's main guns.

"All right. Power up."

The deck under the keel gun battery shuddered as the crewman activated the control diverting power from the engines to the guns. Silarski sighed, and gave the command to Hassan, the pot-bellied, middle-aged crewman who'd given up a cushy job as an engineer to sail toward eternity with a shipload of fools.

"And run the diagnostic."

The giant bank of computers that controlled the gun battery suddenly blinked to life. Whirring and clicking, the ship's vast array of electronic brains and nerves ran the keel battery through every permutation of every command. Beneath his feet, Silarski felt the deck vibrate and shudder, with each change in the energy matrix and every alteration in dispersal. Five seconds later, the computer spat its verdict onto the display screen over the lead gunner's console.

"Verifying...KB2040MBets–chkKB41neg–chkKB42neg–altKB41neg–altKB42neg–ctrl41neg–ctrl42neg–chk:KB2040altKB43,44,45,46,47,48,49,50...neg,neg,neg,neg,neg,neg,neg,neg," read the display.

"Son of a bitch," Hassan whispered. "Son of a bitch. Sarge, do you see it?"

"Run it again," Silarski said. "Just to be sure."

The crewman ran the diagnostic again, as the rest of the tired, sweaty repair team crowded around the display screen. When the computer again signaled that it could find nothing wrong with the gun battery, the entire team gave a loud cheer that was heard through the airlock, and half-way down the hallway leading to the ship's interior. Quickly, the yeoman stepped over to the intercom and depressed one of two red buttons next to the speaker.

"Tell Mr. Malik we think we've done it," Silarski said into the microphone, trying to make himself heard over the shouts of his repair team. "He should come down to check it, right away."

"Roger," came the reply; Silarski recognized the voice. It was the Chief Engineer himself. "I'll be down in ten minutes—and the Skipper's back, so he may be with me."

Grinning broadly, Silarski clapped Hassan firmly on the back. "Well, I think we did it, Tony. I don't know what the hell we did, or how we did it, but we've done it, nevertheless. If it checks out, we can copy the configuration to the other gun batteries. And if it holds there, then we've got ourselves a starship."

"Not enough to earn a rest, though?" chided a crew member coming down the rampway leading to the console. It had been weeks since any of them had a chance to spend a whole hour doing nothing. By the looks of it, they'd be too busy trying their solution on the other guns to have any time to rest any time soon.

Silarski laughed—a strong, hearty laugh, one he thought he'd never hear come out of his chest again.

"Freddie!" he exclaimed, raising his voice to be heard over the cheers of his men. "All of you—take the next five minutes to rest, if you need it. What the hell—take ten. In another week, you'll have all the rest you could ever want. Either you'll have earned it—and I've heard the Admiral is no piker, once the job's over—or you couldn't escape it. Me, I'm betting on the Admiral. If the rest we earn ourselves isn't of the eternal variety, I'll buy everyone here a beer in any bar on Isis you fools manage to drag me to.

The shouts of his men ringing in his ear, Silarski beamed proudly. His crew had done it, he was sure of it. And if things were starting to fall into place for the likes of them, then Luck would surely smile on the Admiral.

* * *

THE SOOTHING strains of ancient music seemed like an enveloping balm in the darkness. Cook stroked Janet's back, smiling as he rediscovered each rise and undulation. Her breathing, silent and rhythmic, made her body pulse in counterpoint to the music.

Janet stretched her body, and nestled herself into her husband's arms. She'd spent so much time wondering whether they'd ever have a life together, and it was nice to be able to relax without worrying about anything past tomorrow. There was so much left unsaid, so much she couldn't express, but everything could wait. Nothing mattered to her anymore, except for the fragmentary moments of time she could steal from the war, and the Ship, and everything else that had made her life a living hell.

Her head rested on his chest, rising and falling with each breath he took. They'd seen so much of the Universe together, so much beauty, so much death. Now, she tried her best to stay calm, to help him fight off the evil threatening everyone around her. Yet through it all, she could never imagine anything bad ever happening to him;

he was too big a part of her life to admit the possibility. He was always so strong, commanding events as if ordering filing clerks about. Listening to each passing beat of his heart, she felt warm and safe. Her mind was hungry for comfort and reassurance, and despite all the things she wanted to say, all the calming things she wanted to hear him tell her, she found herself basking in warmth and love, and slowly drifted off to sleep.

Silently, Cook kept stroking his wife's back, occasionally smoothing her hair. He stared off into the darkness, his thoughts filled with the coming battle. His mind churned with the countless things he still had to do.

With work on the shields and guns falling into place, he needed to master timing the energy transfers between gun batteries. He had to impose his routines on the Bridge—not that Janet hadn't tried her best, but he had to make sure that the crew would do things his way, on his schedule, at his command. The corridors were littered with cables and wires, and the call to battle stations would be chaos until the halls were cleared of debris. The ship's repair teams needed to know their posts—and if he didn't give them some feel for the belly-wrenching maneuvers he'd need for battle, they'd be no use to him when the shooting started. And he had yet to practice any of the hundreds of standard evasive measures he'd perfected for the Terrans to use against their enemies, maneuvers he'd need himself, going up against the Cosmic Guard. The battalions of small craft would have to fend mostly for themselves, he concluded; even the frigates would have to do without him. He'd done all he could to prepare them for the coming fight; the rest of the time, he'd have to ready himself and his ship for combat.

His heart was pounding like a kettle drum. He was convinced he could pull it off. His ragtag little fleet had the heart of a whole battle wing, and were fighting for their homes and everyone they loved. He just prayed that he hadn't cut it too close this time—that now, with everything at stake on one Cosmic dice roll, he wouldn't be caught up by all the little details he always left until the last minute.

The minutes raced by, his mind racing ahead of them. With events swirling around him, he'd never felt such exhilaration in the simple fact of being alive, so desperately needed, so much in command of himself and everything around him. But even with his body wrapped around the woman he loved, he'd never felt quite so alone.

Looking out the porthole, the young boy was struck mostly by the colors: the reddish swirls of the massive clouds of Nakahashi, the clear, jewelescent hues of the distant stars. And the breathless sweep of the Milky Way, stretching from the west until it disappeared behind the clouds.

"Grandpa?"

"What is it, Roscoe?"

"How can the night sky be so colorful in space, and so black and white at home?"

Turning away from the controls, the old man chuckled. The boy had been quiet all day, just staring out the porthole at the passing skies. Three years old was a bit young to be whizzing across the heavens, the boy's father had told him; and if it hadn't been for the fact that his son and daughter-in-law needed a babysitter for the weekend, it would have taken him forever to get their permission to take his grandson sailing.

"Lots of things are more interesting, when you examine them closely, Roscoe," the old man said, taking his grandson onto his lap. "Look at an anthill for a while, and you see an alien city. Look at water through a microscope, and you find an invisible world just waiting for someone to come and explore. But the stars were here before the first humans walked the Earth, and they'll be here long after we're all gone. So it's not surprising that you have to come out here, high above the clouds in the skies of home, to see them in all their majesty and splendor."

"In all their what?"

The old man laughed and so did the boy, though the lad didn't really know why.

"To see how neat they are. And you know," he continued, "in space you can go just about anywhere you want. Just point the ship in the right direction, and you can sail through the darkness, toward anything you can see."

"What's over there?" the boy pointed toward a hole in the distant clouds. "It looks like a secret cave."

"It's called the Western Channel," replied his grandfather. "Or 'Paddy's Pass.' It's a giant tunnel through the Clouds, The grownups call the whole thing Gutterman's Gap. Some say it's a natural formation, but me? I think the Ancients carved it through the storm."

The boy's eyes lit up like a Founder's Day skyrocket. There wasn't a child on the whole planet who wasn't excited by the old alien ruins, or the thought that some of the first Isitians might still be watching over them.

"The Ancients?"

"Want to go take a look?"

"Can we?"

"Sure. "

His grandson on his lap, the old man turned to face the controls. "Just turn the wheel till the ship's nose points toward the cave in the clouds—gently, now; don't overdo it—and we can just sail right over there."

Of course, he thought, Andrew and Emily would kill him for keeping their son out for so long. But it was like pulling teeth to get anyone else in the family to come with him for a weekend among the stars. And the boy did seem to be enjoying himself, so.

Chapter 10

S-144— REPORT?"

"Skies clear, no signs of the enemy. S-144, out."

"Roger; *Avenger*, over and out."

* * *

"COMMANDER—YOU really should get a look at this."

"On my way."

Suppressing the urge to scold his systems officer for disturbing his attempt at rest, Barnes rose wearily from his bed and strode through the door into the Main Corridor. The old frigate did not have the commander's quarters directly beside the bridge; in fact, there were no living quarters on the Conning Deck at all. The early engineers, to conserve life support resources, had arranged the ship to concentrate the crew's cabins just above the Engineering Deck. Unfortunately, this had the effect of doubling the time it took to muster all hands to stations, and it struck Barnes as loony to stick the ship's skipper where he'd have no chance to take a proper nap. By the time he made it to the bridge, he was in a foul mood. The goofy grins that greeted him when he stepped through the entry doors just made him testier.

"This way—sir, over here," Hodding, his first officer, beckoned him to the tactical monitor.

Barnes stomped over to the display screen. There he saw the Navy's two starships, doing nothing in particular as far as he could tell.

"You fools got me out of bed for this?" he demanded sourly.

"Wait," said Hodding. "Just wait."

A few seconds later the two ships began moving—slowly, silently through the sky, in single file, one slightly behind, to the side and slightly atop the other—only to come to a halt less than two astrometers later. After a short pause, they repeated the maneuver—this time, in a different direction, at an increased speed.

"They've been doing that for the last hour," said Addison, the systems officer. "For the life of me, I can't make heads or tails of it. Mr. Hodding says it looks like a mating ritual."

"Like the sea pigeons—there's no place for them to land," grinned Hodding. Barnes, too cranky to find anything very funny, was still curious. The Admiral wasn't one to waste time; this close to battle, he'd surely be concentrating on polishing any battle plans he might have. He thought a moment, then turned to the radio officer.

"Gates," he said, "scan the ship-to-ship channels. If they don't have this too badly scrambled we can listen in."

Gates nodded, and a few seconds later they heard the scratchy sounds of interstellar static, not quite obliterating the conversation between the two starship commanders who would lead the fleet to victory or disaster.

"With all due respect, sir— "

"Landis, you nitwit!"

They all recognized the voice of the Admiral.

"Straight—just steer your ship straight! That's all you have to do. Well not quite all, perhaps, but that should be quite sufficient for right now. Sail as straight a line as you can manage. I want to see exactly—and I mean exactly—how much range you can cover, if I'm off to the side, like this."

"I fail to see the purpose— "

"Just shut up and steer your damn ship, Commodore. I don't need you to see the purpose. For that matter, it takes at least three starships to run this maneuver properly, so we may very well be wasting our time after all. But as long as we still have the time to spare, we may as well try the one maneuver we can actually do together on such short notice. At the very least, it will help me get my timing down, as well as nailing down Kill Zone coverage for both of us. In other words, now that I think of it, it may actually *minimize* any wasted time and effort."

"I beg your pardon, Admiral, but in my opinion— "

"Just steer your damn ship, Commodore. On my mark."

"But— "

"Steer your ship. *Avenger*, out!"

As the communications channel faded into nothing, even Barnes couldn't help but chuckle. It was refreshing to see Landis get his comeuppance: before the Admiral's arrival, the commodore had always played the supercilious twit with the regular Navy. It was a welcome change to see Cook skewering Old Fusspot's pomposity.

Still, Barnes was curious about the exercise. Despite himself, he had to agree with Landis about one thing: there didn't seem to be much point in it.

"What do you make of all that?" Hodding asked him, grinning like a schoolboy. The two starships began gliding through the blackness once again, though the scene reminded Barnes more of mating whales than sea pigeons.

"I don't know, and I don't care," the commander replied. "I'm sure the Admiral has his reasons. If we survive the next few days, maybe we can ask him. Until then, back to work.

"Mr. Hodding, you have the chair. I'll be in my quarters."

* * *

"AVENGER, THIS is S-449. Priority-one."

"Go ahead, four-four-niner."

"I'm in Sector 7. I'm reading movement on my screen. Looks like smaller craft. Scouts or escorts, I think. It's kind of hard to tell at this distance."

"S-449, please hold for the Admiral.... "

Bill Bohley took a deep breath. In the four months since he enlisted he'd been abused, prodded, and harassed almost beyond his endurance. Now he felt exhilaration like he'd never known before. He'd seen the Admiral twice: once at a physical training session, and once when the Admiral came to address his company during a simulator session. But he'd never had the Admiral's attention. And he never thought the man everybody called the Skipper would be interested in anything he had to say. Not in his wildest dreams. He looked at Tim Martin, his navigator; Tim was grinning from ear to ear and gave him a thumbs-up, signaling him to speak his mind, whatever goofy babblings might come gushing out.

Soon, a strong, clear voice called him back to reality.

"This is Admiral Cook. Who's on the line?"

"Lt. William Bohley, Sir."

"Bohley—who else is in your sector?"

"Two other scouts. Carter and Kruse in S-198, Vaillancourt and Schelling in the 979."

"All right—listen to me closely. You and Carter approach as closely as you can, remaining in constant contact with Lieutenant Vaillancourt. Watch out for enemy small craft, particularly escorts. The scouts can pinpoint your position, but the escorts are quick, maneuverable, and nearly as well-armed as frigates. Stagger your formation, and set up a communications relay, if you find it useful. I want information on formations, numbers, and precise locations. And if the Terran commander divides his fleet, I need to know immediately. From now until you're relieved, stay in radar contact with the Terran fleet. Stay undetected, if you can manage it. But I'm sure they know we're out here, and the intelligence you uncover is more important than staying hidden."

"Understood, Admiral."

"One more thing, Lieutenant: if you can manage it, I want to know exactly how many starships and cruisers we'll be facing. More than anything else, that will dictate our tactics, so the sooner I know, the better."

"I'll get the numbers, Admiral. One way or another, you'll have the information by the end of the day."

"Good luck, Mr. Bohley. I know you'll do your best."

"Thank you, sir. We're all doing our best."

"Then may you find a charmed star to guide you, Lieutenant. We're all going to need one very soon."

"I'll do my best about that, too, Admiral."

As he signed off, Bohley felt a wave of excitement. He had no illusions about the dangers they'd be facing. If they didn't stay hidden, the Terries would light the skies with them; but if they didn't do the job they volunteered for, the Terries would sack Isis in a matter of days. The Admiral didn't need to tell them that. Everyone understood it, with painful clarity.

He looked at his navigator and winked. "Ensign Martin," he said, a cocky grin on his face, "plot us a course, and let's get moving. The sooner we get started, the sooner we put it behind us—one way or another."

"Don't go regular Navy on me, Billy Boy. Not now. That's the last thing I need." Tim fiddled with his controls, readjusting his readings to the skies they'd be sailing.

"I'm as irregular as anyone."

"I don't know, Bill. Sounds to me like you're another one trying to shit granite all over everything. Just like the clowns in the frigates. Only one I know who can pull it off is the Admiral—and I bet even he doesn't take all that stuff seriously."

"Tim— "

"Course plotted, Bill. Just keep us away from the Terries."

* * *

COMMUNIQUE

Date:	cc:144.8012.5
From:	Adm. R.A. Cook
	Commander, Isitian Interstellar Navy
To:	I.N. McInnis
	Chancellor
Re:	Status Update

We have made radar contact with the Terrans. Morale is high; readiness is better than I envisioned. I expect to engage the enemy within the next two days.

This will likely be my last communication before the battle. I hope to be in a position to transmit a communication afterwards—but War, like life, is unpredictable.

Wish us luck.

COOK LEANED over the shoulder of Jarvis, his radio officer, and reread the communication one last time. It was sterile and a tad pretentious, but he had more important things to worry about than polishing his writing.

"Send it," he ordered. "Then broadcast the stand-by command to the advance scouts." He turned toward the entry hatch and strode down the ramp.

"Mr. Nielsen,," the Admiral said brusquely, "take the chair, and page the second team to the bridge. The rest of you, stand down until further notice.

"And Nielsen— "

"Admiral?"

"I'll be in my quarters. I am not to be disturbed, except on the Commodore's say-so. Anyone who tries will be thrown in the brig—or shot." Cook turned and strode from the bridge, leaving his crew puzzled by his abrupt change in manners. As usual, he left it to Janet to explain.

"He's going into seclusion, until the eve of battle," she said at last. The rest of the crew simply nodded their heads.

"Plotting our strategy?" Nielsen said, knowingly, rising from his place at the weapons station.

"No," Janet replied, smiling. "Just going to sleep. I suggest the rest of us follow his example. He'll need us all alert and rested, if we're to have a chance at pulling this thing off."

Chapter 11

RANGE?" BOHLEY LOOKED at his navigator; Tim Martin quickly took a reading, and reported the findings.

"Terries are still half-a-parsec away, Bill. Not much detail from this distance."

"Damn!"

"Slow down. We don't want to draw their attention. Remember, their radar is a lot more sensitive than ours."

Bohley wiped the sweat from his brow. The enemy fleet filled the entire bottom half of his sensor screen. Through the blackness, the Terrans were still invisible to the eye. But they were there; he could feel their presence. He leaned forward and spoke softly into his communications microphone.

"Carter?"

"Here."

"You see any good vantage points?"

"Afraid not, Bill. There's that isolated nebula off the starboard beam, a few odd rocks here and there. Two small stars off to port—the Caldwell Binary. But I've been there, and— "

"I wouldn't want to hide there, either."

Bohley shook his head wearily. The Caldwell system was barren—two small red stars, barely bigger than a good-sized Jovian planet. They were running out of time, but there was nothing, not even a decent asteroid, to confuse any enemy radar. If the Terries got a whiff of them—

"Bohley to S-979," Bill called into his mike; Vaillancourt, the pilot of the S-979, would be monitoring their communications, but was not broadcasting toward the Terran positions.

"Vaillancourt, we're going to have to give this some thought. They'll spot us if we get much closer, and we can't tell anything from this distance."

"What do you think, Bill?" asked the navigator, his eyes large and worried.

"I don't know, Tim. I just don't know."

"INCOMING LONGWAVE transmission, Doug."

Instantly, Doug Reynolds was wide awake. Clapping his hands to summon the lights, he felt his eyes ache for a moment, as he struggled to find the intercom.

"On my way, Eddie," he said. Springing to his feet, he grabbed his trousers. Hopping as he donned them, he nearly crashed into the wall in the process. Once through the hatch, he sprinted from his cabin to the bridge.

This was a day he hoped he'd never see. Yet once he'd seen the Terry fleet sail past him, he knew it was inevitable. He'd reviewed the procedures a hundred times in his head. Now it was a simple matter of receiving the order and executing the command.

Arriving on the bridge, he glanced over the shoulder of his navigator. The signal was coming in, strong and clear, on Long Range Channel 12. Their briefing had been quite clear on the next part of their mission. Aside from providing information on enemy movements and strength, the advance scouts were responsible for disrupting Terran communications when the battle was imminent. To keep their position and intentions secret, the commands would come in the form of predetermined long-wave subspace radio signals. And the Admiral had reduced the possibilities to a sequence of single letters: "M" meant to cancel all orders and return home; since a cancellation of hostilities eliminated the need for secrecy, nobody expected to receive that command over long-wave radio, but the Admiral wanted to be thorough. "N" meant that trouble was coming, and all advance parties were to find a new hiding place and stay hidden until contacted again. "T" was a four-hour attack notice; and "E" meant to attack the Terran communications relays at once. Anything else was noise—or the enemy—and could be ignored.

He'd expected the Admiral to be broadcasting daily, if only to confuse the Terries. But the long-wave signals had been silent—until now.

"First signal duration—forty-five seconds," said Eddie, the navigator. "That makes it a long." Though short blasts usually lasted five or ten seconds, he recalled, anything over thirty seconds was considered a long; that eliminated the attack command: "E" for attack was one short signal; the others all began with a long.

With growing anxiety, the two men watched and waited. Long wave transmissions usually used two-minute segments between signals. The next signal would determine the message: another long, "M," meant they could go home; a short, "N" meant they should head for cover.

When two minutes passed without a signal, the two men looked at each other, sharing a worried look. Three minutes later, they had their answer.

The signal read "T": they had four hours to move into attack position.

"I guess it's starting," Reynolds sighed. Without another word between them, he began easing them into the open skies around the large star system they were using for cover, as Eddie plotted the course to the nearest Terran relay buoy. His team had isolated a half-dozen relay buoys that were floating freely in space, completely undefended. Yet though far away from the scene of fighting, he felt his heart beating furiously. Things would be getting very intense very soon. And the fate of his home, his family, and his future would be decided without him, a long way to the west.

Maintaining strict radio silence, he guided his ship into position to attack the nearest communications buoy. He and the rest of his team had already divided up the relays; by the end of four hours, they would all be within two minutes of their first designated target, awaiting the command to attack.

* * *

"BOHLEY?"

"Here."

"My computer confirms your estimate. Looks like two divisions from this side, as well. The troop transports throw off the precise numbers a bit, but not enough to change the overall picture."

"Any better luck with the array?"

"I get one starship confirmed. Nothing else. Can't even tell if the ships are cruisers or frigates. Not at this distance."

"Damn."

"I know, Bohley."

"Vaillancourt—if you're listening, relay the information to the Admiral and continue monitoring."

"Bohley— "

"I know, Carter. I know."

"That cloud down there might provide an escape. If we're lucky."

"If one of us is lucky, Carter. No need getting us both killed. At least, not at the same time."

"Any idea how we go about drawing straws through space?"

"How about reverse alphabetical order?"

"Nice try, Bohley."

* * *

"INCOMING MESSAGE from the scouting detail."

"Let me see." Janet leaned over the radio officer's shoulder and stared into the monitor. She was too nervous to relax; everybody but the Skipper was too nervous to relax. But good old Cook—ice water in his veins—was still sleeping like a baby.

Impatiently, Janet waited for the cryptography program to finish decoding the message. Finally, the screen showed the results:

```
///I/PRIORITY DISPATCH
/I/I/I/s-979 to ss-avenger/est t-fleet two divisions/unknown
array/troopships confirmed/one t-ss confirmed but info soft/will
proceed to better look/will update/s-979 vaillancourt lt over/
```

He was right again, Janet told herself. Two divisions—about 250 warships. They'd still be badly outnumbered, but at least the odds weren't hopeless. And with a little luck....

"Commodore?"

Janet looked down at the radio officer's upturned face.

"Good news or bad?"

"Hard to say," Janet smiled. She leaned against the console and took a deep breath. "Actually, it's good news, I guess. Two divisions are more manageable than ten. And two is exactly what the Admiral was expecting."

"Shall I page him with the news?"

"Heavens, no!" Janet exclaimed, surprised at how much better she felt, now that she had a better sense of the odds against them. "He'll lock us both in the brig if we do that. He's always cranky when he wakes up."

The crew laughed nervously.

"We'll wait until we have more information on the array," she continued. "He won't decide how to deploy our ships until he knows how many starships we'll be facing. I'd rather wait until then to wake him. We need him well-rested. As long as we have nothing to change his assumptions, I'd rather not disturb him."

Janet stretched, and walked back toward the command chair. Still too anxious to relax, she was having a hard time sitting still. Though it had driven her to distraction at times, at times like this she envied the Skipper's ability to sleep anywhere at anytime.

And actually, a bit of rest might do them both some good, she smiled.

"Mr. Wasser, take the chair," she announced blandly. "I think I'll try to get some sleep myself.

"Yes, Ma'am."

"Keep a sharp watch on the scouts, and an eye on the clock. I'll be back in two hours. If we've heard nothing by then, we'll consider dispatching another scouting detail."

"Roger."

BOHLEY LOOKED at the computer screen again. He didn't know whether to be glad for the chance to be a hero, or to curse his luck.

"Nine," read the screen; since he'd selected "even," it meant he drew the honors. He'd be the one dashing across the sky for a closer look at the Terries.

"Wish me luck," Bohley said at last.

"Break a leg," said Carter, trying not to jinx his companion, and struggling to keep the sense of relief out of his voice.

Starting to edge his sloop toward the Terry fleet, Bohley glanced at his navigator, who shrugged and shook his head. "Playing rounders, I always wanted to come to bat with the game on the line," said Tim.

"They don't shoot at you, when you're on the ball field."

"No...but then, there weren't any Earthers in the neighborhood."

Laughing as bravely as he could, Bohley came about and sent his ship hurtling toward the Terrans. "Keep the channel open," he said into the microphone. "I don't want you fellows to feel you're missing anything."

His heart pounding furiously, the young lieutenant watched his tactical screen for the first sign of trouble. He slowed his ship to a crawl, hoping to coast into position to take a good reading as the Terrans drew nearer. He passed in front of two distant star systems in short order, keeping along their solar plane as best he could, using the static from the stars to mask his presence. He knew that the Terran radar operators would be watching for the slightest sign of movement. Once past the second star, he had to pass into clear skies. It was only a matter of time before the Terrans realized that they had company.

AN ETERNITY LATER, the Terran fleet finally showed signs of life.

"Christ," Bohley muttered under his breath. He almost thought they'd make it; for twenty minutes, they'd managed to stay hidden. Twenty minutes, as he inched his way to within a thousand astro-kilometers of the Terran fleet.

Of course, one thousand klicks was the outermost limit of CosGuard's Class-C sensors. Five seconds after he crossed the line, the Terrans scrambled to respond: a heartbeat later, a squadron of frigates and a company of escorts were heading directly to intercept him. He fired his engines to come as close to the Terrans as quickly as he could.

"Watch the escorts," came Carter's voice over the speakers. "You might wriggle free of the frigates, but those escorts can nail you."

"Roger," said Bohley, trying to concentrate on his job, struggling hard not to think of the consequences of a wrong move. He looked at the tactical plot that Tim had put on the screen for him. On his present heading, the Terries would intercept him well before he'd anticipated. If he didn't do something, he'd never get close enough for a good reading. And if the Terrans realized he was heading toward the small nebula off to starboard, they could easily move to cut him off before he ever got there.

"Coming about," he said to his navigator.

"Oh, Jesus."

"Let's worry about one thing at a time, Tim. We need to get closer."

Bohley cut sharply to port, nosing the sloop directly toward the Terran fleet and coming well inside the Terrans' heading. There was, he realized to his horror, no turning back. But if the Terries were going to kill him anyway, he'd make damn sure the Admiral got his information.

"Into the valley of the shadow of death," Tim said grimly.

"I don't like it either."

Bohley gunned his engines to full throttle. Gritting his teeth until they hurt, he forced any tears of regret back into his eyes.

"Watch the monitors," he told his navigator. "I won't need you until we start heading toward the nebula. And I sure as hell don't want us to miss anything."

"Roger."

Bohley focused his eyes on the tactical display. He couldn't see enough out the forward windows to matter, and he wanted to know exactly how the Terries were moving in for the kill. He saw the escorts split into five squadrons, and circle round to cut off his lane to the cloud. Meanwhile, the frigates, larger and less maneuverable, moved in for the kill.

Interesting, he thought. They don't think they need the added flexibility. It appeared to be something of an insult, he smiled glumly. All it did was make him angry.

"Range, seventy-five klicks," said Tim into the radio. "Sensors show a second starship. Entire enemy fleet is formed into a single battle wedge, with the starships in support behind the point."

Bohley saw the frigates moving toward him at flank speed. Racing his own engines at full throttle as another company moved to intercept him, he realized that in a few moments he'd be within full sensor range of the entire enemy fleet.

"Fifty klicks," said Tim, "and no cruisers showing yet—wait! I show three starships, repeat three starships showing at thirty-five, thirty...still no cruisers."

Suddenly, two more companies of frigates broke away from the main body of the Terran fleet, heading straight toward the lonely Isitian scout.

"Breaking off," barked Bill into his microphone. "Tim— "

"S-449 breaking off approach at twenty-two klicks," said the navigator, working furiously to plot the direct course to the nebula and safety, his heart knowing that they were dead men. He slammed into the side of his seat as the small ship veered desperately to starboard. Holding tightly onto his speakerphone, his fingers worked feverishly at the console as he broadcast one last report into the heavens.

"Enemy strength confirmed at two divisions, Standard Formation; three—repeat, three—starships. No cruisers—repeat, no enemy cruisers in formation. Ten troop transports confirmed, twenty-percent probability of more. Give our best to the Admiral—and wish us luck."

"We'll need it," Bohley muttered under his breath. He gunned his engines to maximum speed, heading directly toward the wispy cloud that was the only cover for three parsecs in any direction

"We'll need more than luck," Tim said grimly.

THE STARS hung in the sky like distant jewels. In the broad clearing that led toward the Great Nakahashi Cloud, the one-sided pursuit marked the first excitement the small Terran fleet had known since their last night of liberty at Zarathustra Command.

As the Isitian sloop made its frenzied dash for safety, the Terrans calmly slipped into position. Realizing that the rebel ship's only hope was to make it to the small, reddish gas cloud hanging just west of the main body of the fleet, the Terran commander ordered his escorts to form a barricade line one astrokilometer east of the nebula, and sent his remaining interceptors toward the enemy scout. It seemed like overkill to the rest of the attack force, but their commander knew that other Isitian scouts were probably watching, and wanted to give them something to report back to their own feckless leaders. If they made an example of this one scout, it might even eliminate the need for the entire exercise—although it would be hard to restrain the Army commanders from practicing their troop landings, and some of the rookie frigate skippers would not appreciate coming all this way for nothing.

As the Terrans closed on their quarry, the small sloop raced headlong toward the line of escorts standing as a picket between its two-man crew and the safety of the nebula. In desperation, the scout began dropping decoys, scattering debris along its wake, hoping to divert the approaching Terrans from their pursuit. But the Terran frigates and attack escorts kept on a tight intercept course, drawing nearer—nearer—until they were seconds from firing range.

Suddenly, without warning, the Isitian scout cut its engines and immediately slowed to sublight speed, dropping off the Terran's subspace radar. Half of the frigates slipped past, their skippers too slow to react to the rebel's cunning change of tactics. But all the escorts were able to come about before racing out of range. Soon the skies were flooded with Terran attack ships, combing the heavens for signs of the lone enemy scout, filling the sky with their sensor probes, knowing that the pristine clarity of the surrounding void would be the death of their quarry.

Their search did not last for long. Apparently realizing that it was only a matter of time before he was discovered, the scout fired his engines again, accelerating toward the safety of the nebula with all the power he could muster. From all sides, Terran guns blasted at the small ship as it bolted; within a second, the small rebel ship was consumed in a fireball.

A signal from their fleet ordered them back to formation, and the Terrans slipped through the blackness toward their fleet, leaving ashes and scattered debris to mark their enemy's passing.

But among the debris left unattended was a small, box-like object, ten meters across, ejected with an unseen load of chaff just before the ship's autopilot took over. Its tiny thrusters, like its distress beacon, was dormant for the moment—and its two terrified occupants were left alone to pray in the darkness that the twenty days of air and water they had in their lifeboat would be enough, and that help would find them before they were left to wander through Eternity, as cold as the blackness of space.

* * *

"A<small>DVANCE SCOUTS</small> should be into position to kill enemy communications by now, Admiral."

"Two divisions is nothing to sneeze at, Commodore."

"But if you consider— "

"As the Admiral said, we're not going against their varsity."

" —but on the other hand— "

Standing a short distance from the conference table, Cook's mind was a million parsecs from the situation room. He didn't notice the chattering of his subordinates, and paid no attention to the passage of time. His entire being was focused on the holographic star map in front of him, and on the message relayed from the scouting team.

He looked down at the piece of paper once again:

///I/PRIORITY DISPATCH
/I/I/I/s-979 to ss-avenger/confirm t-fleet at two divisions std battle formation speed c-10/confirm ten transports 25% probability of more/confirm no enemy cruisers/confirm t-ss at 3/ close approach 21.9ak/s-449 observed destroyed by t-intercept/s-979 vaillancourt lt over/

Cook made a mental note that, dead or not, the scout crew obtaining the information deserved a medal. Coming within spitting distance of the enemy fleet like that was so foolhardy as to be heroic.

But that was in the future. The distant future. For now, his Universe was the threat to his planet, and he was drawn to the specifics of what his scouts had told him:

The Terrans had no cruisers in their attack wing.

And they had three starships.

Three starships.

As his command staff analyzed all the available data, from all available angles, Cook quickly dismissed most details from his mind.

Three starships.

Oblivious to everything but the star map, he began visualizing the battle, struggling to discard every preconceived thought he had about the Cosmic Guard and interstellar war, every contingency he'd envisioned about Terran battle plans and tactics, every idea and anything he'd ever done in any battle in the past.

None of that mattered now.

Three starships; three starships and no cruisers.

His staff kept debating the possibilities, prattling endlessly as they analyzed and re-analyzed the information they'd received. But Cook wasn't interested in anything they had to say. He was no longer planning simply to turn back the Terrans. That was past history and not worth remembering at the moment.

In his mind, he was even not visualizing victory. Not any longer. Projecting his imagination into the skies around him, the prospect of merely stopping the Terrans had faded into the background.

Three starships, no cruisers, and ten transports.

He was imagining a rout.

Chapter 12

A VENGER, THIS IS S-917. Priority-one."

"Go ahead, nine-one-seven."

"I see movement in Sector 3-Alpha. Looks like the main body of the enemy fleet, nearing the eastern approach to the Gap on Heading 752, north 5 degrees."

"Range and speed?"

"I show them approximately one-half parsec from the opening, maintaining a steady C-11—repeat, Cee-One-One. Estimate arrival time in the Eastern Channel in 2.5 cosmic hours. No change in reported enemy formation. Still no trace of enemy scouting in this sector. I am proceeding to a safer location, further off their projected course heading, and will continue monitoring from a distance. I estimate my safe broadcast time remaining to be seventy-five minutes."

"Nine-one-seven, you are ordered to cease all transmissions in fifty minutes—repeat, five-zero minutes. Please acknowledge."

"Roger that, *Avenger*. Five-zero minutes to radio silence. S-917 over."

"Keep us posted until then, nine-one-seven. *Avenger*, over and out."

* * *

"HURRY, COMMANDER!"

Barnes hopped down the corridor, pulling at his boots as he scurried to the bridge. He tried not to think about how much he hated the engineers who designed his ship, but it was quite apparent that whoever was responsible for the layout of this frigate had a warped sense of humor. Sticking the crew's quarters on the wrong end of the rusting old frigate was bad enough. But putting the head at the far ends of the corridor—especially the far end of the Conning Deck—didn't strike him as the least bit funny.

"It's him, Commander."

Christ! thought Barnes. He paused to take a breath. There was no reason to panic, he kept repeating to himself. It seemed as if he'd been training for this for ages. And he'd brought these present burdens entirely on himself. Nobody made him spend so much time practicing the art of starmanship. For that matter, the only fool he could blame for being in the Navy in the first place was the idiot who looked back at him every day in the mirror.

Striding boldly through the hatch, Barnes paled when he looked up at the monitors. The entire command staff was staring at him from the communications screens—the command staff, and all the frigate squadron leaders. The look of impatience on the Admiral's face told him that the whole Navy was about to have some very rough days in the very near future.

"Thank you for joining us, Commander," said Cook, peering regally from the monitor.

Feeling himself blush, Barnes knew that trying to explain his delay would only make him seem even more foolish.

"If we can now proceed to the matter at hand," Cook continued, his stern image fading to a tactical projection of the outermost pass through the storms. The screen showed the twin bottlenecks of Gutterman's Gap—the wide, eastern passage, opening to the narrows of Parson's Ridge; and the narrower western passage near the Paddington Shoals.

"As you can see, the Terran fleet is about to enter the eastern end of Gutterman's Gap," Cook said sharply, his voice crisp with confidence. As the Admiral's voice gained intensity, Barnes found his fear vanishing.

"I'm positioning the smaller craft at various locations throughout the western passage, just west of the shoals at Paddington. I'm detaching one squadron of frigates—Mr. McAllister, it will be your squadron—to be my personal detachment. Your mission is to keep the small fry away from me."

Barnes saw McAllister pale, and take a deep breath before venturing his question.

"How do I—?"

"I don't care how," Cook snapped. "I leave those details to you, but I suspect we'll all be very busy. Even if everything else is going smoothly, you'll probably have one of the day's toughest assignments. I've yet to fight a battle where the enemy didn't come gunning for me, and I have no reason to believe this one will be any different. I've assigned myself quite a tall order of things to do, and—immodest as this sounds—even if we can't win this thing without me, I can't do it all by myself. Your mission is to watch my tail and my flanks, and do your best to keep the enemy frigates from slipping close enough for a cheap shot. Once I've accomplished my main missions, I'll release you to something easier. That is, If you're still with us."

McAllister's jaw locked firmly; Barnes could see the fire in his eyes. "Yes, sir. We won't let you down."

"Barnes?" Cook's eyes turned until they bore right into the soul of the young officer.

"Sir!" Barnes felt the words come out before he realized he was speaking.

"You are the company commander for all the remaining frigates. Your assignment is twofold."

"Yes, sir."

"First, you will take a position here— "

Barnes looked at the tactical monitor; the Admiral had moved the cursor to the west-center edge of the Gap.

"—on our right flank. At the outset of the engagement you will stand fast with the *New Alexandria*, keeping Mathieson's division of sloops between you. Don't move—don't move at all—until the enemy comes within spitting distance. When the command comes to attack, I want you to hit a company of enemy frigates—hard!"

"Yes, sir. Which company?"

"Any damn company will do, Commander," Cook said impatiently. "Pick the closest one, and hit them—hard, damn hard—and keep attacking until our jamming begins. Until it actually begins."

"Jamming?"

Shaking his head, Cook snorted and continued.

"I will be giving two commands on unsecured channels to all ships. The first—'Jam'—is your signal to attack. It has other meanings for other companies, but that won't concern you. But do note this, Mr. Barnes—it means nothing to the communications ships. Nothing at all. The second command—'Commence Jamming

Now'— is their order to commence jamming operations, and your command to disengage as soon as possible, and redeploy your forces."

"Disengage—??"

"Disengage, Mr. Barnes," Cook said harshly. "In other words, pull back and redeploy, on the signal: `Commence Jamming Now.' "

"Commence— "

"It may have other things mixed in, Commander, depending upon how the mood strikes me. But the signal—'commence jamming now'—those three words in that precise order— is your command to disengage the enemy and move into position here...."

His mind a hopeless jumble, Barnes felt panic creeping into his brain. He looked at the tactical screen. The cursor was at the extreme western edge of Gutterman's Gap.

"This is your primary assignment," Cook said. "You are assigned to defend this channel—Paddy's Pass, the western passage from Gutterman's Gap into the clear skies beyond. Until you are relieved, you will defend that pass *to the death*. Am I understood?"

"Yes, sir." Barnes was instantly alert. If he understood little else about his assignment, he understood the need to hold the western passage.

"You may take a position slightly to the east if you choose, to give yourself some wiggle room. In fact, I recommend that you do so, but I prefer leaving such details to the commander on the scene. The passage narrows to less than two astrometers near the end of the channel, which will let you keep the enemy in front of you at all times, gives them no room to maneuver, and will keep them from trying to turn your flank. I'll try to drive them away from you— eastward, and away from Isis. But mark this, Commander: you *cannot* permit the enemy to slip past you. That will compromise our tactical position and give them a clear approach to the Planet. This means that you may not retreat past the channel opening. And I expect you to hold your position to the last ship."

"I understand, Admiral."

"Commodore Landis?"

"Yes, sir."

"Once the battle begins, your mission is to occupy one enemy starship."

"Sir?"

"Just keep it busy until I'm able to come for it. I'd have no trouble, beating two starships," Cook smiled wanly. "I think I'm the only starship skipper who's ever done so—even if it's only been on the computer. But I can't always beat three, so I'll need you to pin one of them down for me. Once I've dispatched her companions I'll come relieve you, and decide your new assignment at that time.

"And Commodore?"

"Yes, Admiral."

"Not to alarm you," Cook said, all humor gone from his eyes. "But in the event that my ship goes down, your assignment changes accordingly. You are to ram—repeat, ram—your enemy starship. And before you do, you will order our remaining frigates to ram any starships I may have left behind. I leave the details to you, if it comes to that."

His jaw set firmly, Landis took a deep breath before replying.

"Yes, sir."

"One last thing."

Cook's fierce eyes and unswerving manner filled Barnes with hope and abject terror. The young commander had never seen such bitter resolve on anyone's face in his life. None of them had. Each of them hoped that they'd never see such cold fury in anyone's eyes again.

"Once our jamming operation starts, every Isitian ship will broadcast and monitor three channels—medium wave channels 124, 133, and 199. Our communications ships will be jamming those three channels randomly—and all other medium channels completely. Instruct your people to listen to all three channels, and to broadcast any messages on all three simultaneously—scrambled, but simultaneously. Any signal from a ship doing so should come through without trouble. Routine communications within or between units should be by short wave communications only—Channels 1015, 1019, 1022, 1044, 1045, or 1077. Those channels will be kept clear, and all other short wave channels will be blocked, as soon as the fighting starts. And be sure all transmissions are scrambled; the scramble pattern we've programmed will duplicate static until it's decoded, so if we're lucky the Terrans won't be able to crack our communications until it's too late. All IFF transponders will be set to the signal 'Lilac'—in honor of the season back home. Be sure your people get the signals straight."

Cook leaned back in his command seat. For the first time since he'd arrived, Barnes noticed, the smugness had vanished from the Admiral's bearing.

"This last point is rather important," he said quiety. "Our only chance in this whole affair is to keep the enemy confused, for as long as possible. I will move as quickly as I can manage through the enemy ranks, slicing them up as best I can. But once the fighting starts, I can't always take a second look at the ships I'm shooting at. So everyone—and I mean everyone—had better have our communications protocol mastered. When the dust settles I'd rather not have any Isitian souls on my conscience. If we lose communications, I'll issue a signal—the letter `M'—in long-wave Morse code, followed by a three-digit number. The number will be a numeric anagram of a medium-wave channel, and all ships will tune to that channel for further instructions."

"Questions?"

Barnes was amazed to find himself speaking out. "What about the small craft, Admiral? After all the time we spent drilling with them—"

"The small craft are not your concern at the moment, Mr. Barnes. Your own assignments should keep you busy enough, especially once the enemy starts shooting at you. I'll be giving them their own assignments in a moment."

"But shouldn't we know that they're doing? I mean, just for the sake of...."

Smiling patiently for the first time since the briefing began, Cook shook his head and chuckled softly. When his gaze returned to the screen, Barnes saw an ironic twinkle in the Admiral's eyes.

"Mr. Barnes," he said, his eyebrows arched wryly. "I'll let you in on a State secret, one that I expect everyone here to guard with his life. I expect I'll use them to confuse the enemy about our intentions, tactics, and numbers. But Mr. Barnes, until I see how the enemy reacts I can't be sure just what I'll have them doing. I have a lot of ideas bouncing around my head on how to use them, and I do know, more or less, where I want to put them. But I won't be sure exactly what I want them all to do until I finally give the command. And that, Commander, is God's own truth."

* * *

"R-1277, OVER and out."

Lt. Randy O'Dell was sweating as he looked at the monitor screen. He tried his best not to think about the future. Thinking just made him worry, and worrying only made him sweat even more.

"Move into position?"

O'Dell turned to look at his navigator, who was sitting at his post; the rest of their 6-man crew gathered behind him. The Admiral's orders were still echoing in his brain: once in position, all radio ships were to maintain their location. If the enemy approached, they should cease transmitting and hope for the best.

They can quickly trace you to a cubic astromillimeter, the Admiral had said. After that, they'd have to rely on their sensors, or track you down foot by cubic foot. In the heat of battle, they probably won't have time to acquire a target, if the ship stayed motionless and didn't broadcast a peep.

That might well be true, O'Dell thought to himself. But the prospect of staying calmly in place while the Terries milled about trying to kill him was not a pleasant one. As they monitored the transmissions and movements going on around them, it was obvious that they wouldn't have to wait much longer.

"Come about," he said suddenly. The sharpness in his own voice surprised him, and let him hope that the rest of his crew wouldn't notice how frightened he was. "Heading 490; lay our relay buoys behind the regiment, then move into battle position just east of the last company of small fighters."

"Aye, aye."

"All right, people—Isis needs heroes, not a gaggle of hens. Vinnie, you ready the buoys; Papineau, stand by the airlocks. The rest of you, stand by to check the relays.

"And double-time—move it!"

* * *

"F-3766, ACKNOWLEDGED. Alpha Company, this is Blue Leader; fall into position, Block-L formation—Blue and Green take the tail, all others, take the base—mark."

"Green-2, acknowledged."

Greg Garrity, of Division Green, Naval Militia, watched his tactical monitor as the rest of his company moved into their assigned formation, easing his ship into position. The red clouds of the Nakahashi storms loomed menacingly in the distance. Ahead of them to the east, the shoals lay hidden, a grayish dusting on the face of the giant, swirling gasses that stretched out toward the approaching Terrans. Out his viewing window, he could see hundreds of tiny ships slicing through the dark skies. He had no idea what was planned; he doubted that anyone did. As far as he could tell, the Admiral seemed to be stringing fighter brigades randomly throughout the clearing. And as he studied the pattern of movement on his sensor screens, he could detect nothing to ease his fears. The small crafts designated as fighters darted toward their assigned locations for the coming battle, but their puny guns could never decide the outcome. For all their numbers, they could never stand against Terran warships.

"Image enhancers checked," called Tommy Reed, navigator and first officer on the tiny schooner. "Shields checked...primary guns checked...."

As his crew went down the checklist, Garrity entered it all on the ship's log. It seemed a waste of time. Nothing they did would make the slightest difference. Fighting his feelings of hopelessness, he remembered his mother and father back home—how they'd both wept uncontrollably as he stepped off toward the transport deck that would send him up to the Navy. He'd thought them mawkish and sentimental when he'd hugged them goodbye; he'd had to pry his mother's arms from around his neck. And his dad, the same man who seemed cold as a stone when his grandparents passed away, had a throat so tight he couldn't utter a word through the flood of tears that flowed down his weathered cheeks.

That was months ago, Garrity reflected. Nearly a lifetime ago. Back when a twenty-year old could actually think he knew everything life had to teach him. Now, he'd give anything to touch them one last time.

"BLUE LEADER to Green Leader—get your squad moved back toward the base of the 'L.' I don't want that big a gap between us and the rest of the company.

"And Red Leader, get your people lined up, for crying out loud. We've got company coming, in case you've forgotten. The Admiral wants our tables neat, and our knives sharp and ready for them."

"Roger, Blue Leader. We don't want them to think we're slobs as well as sissies."

"Let's just keep our end of the table straight. The Admiral will set the Terries straight on the rest."

* * *

"BARTA'S BRIGADE reports all ships in position."

"Sheiko has his ships moving toward the western pass. He estimates they'll arrive in another five minutes."

"Alberts reports the communications buoys are arrayed along the southern end of the channel."

Cook paid little attention to the progress reports as they arrived. Standing by himself, away from the buzzing activity around the monitors in the Situation Room, he kept quiet as each new communication arrived, confirming that his rag tag fleet was slowly moving into position for the coming fight. His eyes focused on the large projection of the local skies. He watched as *Avenger's* sensors converted the movements of the tiny ships into small points of light, and placed them in their proper place on the holographic map. He'd gone through this before every battle, watching his people deploy, following their every movement to make sure they were positioned properly. As in the past, everyone was counting on him for a miracle, and thousands were ready to die on his command.

But this time was different.

This time, the stakes were incalculably higher.

And this time, he knew each and every soul on every ship.

"Admiral?"

Noticing the change in Jarvis's tone of voice, Cook turned to face his young radio officer.

Young, he mused—not that any of the faces around him were old. Except for himself, of course: suddenly, he felt as old as Methuselah.

"What is it, Mr. Jarvis?" Cook's voice was stern and unforgiving. War was no time for sentiment. And if his world was going to survive, his own mortality would have to wait a bit longer.

"You wanted to know when the last of the Terries have slipped into the Eastern Pass? The scouts report— "

Without waiting for the young man to finish, Cook bent down to speak into his communications cylinder. He pressed the setting for Universal, broadcasting his words to the entire fleet.

"This is the Admiral," Cook said, speaking slowly, to give his people time to realize the gravity of what he was saying.

"The enemy is almost upon us, and I'm about to move to my own assigned position to await them. This will be the last time I speak to all of you before the battle, and the last time I speak at all to some of you."

Unconsciously, Cook began pacing about the command room, oblivious to anything but the star map and his thoughts.

"I know you're all frightened, and hoped this day would never come. What awaits will be the most terrifying experience of your life—but also, if you live to tell about it, the most exhilarating. We have the chance to save not only our world, but also everything we have ever hoped to be, or dreamed of becoming. Our enemy has a reputation for invincibility and, with few exceptions, has been unstoppable. But this reputation is built on sand—and I, better than anyone else in this Universe, know exactly how to beat them.

"I'm not planning just to stop them. I intend for us to humiliate and destroy them. I know how to do it, but I can't do it alone. I need the courage and daring of each and every one of you, to pull us through. I've trained you all, and I know what this Navy of ours can do. If we face them, strong, united, and brave, whatever the odds against us, we will not fail."

"Don't think of the forces we'll be facing; think instead of their weaknesses—and their weaknesses are legion. CosGuard Central Command is staffed by fools, and their fleets are commanded by idiots. They react slowly in times of crisis, and rely upon brute strength to win in battle. Neutralize that strength and they will founder about, as helplessly as fish on dry land. Their weaknesses become our strengths. And beyond that, we come to this fight not as invaders, but to save our homes and families—all of whom need us every bit as much as we need each other.

"I can't promise that we'll all return home to the hero's welcome that awaits us. But death will come to all of us, one day; if not today, then perhaps tomorrow. Our fight today is for freedom, and decency, and civilization. This fight is one of philosophy as much as courage, and can never be won by pointless sacrifice or mindless slaughter. But if Fate decrees that today is your day to die—or mine, or someone else's, down the line—let's promise each other that every death of ours will count for something good in this Universe."

Cook looked up to see the faces of his command staff, silently watching their commander speak what was in their own young hearts. Looking from face to face, he continued speaking into the transmitter.

"May we meet again, at the battle's end," he said, his eyes softening for the briefest of moments. "And may God sail with each of you."

In an instant, Cook's eyes blazed with the fire of battle, and his voice rang with the steel of command. Changing the setting on his radio, he paged the bridge.

"Janet—sound battle stations," he said gruffly. "Come about to heading 595, and take us into the edge of the clouds. Just enough to mask our presence from enemy sensors."

"Yes, sir," came the reply, over the speaker.

"Mr. Jarvis," Cook told his radio officer. "Inform Division Green to take cover in the western rim of the Paddington Shoals. They're to wait among the rocks until the last enemy ship passes the rocks, into the western channel. They're not to budge—not even if they're attacked—until they see us leave the clouds. And then they're to move, quietly as possible, directly toward the rear of the Terran fleet."

"Yes, Admiral."

"Then radio the *New Alexandria*, and tell Commodore Landis to broadcast the attack signal to the advance scouts. It's time to cut their communications."

"Aye aye, sir."

* * *

EIGHT SECONDS."

Looking at his navigator, Reynolds took a deep breath and leaned back in his seat. Without another word, Eddie put the final course plot to the Terran relay buoy on the tactical screen, and pressed the switch to activate the ship's guns.

"Guns charged," he said, when the red light appeared.

Moments later, the young men watched as the remnants of Relay Buoy 4 briefly lighted the skies. Without a word, they moved the ship off to port, heading toward Relay Buoy 3 and their next assignment.

* * *

STANDING BY the giant bay window overlooking the gardens that filled the southern yard of her official residence, the Chancellor reread Cook's latest message. She had gathered her senior staff together to go over the last details of their contingency plans, in case Cook proved to be no miracle worker. But by the 14th of May, Isis was overcome with lilacs, filling the air with the fragrance of Spring. Looking out over the lilacs in bloom, feeling their sweetness at work even through the walls of the mansion, she found herself unable to concentrate on anything beyond the words of the man who held the future of Isis in his hands. So she'd cancelled the meeting and, except for those few ministers she considered friends, dismissed everyone for the day.

It was, she told them, a day for friends and family. And so, she kept George McKenzie, her friend from the old days, and Reggie Ross, her protégé for the future, close at hand. She told them to send for their own families—and had the servants and personal staff send for their loved ones as well, to spend the night at the mansion. Nobody should be by himself today. Nobody should have to face the morning alone.

Unfolding the paper, she read the message once again.

COMMUNIQUE

Date:	cc:144-8014.1
From:	Adm. R.A. Cook
	Commander, Isitian Interstellar Navy
To:	I.N. McInnis
	Chancellor
Re:	Final Thoughts

I have finished deploying our forces, and have given the order to cut Terran communications with their base. The battle will begin at any moment.

I am sure we have all, in the past, recalled the proverb which says that Heaven protects lunatics and small children. I had long hoped to find some mention of Isis, if only in a footnote. My wife, however, tells me that I qualify on the first two counts, as well, so I suppose it should make no difference to the outcome.

"Well, George," she said at last, "I suppose there's nothing to do but wait."

"Well, there is that old subspace radio in the storage cellar," the defense minister chuckled. "It's a tad past its prime, but it may still work if we can get the staff to dust it off a bit."

"You mean, we can listen to the battle? I'm not sure I have the nerve."

"We'll be lucky to raise a signal on the damn thing," McKenzie laughed. "Between the blasted radio, and the Nakahashi storms, we may not get much of a signal. Even if we do, we'll be lucky to make sense of anything. But at least it will give us a way to pass the time."

Shaking her head doubtfully, the Chancellor closed her eyes, and wished that when she awoke it would all be a bad dream.

"Why not?" she said at last. "Why not, indeed?"

Chapter 13

THE CLOUDS OF NAKAHASHI, blood-red and mottled by dust and swirling clouds, loomed menacingly in all directions, punctuated by an occasional flash of interstellar lightening.

As the Terran fleet entered the eastern channel of Gutterman's Gap, their commander cast a wary eye on the shoals that lay ahead of them. The Donnelly Shoals stretched into a clearing that ballooned nearly as far north as the entire gap was long. It was the perfect spot for an ambush: the broad length of the shoals was a perfect hiding spot for an enemy fleet, and the rocks narrowed the channel to only five astrokilometers. It would provide some room to maneuver, but not enough for the invaders to do anything but plow straight ahead, into the clearing at the heart of the storms.

When their scouts reported the channel clear, the Terrans marveled at their good fortune. The Isitians, it seemed, were too inept at warfare to pick the right spot for a battle, for the only other place for a stand was near the other set of shoals—the Paddington Shoals, a long, thin stretch of rocks and ice that guarded the passage into the western channel. Once into the clearing, the Terran scouts quickly raced ahead, taking a vantage point well inside the Gap. There they saw the Isitian fleet, waiting for them halfway down the western channel.

Aside from a single starship, the scouts reported just three companies of frigates, all arrayed south and center of their flagship. The Isitians were well past the narrows at Paddington, and had taken a position to defend the narrow passage opening into the clear skies leading to the rebel planet. It seemed that the 'Sissies were determined to fight, but the mispositioning of their forces promised that the battle would be as short as it would be one-sided.

The Terran commander noted that passing into the clouds seemed to have severed communications with the base at ZarCom. All the same, he saw no need to worry. His orders were direct and to the point: occupy the planet, and crush any resistance by any means necessary. There would be plenty of time to reestablish the relay once the renegade planet was secure.

* * *

"TERRIES ARE into the clearing, Commodore."

Landis nodded his head, and closed his eyes. His heart was exploding, and he felt warm and very weak.

But his orders were clear: do nothing. Do absolutely nothing. Wait for the Terries to enter the western channel, but do nothing in the meantime.

"Companies Alpha-1 and Bravo-1 report engines starting to overheat," reported Ehrlich, the radio officer.

"Tell them to stand down on the enhancers," Landis replied. "Give them a mark, and have them switch with their seconds."

"Aye aye, sir."

Well, he smiled to himself, almost nothing.

"Alpha-2 and Bravo-2, ready your enhancers; Alpha-1 and Bravo-1, prepare to stand down. All ships, execute on my command."

Landis leaned back in command seat of the *New Alexandria*. He hoped the deception would work. For months, he'd thought Cook a fool for spending so much time and money retrofitting the tiny ships of their Naval Militia. But he had to admit that the Admiral was right about one important thing: imaging technology had spent hundreds of years minimizing the subspace radar images of warships—trying to hide the presence of a starship from an enemy, real or imagined, or making a band of pirates think a frigate was an ore freighter. Nobody ever thought much about using a ship's engines to inflate its image on a radar screen.

"All ships—execute."

At least, Landis chuckled to himself, not until Admiral Cook.

"MOTHER OF GOD— "

"Steady, Lund."

"—Mother of God— "

As his navigator faded in and out of lucidity, Lt. Jeff Jason watched his screens carefully. With each passing second, the Terran fleet edged closer and closer to his company. And each second took an eternity to pass. From their vantage, at the anticenter tip of the shoals, they could see the approaching Terran fleet. It looked huge. When he thought about exactly how few real warships Isis had, he wanted to close his eyes and be done with it all. It took all his strength of will to force himself to concentrate on what the Admiral had stressed in the training manual: fear is a paralyzer; hope is a liberator; and nothing—not even the prospect of death—is ever as hopeless as it seems.

Jason looked across the passage, toward the red clouds on the other side of the narrows. There, the Admiral was hiding with his ship, waiting for the Terrans to pass into the western channel. Once the last of the Terran fleet had passed, they'd have to force themselves out of their safe hiding place in the Shoals, and venture out into the open.

The young man stared at his screens. The Terran warships looked so big, so menacing. Armed and glistening in the darkness, the enemy fleet looked more powerful than he'd imagined. Every cell in his body screamed at him, begging him to stay safely hidden. Telling him how foolish it was to think that their rag-tag collection of broken frigates and pleasure boats could stand against the greatest war machine in human history.

He didn't want to do it.

He didn't want to think about it.

Instead, each time he felt his heart beat, he thought of his seventh Christmas—the toys and the singing, and the magic of a season when he was old enough to understand, but young enough to believe. And each time he took another breath, he savored it as if it were his last.

BARNES WATCHED the screens intensely, barely able to stay in his seat. Too agitated to sit still, he knew he couldn't leave his chair without distracting the rest of his crew.

"Addison?" he snapped.

"Range, five hundred klicks," responded the systems officer. "They're slowing to C-3 and drawing into a battle wedge."

"Are they past the bend?"

"Not yet. Some of their scouts may be through, but it looks like their point is just nearing the bend right now."

Barnes didn't hear the rest of the report. He'd heard enough to know that it would seem like forever before they could move.

The Admiral had been explicit: don't move; maintain position until ordered to attack. The waiting was driving him crazy, and he took no solace in the fact that the fighting might be even worse.

"Gates?" he barked at his radio officer.

"Nothing yet, Sir," Gates replied. "I'm watching all the channels, but I don't expect any word until— "

"I know," Barnes said, dismissing the young man with a wave of his hand. It was nobody's fault that there was nothing to report. But it was hard to stay calm when eternity was calling them, and time insisted on standing still.

* * *

As the Terran fleet neared the point of the Paddington Shoals, a small magnetic storm raging to the east sent ripples of interstellar lightening across wide stretches of the Clouds. Fanning out into a full battle wedge, the Terrans gathered their troop ships and support vessels to the rear, away from the likely point of battle, and posted one of their three starships beside them to stand watch. It seemed a needless precaution, but their commander didn't want to take any unnecessary chances with the ten shiploads of Terran soldiers they'd be landing on the rebel planet. Besides, it would provide a good vantage from which to steer the course of battle, and he wanted to let his two junior captains settle among themselves who should be the second-ranking starship commander. And so he assigned Captain Chen the left flank, and gave Captain Rodriguez the right—and told them that whichever side gave the best account would earn bragging rights for the rest of the mission.

For himself, he'd already seen enough action to last a lifetime. He'd been first officer on several ships of the line, up and down the Crutchtan front. And before his promotion, he'd helped Captain Stark and his battle group stick a few divisions up the Glinci's rear. Of course, that was when he commanded the *San Francisco*—a well-trimmed cruiser with a crack, veteran crew. Though he wouldn't share it with a single soul, he felt unprepared to be a starship skipper, let alone to command an entire invasion force. But that was one of the reasons why Central Command had tapped them for the assignment. With the challenges awaiting them on the alien fronts, they needed all the experienced skippers they could muster; and a practice exercise like this—using real, fully powered guns against an opponent who was playing for keeps—would be invaluable training for all of them.

Slowly, the Terran fleet edged forward toward the small rebel force sent to stop them—then stopped, just beyond the point at the edge of the Paddington Shoals. As the three starship commanders conferred on a plan of battle, the storms of Nakahashi raged around them, casting a dull, reddish glow throughout the length and breadth of Gutterman's Gap.

* * *

His own stomach dangling over a precipice, Barnes looked across his bridge. He saw panic in the eyes of his crew, and fear was etched into their faces. The Terrans, moving steadily toward them, now filled their forward screens. He had to do something—anything—to break the tension.

"Sound the klaxons," he told his radio officer. "And broadcast the order to all ships."

"We're already at battle stations. Everyone's at battle stations."

"Sound them anyway!" he thundered. "If we're going to charge headlong against that many ships, we can damn well make some noise."

As the alarms sounded, Barnes closed his eyes and took a deep breath. He didn't know how he was going to make it; he didn't know how any of them were going to make it, but there was no turning back. If they were going to die, they could do their best to make everyone back home proud of their last moments in this Universe.

Landis drew a deep breath and opened his eyes. The Terries were nearly to the designated point, and he couldn't delay things any longer. Swallowing to moisten his mouth, he cleared his throat and spoke as confidently as he could.

"Mr. Ehrlich, open a hailing channel," he said, drawing strength from the sound of his own voice. "Put the bastards on the screen. Let's all see the kind of rubbish the Terries are sending out to do their dirty work."

As his radio officer hailed the enemy flagship, Landis felt everyone looking to him to carry the fight forward. But the Admiral's instructions left little to his discretion: he was to order the Terrans to withdraw, but do nothing until the *Avenger* slipped behind them to cut off their retreat. Even then, he was supposed to wait for the Admiral's attack command before moving from his present position. None of it mattered now. Not the whispered doubts he heard down the corridors. Nor his own feelings of inadequacy when he compared his own skills to Cook's.

Nobody really knew what the Admiral had in mind for any of them. Though he'd had his own doubts about the Admiral and his plans in the past, Landis smiled to think that the blind faith the Isitian fleet had in their commander was, in the end, highly contagious. Every fiber of his being insisted that attacking a vastly superior force, a force outnumbering you tenfold, was madness. Particularly when you were sealing the only lane of retreat, and forcing it to fight. It made more sense to him to fight the Terrans by the Donnelly Shoals, ambushing them near the eastern passage where they couldn't see you coming, and had an easy way to escape if the battle turned against them.

But from the day Cook returned to Isis, Landis knew he just a bit player, fighting whatever battle lay ahead on the Admiral's terms. In a way, it was a relief not to have the responsibility. They'd all live or die with the Admiral, and if Isis needed someone to present a strong front to the enemy—keeping the Terries occupied, and their attention away from the door swinging shut behind them—then he'd be the best damn distraction in the Universe.

"Channel open, sir."

"This is Commodore Landis of the Isitian Interstellar Navy," Landis said, his thin face and graying hair contrasting with his strong, clear baritone, "commanding the Starship *New Alexandria*, to the commander of the unidentified fleet now on Heading 752. You are trespassing on space claimed by the Republic of Isis. You are ordered to identify yourselves immediately and give assurances of non-hostile intent, or prepare to suffer the consequences."

* * *

As GARRITY WATCHED his monitor, his palms were moist, and he felt droplets of sweat forming on his forehead. They were safe for the moment; the Terrans still hadn't seen them. The enemy fleet had lumbered past his position along the edge of the channel without beaming so much as a strong probe in their direction. Now his whole division was lined up along the enemy's flank.

Not that it was likely to do them any good—the thought kept forcing its way into his brain. Setting a thousand or so ships along either Terran flank wouldn't change the disparity in firepower. Not as long as it was sloops and schooners going against warships.

Big warships, his eyes told him, for the frigates were three-hundred yards long, and nearly half that distance across. Those powerful guns would shatter a sloop's meager shields with a single salvo. And Commodore Landis was hardly making the enemy nervous.

"You are in no position to be making demands," sneered the Terran commander. Garrity thought the Terran looked like he was enjoying himself: a tight smile seemed to betray his amusement that a collection of old CosGuard rustbuckets would dare stand against a full array of Terran firepower.

"You are only making things difficult for yourselves and your fellow cowards." the Terran continued. "If you won't do your duty without outside encouragement, you can hardly complain when someone comes to hold you accountable. And if you insist on upholding the treasonous designs of your planet's leadership, you will share in their destruction. You, and all the other blind fools on your miserable, self-important world."

"You are trespassing," replied Landis, his eyes cold and angry, his voice firm and defiant.

"And you are a traitor," came the cold, sinister reply. "A traitor, as well as a fool."

We're all fools, Garrity thought to himself. Every last one of us—the Terries as well. If any of them had an ounce of sense, they wouldn't be here, moments away from trying to kill one another.

As the two opposing commanders continued their verbal sparring, Garrity was on the verge of panic. Attacking the Terrans seemed like certain death; but turning and running would mean certain death for everyone he knew—back on his homeland, as well as those along-side him.

He wanted desperately to return home, to bury himself in the arms of the first pretty girl he found and stay there forever. The thought that he couldn't, the mere thought of leaving his friends stranded in the face of an enemy that would kill them if he left, made him angry. The realization that he wanted nothing more than to run and hide made him want to crawl into a hole and die.

"—AND ONCE AGAIN, Captain, I insist that you withdraw your forces, and go back to wherever you came from."

Landis paused a moment, and looked directly at his counterpart. Stalling for time, Landis hoped his uneasiness wasn't evident to his opposite number. He'd expected Cook to appear before now, and it was a constant struggle not to keep glancing toward his systems officer to check the ship's radar.

"You're beginning to bore me, Mr. Landis," said the Terran. "I suggest that you and your little party of daisy-sniffers stand aside and let us pass."

SITTING COMFORTABLY in his command seat, Cook rocked back and forth, contemplating the image on his communications screen. He knew the Terran commander; he knew him quite well, in fact. And the more he thought about how well he knew him, the angrier he got.

Angry at the Terrans, for coming to destroy everything he loved.

Angry at himself, for taking things so personally.

And angry at the Cosmic Guard, for promoting a twit like Ronald VanderMuelen to the command of a starship in the first place. Vandy had been one of his tormentors during his Plebe year at the Academy, Cook remembered. A bigoted dullard who thought Isitians were fit only for raising flowers and masturbating, and who ridiculed the only Isitian he'd ever met for splattering blood over the boots and fists of half the senior class. Vandy still ranked among the meanest, most ignorant people Cook had met in his life, and the Admiral found it deliciously ironic that Central Command would choose someone like VanderMuelen to command the fleet sent to conquer Isis. But with an idiot like Weatherlee now in charge of the Cosmic Guard, perhaps it made perfect sense, after all.

"Don't you think—, " Janet began, for the tenth time since they emerged from the clouds into the edge of the clearing.

"Just another moment," Cook interrupted, also for the tenth time. He didn't want to start things just yet.

He wanted to get a sense of how his old nemesis would react, when pressed; and so far, Landis seemed to be doing a remarkable job of goading the sub-moronic rotter.

Most of all, though, he didn't like the prospect of beginning this dicey a project with the old feelings of resentment swirling around inside him. It was better, he had learned, to act when his head was clear. Thoughts of revenge might have kept the young Plebe awake nights, many years ago. But if hatred was a powerful motivator, it could also make him careless.

Better to let things simmer, he told himself. If he calmed himself down, the added edge that the Twit's presence provided might make him sharper; the added personal score to settle would make victory all the richer. And, he smiled to himself, if he waited a little longer, VanderMuelen would probably give him the perfect entry line to make his appearance.

"Start easing us into the channel," he said at last, rising from his chair to stretch his legs. "One-quarter sublight, heading 040 by 2 points north. And Jarvis...?"

"Sir?"

"Stand by to cut in to Commodore Landis' hailing channel. And ready the signal for all ships to begin operations."

"Aye, aye."

TRYING HIS BEST not to show his discomfort, Landis felt himself sweating. It was obvious that he was stalling; and the Admiral was certainly taking his own sweet time before showing himself.

"You have no business in this sector, Captain. I demand that you leave immediately."

"Mr. Landis, I am at the end of my patience with you and your treasonous breed. You will either stand aside, or you will stand as targets for my gunners. Either way, I am declaring this charade at an end.

"If you choose to act rationally, we will post a guard to make sure you don't get yourselves into trouble. But you, Mr. Landis, have become tiresome and obnoxious. And since you have stopped being a source of amusement, I will not let you stand in our way any longer."

As Landis opened his mouth to reply, the image on the screen dissolved in a burst of static. When the static cleared, he was never so relieved to see anyone in his life.

"I can see that the years haven't improved your manners," Admiral Cook said in a pleasant tone of voice, his image smiling from every screen monitoring the channel.

Immediately, Landis signaled his radio officer to terminate his own transmission. Then he sank back in his seat, emotionally drained. He knew he'd have just moments before he was needed again.

COOK STARED into VanderMuelen's widened eyes, each sign of reaction etched into the Admiral's memory. The Terran captain's face was ash white, and Cook almost felt sorry for his old tormentor. But his instincts told him that he'd achieved his first objective: complete tactical surprise. The Terrans were obviously shocked to see him, and had no idea they'd be facing a second Isitian starship. All that mattered now was pressing his advantage, and blowing the Terrans from the skies before they had time to regain their wits.

"Hello, Vandy," Cook said coldly. "It's been a long time."

"You—you're supposed to be dead," VanderMuelen whispered.

"Sorry to disappoint you," Cook smirked, his eyes hard and menacing. "And I hate to seem inhospitable. But with your own patience at an end, it seems to me that we've been more than patient, as well. And so now, I have two things to say to you."

Cook's eyes narrowed mercilessly as he kept his gaze focused on his adversary's eyes. His voice dropped to a whispered snarl.

"The first thing, Captain VanderMuelen, is that you are not laying a finger on my planet. And the second is that if your entire fleet does not surrender immediately, you and most of your people are going to die."

"Once again, Midshipman Cook," VanderMuelen said, his face blushing as he fought to regain his psychological edge, "you overestimate yourself."

Glaring contemptuously into the screen, Cook snapped his fingers; immediately, Jarvis broadcast the command "jam" across all communications channels. A second later, the Terran radar screens showed the Terran fleet beset on all sides, surrounded by five divisions of Isitian frigates: one division just aft of Cook's starship, two divisions moving up beyond the *New Alexandria*—and a division lined up along either Terran flank.

Cook watched impassively as the enemy bridge dissolved into chaos, and saw VanderMuelen look about in confusion, from screen to screen to screen. Sensing the chance to disrupt the Terran's command lines before the battle began in earnest, Cook seized the moment to plant one last thought in the enemy fleet.

"Your choice is clear, Captain: you can surrender, or you can die. All Terran ships will be destroyed, unless their commanders drop their shields, drain their engines, and cease all operations.

"Cook, of the *Avenger*, over and out."

As the screen faded to black, Cook swiveled his chair to face his weapons officer.

"Nielsen—keep all shields at full strength; they're going to come after us with everything they've got.

"Helm—hard to port, bearing 990, at C-8. There's a starship on the Terran left flank—head for it, then slow to sublight when we come within five-hundred astrometers.

"Jarvis—repeat the command 'jam.' And repeat it over all channels every fifteen seconds until further notice. Tell all division commanders to switch enhancement brigades at their discretion—but not to let more than a hundred twenty-five of their own ships show on the screens at the same time. And tell Division Green to begin advancing toward the enemy's left flank; I want their first starship pinned, if we can manage it.

"Mr. Wasser—put enemy movements on the communications screen. The big one, up front. I want to know exactly how they're responding to all this—and I want everyone's attention. Quickly."

Cook looked sternly about the room. All eyes followed his every movement. His voice betrayed no trace of doubt, no hint of any emotion beyond unforgiving determination.

"My guess is that we have about twenty minutes before they reestablish their communications. By then, someone should have figured out that something's wrong with their screens, and that their sensors are feeding them false information. By that time we'd damn well better have the battle won. That gives us twenty minutes to take out their three starships. It means we've got to hustle—everyone's got to pull twice his own weight—and we can't afford a single screw-up on this end."

As Janet took the great ship racing toward the first enemy starship, Cook leaned back and closed his eyes. His heart pounded wildly in his chest. The die was cast, he told himself, and he was well aware of the stakes. He hoped he'd chosen wisely but knew it was too late for second-guessing. One way or the other, it was time for them to seize their fate; it was time for them to attack.

THE SIGNAL bell sounded at the radio console.

"Jam!" came the message, across the speakers—just as Addison, the systems officer, screamed another warning.

"Incoming fire!"

The ship shuddered under the impact of Terran guns. Barnes, shaking his head as he tried desperately to regain his wits, breathed a sigh of relief that he was still alive.

"Gates!!"

"Still nothing, Commander," came the reply. "They're still broadcasting the old signal."

Barnes took a deep breath to calm himself. This attack was not going well at all. In three minutes, they'd lost two ships—and he'd nearly succeeded in killing himself off, as well.

"Shields?"

"Still holding," said Hodding, the weapons officer. "But they're down to 70 percent. A few more blasts like the last one, and we'll be history."

Barnes glanced at the tactical monitor. Immediately, his heart sank, and he struggled to shake off his sense of growing alarm. This wasn't like the simulator at all. The Terrans weren't responding at all like the computer, and he couldn't freeze the frame, or replay the action if he didn't like the outcome. Nothing prepared him for watching people blown to bits, and it was impossible to do more than react to the Terrans' movements. Worst of all, he found himself too worried about his own ship to monitor whatever else was going on around him.

It was, he realized in a sickening moment of insight, a disaster in the making. They were fools to think they could stand against the Terrans. And there was no way out, no means of escape. They were all going to die.

Suddenly, the alert bell on the communications station signaled. Gates pressed the button to put the message on the speakers.

"All ships—this is Admiral Cook," came the message, in Cook's own voice. The Admiral sounded angry, and Barnes felt the blood draining from his brain.

"Commence jamming now, *dammit!*" the Admiral said, sternly; instantly, the transmission ceased and the channel fell silent.

"Commander— "

"I heard," said Barnes. "Give the command to withdraw to the rally point. Let's get the hell out of here."

"All channels now jammed," reported Gates. "Except for our designated communications network."

"Recalibrate communications," Barnes barked angrily.

"Recalibrating to make the adjustment."

As the Isitian ships came about, Barnes sent a squadron over to cover their retreat. After another flash of Terran guns, he saw Wes Hendrick's ship, the *Columbus*, disappear in a fireball.

Immediately, he thought of Jim Nelson, a junior gunnery officer on the *Columbus*. The two of them were in the same class at college—and once shared the same girlfriend for nearly a week, without knowing it. Part of him wanted to die, to end the pain of seeing friends dying around him. If it was hopeless anyway, perhaps a quick death was more merciful than a full day of torment.

Suddenly, something in the Admiral's message jolted him out of his torpor of self-pity. The Admiral sounded angry—as if his commands had been ignored. But he'd been very explicit about the matter—even specifying the exact wording of the command to withdraw, ahead of time.

Slowly, Barnes began to relax.

Perhaps things weren't out of control after all. If the Admiral's anger was just for show, he thought, maybe their attack was just for show as well.

"All ships ahead, flank speed," Barnes said, his voice and mind now firmly back under control.

And if their attack was just for show....

Barnes began to chuckle to himself. For the first time, the pieces were beginning to fall into place for him. For the first time, he saw in his mind a hazy outline of what the Admiral was doing.

And for the first time, he realized just how big a responsibility he'd been given—and just how important their initial, clumsy thrust toward the enemy had been: the one attack by a company of actual frigates, just before the Terries lost their communications.

"Mr. Addison, put a tactical display of the entire Western Passage on the screen. Let's see what we can do to guard this end of the box for the Admiral."

"CAN YOU TELL—?"

"I can hear— "

"Yes, but there's so much babbling on the line. And there's quite a lot of static. I think they're jamming most of the channels. How can anyone— ?"

The Chancellor tried her best to ignore the chattering of her companions. The mansion, dimly lit as the night passed toward dawn, was hushed as a graveyard, as everyone gathered around the small radio, listening to the tinny sound of transmissions coming through the Clouds.

It was fascinating, she marveled, her heart racing madly. The future of her world and its people was being decided in distant skies. And it was thrilling to be a witness to history, even if she didn't know whether she should cheer or vomit.

Of course, she hadn't the foggiest notion of what they were hearing, what was going on, or what any of it meant. None of them had a clue about tactics, or deployment. Even old George McKenzie, the defense minister, had to admit when pressed on the subject that he couldn't follow anything, either—though at times he thought he could pick out the Admiral's voice through the static.

But it was fascinating. Absolutely fascinating, nevertheless.

Chapter 14

EVERYWHERE ALONG THE LINE there was chaos.

"Enemy advancing, Commander. Range, two klicks and closing."

The young officer closed his eyes and fought the urge to panic. The neat, trim skirmish line he'd set for his ships had already dissolved into a dozen or more thin waves, with gaps between his companies widening by the minute. The Terrans approaching on his monitors were not coming to pay their respects. Under the strain of impending attack, he didn't know if he could hold everything together.

"Mr. Davis," he told his radio officer. "Signal Companies B, F, and G. Tell them to move off more to the right, so they'll be on the Terry flank when they pass. Hurry, now!"

"Aye, sir."

"First wave is reporting engine fatigue."

"Second wave, on line," the commander replied. "And tell G Company to stand by for my mark. "They'll be first up, on the flank."

"Yes, sir."

He should be off studying algae, he groaned. Or whales, or skuttlefish, or some other damn thing. He'd been a semester away from graduating as a marine biologist before the Crisis—and in his darker moments, he regarded it as his particular misfortune to realize that his training in a bathyscaphe might be useful to the Navy. Now he could barely manage to keep his bladder under control.

"Terries are within five-hundred metes."

"All ships—blank their engines!" the commander ordered. "Davis, tell G Company to fire their enhancers in ten seconds—Mark!"

As the Terrans surged forward to meet the advancing Isitians, their sensor screens went blank. Lost in the storms of Nakahashi, the rebels had simply vanished. Struggling to overcome the infernal jamming that was disrupting their communications, the Terrans fired wildly into the open skies, certain that the Isitians had to be there somewhere.

As the Terran line moved toward the position their eyes had told them must be occupied by the enemy, the Isitian division appeared again—this time, advancing on their distended flank. Wildly, with no way to make a graceful pivot and still trying to reestablish communications between their ships, the Terran line thrashed about in the blackness, watching as their monitors showed a slow, inexorable advance by the Isitians toward the gaping holes in the Terran lines. Events were happening too quickly for the Terrans to absorb, and most ship commanders found their bridge teams gripped by the notion that the Isitians had, in complete secrecy, mastered the ability to mask their presence from a sensor scan.

And if the Isitians could turn a pivot that sharply, indistinguishable from the emptiness around them, all the while maintaining total radio silence, the battle was hopeless. Each Terran bridge felt a wave of cold fear at the prospect of facing a trap sprung by the likes of Roscoe Cook, the one wing commander who had never lost in battle.

Using signal beacons as semaphores, the Terrans regrouped, and turned to face the advancing Isitians. As they reformed their battle lines, their momentum carried them away from the main body of the Terran fleet; realizing that they were cut off from help, and still could not talk to each other, panic swelled on every bridge in the fleet.

Among the Terrans, no one noticed that for all their maneuvering, the Isitians had yet to attack. But watching the Isitians make their relentless advance, nobody in the Terran fleet harbored any doubt that they were in a battle none of them expected, and were fighting for their lives.

"BARNES REPORTS they've taken their position at the western rim, with a loss of three frigates."

Cook stared intently at his own sensor screen, oblivious to the frenetic activity on his bridge. The subspace static might help their deception, he worried, but would do no damn good if it kept him from finding and killing the Terran starships before the enemy realized what he was doing. Ignoring his radio officer's report, Cook rose from his seat and paced from station to station, coming to rest at the systems desk. Leaning over young Wasser's shoulder, he scanned the instruments, then stood, tall and erect, towering over the nervous young lieutenant like a mountain over the sea.

"Still no sign of the starship?"

"No sir. In all this mess— "

"Keep trying, Mr. Wasser. Jarvis, radio Barnes, and tell him to move up the pipe another half-klick. He's going to need some wiggle room, if the Terrans slug their way down that far. Wasser— "

"Sir?"

"One klick to the first battle line, isn't it?"

"One exactly, Admiral."

"Helm—take us through our own line, right into the heart of the enemy formation. If we can't find a starship the easy way, maybe we can flush them out by lighting up a few enemy frigates."

"Aye, aye."

"Weapons?"

"Shields amain, forward guns already charging."

"Charge all the guns, Mr. Nielsen. We may not be able to stay very long. But we can damn well put the fear of God into them while we're here."

"Yes, sir."

"Mr. Jarvis, radio the sloops up ahead. Tell them to scatter on our signal. I'll tell them how, when I see how the Terrans are responding."

"Aye, aye."

"Janet—jump to C-12, on my command."

"Yes, sir."

As the ragged Terran flank began to advance on the charging Isitians, discipline and training gave the Terrans an edge they had not expected. Without adequate room to maneuver, even without normal communications, they needed only a few short signals to reform and begin one of their many prearranged battle sequences. As the Isitians massed to the center, the right side of the Terran battle line charged boldly toward the enemy's flank, while the left swung sharply to the side, hoping to catch the Isitians in a pincer in order to divide their forces. The maneuver, known as "Left-P-1A" in the shorthand of long-wave transmissions, seemed to catch the defenders napping, as the Isitians stood their ground without reacting.

Without warning, the Isitians bolted forward, outrunning the pincer as it closed behind them, and dashing toward the edge of the cloud cover only to disappear into the darkness.

Left behind was a lone Isitian starship, dodging their tiny fire while her guns slashed mercilessly against the advancing Terran frigates. As she danced and swayed in the darkness, raging against the Terran advance like a cosmic storm, none of the Terrans doubted that the starship was Cook's *Avenger*. Soon, the death embers of a dozen Terran frigates dimmed into blackness, while another half-dozen found themselves listing badly, and unable to maneuver. The Terrans retreated instinctively, their ranks closing to protect their wounded comrades. Seconds later a bright, shining point of light was thundering toward the front, coming to rally the Terrans.

* * *

MCALLISTER STARED at the monitors, his fingers clenching his armrests so energetically that his forearms began to ache. He was painfully aware of the desperate need to keep Admiral Cook alive and the *Avenger* secure. But it was hard enough to keep up with the Admiral when he was simply dashing about the skies. Staying with him as he skittered around in the middle of battle was impossible. And now, with a Terran starship heading right for them, he knew his job had just become hopeless.

"Huntsman!" he said sternly. "Keep on her portside. We can't leave her flanks unguarded."

"We can't keep up with her," the helmsman retorted sharply. "You get him to stand still, I'll keep us in formation."

"Shortwave transmission, incoming," announced Hollander, the radio officer. "No—sorry. It's not for us."

"Put it on audio, anyway."

"Sorry, sir. It's over."

"And?"

"He told the sloops to form along the flanks. And he said to— "

"She's moving, Commander."

"Keep with her, dammit!"

"Sorry."

"Don't be sorry, Huntsman, just stay with her."

"I can't promise— "

"Just do it!"

SLICING PAST the incoming enemy guns, *Avenger* ignored the Terran frigates and headed straight for the Terran starship. Bursting through the Terran lines, she beamed a low-wave signal, commanding the Isitian flanks to begin an advance. The Terran gunners struck hard against the squadron of frigates she trailed in her wake, cracking the shields of two of them. But the sudden appearance of the Isitians along their flanks froze the Terrans in place, and they moved to gather their lines to meet the coming onslaught. With the enemy frigates occupied astern, *Avenger* came upon the enemy starship alone, her guns fully charged, her commander sensing that his opposite was about to make a fatal mistake.

As the Terran ship fired a full salvo from its forward guns, *Avenger* rolled beneath her shields to deflect the blinding, blue flash that would briefly drain her adversary's guns, then quickly slipped inside the enemy's optimum targeting range and commenced a rolling barrage, firing and charging her guns in a tight, deadly sequence. As the enemy starship struggled desperately to rearm its weapons, Cook brought his ship nearly to point blank range. Again and again, *Avenger's* guns crackled and snapped through the surrounding heavens, battering her helpless foe with a merciless torrent of fire. Soon the sky glowed with a blue flame that shredded the buckling enemy shields, ripping heat tiles and viewing tiles and reinforcement cables from the shattered hull of the dying starship, tearing the luckless ship into splinters and shards of mangled debris. After twelve seconds of fury, the Terran ship exploded in a fireball of death.

Before the enemy's flames could reach their crest, the Isitian ship snapped into a sharp turn and headed anticenter-north, toward the Terran forces gathering for a run against the division guarding the eastern edge of the passage, blocking their retreat to open skies. As the *Avenger* sailed off toward her next target, her slightly battered escort in tow, the rest of the Isitian frigates suddenly vanished into the darkness, leaving a dazed and shaken enemy behind to watch the ashes of their leader's ship fade and disappear amid the clouds of Nakahashi.

* * *

"Incoming—!"

The deck of the *New Alexandria* shook beneath his feet, from the impact of the enemy guns. Quickly looking to the systems console, Landis was reassured by Lt. Hays' cocky grin.

"Not a dent," scoffed the young systems officer.

"Shields holding at full power," reported the weapons officer. "Forward guns charged and locked on target."

"All forward guns—fire and recharge!" commanded Landis. The bridge lights dimmed briefly, and he felt the deck shudder ever so slightly. Looking to the monitor screen, he saw two Terran frigates explode where they stood, and heard loud cheers sounding across the bridge. It was the first time the *New Alexandria* had fired her guns in battle. And it was, so far as they knew, the first Terran casualties of the engagement. He tried his best to keep from getting giddy with their apparent success as a warship, but found his crew's enthusiasm contagious.

"Enemy company falling back, heading 240," reported Hays.

"Helm, keep on their tail. Weapons, prepare to finish off any wounded ships you come across. Mr. Hays, any sign of that enemy starship?"

"Negative," Hays replied. "With all this activity, the screen's a blur. Nothing but frigates within close range, and there's too much static to do a wider sweep."

"Keep trying, Lieutenant."

As the *New Alexandria* closed on the retreating Terrans, Landis looked at the tactical display. The screen showed a seamless mass of enemy warships, streaming toward the eastern edge of the channel in a chaotic jumble . He shook his head grimly: if the Terries were determined to fight their way to open skies, the thousand or so sloops and schooners that made up their phantom division could never force them back. Once clear of the channel, they'd have clear sailing all the way back to ZarCom.

Suddenly, a bright image lit the monitor, and his systems officer shouted with alarm.

"Starship on the screen, bearing 490, range fifteen klicks."

"What's his heading?"

"He's circling around the rest of them—like he's trying to head off their retreat and rally them to the attack."

Saints be praised, Landis thought. From such little shreds of blind luck, Cook might just pull it off.

"Hays, keep an eye on the starship. Helm, hard about—come to 120, ahead at flank speed, then arc past the enemy lines from the other side. If the Terries are going to herd their own ships for us like cattle, the least we can do is help them."

As an animal yell filled his ears, Landis sank back in his chair and breathed a sigh of relief. The Terry starship might still be the death of him, but at least they'd go down fighting.

* * *

THEIR COMMUNICATIONS cut, and seeing the enemy on all sides, the Terran divisions began to fragment. Disciplined by endless drilling, each squadron managed to stay in formation clinging together out of desperation. But as they milled about, they were unable to form any cohesive battle groups. Sensors could barely penetrate the static and subspace fog of the surrounding storms, and individual companies soon lost track of their division. Realizing that the nearest open skies were to the east, and that most of the Isitian ships had appeared to the west, they staggered eastward in a mad, chaotic scramble. Groping through the darkness, the Terrans kept a careful watch on their sensors, and the Terran frigates kept probing desperately for signs of the nearest starship: knowing that Cook had appeared to their east, most Terran skippers feared that they'd have to face him alone, without cover from their own witless commanders, and knew that their shields would never survive a full salvo from a starship. And so at the first sign of a starship on their screens, the Terran frigates came sharply about, racing in the opposite direction like a flock of terrified birds trying to evade a hawk. If their leaders couldn't break the enemy's incessant jamming, their only hope lay in making their way to clear skies, where they stood a chance of fighting their way free—and their radios might just be able to break through the static.

But as first one starship, then another appeared on their screens, circling around from the opposite direction, the Terrans became confused, then terrified. The Isitians had, after all, suddenly appeared with two starships. As Cook's ship would never go down without a massive, coordinated attack, the Terrans concluded that the Isitians were trying to catch them in a quick, deadly pincer—and that their only hope lay in retreating to the west. In the agitated flurry caused by the massive, shifting swirls of warships, a host of fiery collisions swallowed a dozen frigates, and a stampede through a hidden mass of small, Isitian vessels caused a dozen more collisions. The Isitians, firing their tiny guns incessantly, did little damage to the Terrans; but the wild exchange that followed claimed nearly as many Terrans as Isitians, as the cross-firing salvos through the Isitian brigades registered on Terran frigates obscured by the dense mass of small enemy ships, resulting in ever more deadly exchanges before the Terrans realized they were firing on their own people—and that, in the meantime, the Isitians had once again mysteriously disappeared into the blackness.

"Starship showing aft."

Casting a stern, practiced eye toward the aft monitor, Cook recognized the vessel and decided on his course of action before Wasser could confirm the identity of this newest sighting.

"IFF response, negative. Configuration is— "

"Helm—hard about."

"— consistent with a Terran— "

"Increase speed to C-12."

"— starship, *Covington*-class."

"Landis reports a stampede of enemy frigates heading our way," reported the radio officer.

Damn! thought Cook. He'd done all he could to make them retreat to the east—away from Isis. He'd put most of his apparent strength to the west—he even abandoned his position to the east, for the love of mercy. Now all that foresight was shot to hell.

"And he says he's sitting on that last enemy starship. He thinks it's the leader."

Wrong, Cook smiled coldly. The leader was just astern of them. And as bladder-brained as ever.

"Weapons?"

"Guns still charged."

"Blank all rear guns, divert power to the shields. Janet, stand by to give our uninvited guests a final lesson in starmanship."

"Yes, sir."

"Aye, aye, Skipper."

"And Jarvis?"

"Sir?"

"Radio Divisions Blue and Green. Have them move to reinforce Barnes. Then radio Division Gold, and tell them to advance westward down the channel. After all my calculations and all that bother about making our first score on the enemy's centerside flank, if the enemy is off bolting toward Isis after all, they may as well think we've cut off their retreat."

"Aye, aye."

Maybe they'd done too good a job jamming their communications. Or maybe they did so well confusing the poor bastards that the Terrans couldn't tell which end of the channel was which. It was too late to worry about such details now. As long as the battle was still in doubt, it was hardly time to start his post-mortems.

"FIRE!"

The blast from *New Alexandria's* guns lighted the skies, as the Isitian ship found and destroyed frigate after frigate. Landis, keeping a close watch on the Terran starship, felt his palms sweat and his heart begin to race. The Terries had not conquered half the known galaxy by being totally witless. It was only a matter of time before they regrouped and counterattacked. And watching the enemy starship circle around his own position, guns fully charged and shields looming large and impregnable on the tactical monitor, he wondered how long it would take the Terrans to begin the assault. Suddenly, all his training and all his preparation seemed paltry and inadequate. His entire life dangled over a precipice nearly an astrokilometer wide—the distance between the *New Alexandria* and the enemy starship. But to his surprise, he was more terrified by the prospect of disgracing himself in the eyes of his crew than by the likelihood of dying.

"Terry's increasing speed," reported the systems officer.

"Helm, hard a-port. Mr. Molnar, blank all guns and keep our shields toward the enemy."

The Terran ship thundered past them, its guns scoring direct hits on two of their shields, causing the lights on the *New Alexandria* to flicker. In the joy of realizing that they'd survived the starship's initial pass, Landis felt all sense of fear leave him. They'd taken the enemy's best shot, and were still kicking. Now, the thought that the Terrans were trying to kill him made him angry; and the thought that they were trying destroy everything he loved filled him with hate. Nothing else mattered: not death, not danger, not the prospect of spending eternity drifting about the cosmos as a scattering of dust and ashes. Isis needed them to stop these monsters, and he'd die before he let them escape.

As their shields firmed, and the Terran ship slowed and came about for another pass, Landis decided that he couldn't simply wait for the Admiral to come to his rescue. Cook had brought victory within their grasp, by willpower or magic or some mystical powers that none of them could comprehend. But Cook had enough to worry about, Landis thought. For months, they'd hoped that the Admiral could somehow win this battle for them single-handedly. Now, it was time for them to stop depending on him to work miracles all by himself. Whether his crew lived or died defending their homeland, this enemy ship belonged to the *New Alexandria.*

"Shields firming. Seven and Twelve coming back to full power."

"Hard about—charge two aft guns. Mr. Conrad, prepare for another evasive maneuver on the next pass, this time, due south, two-hundred fifty degrees. And Mr. Molnar?"

"Sir?"

"Let's have a surprise waiting for Terry when he crosses our mast."

"Aye, aye, sir."

* * *

The Admiral watched the Terran flagship circle cautiously, keeping a steady distance from the *Avenger.* VanderMuelen might be an idiot, but he was not a complete fool. Most likely, Cook thought, Vandy well knew that the Terrans' only hope was to hold their forces together—and, more importantly, to keep their starships alive until they could restore communications. Any minute, the Terrans could break through the jamming. Cook was reluctant to press his luck any further.

"Mr. Jarvis?"

"Sir?"

"Radio a message to the communications ships on Channels 133 and 199. Tell them to broadcast random, computer-generated words along with their jamming. That might make the Terrans' job of breaking through a bit easier, but we've kept them in the dark for longer than I'd hoped. I'd just as soon have them compete with babbling, if and when they finally do restore communications."

"Yes, sir."

Returning his attention to the Terran flagship, Cook fought the urge to rush. With one starship down, and Landis keeping track of the other one, there was no need to race the clock, no reason to start taking foolish chances.

Steady now, he told himself, over and over again. No need to press, no need to hurry, no need to jeopardize victory with anything so foolish or petty as a schoolboy's pride. Though his own forces were badly outnumbered, those numbers meant nothing. The Terrans still had no idea where the real fight would be, or how easily they could still turn the battle if they could concentrate their forces. Dazed and confused by the successful misdirection, they didn't realize how close they were to losing everything in the next few minutes. Milling about in a panic, they had no idea that the real battle was just now getting underway—and that they'd be in no real danger until that battle was over.

* * *

THE TWO ships circled warily, each cautiously respectful of the others' powerful guns. The red clouds, billowing in the distance, cast a dark, sinister hue across the hull of each. As the surrounding skies flared with lights from occasional blaster fire, the starships focused their attention on each other, their commanders mindful of all that was riding on the encounter.

Suddenly, the Terran ship banked hard to port. Sensing an opening in her opponent's defenses, she raced forward with guns charged and all shields raised. Dropping quickly below the plane of approach, the

New Alexandria pivoted to keep her forward shields facing the enemy, accepting two quick, powerful thrusts against her defenses, before firing all aft guns against the retreating enemy. The two ships parted and circled around for another pass, both hurting, and each with shields drained. As the damage reports funneled into their respective bridges, each commander worried that another pass would leave them too weakened to press the fight.

"NUMBER TWELVE is stuck at 50 percent power," reported Hays, the systems officer. "Seven is holding steady at 80 percent, but the reserves are gone. With enough time, we might get it back up to full power.

Landis watched his adversary carefully, etching every sight and motion into his memory.

"Any readings from Terry?"

"Too far away, Commodore. I can't get anything accurate at this distance, and the hit we took wiped out our sensors for a second or two. I can't call anything up to fill the gap in our readings."

"Molnar?"

"I think we hit him pretty good," replied the weapons officer. "Seemed like most of his spare power was in his forward shields."

Landis gazed intently at the monitor screen showing the Terran ship as it came about. To his relief, Terry began circling to port, rather than heading directly into another pass.

We did do some damage after all, he thought, with grim satisfaction, even with a rickety old ship that belonged in mothballs. Of course, too many more hits like that and they'd fall apart. But if it was to be a fight to the death, at least they'd proven that Isis grew more than daisy-sniffers. And that Cook wasn't the only warrior on the planet.

* * *

"LOOK'S LIKE we're going to have company."

Cook cast a glance aft, to see the mass of Terran ships heading their way. They were still several minutes away, and wouldn't be a factor in the fight with the enemy flagship: their course would carry them too far to anticenter. Still, he made a mental note not to dawdle in bringing things to a head. Those enemy ships were racing headlong toward the Western Passage; he doubted that Barnes could hold them off very long all by himself.

But he found himself drawn to something else appearing on the screens. Something his instincts told him he shouldn't ignore. "Looks like they already have company," he said, peering at the starboard monitor. Faintly visible through the static, he could just make out a half-dozen or so images on the screen. They were faint in the distance, and appeared to him to be trying to hide amid all the static that was fouling everyone's instruments.

"Mr. Wasser, try to get a better look. Helm, increase your arc by 20 points, and swing us wide to starboard.

As the systems officer fiddled with his sensors, Cook watched the blurry images fade and reappear. Gradually, even before Wasser could pull them into focus, he began to feel his lips curl into a grim, humorless smile.

VanderMuelen wasn't just being careful, Cook thought, shaking his head and sinking back into his command seat. He was trying to protect their little fleet's most vulnerable asset.

"I think we've just found our secondary targets," Cook said quietly.

As he spoke, Janet reached the apogee of their arc, and the systems officer was finally able to put a crisp image on the screen.

There, plain as day, were ten troop transports, each holding up to a hundred-thousand men—ferrying the Terran invasion force toward their rendezvous with Isis.

"Helm, hard to port, prepare a jump to C-15—and stand by to cut it short.

"Weapons—full power to forward shields, stand by to blank all main guns except the aft batteries, and a single forward gun. And make your shot count, Mr. Nielsen; I want to do this in a single pass. We have a lot to do—and we still have to go help Commodore Landis. So remember to— "

"Watch for the seams—yes, sir."

As *Avenger* banked steeply and began her charge, a massive burst of static poured across the skies. Deep within the clouds, an interstellar flare was surging, obliterating most radio bands and sending dials and monitors into spasms of electromagnetic convulsions spanning the length and breadth of the channel.

* * *

ALL BUT one of his shields had returned to full power, Landis knew. But with Number Twelve stuck at 50 percent, he had a gaping hole in his starboard defenses. As he watched the enemy slice through the skies, watching for an opening, he suddenly found himself faced with an entirely new set of problems.

"Storm flares are causing power surges all down the line," reported the systems officer. "Rating them as Class-C. Until they subside, I can't promise we'll have all systems operational."

Damn! thought Landis. He didn't need any more problems. Flares like this could last as long as five minutes. By then, the Terran ship might well have returned to full power—if it hadn't already. He looked at the chronometer: Cook was already overdue. And each minute that passed carried them further beyond the twenty-minutes the Admiral had allocated for this entire phase of the battle.

"Ehrlich—call *Avenger* and ask the Admiral when he'll finally be ready to lend us a hand."

"Flares are interfering with communications, Commodore. Until they pass, we're as deaf as the Terries."

"Try anyway."

As the radio officer tried to raise the *Avenger* without success, Landis struggled to keep himself calm. He was on his own; this time, he was really on his own. He didn't know how his ship would react to the disruptions in its systems. And he wouldn't know the operational status of his adversary until one of them attacked.

"Hard astarboard," he called suddenly, surprised at the strength and power of his own voice. "Charge all weapon systems, and keep funneling all reserve power to the shields. Cut power to auxiliary systems, if you have to.

"Helm, come about and increase speed to C-5. And keep our starboard shields away from the enemy."

"We don't know how the storm's affecting the Terries—, " protested the weapons officer.

"Then we're both laboring under similar handicaps, Mr. Molnar. But I suspect that Terry is more experienced than we are. If they're not attacking, they must have a reason—and that's reason enough for us to keep up the pressure, until the Admiral arrives."

"Range, two klicks and closing."

"Mr. Molnar, prepare to fire on my command."

"One klick and closing."

Helm, cut speed to C-2, and hard aport. Weapons—commence firing, sequential barrage. All ancillary gunners, fire at will."

* * *

COOK PUSHED all thought of storms and flares from his mind. The flares might play havoc with their sensors, but weaponry and shields were internal systems and would be unaffected by anything going on around them. If anything, he smiled coldly, the disruption would give him an unfair advantage over his old tormentor. Perhaps not as unfair as the four-sided pummelings he'd received as a plebe. Back then, VanderMuelen was never one to pull a punch; with the future of his world riding on the outcome, Cook wasn't going to fret about using every gift that Fate had given him.

"Sound the klaxons—cut gravity—and hold fire for my command, Mr. Nielsen. Display targets, all guns, on the tactical screen."

"Yes, sir."

"Now, Janet—hard about, spiral left. Mr. Nielsen, watch for the enemy coming up aportside."

The *Avenger* threw her crew violently against the wall as she turned inside her own arc of motion. Cook felt his body press against the side of his chair, as his ship first carried itself just beyond the killing range of the enemy guns, deflecting the Terran guns with her aft shields, then wrenched through its own course heading and came back across the Terran's bow, as the Terran guns struggled valiantly to recharge for another salvo. All the while, he kept his eyes glued to his tactical monitor.

"Fire forward gun; stand by aft batteries"

"Aft guns amain."

Avenger ran close athwart the Terran's bow, her motion continuing in a tight spiral, her first small blast summoning a surge of power to the Terran's forward shields. As the spiral brought them quickly port-to-port alongside the enemy, the Terran commander tried desperately to bring his charging guns to bear on the Isitian ship, not realizing that his shifting power relays were stretching the seams all along his circumference.

"Stand by, Mr. Nielsen."

As *AVENGER* circled round the Terran's aft and came upon his starboard, a lethal hole had opened in the enemy's starboard shield. With the instruments down, it was quite invisible. But Cook knew it was there; he couldn't see it with his eyes, but his mind could touch it, and as he gave the command he felt a cold shiver of contempt for all things Terran, and anything reminding him of his previous life among them.

"Mr. Nielsen..."

Cook's eyes were fixed on the monitor, waiting—waiting—until—

"Target dead on the starboardside guns. Fire main aft batteries!"

"Firing aft!"

"—and recharge all guns. Helm, increase speed to C-3, full ahead."

As *Avenger* powered her engines, bringing her out of the spiral and safely away from her quarry, the Terran ship exploded in a cataclysmic blast. Cook looked astern, the cheers of his crew ringing in his ears, but he felt empty inside, as if part of his past had died along with VanderMuelen, a past that had not yet lost its innocence. He was surprised to feel no satisfaction in killing his old nemesis, and chided himself for worrying about it. He'd killed so many times, telling himself it was all in the service of humanity, that death had become his albatross. If VanderMuelen's death would help save his home, he could smile at the irony. But he'd destroyed enough lives to last a thousand lifetimes of atonement, and death had meaning for him only as a source of tragedy.

Suddenly, he winced under a bright flash of light from the port viewer. Forcing himself to look, he realized instantly that there was only one possible source for an explosion of that magnitude: it was the death blast of a starship.

"Helm—hard to port, heading 246, flank speed. Weapons, blank guns astern, all power to shields. We're still in a fight, people. And I suspect things just took a turn for the worse."

"Storm abating," reported the systems officer. "Estimate communications restored in two minutes."

In two minutes, thought Cook, they'd be upon the surviving starship. And if the Terrans kept going on their present course they'd be nearly to the western rim.

Damn! he pounded his fist against the arm rest. He'd been so smug and self-indulgent he'd almost forgotten everything else. So long as there was still one enemy starship lurking about, the battle was far from over. The Terrans still had their invasion army intact, Isis was still in danger—and Barnes and his tiny company of rusty frigates was about to face the brunt of the Terran armada quite alone.

"Helm, jump to C-17 and prepare to spiral quickly about. Mr. Nielsen, stand by all forward guns for a full barrage on my command. This next one is apt to be like the first, people—short and ugly. But we've dawdled too long already, and we've got to make up for lost time."

As acceleration pressed his body against the familiar padding of his command chair, Cook kept his eyes ahead, watching the monitor for the first sign of trouble. He felt tired and alone, and wanted nothing so much as to collapse into Janet's arms and fade into oblivion. But there was too much to do. Too many lives were dangling by a thread, ready to live or die on his command. He could smell victory, even through the void of space; he could smell her and taste her, and felt her warming presence all around him. But he'd snatched too many victories from the blackness to think her anything but a phantom that would fade without a trace unless seized and cherished. It was not the time to relax, he told himself; it was time to be twice as strong, twice as bold, twice as fearless.

That was what victory needed; and, he promised himself, he would not relax again until the threat was destroyed, and his home, and everyone on it, was safe.

* * *

"COMMANDER—I don't like this."

Taking a deep breath, Barnes looked up from the control monitor and cast a glance at his systems officer. Immediately, the young commander saw what had him so worried.

There, on the screens, he could see the mists of subspace static beginning to fade. But in place of the static, he saw Terrans.

Terrans.

Nothing but Terrans, as far as the eye could see.

"Communications?"

"Still out, sir," confirmed the radio officer.

Moving toward the systems desk, he took Addison aside. None of the others on the bridge had seen the sensor screen, and he didn't want to alarm them needlessly.

"How many?" he whispered. Addison's ashen face confirmed his worst fears.

"No way of knowing, Commander," he said, trying his best to keep his composure. "But they had two divisions—and I haven't been able to come across anything else. Every ship in sensor range is heading right for us. And those two big explosions we just saw? I'm almost certain they were starships. And right now I can't locate either of our two big ships."

Barnes stepped back and desperately tried to think. They could never hold the line against two whole enemy divisions. And if the *Avenger* had been sent up, the battle was already lost.

But he had his orders. They were to hold the pass to the last ship. And he refused to believe that the Terries could ever kill the Admiral. Not like that; not without trapping him like a caged animal, and concentrating all their forces on the effort. Until he heard otherwise, from the Admiral himself, they would maintain their line—all of them. Whatever doubts he had, he'd never let his crew, or his command, know how scared and alone he felt.

He returned to his chair and sat down. They couldn't retreat, and the Terries were hurling too many ships at them to make a stand. Whatever happened, he'd feel responsible. He consoled himself with the thought that if it turned out badly, he wouldn't live long enough to suffer very much. But his training hadn't prepared him for the doubts churning in his belly, or the thought that his friends—those he'd lived with and trained with for the past few months—were depending on him to pull them through. There seemed no way out, not without violating his duty. No way out but certain death.

"Mr. Gates?"

"Communications are clearing, Commander. I can patch us through, short-range—but that's about all."

"Then do it."

Clearing his throat, Barnes took a deep breath and waited for a nod from Gates. He could feel his heart hammering in his chest, and stared hatefully at the images of the approaching enemy on the display screen. By the time the communications channel was clear, he'd calmed himself just enough to keep his voice from rising in pitch, and kept reminding himself to speak slowly and clearly. Whatever the odds, they wouldn't just wait to be slaughtered. He might not be able to save any of his command; it was quite possible that every one of his ships would be destroyed in the next few minutes. But if they were going to die, they'd go down fighting.

"All ships will stagger the line, and maintain open fields of fire," Barnes said, trying his best to appear confident, hoping that his people would rally to the sound of his voice. "Seems we're about to have company, very soon. I suspect they anticipated an easy time of it—much too easy a time of it. By the looks of things so far, they didn't prepare for much of a fight, and this is probably their last gasp at breaking out of the Admiral's trap.

"I expect the Admiral's right on their heels," he continued, hoping to God that he was right. "If they're trying to run the channel, they're probably heading for the clear skies beyond us. That's the only way they can regroup. But we're charged with guarding this pass for the Admiral, and guarding it with our lives. And if we're going to die defending it, then we're damn well going to push them as far back toward the *Avenger* as we can manage.

"Small craft, form behind the frigates, fire your engines and stand by to engage your enhancers. If our training taught us anything, it was that we don't lose the initiative—we don't let the enemy set the terms of battle—and we don't lose heart, ever, under any circumstances. And above all, keep doing the unexpected—whatever the odds, whatever the outlook. We'll be facing as many as two enemy divisions—two divisions that outnumber us, nearly ten to one. The Admiral ordered us not to let the Terries pass, but we can't hold the channel against a force that large. So we won't even try to hold the line here. Instead—we're going to attack!"

Barnes rammed his fist onto his armrest. He was startled to hear shouts and hollers of approval ringing in his ears, and pouring over the open communications channel.

"All ships, prepare to advance on the enemy. C-Level 2, on my command."

* * *

"MY GOD, Cook—but it was glorious!"

The scene on the screen from the *New Alexandria* startled everyone. Landis, delirious from his brush with death, was prattling on endlessly, gushing over every last detail of his fight with the last

Terran starship: how the starboard shield buckled, how the Terran ship tried to come about, how the last shot scored just as their main shield stood on the verge of collapse. The rest of *New Alexandria's* bridge was unable to contain their glee at the simple joy of survival, and was busy celebrating its good fortune by turning their bridge into a pigsty.

"Inches away from total disaster! But you know what finally did it? It was those bloody small guns—the gunnery officer sunk a shot down their windpipe, just like you wrote in the damn briefing book! My God, but it was glorious."

The effect on *Avenger's* crew was as predictable as it was contagious: the junior officers were on the verge of dancing themselves. But Janet didn't expect the effect it had on her husband, and it was enough to keep her from joining the celebration.

"What—what—what do you mean—?" Cook sputtered. The Admiral, it seemed to her, was livid, and she'd seen the venom in his eyes before: it meant he was about to lower the boom on some misbegotten fool. Quickly, she cut the engines, stepped to the command seat, and dug her nails into her husband's forearm.

"What the hell are you doing?" he demanded, immediately turning his anger toward this new source of aggravation.

"Hush for a moment, unless you want to make an ass of yourself in front of the entire crew," she whispered, careful not to be overheard. She saw fury raging in his eyes, and knew she had to be brief.

"Think—Cook, you bloody idiot, *think*! Just what are you so angry about?"

Snorting derisively, Cook forced himself to answer the question. Janet had never done this before—fronting him directly like this.

"They were supposed to keep the enemy busy," he snapped. "The risk of his engaging the third ship—"

"They kept the enemy so busy they destroyed him. So what, if they took a foolish chance? This is no time to chew them out—and for what? For being brave? Isn't that just what Central Command did to you, once upon a time? And you know—everyone on every ship in the whole damn Navy is doing it all for you. Every single thing they do, they do to make you proud of them—even if your own skull is too thick to see it. Or are you just mad because you didn't get to do every last little thing yourself this time?"

Seeing her husband's brow furrowing angrily, Janet knew she couldn't push things any further. Not without causing a major disruption in the middle of battle. She had to hope the fool she married wasn't a complete fool. She resumed her seat, and turned away, watching the celebration continuing on the bridge of the *New Alexandria*. She didn't want him to feel threatened, or pushed. At least not now. Not in public. And not until they were all out of danger.

A few seconds later, her heart sank when she heard her husband pound his armrest loudly. She didn't relax until she heard his voice.

"Landis, you fool," Cook said, his voice brimming with rough good humor. "Get a grip on yourself. You can't gloat forever—and the battle's only half-over, you know."

"Admiral, you wouldn't believe— "

"No, I wouldn't," Cook interrupted. "Not until the job's over and done. Now, Commodore—you come to heading 268, and circle back toward the western outlet. Don't trouble yourself about any enemy stragglers you meet along the way—that's mop-up, and we still have to deal with the main enemy contingent. Proceed to the center of the channel, five astrokilometers behind the last ship in the enemy formation, and wait for instructions. Once the static clears, contact Barnes, and tell him help's on the way. You're free to assess his tactical situation when you arrive—but remember: your shields are already weakened. You can't confront all those frigates by yourself. I'll leave anything else to your own discretion. But keep in mind that we'll be about five minutes behind you.

"Aye, aye."

"And Commodore?"

"Admiral?"

"Well done, Commodore Landis," the Admiral smiled and nodded his head. "Your country owes you a debt of gratitude—and so do I." Seeing his subordinate's eyes water, Cook realized just how close he'd come to being his normal, arrogant self.

"Thank you, Admiral," Landis beamed. "Thank you very much."

"We'll meet you at the rendezvous, Commodore. Do be on time. And do try to leave some of the enemy for us this time, won't you?"

Cook watched the Commodore and his entire bridge crew laugh. Relief was in their eyes, and he could see the pride and wonder in their hearts. As the *New Alexandria* came about, Cook turned his attention to the one objective remaining—the only task left before he'd consider the battle won. The transports, he thought darkly. The army of invaders, sent to conquer Isis.

"Helm, come to heading 740, ahead at C-2. Systems, set sensors on active probes, maximum intensity. The flare from the storm should be dying—and I don't want to leave the enemy free a second longer than it takes for us to penetrate the static."

"Yes, sir."

"And Mrs. Cook?"

Janet turned in place, to face the command seat. This was not the time for sentiment, she thought to herself, hoping that he'd make a fool of himself anyway.

"Thank you, Helmsman."

Shaking her head as she smiled, Janet returned to her instruments. "Comes with the job, Admiral," she laughed. "Ahead C-2, heading 740."

Chapter 15

BATTALION A, FIRE your enhancers and move up to the line. All ships, fire at will."

As his ships moved into position, Barnes cast a painful glance at his tactical monitors. The Terran lines looked invincible, a wall of fire and titanium moving in battle formation. Closing his eyes, he called to mind his home, and his parents, for a last goodbye. Even without their starships, the Terran battle wedge was a frightening sight; Terran fleets had conquered half the known galaxy, and he wondered how much they owed to the size of their formations and their ability to light the heavens with their guns.

"Range—five-hundred astrometers and closing."

"Mr. Gates?"

"Communications are coming back, Commander. The channels are nearly clear."

"Broadcast a request for assistance on the battle network," Barnes ordered. "Advise them of our situation, and let's hope there's someone out there to hear it.

"Then relay the order, down the line—all sloops, fire their enhancers. All ships attack."

"Yes, sir."

Barnes took a deep breath, then turned to look at his tactical screens. The Terran thrust contained more than a full division. As the Isitian line surged forward, and their image enhancers inflated the size of the tiny ships that comprised the bulk of their Navy, he saw a small crack appear in the Terran wedge. He smiled weakly as he saw first one squadron, then several, break away from the line and peel away. Soon, more then two dozen of the Terrans had bolted, turning sharply and scattering as they headed back toward the opposite end of the channel, fleeing from what appeared on their screens to be five divisions of Isitian frigates.

So the Terrans weren't supermen after all, he mused. The poor fools didn't know how few warships the Isitians really had. It might not make death any less final, but at least he had the satisfaction of seeing a mob of daisy-sniffers face down the enemy. And when time came to stare into the face of death, it wasn't the daisy-sniffers who turned tail and ran.

"Incoming!"

The ship shuddered under the impact of an enemy barrage. All around him, Barnes saw the funeral fires of friends and comrades, lighting the sky with death. Determined not to spend his last moments alive cowering in the face of the enemy, he summoned all his strength and forced the words from his throat.

"All guns—fire and recharge, constant barrage. Mr. Gates—order all ships to fire at will, and to keep firing. Small craft as well. If we're going down, we're taking as many of the Terries with us as we can."

COOK LOOKED at the Terran troop ships coming up on his sensor screens, wallowing helplessly in the middle of the channel. With the enemy starships gone, the transports were the only remaining threat to his planet. He had no doubt about the devastation an army of Terran blighters would cause if they managed to land, and with Barnes facing the full force of the Terran attack at the edge of the channel, he couldn't dawdle. But while he didn't want to place any more Isitian lives at risk, he hated the thought of frying a million Terran soldiers without giving them the chance to surrender. Turning to the communications screen, he saw his young squadron commander; by the looks of it, the boy was dying to see some action. Cook hoped it wouldn't make him bloodthirsty.

"Mr. McAllister?"

"Admiral?"

"A bit less hectic than you expected?"

"Yes, sir."

"I'm a bit surprised myself. I guess they weren't nearly as well prepared as I thought they'd be."

"I'm not complaining, sir."

"Well then, neither will I," Cook laughed, and motioned for McAllister to watch his tactical screen. "Circle your frigates to the left," he said, "to cut off their retreat. I'll keep them pinned where they are."

"Aye aye."

"Monitor our communications. And keep watch along our flanks. There may be some stragglers lurking about."

"Yes, sir."

Edging the *Avenger* to within eyeshot of the floundering Terran ships, Cook opened a hailing channel to all vessels. Soon, he saw the ashen faces of the Terran transport commanders, their eyes wide with fear.

"Weapons, lock on all enemy transports," Cook said sternly.

"See here, Cook—!" protested one of the Terran skippers, a plump, middle-aged woman sporting commander's bars on her epaulets. The Admiral turned to face her, choosing to address her as the leader of the group. The Terran's face, sweating profusely, was a mixture of rage and terror. Cook's narrowed eyes showed no hint of emotion, no trace of pity.

"Commander, you and your people will drop your shields and drain your engines—all of you, immediately. Or you will be destroyed."

"Listen to reason, Cook. Do you have any idea how many people we have on board, here? I can't just let you— "

"Mr. Nielsen," Cook said, staring directly into the bulging, desperate eyes of the Terran commander. "The enemy has five seconds to surrender before we open fire. Target the Commander's ship, and tell me when five seconds have expired."

"Yes, sir."

"You can't do this, Cook!"

"I'm not the invader, Commander," Cook replied coldly. "And right now, I can do pretty much as I please."

"Cook...listen to me, Cook... "

"Five seconds, Admiral."

"Are the enemy shields still up?"

"Yes, Admiral."

"Fire."

Nielsen hesitated, his mind recoiling at the thought of killing a hundred thousand people in one flash. He was surprised to feel the ship shudder anyway, and see the Terran ship explode in a massive blast. Spinning his seat around to face the command chair, he saw the Admiral remove his finger from an override control on his own console. Immediately, the young man felt like a failure, and wanted nothing more than to fade away like the embers of the dying Terrans. Expecting to see anger, he was surprised to see a look of patient understanding in the Admiral's eyes. The look disappeared as soon as Cook opened his mouth to speak.

"Mr. Nielsen," Cook said, his voice stern and unforgiving, "target all remaining ships."

As he did so, the nine remaining transports immediately dropped their shields, and the young weapons officer noticed the energy readings from their engines start to plunge. The Admiral noticed it too, for he winked at the young man and motioned him simply to stand by.

"Lt. Commander McAllister, would you please join us?" Cook said, still on the hailing channel. Two seconds later, McAllister's face appeared on the screen. Cook hoped the young man was bright enough to follow his lead, but soon realized he was worrying needlessly.

"Admiral?"

"You and your squadron will remain here, to guard the surrendering enemy transports," Cook said, choosing his words carefully, for the benefit of the Terrans monitoring the channel. "If any one of them begins to fire his engines, raise his shields, or make any move you have not authorized, you will destroy all of them. If any one of them tries to contact any vessel other than yours without your permission, you will destroy all of them. If any enemy frigate appears on the scene, and makes any movement you deem threatening, you will destroy all of them. And if any enemy ship does anything to make you the least bit nervous, you may destroy any or all of them, as you see fit. On the other hand, if they behave themselves, you will see to it that they come to no harm."

"Do you have any questions?"

"None, Admiral."

"Do you know what these transports are carrying, and why they are here?"

"Yes, sir."

"Do you understand how many Isitian boys would die, trying to keep this army of invaders from destroying our home?"

"Yes, sir."

"And do you think sparing them is worth risking a single Isitian life?"

"Absolutely not, Admiral."

"Very well, Mr. McAllister," said Cook. "I leave matters to your discretion. Once we have things more securely in hand, we'll decide precisely what to do with all enemy prisoners. For now, watch your flanks, monitor the designated channels—and keep your guns fully charged and your targets fully locked."

"Aye aye."

"Helm, hard about; we have business elsewhere. Mr. McAllister, so long—and thank you for all your help."

"Good luck, Admiral. And thank you, sir."

* * *

"Oh, my God."

Landis rose from his seat, and walked toward the forward viewer. From one end of the screen to the other, the flash of guns split the blackness, and the sky glowed as if space itself were on fire.

"Ehrlich?"

"Channels are clear, Commodore," said the radio officer.

"Raise Barnes. Quickly."

As the seconds passed, Landis could see the Isitian line bowing precariously. The center was about to collapse under the constant enemy hammering. The poor sloops and schooners were firing away madly, bless their hearts. But they could barely slow the Terran advance, much less stop it. Their one saving grace was positioning: somehow, the Terries had stretched their own lines wide, rather than focusing their attack in the center. Probably a result of the wide line of attack Barnes had ordered, Landis thought. If he hadn't done that, the bastards would be through the channel by now, and halfway to Isis before the Navy could catch them.

"Barnes and the others are fighting for their lives, Commodore," Ehrlich said at last. "His radio officer is on the verge of hysteria. Sounds like they're about to break, if you ask me."

"Helm—take us right to the heart of the battle. Flank speed."

"We can't take them all on," protested the weapons officer, as the *New Alexandria's* engines fired, and the ship began its approach. "We don't have the shields for it."

"Quarter power to forward guns, all available power to shields," Landis said, striding resolutely to his chair. He took a deep breath, and hoped that he wasn't about to kill them all.

"Commodore!"

"We don't need to turn the battle ourselves, Lieutenant," he snapped. "Once the Admiral gets here, I suspect we can go along for the ride. But our countrymen are getting slaughtered out there, and I'll be damned if I sit idly by and watch."

"But— !"

"Lieutenant—you're relieved. Mr. Radnick—take over the Weapons station.

As the young ensign moved to assume the weapons console, Landis felt his head swimming. Events were moving too fast. In all their drilling, they'd never done anything like this. He didn't even know if what he wanted to do was possible—or how to change it, if it wasn't. He barely had time to react as events swirled around him. If only he had enough time to think.

"Helm, prepare to pull us up, just as we come within range. Mr. Radnick?"

"Sir?"

"Scatter your shot as widely as you can," Landis said, staring intently at his tactical screen. "Make as big a show of our presence as you can. We can't do much by ourselves, but we can have a go at disrupting their attack on this end. Maybe that will give Barnes the chance to regroup."

"Yes sir."

As his ship sped forward, Landis took a deep breath, and hoped for the best. He had no idea if any of this was going to work. He just hoped that the Admiral's habitual tardiness was limited to meetings and briefing sessions, and not the skies of battle.

* * *

"HARD APORT!"

As the ship banked violently to the left, the force of the explosion pushed them nearly out of control, and sent the overloaded instruments and circuits into a frenzy. Greg Garrity sweat coursing down his face, pulled himself back into his seat and tried to fix the latching that was supposed to secure him to the pilot's console. The safety belts were probably cheap enough to save the ship's original owner five or ten credits, he thought; but factory seconds had no place in combat.

"Damage report!" he barked. Looking over his shoulder, he saw that the rest of his crew was in worse shape than he was. Tommy Reed, his best friend and navigator, lay sprawled on the deck, a five-inch gash cut into his head. They'd been less than four miles away from the *London Dancer* when the Terry frigate came upon them; and the size of the blast left no hope that the Terran ship had missed its mark.

Smelling smoke, Garrity spun around and saw a billowing, black cloud pouring out of the engine room. His first thought was to get his people out, but he soon realized that the hatch had been blown clean off its casings, and anyone able to escape the fumes would have no reason to dawdle.

Looking at his console, he saw that he still had maneuvering thrusters and sensors. His tactical screen was intact, and he saw the Terran frigate coming about, looming in the blackness, moving to bring its heavy guns to bear on his crippled sloop. He could move in place, he realized, but without his engines he'd never be able to escape.

By reflex, he cast his latching aside and gripped the helm with both hands. Straining to bring the ship about, he hurled himself against the wheel with every muscle in his body, fighting to turn the ship. With the engines down, coming about was a struggle, and as he wrestled with the wounded ship's controls, his soul filled with hate for the evil stupidity that had brought them to such a turn. Wiping the sweat from his brow, he stared at the frigate as it appeared, sliding into his view just beyond the ashes of the *London Dancer*. He hadn't known the other ship's crew, but he'd felt their death quite vividly. He knew that he'd never make it home, either.

Firing his thrusters, summoning whatever power remained from the ship's dying batteries, he aimed straight for the bridge of the enemy frigate and closed his eyes.

"I love you, Mom and Dad," he whispered. He took and held a deep, trembling breath.

EXPLOSIONS FILLED the skies, and Landis aimed his ship into the center of the action. The Terran ships scattered at their approach, and the dispersal of the weapons fire kept any of their hits from scoring effectively. As the *New Alexandria* circled about, trying her best to break up the Terrans' attack, Landis kept his eyes darting between the tactical screens, and the aft monitors, where he hoped to see the bright light that would announce the arrival of the Isitian flagship.

He wasn't prepared for the message when it came; and he was devastated by the order it carried.

"*Avenger's* on the line, Commodore."

"Put him on the viewer."

"Sorry—they've already broken the contact. We're to withdraw immediately, and circle back around the centerside flank."

"What!"

"They even gave us a course heading—610—and a new point of rendezvous. We're heading right into edge of the cloud."

"Oh, my God!"

His mind spinning, every cell in his body rebelled at the thought of deserting his comrades in their moment of need, leaving them to die in torrents of flame and ash. It was the cruelest thing he'd ever had to do. But Landis nodded, and forced himself to give the order to come about. He had no idea what the Admiral had in mind, and could think of nothing but the brave souls who were going to die if he left. It took all his strength to keep his composure, and he clenched his jaw bitterly, hoping to vent some of his anguish. He was sure he was condemning thousands to death. Try as he might, he knew he'd never be able to put the thought out of his head. Not for as long as he lived.

"Arcing astarboard, bearing 610."

"Flank speed, helm. Take us away."

"Aye, aye, sir."

As the *New Alexandria* sliced through the blackness, Landis kept his watering eyes away from the aft and starboard screens. He couldn't bring himself to look at the massacre that would certainly follow. His only consolation was the hope that the Admiral knew exactly what he was doing.

"COMMANDER!"

The anguished call of his systems officer went unanswered; across the bridge, the horror was palpable, and threatened to leave the ship foundering in space. It was all Barnes could do to try to bring them back to the business of running the ship. He knew if he gave himself a moment to think he might lose himself to panic, as well.

"Helm—hard aport, heading 110. Mr. Gates, broadcast the order to hold the line. We can't let the Terries break us."

"They just left, Commander. They're leaving us all to die."

"Addison—you're relieved. Fields—take over the systems station."

Barnes turned his chair to face his starboard screen, and watched the starship disappear. He could feel the courage draining from his soul. They'd all cheered when they saw the bright light of the *New Alexandria* appear on their sensors, every last one of them; it meant that help was on its way, that the starship would soon be able to fight her way to the thick of the battle. They'd kept up the fight even as other ships kept dying all around them. The Terrans had scattered, at first. And though the Isitian starship had pressed most of the enemy frigates further into the line of battle, Barnes had known— he'd just known—that the starships would tip the fight in their favor.

Then, as suddenly as it appeared, the ship just sailed off into the darkness. Running from the fight, and leaving the rest of them to pay the price. Barnes felt as if a great chasm had opened beneath his feet, and they were plunging headlong into a deep pit.

"Ziegler wants to know if we can retreat."

"Hold the line!" Barnes snapped, his eyes filling with tears. "I don't know how many times I have to repeat myself." Fighting grief as well as the Terrans was more than he could bear. Maybe they should have kept their position, further down the channel, he thought. Maybe he shouldn't have worked so hard, just to be the one giving orders when he didn't really know what to do. Maybe he should have just gone home, and left the fighting and dying to fools who didn't know any better. But he'd made his choice; and it was heartbreaking to watch help come only to vanish like a mirage.

"Commander!"

And he knew that none of them would ever forgive the *New Alexandria* for deserting them. It was unforgivable. Indefensible. Treasonous. If any of them did survive, he promised himself, the name Landis would become a synonym for coward.

"Commander—!"

Barnes didn't hear his radio officer; he was too busy watching the starboard screen, etching the sight of the fading point of light to pay attention to anything else. It came as a shock when Gates, acting on his own, put the incoming signal on shipwide audio.

"Clear the zone; clear the zone; clear the zone...."

It was the Admiral's voice. It was obviously a recording, looping back on itself. And it was scratchy and distorted, from the lingering effects of the Nakahashi flares. But it was unmistakably the Admiral's voice. Throughout the ship, the effect was electric: animal cheers shook the walls on every deck, even as the ship shuddered under the impact of Terran blasters. Barnes felt himself rock violently from side to side, held in his chair only by his safety straps. The ship's lights faded ominously, then stabilized.

"— clear the zone; clear the zone— "

What zone? Barnes wondered to himself.

"We're just getting a visual, coming through," the communications officer announced. Instantly the viewer filled with a tactical grid, showing the battle line as it stretched toward the anticenter clouds. On the western side of the line, a long, red, misshapen rectangle was blinking.

"— clear the zone; clear the zone— "

"What in blazes?" Barnes wondered aloud, only to be cut short by a change in the transmission.

"Commander Barnes—and all ships on the battle line—this is Admiral Cook," Cook's voice came, clear and strong, over the pulsing tactical display. "Help is on the way, and will arrive approximately twenty seconds after my mark. All ships can begin retreating—immediately. It is imperative that everybody—repeat, *everybody*—leave the zone indicated on the tactical display not later than twenty seconds after I give the signal. If you can manage it, your ships should jump speed somewhere between the fifteen and eighteen second mark. But it is absolutely critical that you open a gap of at least ten astrometers between our ships and the enemy. Any ship that cannot—repeat, cannot—clear the zone on time must— repeat, *must*—stop its engines and drop its shields. Ships can scatter in any direction their skippers choose, though a westerly retreat will best allow you to regroup at a designated rally point."

Barnes saw ships peeling away from the battle, all down the line. The sloops, turning quickly and racing westward, were already opening a gap between the contending lines; their frigates, coming about more slowly, were narrowly avoiding themselves and the enemy in their haste to escape the carnage. In many ways, he thought, it looked like panic was sweeping over the Isitian fleet.

"Helm—full about, heading 752," he shouted, feelings of relief washing over him like warm, soothing water.

"At the end of this transmission," the Admiral continued, "we are changing the communications protocol. Radio ships will cease all jamming until further notice. Channel 124 is reserved for myself, Channel 133 for Commodore Landis, and Channel 199 for Commander Barnes. No one will broadcast on any of those Channels, except those designated officers or their ships.

"Don't lose heart, people. Fight to hang on for a little while longer. Remember—twenty seconds; the worst will be over twenty seconds from...*Mark*!"

Rally points—communications—regrouping—Barnes felt his mind swimming and his brain become numb. Fighting the urge to relax, he summoned every ounce of energy left him. He had no idea what the Admiral was doing—and, he thanked the heavens, he didn't have to worry about it any longer. But there was still much to do, to keep his people safe and together. Pounding down on his armrest, he activated the communications override, and set the transmission for Channel 199.

"All ships set to jump speed two levels on my mark," he commanded, nodding to the radio officer. "Rally point—one mete this side of the opening."

He felt himself press against his chair, as the ship's engines strained to change course in time. As the seconds ticked, he glanced at the screens to see the battle line collapsing, as the Isitian ships began heading west at flank speed. He searched desperately for any trace of the Admiral—and became increasingly concerned when he didn't see a trace of either Isitian starship.

Had it been a mirage? he thought—or maybe a wicked Terran trick, to turn the battle into a rout. But how could the Terries know about their reserved communications channels? He kept his eyes riveted on the aft viewers, trying to bring his mind into focus. What he saw filled him with horror. Terrans filled the sky; from starboard to port, the Terrans stretched in a long, unbroken line. They were all heading west—right after the fleeing Isitians.

"Ten seconds," said the new systems officer. "Twelve—thirteen—fourteen—fifteen— "

"All ships," Barnes shouted into his receiver "—*Jump*!"

"—venteen, eighteen— "

As the ships lurched into hyperdrive, a narrow gap opened between the formless rush of retreating Isitians and the long, extended Terran line. Looking aft, Barnes saw two bright lights appear to port, on the Terran's centerside flank—one slightly above and slightly west of the enemy line, the other just below and to the east.

"Two starships... ," began Fields.

Suddenly, two whitish-blue, parallel streaks screamed across the screens—trailed by the flash of a long, giant explosion so blindingly bright it forced Barnes to shut his eyes. When he forced his eyes open, he saw the explosion had resolved itself into dozens of smaller ones. Confused, he searched for the two bright lights, and was surprised to find them now far to starboard—one, idling patiently just west and above the line of explosions, the other, now tinged red and well past the first, clumsily circling back toward its companion in a wide, undulating arc.

"Well that's odd," Fields remarked. As he searched for the Terrans through the clouds of fire and ash, he and Barnes realized that they were already looking at what was left of them. Simultaneously, both men jumped from their seats, shouting at the top of their lungs. As the rest of the bridge crew cast their eyes aft, confusion was soon replaced by a complete breakdown of discipline. Wild screams and shouts soon began to hurt everyone's ears. Before long the intercom was ringing with inquiries from the rest of the ship, wondering what was happening on the bridge. But the lights on the intercom board danced unanswered, as the bridge of the *Bristol Bay* surrendered to emotions they had no reason to hold in check.

"Gates—put Channel 124 on the speaker. The Bridge speaker only," Barnes laughed, wiping his eyes. "I don't know how much of this we're supposed to hear."

"I doubt we'll hear any of it," shouted the radio officer, vainly trying to be heard over the celebration. But Barnes didn't care. Tears streamed down his face, and he leaned back in his chair and began to laugh uncontrollably. He was relieved at having survived, and desperately happy that it was the Terrans, and not himself, whose ashes were now scattering in the cosmic wind. He was curious to know how they had done it, and what had actually happened to the

Terrans. Mostly, he just wanted to hear the Admiral's voice, and make sure he wasn't dreaming.

* * *

"....AS I tried to tell you. It's just like a harvester cutting a row of corn."

"What did you call that, again?"

Cook smiled and shook his head. Explaining things was not one of his strong points; confusing the issue was always more fun, at least when lives weren't on the line. But he was grateful that Landis had the wit not to quibble in the heat of battle, and so he tried his best.

"Well—I guess we'll call it a 'straddled enfilade,'" he said.

Janet smiled and shook her head. A lot of talk for simply turning the enemy's flank, she thought. But Skipper had every right to be proud of himself, and she didn't want to spoil the moment for him.

"That's why CosGuard moves in battle wedges, and not in a straight line," Cook continued, "although as far as I know, the move's never been done with a starship before, and they've probably quite forgotten how that particular bit of tactical dogma arose in the first place."

"I beg your pardon?"

"Actually, since pirates never move in straight lines, they don't really teach it at the Academy—not the way they should, at any rate. And, in fact, the Crutchtans aren't stupid enough to line up in a row like that either, so the only records of the maneuver I know are found in some dusty old textbooks on military tactics. From the days of cavalry charges, mostly, when the weapons were less potent and the terrain largely dictated your methods. But it seemed like the thing to do, you know—even if we didn't have any horses handy."

Cook saw Landis laugh on the screen—a rich, hearty laugh that lit his face like a candle on a birthday cake. It was the first time he'd ever seen him laugh, he realized. But perhaps it was the first time since the two men met that Landis had any reason to laugh. He winked at Janet, the only member of his bridge crew able to keep any sense of order. She smiled radiantly, he thought—and even if the two of them were the only ones who knew just how one-sided the fight had really been, it was quite a relief to have this whole business behind them.

"And you do know, of course, that you should probably get a Terran medal for saving more lives in this engagement than any of the enemy commanders."

"Oh, really, now?"

"Well, I was all prepared to make a second pass to thoroughly bash the rotters, but when you took your time coming about, I took the chance to take stock of our situation. Out of all the frigates in their battle line, we'd left only three dozen or so behind on our first pass, at least by my count. And we damaged a good fraction of them, besides. Then, what with *Avenger* sitting here for the longest time and all, it seemed to me that they'd pretty much lost their stomach for tangling with a starship any time soon. I doubt we'll have any trouble with the rest of them. And it dawned on me how handy all those extra frigates might be someday, manned with Isitian crews and sailing with the Interstellar Navy. In fact, by the time we're done mopping up we might just triple the size of our fleet."

"I didn't realize how devastating a starship could be."

"Neither does the Cosmic Guard," Cook laughed. "That's why I always led with my starships—and why every other CosGuard commander takes forever to win a battle. They don't know how to play with the toys they have, and their brass is too stupid to realize what they don't know. They could beat the universe with open skies and two dozen starships—but the damn fools are so afraid of losing that they never quite learned how to win. In the end, that's why they'll lose their war. And why it seems they didn't have much of a chance against us, either."

"Admiral— " Landis began, his eyes starting to moisten.

"Acch—don't get mushy on me, Landis!" Cook said, with a wave of his hand; Janet, though, could tell from the smile in his eyes that he was quite proud of himself. "Not while there's still work to be done."

"Yes, sir."

"I want you to take charge of the operation here. We'll be broadcasting a message to the rest of the Terran fleet, telling them that the time has come for them to surrender or die. There should be a few isolated pockets of enemy frigates scattered about, perhaps as much as half a division or so, and we need to mop them up before they have a chance to coalesce.

"You and Barnes can start rounding up the enemy stragglers.

Don't underestimate them: they're still dangerous, and I don't want you taking any foolish chances. Have them drop their shields and drain their engines, and tow them into a central holding area. Transfer the officers to one or two of our frigates, and hold them in the hangar bay. Once we're done mopping up the channel, we'll effect a transfer of prisoners to their own troop transports, and send our people to man the captured frigates."

"Yes, sir."

"And Commodore," Cook smiled grandly, his voice still ringing with the steel of command, "I thank you for your invaluable service. Since I'll be busy rounding up Terries for the next hour or so, I want you to have the honor of sending our victory message back home."

"No, Admiral. I couldn't...."

"Wait until you've wrapped things up here, of course. No sense rushing things, after all—and you might find it embarrassing to interrupt your transmission, in order to dispatch a few more Terrans. Make it short and direct. That will drive the reporters and politicians crazy. But don't dawdle too much. I imagine the folks back home will be anxious to hear from you, as soon as you find it convenient."

"Admiral...."

"I leave the details to you, Commodore Landis. Right now, I can do more good relieving Gold and Silver Divisions than I can jibber-jabbering with a bunch of politicians. So, now that we're facing a gaggle of idiots instead of an enemy fleet, I defer to your superior tact and discretion."

"Yes, sir," Landis smiled proudly.

"Carry on, Commodore."

"Thank you, Admiral."

As the crew cheered all around them, and on every deck and corner of the ship, Janet rose from her seat and walked over to the command chair. Tossing her hair aside girlishly, she sat down on her husband's lap and kissed him warmly. Nestling herself in his arms, she looked up to meet his eyes and smiled.

"Don't think I'm not proud of you," she said coyly. "I'm as proud of you now as I've ever been—and, today, I think I'm just about the luckiest girl in the Universe. But could you tell me something?"

"Sure—anything."

Janet looked him squarely in the eye. "Exactly what are you up to?"

"What do you mean?"

"Skipper," she whispered, careful not to disrupt the celebration going on around them. "You're a terrible liar."

"I'm not a liar!"

"You may be able to fool everyone else, you know. They don't know you like I do, and they're too drunk with hero worship to begin wondering what you're doing."

"I'm not doing anything," he smiled wickedly in spite of himself, shocked at being caught so easily. "Well, hardly anything. Just—well, mop-up."

"Right—just like I'm sure you just can't bring yourself to send the victory message," Janet said, skeptically.

"Well, actually— "

"And that 'gaggle of idiots' nonsense was enough to make me gag myself. You like nothing better than to let a real idiot know exactly what you think of him. And besides, I know for a fact that you actually like the Chancellor."

"I just thought I'd give the honor to Landis. He really was a lot of help, you know. And it frees me to concentrate on—well, on mopping up. You know—mopping-up operations."

"Mopping-up operations?"

"That's right. Mopping-up operations."

"You can't spare the ten seconds it takes to transmit a written communication back home? That's too much of a bother?"

"Well, not a bother, actually."

"Not a bother?"

"More like a pitfall."

Frowning regally, Janet looked skeptically into Cook's eyes, refusing to budge until he was more forthcoming. Cook realized at once that his tactical situation was deteriorating by the moment.

"Well," Cook winced, not quite sure how she would take the news; absently, he began to stroke her hair, and face, and neck. "Up to now, you know, I've had pretty much a free hand to deal with the Terrans as I deemed best. And I see no reason to change that. Not until we're done mopping-up."

"By any chance, is this little mop-up likely to take longer than everyone expects.?"

"Oh, no. Certainly not."

"You're sure about that?"

"Quite sure. At least, not for everybody."

"Just for us?"

"Well...."

"How long?"

Furrowing his brow in thought, Cook took a deep breath as he ran the estimates in his head. "About two weeks," he said at last. "If we can avoid any hangers-on. It'll all be so much quicker if we do this alone, you know. Provided there are no further complications."

"Two weeks?"

"More or less," he nodded.

Closing her eyes, Janet melted in Cook's lap, trying to ignore the gentle sensation of his hand against her cheek. She knew he was trying to distract her, and knew he would do as good a job as she'd let him. But something in her brain told her the answer was staring her in the face. Two more weeks, she thought idly. Did he mean fourteen solar days, or twenty cosmic days? And if the starship could cruise at a speed of four parsecs a day, a twenty-day round trip would bring them into the vicinity of—

"*ZarCom!*" she said accusingly, bolting upright in his lap.

"I beg your pardon?"

"You're going," she suddenly dropped her voice, to avoid disturbing the others, who were taking pains to let them have their moment alone, "to take out ZarCom?"

Cook cleared his throat and grimaced. Now that the element of surprise was gone, he figured, he might as well just forge ahead fearlessly.

"Well, granted, this Terran fleet did cause us a real spot of trouble," he shrugged. "But essentially they're just a short-term problem. ZarCom is the real long-term strategic threat. It's the only starbase for a hundred parsecs with a dry dock big enough for a starship. Eliminate ZarCom and they have to come all the way from Earth to attack us. And as long as the invasion force came from Zarathustra—and the Terran fleet used Zarathustran space for a staging area—well, right now we do have the reason, the excuse, and the opportunity to really mop this thing up properly, don't you think?"

"*Skipper!*"

"Besides," he laughed, "as I recall, even for a starbase ZarCom's defenses are pretty pathetic. Shields can't stand up to blaster fire from a starship, and their own guns were designed to repel pirate ships, not warships. We can blast them all day from beyond their firing range and they won't be able to touch us."

"So now we're going to destroy a CosGuard starbase?"

"We won't be in any real danger, so we can let them evacuate. It's the base we want to destroy, not the poor slobs who live on it. And if they rebuild it, we'll just send up the new base, as well. Without an existing spot to moor a starship, you know, they really won't be able to defend an uncompleted one. And with all their troubles on the eastern front, I rather doubt they'll spend much more time worrying about us."

"Have you cleared this with the Chancellor?"

"I beg your pardon?"

"You didn't clear this, did you?"

"Well, my orders *are* pretty vague— "

"I don't believe this."

"But our mission is to defeat the Terrans. So I figure that until we actually finish mopping things up...."

Despite herself, Janet started to laugh. Relaxing, she buried herself in her husband's lap and closed her eyes as the cheers rang loudly around them. In her heart, she knew he was right, though she doubted that most politicians would see things quite so clearly. But it wasn't her problem, she told herself.

For tonight, and tomorrow, and as many tomorrows as she could manage after that, it wouldn't be her problem, any longer.

* * *

THE MIST hung low above the veranda overlooking the gardens. The Chancellor, too happy to feel exhausted, walked to the railing and breathed deeply in the damp, morning air. Even through the fog, the scent of lilacs filled the air, and she remembered the Springs of her girlhood, when life was an unending succession of crisis and ecstasy. The lilacs were the same, and above the clouds, she knew that the golden sun was as warm as ever. But never, she thought, never had she known such a glorious dawn.

Looking down, she read the message once again.

cc:144.8015.2
To Chancellor McGinnis:
From Commodore Anthony J. Landis
On this date, the Isitian Interstellar Navy met and destroyed a superior force of the Terran Cosmic Guard in the channel west of the Paddington Shoals.

More details will follow, once Admiral Cook has concluded final operations in the channel.

The nightmare was over, she thought. Landis would never send a message like that on his own. And if Cook thought the battle was over, then it was really over. And after working his miracle, the Northlander was simply too generous not to let others share the glory of the moment. As she stood over the railing, she heard a lone church bell start ringing in the distance, and smiled quietly to herself. Some things, she thought, could never be kept a secret; and some things were simply meant to be shared.

"George——!" she turned and called. Bleary-eyed and weary, the defense minister stepped out onto the balcony, carrying a half-filled bottle of champagne, followed by Ross, Henderson, McKenzie—and most of the cabinet and their families. As they entered, the lone church bell was joined by another; soon, another, then another began to sound. All across the city, as the news quickly spread, the bells rang gladly, until their sounds filled the air. Her tired, tearful eyes looked out through the mist to see every street in sight filling with people, laughing and dancing and crying people, a scene being repeated in every quarter of the city. Apparently, George McKenzie wasn't the only Isitian with a radio, she smiled to herself, and laughed to think that the scene would be much the same throughout the countryside. She had no illusions about the cost of all their good fortune. Thousands of fine young Isitians had given their lives to save their homeland. But this was not the morning for regrets; that mourning could begin tomorrow. Today was a day for rejoicing.

"George, I want you to go and gather up every firecracker, Roman candle and skyrocket in this whole damn city." McKenzie nodded and laughed, summoning the servants to bring more champagne, and join in the celebration.

"Madame Chancellor," cautioned Reggie Ross. "I think you'll find most skyrockets on the planet are already committed— "

"Oh hush," scolded the Chancellor. "I know perfectly well why we have so many fireworks about this time of year. June 1st is Founder's Day...."

"Absolutely. So on such short notice— "

"You still don't understand—do you Reggie?" she said patiently.

"I understand that— "

"What you understand is the past, Minister Ross," she continued. "This—today, May 15th—*this* is Founder's Day." Seeing the servants return from the wine cellar, the Chancellor called for McKenzie and the others. As the champagne was poured, she couldn't resist needling her minister of state for the lack of poetry in his soul.

"You try telling them that there's no reason to celebrate," she teased, pointing over her shoulder at the gathering crowds that were filling the streets, "that the real celebration won't be for another two weeks."

"That's not what I— "

"You think we have more reason to celebrate some stuffed shirts signing articles of incorporation for a little backwater town three hundred years ago than we do today?"

"Well, no—but, dammit! "

"Madame Chancellor!" thundered McKenzie, his throaty voice already hoarse with shouting. "To Admiral Cook—and the best damn fleet in the galaxy."

"Oh, George, that's not a proper toast," retorted the Chancellor. "That sounds more like the cleaned up version of a locker room pep talk.

"To lunatics—," she began, raising her glass along with the others, only to be drowned out by laughter and cheers.

"To lunatics, children, and the Republic of Isis."

Chapter 16

DAYS PASSED.

As he waited yet again for a channel to clear to the Interstellar Navy, a seething Reggie Ross glanced down at the latest communication from the Admiral. He'd never trusted the infernal Northlander, and it made him even angrier that the Chancellor seemed to take it all as a colossal joke. Each time he reread the communiqué, he became enraged:

COMMUNIQUE

DATE: cc:144.8129.2
FROM: **Admiral Roscoe Cook**
TO: **Chancellor Irene McGinnis**

I am resuming radio contact, now that ZarCom mission is accomplished and hostilities are finally at an end. Hope you didn't worry needlessly, but radio silence was necessary to ensure the element of surprise.

I apologize for not responding to your earlier broadcasts, but your messages seemed to be garbled in transmission. I am, however, glad to report that our mission was a complete success: we eliminated the Terran base at ZarCom without any loss of life; and we destroyed Zarathustran planetary defenses with minimal casualties on the ground, permitting me to address the planet and tell the Zarathustrans the truth about Paddington and related matters without interruption by the local authorities.

You might like to know, by the way, that we have monitored news reports that the Crutchtans retook Girshoona yesterday; and two days ago, the Glincians finally managed to fight the Terrans to a draw. As I doubt that we could stand alone against the entire Cosmic Guard for very long, I regard this as extremely good news—provided that the Crutchtans do not take it into their heads to thrash us, along with the Terrans. But given your penchant for diplomacy, and our own unwillingness to enter the conflict against them, I see no reason to believe that we cannot make peace with the Crutchtans, and regard this risk as unlikely to materialize.

En route to Zarathustra, we rescued Lt. William J. Bohley, Jr. and Ens. Timothy W. Martin from a lifeboat adrift in interstellar space. Both men were tired and hungry, but otherwise well. Kindly inform their families that they have already received personal citations from me, and will be home as soon as *Avenger* puts to port.

"Any l–luck?"

"Afraid not, Minister Ross. I'll keep trying."

Ross took a deep breath, and began pacing about the small communications room. Crowded as it was, he couldn't wait upstairs any longer. Even if the delay in patching through the transmission to the Cabinet Room would only be a matter of seconds, he felt helpless upstairs.

He also realized that he wasn't about to win any popularity contests with the technicians who ran the equipment. In the weeks since Paddington, he'd managed to get himself physically thrown out of the Radio Room twice. Both times for insulting the Admiral.

No one could dispute the magnitude of their victory, he had to admit. Facing an invincible enemy, and with little more than smoke, mirrors, and Cook's imagination, what they'd accomplished was nothing short of miraculous. From an attack wing of two full divisions, the Terrans had lost everything—every single Terran ship had been destroyed or captured. Isis lost exactly nine frigates, and only a few hundred out of the thousands of small pleasure craft they'd conscripted, all but a handful of those losses coming in the last five minutes of the battle. It was, by any measure, a stunning accomplishment, and the whole planet, from Bristol to New Alexandria, was singing Cook's praises. But the Northlander's stubborn refusal to answer any of his transmissions in the intervening days had caused Ross to begin stuttering again for the first time since boyhood. The fact that the Chancellor simply smiled and ignored the Admiral's irresponsibility did nothing to improve his mood. And now the rest of the Navy was giving him the same silent response. It was enough to drive a man crazy.

It was also, Ross thought, quite inexcusable. After dodging disaster at Paddington, Cook couldn't just come home: that would be too pedestrian to suit his taste for adventure. No—the man had to sail off and pick another fight. The fact that ZarCom surrendered without resistance was, so far as Ross was concerned, just further evidence that Cook led a charmed life. That the Admiral would then undertake to neutralize the planet's defenses and presume to speak for all of Isis, informing the Zarathustrans what had happened and cautioning them not to rebuild the starbase—all without proper authorization from the political leadership back home—proved a stunning lack of sensitivity and political reliability. It merely confirmed Ross' opinion, formed over and over again during a young lifetime of activity in Isitian politics, that anyone named Cook was simply not to be trusted.

"Any word from Our Hero?"

Ross looked up to see the Chancellor being helped through the narrow door and down the steps leading to the monitors.

"Madame Chancellor—wh-what are you doing here?"

The Chancellor smiled and stretched out her arm to Ross, trying to steady herself. She looked at the worried face and concerned eyes of her protégé, and wished that the young man would simply learn to relax. She knew that he was not likely to take kindly to her latest bit of news; that was why she felt a duty to tell him herself. But young Reggie could work himself into such a lather that he often invited trouble—trouble nobody else could even see.

"I'm n-not trying to contact the Admiral," he said. "I'm trying to r-raise the Fleet."

"Reggie," she began gently, "you know that you can't always run everything from the capital. People have their own outlooks, their own concerns. In fact, governments trying to do good have caused more trouble in this Universe than all the schoolboys in history."

"What does this have to d-do— "

"I am simply trying, Reggie Ross, to bring you some perspective," the Chancellor continued, regally. "And to prepare you for this," she added, handing him a piece of paper.

Taking the paper, Ross saw at once that it was a letter—a letter from Cook. A personal letter, this time, addressed to the Chancellor.

Damn Northlander, he thought as he began to read:

Dear Chancellor McInnis:
I thank you for your kind sentiments; I, too, wish we'd had time to discuss matters more fully before the battle. Unfortunately, events move quickly in war, and I had to move along with them. I apologize if I've caused you any grief, or if my remarks to the Zarathustrans gave you cause for concern. I did try to make clear that we would welcome ships sent in friendship, and even invited them to send a transport convoy to fetch the prisoners from our encounter with the Terran fleet. (I did tell them, however, that the captured ships themselves would remain Isitian property, as a prize of war; as I omitted mentioning this in my communiqué, I hope this does not give you additional cause for concern. In any case, I will transmit a verbatim text of my remarks, so that you may decide for yourself whether "patching things over" with the Zarathustrans, as you put it, is really "a job best left to diplomats." And if push does come to shove, we can always let them have their transports back; all I really care about are the frigates).

"D-damn Northlander," Ross said aloud.
"Read, Reggie," said the Chancellor.

We are now proceeding westward, and should reach the vicinity of the Nakahashi Storms sometime in the next week or so. I plan, however, to return with recommendations for a series of defensive bases to ensure that we need not face the threat of invasion again: I envision several observation posts along the outside of the clouds, and at least four major bases along the interior of the passage. This will delay our return by several additional weeks—even if the positions I decide to recommend for our defensive positions along the shipping lanes from Zarathustra remain as I envisioned while sailing the skies as a boy. If these sites no longer strike me as practical, it may delay our return even longer.

I hope things are going smoothly back home. I have, you may note, tried to insulate you as much as possible from any adverse consequences stemming from my "mopping-up" excursion to Zarathustra, and will gladly take full responsibility for my actions, should the need arise. But I trust that the folks back home will take the longer view—or, if not, that they'll be too hung over from our brush with disaster to hold much of a grudge. I also apologize for missing all the festivities you described in your letter. It sounds like quite a grand affair that you have planned, and should be an occasion of much well-deserved celebrating. But, to be honest, I find most parties boring, and most parades gaudy and loud. Besides, as you already have a whole fleetful of heroes to celebrate, you don't really need any more. Perhaps next time.

Best wishes,
Roscoe Cook

"*What!*"

"Now, Reggie.... "

"After all this grief, he still has n-no intention of being here?"

"He has other concerns— "

"Other concerns? He's being c-c-completely irresponsible! After going off on his own against the Zarathustrans, he's trying to cover his own b-behind so that— "

"That is quite enough, Reggie!" snapped the Chancellor. "Quite frankly, I agree with his strategic assessment—though at the time I probably would have winced at the thought of authorizing it, myself. In hindsight, it spared us all a lot of grief. And it concluded hostilities on a note of hope and reconciliation, while at the same time demonstrating our steely sense of Isitian resolve. We are once again in his debt. And once again, his instincts have proven remarkably insightful—even if his diplomatic methods are, perhaps, somewhat more unconventional than— "

"*Unconventional?* The man's a loose c-c-cannon."

"He did send a request for instructions— "

"In the middle of the night! After he'd already taken out ZarCom and mere seconds before he attacked the planet!"

"Well, Reggie," smiled the Chancellor, unable to conceal her admiration for Cook's style, "at least he showed a proper respect for form. As for the rest... ."

"Incoming transmission," interrupted the radio technician. "It's the *New Alexandria.*"

"Finally," said Ross.

"Now, sit down, Reggie," needled the Chancellor. "I think perhaps I'd best do the talking for us." She turned to the technician and smiled her sweetest smile.

"Mr.—?"

"Just call me Jerry, Ma'am."

"Very well, Mr. Jerry," the Chancellor said pleasantly. "If you would be so very kind as to put the signal on the screen."

As Ross stomped over to the nearest chair to pout, the Chancellor took a seat just in front of the monitor. It was a small screen, much smaller than she'd expected, and it took her a moment or two of fiddling with a host of unfamiliar dials and knobs on the control panel to adjust the volume to a level she found comfortable. Soon, Commodore Landis appeared on the screen, scowling angrily. His mood changed abruptly, once he saw who was on the other end of the transmission.

"Madam Chancellor!" he said, surprised.

"Hello, Commodore," smiled the Chancellor. "I hear that you are encountering a few delays, coming down to the planet."

Landis averted his eyes and cleared his throat, but said nothing in reply.

"We've already postponed our victory parade twice before," she scolded gently, "and Minister Ross is most upset at the prospect of postponing it a third time."

"I'm sorry, Madam Chancellor."

"We are, you understand, only trying to show our affection, for you and all the rest of our heroic Navy. Honestly, everyone on the ground is most anxious to let out a veritable salvo of appreciation and gratitude, for you and all of your brave comrades. And, to be quite frank, you are not exactly allowing me or my Government to look very good, what with all these last-minute changes and cancellations. I'm sure you understand how we all feel, Commodore. And I'm sure you can't really want everyone on Isis to feel disappointed, again. Not after all we've been through together."

"We went over that—" Landis began, angrily—only to remember that he was no longer speaking to the Minister of State.

"I'm sorry, Madam Chancellor," he said, apologetically, "but we discussed the matter before at length, Minister Ross and I. And I left no question about how we stood on the matter. I'm afraid there's nothing more to discuss."

Perplexed, and unused to having her charms go so unavailing, the Chancellor stared haughtily at the commander of the *New Alexandria*.

"Might I remind you," she continued icily, "that we have captured ships moored at every available base and port of call, and captured enemy soldiers overfilling every facility that can hold them—including the observatory station on the moon Diogenes and a goodly number of our college dormitories! We cannot just let things slide, indefinitely, you know. Isitians are a patient lot, Commodore, but we can't just postpone things forever. Right now, by God, people are clamoring for a parade. And—*dammit*—I mean to give them a parade!

"Besides," the Chancellor continued, quickly recovering her composure, her voice easing into its customary soft, reassuring cadence, "just think of all the families waiting for all their young people to return home. Parents longing for their children. Husbands and wives, friends and loved ones, all wishing desperately to be reunited—and to celebrate our deliverance from the very jaws of disaster. Surely, you must see the reason in the directive to return home."

Landis looked straight out of the monitor and met the Chancellor's gaze directly. "I'm sorry, Madam Chancellor."

"But— "

"No, Ma'am. The Navy won't stand for it. And, as long as we're being blunt about it, neither will I. Every last one of us owes him more than we can ever repay. There isn't anybody here who doesn't owe the Admiral his life—and that goes for the everyone groundside, as well. So I'm sorry, but our families will just have to wait a bit longer. Nobody here's going to budge until the Admiral's back, safe and sound. You can court martial the lot of us, if you like," he continued adamantly. "But he stood by us at every turn. And every last one of us is going to wait, right where we are, until he can return home with us."

"Now, listen to me, Commodore!"

"I'm sorry, Madam Chancellor. But that's the way we all feel. And that's the way it's going to be."

As the transmission ended, the Chancellor found she couldn't help but laugh, despite herself. Our Hero was certainly Cornelius Cook's nephew, she thought—audacious and stubborn, pigheaded and brilliant. Yet in his own way he was the most scrupulously honest man she'd ever met. And he aroused such passion in everyone around him that he was difficult to live with, and impossible to ignore.

Rising to her feet, the Chancellor walked over to her Minister of State, and took the seat next to his. Shaking her head in resignation, she took a deep breath and turned to face him.

"Well, this is altogether too Isitian," he observed in frustration, trying his best to accept the inevitable. "No matter what we do, we can't possibly avoid looking like fools. So how do we serve up this latest plateful of Isitian hash?"

"Reggie, I'm surprised at you," replied the Chancellor, smiling wryly. "We turn it into a feast, of course. We have two parades instead of one. We take public credit for not forcing the Navy down without their precious Skipper. And we pray to God that he's too damn principled ever to go into politics."

Epilogue

Through the shadows of Time, a shining light still lifts the heart of a grateful People.

Inscription above Cook Memorial,
New Alexandria, Isis

...[Y]ou taught us not only the tactics of war, but also that chivalry and honor could exist even in the worst of circumstances. And by leaving this madness when you did, you may very well have saved my people, as well as your own.

Fashenali's Letter, 2560

"Beer! Beer! Beer!" said the crewmen,
  "Merry all are we—
In all the land, there's none so grand
  As Adm'ral Cook's Na-vee!"

Isitian Nursery Song Refrain
Early 27th Century

Epilogue

THIS SKY WASN'T like the black sky, he thought. This blue sky was alive. Alive with birds. And people everywhere. And the air was different. It smelled sweet. It wasn't like being cooped up at home. Not at all. Here, he could run in any direction he wanted. And there were lots of places to hide. And rocks to climb. And trees. And tonight there would be fireworks!

"Come on, Daddy!" he shouted, impatiently.

"I'm coming," his father smiled.

"Hurry!"

"I'm right behind you."

"Don't get lost."

"I won't," the man laughed. "I may be off, somewhere, wandering in a fog, but I'm never lost."

"What?"

"I'm right behind you."

THE THREE-YEAR old girl was so excited that her pretty young mother couldn't make her stop jumping on the park bench.

"Look, Mommy—it's him, it's him, it's him!"

"Hush," said the mother, making sure to catch a glimpse even as she scolded her daughter for making such a scene. "Leave him alone. And don't stare. Everyone's entitled to his privacy."

CLAD IN running shorts and shirt, the man walked wearily down the path, lagging behind the energetic little boy who was dashing merrily from one stand of trees to the next. His clothes, still damp from the recent exertion of running three miles faster than his body preferred, clung to his sides, showing the world that he wasn't quite the graceful young athlete who'd set his hometown course record a generation earlier. The Festival of Knowledge came once every twenty-five years, a time of contemplation and renewal, and with it came the ritual known as the Festival Torch. Among its more bittersweet prizes, he thought, was the realization that youth came but once—even if the memories of youth lasted a lifetime. But then, it wasn't so long ago that he wondered if he'd ever see another Festival.

"Daddy!"

"I'm coming."

"Hurry!"

Shaking his head, he tried his best to hustle up the hill. Though the privilege of starting the Torch procession was intended as an honor, he was lucky he didn't embarrass himself completely. Twenty-five years ago, he remembered thinking that the old-timers on the outward leg—running the torch from New Alexandria's Central Square all the way to Bristol, in the Northlands—were all wheezing derelicts for running such short distances. He'd thought the youth of the planet, those born since the last Festival—the young, strong athletes under twenty-five who bore it back to the capital—should all go on strike. So he'd foolishly agreed to extend his part of the run to the same three-mile distance that the kids would be running, so that he could pass and greet more people along the way. Now, he'd learned another painful lesson from ages past: nothing stops the passing of Time. Or its effects on the human body. Despite being in good shape for a man in his early forties, and training for the past month to avoid making a fool of himself, he found the First Leg course he'd agreed to run to be excruciating. Between his arm, numbed from holding the damn torch aloft, and his legs, deadened from pounding the city streets as fast as he could in front of a cheering throng, it felt as if his whole body was made of wood. He'd laughed when his wife warned him about acting his age; he hoped she'd be done gloating by the time she waddled back from the crafts show at the bottom of the hill, seven months into their second child and full of complaints about every last bulge in her belly.

"Daddy!"

"I'm hurrying."

"No, you're not."

"Well, maybe not, but I'm sure giving it a try."

"Oh, you're just being silly again."

* * *

"William! Come here this instant!"

Secretly hoping that her little boy would do nothing of the sort, the mother dashed across the open field toward the man they'd just seen finish his stint as a torch bearer. She didn't have the nerve to approach him on her own—and it was considered bad form, besides. But now she had an excuse. And all her friends would just die of jealousy.

"Hello."

"Well, hello there."

"My name is Will."

"Pleased to meet you, Will. My friends call me Skipper."

"I thought your name was Adamal."

"Well, people call me that too, sometimes."

"Did you come for the fireworks?"

"That will be exciting, won't it? But it won't be until tonight, I'm afraid."

"William—come here. I'm so sorry, Admiral...."

"That's quite all right, Ma'am. Nice meeting you, Will—have fun at the fireworks, tonight."

"Daddy, do you get mad when people call you 'Animal?'"

"No," the man laughed. "Actually, I'm sort of used to it." Sitting on the grass, beneath the warm, Isitian sun, the man recalled some of the other things people used to call him. It all seemed like such a long time ago. He hoped it wouldn't all come rushing back to him. He didn't want to deal with painful memories just now. Today was a day for sunshine and dreams.

Resting on his elbows, he felt the wind gust gently, and smiled at the sweet, invigorating scent of lilacs dancing through the air. An early immigrant from Old Earth, the lilacs had swept the planet like the wind, mingling with the native plants and animals as if returning to its ancestral home. Whether accident or fate, the man smiled, it was of little consequence in the grand order of things. It made the Isitian spring a glorious celebration of life. Looking at his small son laughing and giggling as he chased imaginary monsters and quested after hidden treasure, the rest seemed of such little consequence.

But, he sighed, he couldn't ignore his responsibilities forever. The Government had to act, soon—and the Chancellor needed his recommendations. Even on such a glorious Spring day, in darker skies to the east the Crutchtans and their allies were closing in on the shipping lanes from Demeter to Ishtar. With the rest of the known galaxy pressing them from three sides, the Terrans were massing their forces against the giant pincer aimed directly at the planets of the old Frontier. The peace feelers Chancellor Ross sent to the Consortium had been received warmly—and the handwritten letter Captain Barnes brought back from the Crutchtan commander Fashenali, expressing the forgiveness and, surprisingly enough, the gratitude of a race he'd grievously wronged, would always be one of his personal treasures. But with their backs to the wall, the Terrans were fighting ferociously. Now the Allies needed a second front in the west, to relieve the pressure on their own fleets and minimize the eventual loss of life when time came for the final thrust into the Terran heartland.

It was just as well for everyone that he was overruled when he wanted to take out ZarCom 2, he mused. Still half-completed, it had never become operational. Now the crisis in the East left it completely unguarded. Ironically, it provided Isis with a good excuse to act—with minimal risk, with the support of most Zarathustrans, and in a way that would actually help bring the war, and all its pointless death and suffering, finally to an end. He might not be able to undo the past, but he could do what he could to help kill this last remnant of Mankind's savage heritage, and help guide Isis toward her future place among the brotherhood of civilized races.

Right now, beneath the warm May sun, he was too tired to care. This might be a double celebration, he thought—the Ides of May, or Paddington Day, as well as the opening of the Festival of Knowledge that would stretch until the last rays of summer. But he was tired, he was hot, and he was thirsty. And he was grateful to see the small refreshment stand, sitting on the pathway near the top of Crescent Hill.

"Want some ice cream?" he asked his son.

Soon, he was panting his way up the hill, trying hard to keep his three-year old son in view. As he finally reached the summit, he turned around to admire the scene. Crescent Hill had the finest view of the city, he thought. In his days as a student here, before he left his home to wander the Universe, the surrounding park had always been his favorite refuge.

Turning toward the vendor, he drew up to the stand and took a deep breath. "One soda," he panted.

"*Daddy!*"

"Oh—and one ice cream."

He smiled as his young son rolled his eyes and sighed impatiently. The boy certainly liked to imitate his mother, he chuckled. And both seemed to love the task of keeping the man of the family from mistaking himself for someone important. He tried not to notice as the vendor gaped at him. He'd gotten quite used to it over the past four years. It still made him feel uncomfortable, but he'd gotten used to it.

JACK MARKHAM felt awkward and embarrassed, but couldn't keep himself from staring. After all this time, after four years of pining away over missed opportunities and lost chances, he'd finally get to meet him.

And it was him! Big as life, and standing right in front of him. Nervously, Jack cleared his throat, hoping that he wouldn't seem as foolish as he felt.

"I beg your pardon, Admiral?"

"One soda, and one ice cream. Chocolate, I guess. The ice cream, not the soda."

"How old is the boy?"

"The boy? Oh, he's three. Just as you'd expect."

"February 15th, or 16th?"

"March 1st, actually. I was all ready, of course. But, as usual, the wife was a bit late. First child and all."

"Well, you were wise to wait until the crowds cleared a bit. Wish I could've talked my own wife into waiting," he said with a wink, pointing to his own three year old, a pretty girl sleeping peacefully on a blanket in the shade of a royal oak tree. "It was a rather hectic week or so at the hospital. Sent half the planet's obstetricians to the pyscho ward, from what I've heard."

The Admiral laughed, and Jack immediately felt relieved. He knew he might not be the most interesting conversationalist the Admiral would meet today, but at least he could make the man laugh. The first Ides of May fireworks didn't end with the last of the skyrockets, he chuckled. And it seemed like the men on the planet would always have at least one thing in common. All of "Cook's Kids" now walking about gave them all something to chat over, in the interlude between Rounders and Football seasons.

"News from the east is bad for Terry, I see."

"I beg your pardon?"

"I said, the news isn't very good for Terry, these days."

"No," the Admiral smiled. "The Terrans haven't had good news for quite a while."

"Actually, I'd say things turned sour for them the day they chased the last daisy-sniffer out of the Cosmic Guard," said Jack, as he went about his business, pouring the soft drink and dipping the ice cream. "Tell me, if you don't mind, Admiral—but I've always been curious."

"So have I," laughed the Admiral. "It's a damn curse, if you ask me."

"I still don't know how you did it."

"How I did what?"

"How you thrashed them. The Terries, I mean."

The Admiral smiled. Some things were so simple, he thought; and yet some things he could never explain.

"We were lucky, Mr.—? "

"Markham, sir. Jack Markham."

"Well, Mr. Markham, ordinary people can accomplish miracles with hope and a little courage. We had a lot of brave people, fighting with all their hearts to keep us from falling into the pit. And we were very, very lucky."

"If you'll excuse me, Admiral—but from what I hear, luck played not one part of it. But luck or no, we were all behind you, you know. All of us."

"Thank you, Mr. Markham."

"You know, some of us wanted to be there with you. A lot of us. Most of us, in fact."

"Yes, I know. It was very gratifying. And you all helped, more than you realize."

"I—myself. I signed up and tested for the Navy. But I washed out. The Gravity Scrambler, and all."

"That was the end for a lot of good people, I hear."

"But we were still behind you, Admiral. All the way. And the militia—well, as soon as I could, I joined up. All my friends did, too. Just trying to do what we could, you know. And we wouldn't have let you down, either. If the Navy couldn't keep them away, we were ready for them on the ground. And we're still at it, you know. Just in case."

"You were a big help, Mr. Markham," smiled the Admiral. "All of you."

He was used to hearing such stories from the people he'd meet; everyone, it seemed, had a story to tell him. And he'd always listen politely, letting them talk as much as they wanted. He never had the heart to tell them that the whole militia would have been cannon fodder if the Terrans had actually landed. But he had other things on his mind, as this Markham fellow talked about his own small children, and his contribution to the defense effort. Quietly reaching into his pocket, the Admiral slowly pulled out his wallet. Perhaps if he did it quickly, he thought, before the man had time to think, he could pull it off this time. Discretely, he slipped some money into his hand, and prepared to sneak it onto the counter.

Just as he'd feared, the vendor drew up stiffly, as if he'd just been insulted. Sullenly, the Admiral steeled himself for yet another pointed rebuke.

"Admiral," Jack said sternly. "You should know better than that by now."

"Look...."

"I'm sorry, sir. Your money is worthless at my stand—and at any other honest shop anywhere on this planet."

"Please—Mr. Markham."

"No, sir."

"But Mr. Markham— "

"No, sir."

"But see here—if you'll just listen to reason for a moment— "

Jack smiled as he looked over the Admiral's shoulder. He'd wanted to claim the irony of telling him it would be "like taking money from the Admiral," the planet's newest epithet for ingratitude. But a more pressing matter interrupted them.

"I don't think you have time for that, Admiral."

"I beg your pardon?"

"I think you have more important things to worry about," Jack said, pointing down the hillside. Turning, the great man suddenly lost all interest in haggling over prices, or trying to maintain a sense of dignity in the face of such universal and unremitting generosity. He now had a real crisis on his hands.

He saw his son—running.

Running down the hill.

Running right toward a big puddle of thick, black, mud.

Bolting like a spooked horse, the Admiral raced after his son, commanding him to stop as the boy giggled and laughed and looked over his shoulder and continued running.

"Jeremiah Cook—you stop this instant!" bellowed the Admiral. "Your mother is going to kill the both of us!"

OVERTAKING THE boy with a few yards to spare, the father lifted his son over the puddle, then rolled onto the ground, both of them laughing with the breeze. With the boy held tightly against his father's chest, and protected by the man's strong arms, the two rolled together down the gentle slope of the hill, a hillside the father had walked many times when he was young. The same hillside where, one day in the distant future, the son would return to cut a ribbon on a magnificent structure of marble and gold—a monument to the funny, gentle giant that other grownups made such a silly fuss over and the boy knew simply as "Daddy," a loving remembrance from the people the giant had saved, standing guard forever over the pretty provincial town that would grow to become the grandest city ever built by the race of Man.

And as the two of them came to rest beside a blossoming bed of flowers, and his son squealed with delight under a barrage of tickling, the man felt so incredibly lucky that all of Life seemed nothing short of miraculous:

It was a miracle to have stumbled through so many hardships and disasters, only to find love waiting patiently for him at the end of all his travels.

It was a miracle to have kept what little sanity he had, and to realize how much the Universe would always have to teach him.

It was a miracle to bring new life into the Universe, and to watch children grow and prosper before his eyes.

Most of all, it was a miracle that fate had brought him back from the darkness to a place he knew he belonged, to which he could return whenever he needed to feel the grass beneath his feet, or the sun and wind against his face: a place where truth and honor and beauty would always sing in the hearts of a kindhearted people, and the wide, green forests would sway to the songs of birds. A place where children would always laugh and play, with wondering eyes and innocent hearts. And a place where a golden sun lit a land filled with hope, and Spring still belonged to the lilacs.

ABOUT THE AUTHOR

JEFFREY CAMINSKY, a life-long resident of Planet Earth, lives in Michigan with his wife and family. His books include a book about soccer officiating, *The Referee's Survival Guide*, and *The Sonnets of William Shakespeare*, a guide to Elizabethan poetry. In an alternate reality, he is a retired public prosecutor in Detroit. His book *The Guardians of Peace* is the fourth and concluding volume in the *Guardians of Peace* science fiction adventure series.